RIVERS
OF
TREASON

BY K. J. MAITLAND

Daniel Pursglove novels

The Drowned City

Traitor in the Ice

Rivers of Treason

As Karen Maitland

The White Room

Company of Liars

The Owl Killers

The Gallows Curse

The Falcons of Fire and Ice

The Vanishing Witch

The Raven's Head

The Plague Charmer

A Gathering of Ghosts

Digital short stories

Liars and Thieves

The Dangerous Art of Alchemy

Wicked Children: Murderous Tales from History

K. J. MAITLAND

RIVERS
OF
TREASON

K. J. Maitland

REVIEW

143

First published in 2023 by Headline Review
An imprint of HEADLINE PUBLISHING GROUP

1

Cataloguing in Publication Data is available from the British Library

Hardback ISBN 978 1 4722 7550 9
Trade paperback ISBN 978 1 4722 7551 6

Typeset by EM&EN
Printed and bound in Great Britain by Clays Ltd, Elcograf S.p.A.

Headline's policy is to use papers that are natural, renewable and recyclable
products and made from wood grown in well-managed forests and other
controlled sources. The logging and manufacturing processes are expected
to conform to the environmental regulations of the country of origin.

HEADLINE PUBLISHING GROUP
An Hachette UK Company
Carmelite House
50 Victoria Embankment
London EC4Y 0DZ

www.headline.co.uk
www.hachette.co.uk

'Ye, your trust is the cause that I have conspired against you in this treason.'

From *The Boke Named the Governour*, 1531, written
by the English diplomat, and friend of Sir Thomas More,
Sir Thomas Elyot. Elyot's book, dedicated to Henry VIII,
is a treatise on how to educate and train those destined
to rule or govern. This line expands on the much older
English Proverb 'In trust is treason.'

'The state of MONARCHIE is the supremist thing upon earth: For Kings are not only GOD'S Lieutenants upon earth, and sit upon GOD'S throne, but even by GOD himself they are called Gods . . . In the Scriptures Kings are called Gods and so their power after a certain relation compared to the Divine power . . .

Kings are justly called Gods, for that they exercise a manner or resemblance of Divine power upon earth: For if you will consider the Attributes to GOD, you shall see how they agree in the person of a King. GOD hath power to create, or destroy, make, or unmake at his pleasure, to give life, or send death, to judge all, and to be judged nor accountable to none: To raise low things, and to make high things low at his pleasure, and to GOD are both soul and body due.

And the like power have Kings: they make and unmake their subjects: they have power of raising, and casting down: of life, and of death: Judges over all their subjects, and in all causes, and yet accountable to none but GOD only.'

King James I, 'A speech to the Lords and Commons of the
Parliament at White-Hall on Wednesday the XXI of March,
Anno 1609'

Author's Note

Dates in this book use the Old Style (Julian) Calendar. Under the old calendar, the year was not numbered from 1 January but from Lady Day, 25 March, which was regarded as New Year's Day. While some countries in Europe had adopted the Gregorian calendar in 1582, England did not change over to the new calendar until 1752. So, what we would now call February 1608 was under the old calendar still 1607.

The Great Frost referred to in this novel began on 5 December 1607 and ended, ten weeks later, on 14 February. Many rivers in England, including the Thames, froze solid. This was the first of the bitterly cold winters, when Frost Fairs would regularly be held on the Thames. *Rivers of Treason* begins in February a few days after the thaw.

Prologue

ANNO DOMINI 1591

A YOUNG COUPLE lay side by side on the short wooden jetty that overhung the river, the girl on her back, the lad leaning over her. Heavy clouds obscured the moon, and they could see nothing more of each other's faces in the darkness than the glitter of their eyes. A sharp breeze dragged the cold and damp air from the surging water across their skins, and the girl shivered, half regretting her refusal to take shelter in the fowlers' hut close by, as they had on other nights. In there, they were shielded from prying eyes, but she always emerged with clothes and hair that stank of stale blood, rotting guts and fish. The stench clung to her all the way home, proclaiming her guilt like a scarlet brand.

Josiane closed her eyes as the young man laid his hand on her cheek, turning her face towards him. His hot breath smelled of roasted meat and wine. He kissed her greedily, but tonight she barely responded, conscious only of the wind whining through the trees above her head and the roar of the river vibrating through the wooden piles beneath her. She should not have come. She was tired. She had missed too many nights' sleep, and in summer, the working hours in the fields were long and hard. Besides she was beginning to suspect that her brothers were right: nothing could come of it, not that she would ever admit as much to them. It was a game, but she was the prize not the player. The boy ran his fingers over her leg, stroking her thigh. She batted him away, her irritation growing.

High above her, the moon made a bid for freedom, escaping from behind the mass of clouds and bathing the trees and grass in silver. Even through her closed lids, Josiane saw the sudden burst of light. She opened her eyes, turning her head to stare in wonder at the river, now transformed to mercury. The lad leaned over her, his weight crushing her ribs, trying once more to plant his mouth on hers, but she pushed him off and sat up.

'Look at the water!' she urged.

'Why?' he muttered, without interest. He was tugging on her arm to coax her to lie down again, but she resisted, shrugging off his grip.

'Look,' she repeated.

He propped himself up on his elbow, and glanced behind him at the twisting current. But the moment had already passed. The clouds had recaptured the moon and the river was black and menacing as it had been before.

'What am I supposed to be seeing?' he grumbled.

Josiane sighed. 'Too late. It's gone now. Moon turned it silver. It was beautiful.'

The lad snorted. 'It's a stream of cow shit like always.' Then, feeling her stiffen, he added, 'Compared to you, because you're the one who's beautiful, Josy.'

And she was. At fourteen, her cheeks still had the plumpness of a child's, but beneath them the high cheekbones suggested that her face, though pretty enough now, would one day be strikingly handsome. Those dark eyes had already mastered the art of flashing in a way that few could resist. And when she untied her mane of blue-black hair and let it tumble down her back on a bright summer's day, it was as iridescent as a starling's breast.

The lad rubbed a strand of that soft hair now between his fingers, then tickled her nose with it.

She jerked her head away from him. 'My brothers do that to me and I hate it!'

'What's the matter with you tonight, Josy? Would you rather be kissing *him*? Is that it?'

'You know it isn't!' But she felt herself blushing and was glad it was too dark for him to see. She got to her feet, brushing dirt from her skirts. 'It's late and I have to be up afore dawn. Besides, Father'll kill me if he finds me missing from my bed again.'

'Stay, Josy! Your father will never know. You said nothing wakes him after he's been to the tavern.'

'Nothing wakes *him*, but my brothers have got sharper ears than any watchdog and they've twice the temper on them that Father has. They'd be as mad as a nest of hornets if they found out I'd been with you again.'

The young man scrambled up and took her hand. 'Stay a few more minutes, Josy. It's not easy for me to get away either, but you know I'd risk everything for you. Surely, I'm worth just a little trouble?'

Josiane shook her head impatiently. 'It's not a *little* trouble that worries me, it's the great stinking midden of it that'll likely get stirred up.' She pulled her hand from his. 'Now you get off home afore we're both mired to our necks in it.'

She turned away so sharply that she slipped on the boards of the jetty and almost tumbled into the river. He flung an arm about her waist to steady her. Furious with herself that she'd given him cause to save her, she lifted her head and stalked away without looking back. Behind her, she heard his grunt of frustration and the sound of his boot hitting wood, and guessed he had landed a hard kick on one of the jetty posts. For a moment, she expected him to come marching after her, but she heard his footfalls stomping rapidly down the path away from her.

Her own steps were equally swift, but almost as soon as she had stepped off the small wooden landing stage on to the bank, she was forced to slow down. The night seemed darker than usual and the path along the bank of the surging black river was narrow. Tree roots rubbed smooth and slippery by the passage of feet lay ready to trip her, and bushes and brambles snagged her skirts. Several times she stumbled, fearing that she would plunge into the swift, cold current. She breathed more easily once she reached the place where the path branched off, leading away from the riverbank through a coppice, though it was even darker under the canopy of leaves. A branch whipped back in her face, and she cursed at the sting of it, hoping it hadn't marked her. Her hand pressing against the trunk, she rested for a moment, catching her breath. The wind whistled through the treetops above her and she could still hear the low rumble of the river, though muffled now by distance and the thick vegetation. She was so tired she was tempted to lie down where she was to sleep.

'Jo . . . si . . . ane.'

The cry was faint. She wouldn't have heard it had she been walking. It came again, but it didn't sound human. It was nothing more than the breeze among the leaves. At home when she was lying in bed and heard the wind singing over the roof of their cottage, she often fancied she could hear words in it, though she could never make sense of them.

She pushed herself upright and plodded on down the track, holding one arm out in front of her to protect her face from branches.

'Jo . . . si . . . ane!'

She froze. The cry was louder, more distinct, but she couldn't tell where it was coming from.

'Leave me be,' she called out. 'I told you, I'm away home.'

From somewhere out there among the dark trunks came a crack of twigs snapping and a rustling in the dried leaves. A rat, she told herself, and so as long as it wasn't a human-rat, the furry little creatures were nothing to fret about. She'd listened to them every night of her life, scrabbling about in the thatch. She knew they were nothing to fear. But those rats did not call out her name. She hurried on, stumbling and tripping in her anxiety to escape from among the trees.

'Where are you, Josiane?' The voice seemed to be coming from in front of her.

She could see nothing moving in the darkness, but she turned, running now, back towards the river.

'I'll find you!' The cry was in front of her again.

Josiane crouched down, pressing herself against the trunk of a tree, though it was too slender to offer a hiding place. She turned her head, this way and that, trying to detect any movement. But the darkness was closing in around her like a cage, trapping her, blinding her. She forced herself to keep still and listen, but the wind was roaring in her ears and the only sound she heard was the hammering of own heartbeat. She rose cautiously, edging back along the path in the direction of her home and safety.

Twigs smashed behind her and she whipped around. She glimpsed the dark figure, saw the brief flash of pale skin, as the rope dropped over her head. The noose tightened about her little neck. She tore at the rough fibres until her nails broke and her fingertips bled. Choking, her lungs burning, blood pounding in her head, her eyes bulged till she thought they would explode. The strength ebbed out of her limbs. Her arms flopped helplessly at her side. Her legs buckled and she crumpled to the ground. But the rope only tightened. Darkness crept out from among the trees and oozed into her head like a black fog. She did not move again.

The killer waited until he was certain that her heart would never make another beat, nor her lungs ever draw another breath. When he was satisfied, he unknotted the rope, turned the corpse face up, and straightened her limbs. He brushed the long curls away from the livid burn that encircled her neck, and tossed the rope into the swiftly flowing current of the river, to become one of the thousands of pieces of flotsam and jetsam that choked its waters. Then he walked into the darkness.

Chapter One

NEWMARKET PALACE, SUFFOLK

17 FEBRUARY 1607

As THE HORSE clattered into the darkened courtyard, a yawning stableboy stumbled out to seize the reins. The rider swiftly dismounted. No words were exchanged; they didn't need to be. The boy led the horse into one of the many stables as the guard, who had been freezing his cods off in the draughty yard for more than an hour, stepped forward.

'Surrender your sword, if you please, sir,' he said curtly.

Whether the visitor was *pleased* to comply with his order or not made no difference to him. No one would be admitted bearing arms, not even the new favourite, if this is who the gentleman was. The guard had not been told the identity of the visitor who was expected in the middle of the night, only where he was to take them.

Holding up the lantern, ostensibly to give the man light enough to unbuckle his sword, he studied the new arrival. The man's riding boots, hose and black breeches were splattered with mud, but that could not be held against him. The roads and fields were quagmires now that the great frost which had gripped England for ten numbingly icy weeks had finally thawed. King James had returned from the day's hunting looking like one of the urchins who scavenged in the silt of the Thames at low tide. Those who rode with him were even more besmirched. James had, as always, led the field at a demonic pace, cackling with laughter when his horse kicked mud in the faces of those who rode too close behind him.

But in spite of the dirt from the road, this gentleman was well groomed. A long silver earring, set with sapphires, bounced against the dark curl of a lovelock, hanging down from beneath a plumed feather hat. His boots were crafted from finest leather, his hose were silk, and the scarlet doublet and short black riding cloak were trimmed with panels of silver stitchwork – striking, but not gaudy, the guard noted with a grudging approval. Not that expensive clothes were any indication of wealth or breeding: the King bought as many outfits for his favourite, Robert Carr, as he did for himself, and that popinjay was little more than an upstart groom.

This man, though, was not the kind who normally caught James's eye. His legs were unquestionably shapely; that would certainly attract the King. But he was of a slight build and neither muscular nor blond, though handsome enough to turn heads. James had better keep him well away from Queen Anne, or he might end up warming both royal beds.

It was not the first time the guard had admitted visitors to Newmarket Palace whose presence was not to be announced, and although most of the household should be snoring on their pallets at this hour, he held the lantern low as he conducted the man to the group of outbuildings, so that no inquisitive servant peering from a casement would glimpse the visitor's face. The guard paused before a door, but did not open it. He considered it beneath his dignity. The man had not uttered a word since he'd arrived, which meant he was probably another Scottish cattle herder using his looks to make his fortune at Court.

'You're to wait in the tennis court.' The guard jerked his head. 'There's meat and wine been set ready.' He remained by the door until the visitor had stepped inside. Then, cursing all the whoreson Scots under his breath, the guard retreated to the other side of the yard, where he could watch for any summons without being accused of eavesdropping.

The tennis court to which Cimex had been conducted by the guard lay in darkness except for the ruby glow of a small charcoal brazier and the flames of the candles set on a table which had been placed at the hazard end of the long chamber. Much of the room was bare and empty except for the tennis net stretched across the playing court. Beneath the wooden ceiling, the curiously sloping penthouse canopies on the walls made the chamber darker even than the night outside.

Cimex stood still on the silent court, her gaze searching along the row of chairs and benches in the dedans booths built hard against the wall, where spectators sat behind metal grilles to protect them from the hard wooden balls. She was looking and listening for any sign of movement, even for the glitter of eyes in that witch-light. Charles FitzAlan was usually already impatiently waiting in whatever rendezvous he had selected, complaining that she was late even if she arrived early. But this time, he would be justified. Although she was almost as skilful a rider as he was, and her horse a big-boned, powerful gelding, she had not been able to ride it as hard and fast as she would have liked in the glutinous mud, for fear that the beast would slip and break a leg.

She had been expecting the old fox to be crouching in one of chairs, hoping to unnerve her by suddenly speaking out of the darkness. That kind of trick amused him, but, satisfied that the chamber was empty, she stalked the length of the tennis court to the far side of the net into the hazards. The solid floor was sticky from the bulls' blood with which it had been coated to give the players a better grip. It made the chamber smell like a butcher's stall. Peeling off her leather gauntlets, she warmed her hands over the steady heat of the brazier. Then, suddenly finding herself ravenous, she took one of the roasted songbirds arranged on the platter, crunching through the flesh and bones until she had devoured the whole carcass, leaving only the twig legs, which she dropped delicately into the voiding basket.

She smelled the wine. It was strong and oversweetened, which FitzAlan knew was not to her taste. But she was thirsty, so she poured a small measure and gulped it down, before consuming one of the venison tarts. He would not offer her food, but he would insist on wine. FitzAlan could hold his drink better than any man and liked to ply those he questioned with copious quantities of it. It was said by the Scots that he was a generous host; others preferred to think that it amused him greatly to watch people get drunk. But Cimex suspected a different motive. Strong wine loosens men's tongues. It strips away the masks of friend and flatterer.

Two chairs had been placed either side of the table. She pulled the smaller and lower of the chairs further back, as if she wanted to be closer to the brazier, though not because she felt the cold. She sat, her gaze fixed in the direction of the door at the end of the tennis court though it was so dark on the service side of the court she could not distinguish it from the wall. Had he fallen asleep or was he deliberating keeping her waiting?

She felt the rush of cold air as the door opened silently and closed again. FitzAlan was wrapped in a heavy fur dressing gown, a round velvet nightcap on his short-cropped hair. He leaned heavily on a stick as he limped towards the glow of the candlelight. His legs appeared to be paining him more than usual, though she felt no pity for him. Neither spoke, and the silence only served to magnify the echo of his footfalls and the stick.

What has four legs in the morning, two at noon, three in the evening? The ancient riddle of the Sphinx floated into Cimex's head. And that great lion-woman could have added *and none when night falls.* And it would fall, it must. For every dawn, there is a sunset. However fiercely the sun burns by day, it must surrender to the night.

Cimex had risen as the door opened and she now moved aside from the chairs. Sweeping off the feathered hat, she bowed low.

FitzAlan did not acknowledge the courtesy; he never did, though he'd have been outraged had it not been offered. He sank into the larger of the two chairs, massaging his grimy fingers in the steady heat of the glowing fire.

He stretched out a hand for the goblet, as if he expected it to fill itself and jump into his fist. Cimex poured a measure from the flagon and gave it to him. He indicated impatiently she should pour another for herself. She obliged, taking only a sip before setting it down.

'So, you finally make your appearance, my wee bedbug.'

'The roads, sir—' she began but he flapped a hand, dismissing the explanation, glancing with evident amusement at her splattered boots, hose and breeches.

'I ken the mud,' he said shortly. 'But it has nae troubled our wee sparrow.'

'Daniel delivered his report to you . . . on Battle Abbey?'

'Aye, though it seems he was in no hurry to do so, but then you did nae make haste yourself to tell me your wee protégé was back in London.'

'I had not expected he would make the journey to London in the great freeze – only a reckless or desperate man would risk a horse on that ice – but as soon as I learned he was in the city, I sent word to you in Royston. But I fear my letter was ill-timed, sir, for I later heard that you had just moved on to Newmarket. I trust my message followed you there, sir?' Her tone was light, innocent.

'Your many pairs of eyes and ears have grown dim and dull, Cimex. You always know where I am lodging before I've even given the orders to go there. So, it would seem I learned that Daniel had returned before you knew yourself . . . Did I?' He took a long draught of wine, his heavy-lidded eyes fixed on her face as he drank.

Her features, though, were now partly in shadow. Cimex knew the moment she walked into the chamber that the placing of the chair and candle prickets had been carefully arranged to illuminate the smallest twitch of her face. But even had she not moved the chair back, FitzAlan would not have been able to detect so much as a flicker of disquiet in those shark-blue eyes of hers.

'I don't doubt you knew of it first, sir. As ever, your sources are impeccable. And the report Master Pursglove made to you – you are, I trust, *satisfied*?'

A trickle of wine escaped from the corner of FitzAlan's mouth and ran down into his short beard. 'That it was truthful, aye. He's too canny to be caught out in a lie. But was it the whole truth? No, I'd wager it was far from that.'

FitzAlan paused, the fingers of one hand picking restlessly at the fur of the dressing gown, like a goodwife plucking a chicken. 'The wee sparrow told me he'd discovered the fate of the pursuivant, Master Benet, who met his death in Battle, and that unfortunate wasn't the only corpse buried there, it seems. Daniel is uncommonly good at sniffing out cadavers, better than any scent-hound. Send him after one, and he'll soon dig you up another. But he's yet to deliver Spero Pettingar's head on a spike as you assured me he could, nor even the treacherous heart of that old dowager who rules "Little Rome" at Battle Abbey. Though he seems to think her powers are waning.'

'That is only to be expected, sir. Lady Magdalen is in her seventieth year. Age and infirmity must be creeping close upon her heels, if they have not already seized her.'

'Aye, Daniel said she looked to be ill, though the stubborn old besom refused to show it. But the power of that nest of priests and vipers who surround her is not diminishing. Likely, that waxes as she wanes. And according to Daniel, the illegal Masses continue. But the Privy Council have known about that for years and still they refuse to move against her. Your wee sparrow could bring me no fresh proof that I could set before them to have her charged with treason and see her precious Little Rome sacked and destroyed.'

As Rome was once sacked by the Vandals? Cimex's expression remained impassive.

'But I can read men's minds as well as God reads their souls. Daniel was speaking the truth in as far as it went, but he's holding a deal back. And it's what a man keeps from me that is always the more valuable. It's no different from when the King exercises his sovereign right to purveyance – the townsfolk and merchants deliberately conceal their best flour and wine and supply the purveyors with inferior goods, claiming them to be the finest they have.' His speech was becoming rapid. Spittle sprayed from his mouth. 'Then they have the gall to complain when they are not paid.' He slammed the goblet down on the table, sending an echo bouncing around the tennis court.

'I imagine the people have been using that same deception since kings first exercised that prerogative, sir.'

And little wonder, when James's men used the ancient right to commandeer food, and wine from any merchant, farmer, city or village, for a fraction of the price the provisions were worth in the market place.

'It is a game of wits that has been played between commons and Crown for centuries,' Cimex added soothingly.

'That it is, and Parliament would think to deprive the King of that sport and of the money too. But he will not be bested. If they want to take the prerogative from him, they will have to pay him for it. Do they think their monarch such a rickling that he'll simply hand over the right of the king and his heirs for no gain? Surrender purveyance to them and next they'll be demanding his palaces and even the crown from his head.'

FitzAlan's voice had risen and in the empty space the words were ricocheting off the walls, floors and ceiling as if it they were balls smashed around in furious game. He suddenly seemed aware of the sound and took another gulp of wine.

'Is it a lass that's sealing his tongue?' He frowned impatiently when Cimex didn't immediately answer. 'At Battle! Has another lass bewitched Daniel like that one in Bristol?'

'I hear Lady Magdalen's young ward, Katheryne, is a pretty creature,' Cimex said. 'But with the old dowager and a circle of priests guarding her virtue, I doubt that Daniel would have managed a moment alone with her. And I do not believe the girl shares her guardian's zeal for the old faith, so, what reason would Daniel have to shield her?'

The truth, and nothing but the truth, but never the whole truth.

'Then what?' FitzAlan demanded. 'You swore to me that your wee protégé had no love for popery either, despite being raised in the house of that old recusant Lord Fairfax. Did you mistake his loyalties or has Battle Abbey corrupted him and coaxed him into turning his coat?'

'He was only there for a few weeks, sir, hardly long enough to convert a man.'

'The playwright Ben Jonson, who writes the entertainments for Queen Anne, claims he was converted in two weeks by a Jesuit priest in Newgate gaol, but since he'd just killed a man, I dare say he was tender meat, ripe for persuasion if he thought he was facing the gallows and hellfires beyond. And Jonson was converted despite being raised a good Protestant, but Daniel was weaned on that papal pap. A few weeks would be ample time to bring him back into the Catholic fold, especially if he'd a whole coven of priests working on him.'

'Not when he hates and despises those priests, sir. And all I have learned about Daniel convinces me that he does.'

FitzAlan scowled at her. He plucked a roasted songbird from the platter, ripped it apart with black-rimmed nails and popped the shreds of flesh into his mouth.

He studied the carcass. 'I could have him persuaded to speak the truth . . . the *whole* truth.'

His gaze flashed up to her face. Had he heard her tiny intake of breath?

'You could indeed, sir,' Cimex said, her voice as devoid of emotion as a cook sending a scullion to kill a chicken. 'Some men can be induced to blurt out all they know at the mere sight of the instruments of persuasion, even hearing the man in the next room scream or glimpsing him being dragged unconscious back to his cell. But Daniel's metal has been tempered in a fierce heat. He has known battle and a great many hardships. It has forged a man upon whom the infliction of pain would only harden his resolve. If you asked him under torture to tell you the colour of the sun, he would stay silent until his final breath, simply because you were forcing him to answer.'

FitzAlan gave a mirthless bark of laughter. 'Few men have withstood the iron gauntlets, as Robert Cecil will attest, and those that have, have been the most fanatical of Jesuits. They embrace agony and death, believing they will soar to the highest reaches of heaven as martyrs on the wings of pain. But you have just told me Daniel has no such faith to bear him up. You do not know men and their weaknesses as I do, Cimex, despite your breeches.' He poked his stick between Cimex's thighs and gave a spiteful chuckle.

Cimex inclined her head. 'That is indeed so, sir, but after such persuasion, Daniel would be of no further use to you, even were he to survive. And what would be the advantage? To discover some trifle now and risk losing a great deal more valuable information later. Put too severe a bit in the mouth of an unbroken horse, drag on the reins too hard, and you will ruin the beast's mouth for life. It will resist all your commands ever more stubbornly.'

'Do you presume to teach me horsemanship?'

Once more, Cimex inclined her head in apparent meekness. 'As you have said, sir, you know both horses and men far better than a mere woman ever could . . . But have you considered that Daniel may indeed have told you all he learned at Battle? Do you have reason to doubt him?'

Cimex took another sip of her wine. Her gaze, which had been fastened on the candle flames, flickered towards FitzAlan.

FitzAlan, leaning back in his chair, studied her for some moments. Framed in the hell-red glow of the brazier, she made an enchanting succubus. When he finally spoke, his tone was soft. Cimex tensed.

'Your wee sparrow has no reason to think I doubt him. He was paid more than generously for his services, and I instructed him to remain in London for now.'

FitzAlan suddenly leaned forward. 'But he did not remain!' he snapped. 'Daniel left the city yesterday morning, riding north and riding fast. He has not returned. Something he has learned has sent him chasing off and nothing he told me would give him a reason to do that, so there must be information he has kept back. Your sparrow has flown, Cimex, but mark this, the King has spies everywhere. Daniel Pursglove will be found.'

Chapter Two

RIVER DERWENT, EAST RIDING

DANIEL PURSGLOVE

Two MEN BURST OUT OF the small coppice and stood squarely blocking the track. One held an axe in both hands, the blade angled towards my horse's neck; the other was swinging a bill-hook.

'You! Hold fast!' the axeman ordered.

I obligingly reined my mount in and waited to see what they intended. Beneath my cloak, my dagger was already in my hand. I could have charged my horse between them, but there was no sense risking injury to the beast from that axe. Besides, I had heard this pair chopping wood from half a mile away as I had trotted towards the grove of trees. If they had any ambitions to become footpads, they would not make much of a living from it.

'Good morrow, brothers.'

The one with the axe scowled. 'It'll not be a good one for you unless you tell us where you come from and what business you have on this road.'

His heavy jowls hung down in folds, giving the appearance that his head was growing straight out of his body. He reminded me of a giant toad, with his thick, muscular shoulders and a bulging gore-belly that contrasted oddly with his long skinny legs. And his tone was beginning to annoy me.

'And what business of yours is it to question mine? I see no sheriff's badge on your jerkin.'

The toad's mouth opened, but his companion took a step forward. His ragged sandy hair seemed to have been chopped with his own billhook and it stuck out from under a close-fitting leather cap. He bore a great resemblance to the scruffy terrier yapping at his heels. He raised his makeshift weapon. The blade glinted and winked in the low winter sun. My horse jerked his head and skipped sideways, unnerved by the flickering light.

'I wouldn't wave that around if I were you, brother. My horse has been trained for the tilt. He is likely to charge straight at you, if he mistakes that flashing blade for a lance.'

In truth, I had no idea what this horse, Valentine, would do. I'd bought him only the day before I'd set out for the East Riding, reluctantly leaving my faithful beast, Diligence, behind. Charles FitzAlan had furnished me with my old horse when he'd hauled me out of Newgate gaol and dispatched me to Bristol to hunt for the gunpowder plotter Spero Pettingar, who alone of all the conspirators had evaded Robert Cecil's clutches. FitzAlan had warned me then, and again when he'd sent me to Battle Abbey after the same fugitive, that he had men following me, tracking my every move, ready to drag me back to the Hole in Newgate if they discovered the slightest sign that my loyalties did not lie entirely with the King. He'd ordered me to stay in London, but I had managed to slip away. I had no intention of cooling my heels there. I had a score of mine own to settle, and it would be weeks before FitzAlan sent for me again, by which time I would be safely back in the city. But FitzAlan's men knew my horse, Diligence, too well. No disguise would have got me out of London unseen if I were mounted on him.

The terrier hesitated, then took a step back, but his sharp chin jerked up to show he was not backing down. 'Business of every loyal man to stop strangers and find out where they've hailed from. King's orders. You could be a . . . a foreigner, a Spanish spy.'

The two men exchanged warning glances and I knew that *foreigner* was not the word the terrier had been about to utter; nor did they have any intention of reporting suspected intelligencers to the King's men. This was recusant country. It was not the Spanish who drove fear into their hearts. At our very first meeting, FitzAlan had taken a malicious delight in reminding me that 'the King has spies everywhere' and these men knew it, as did every Catholic in those parts. My annoyance subsided a little; I couldn't blame them for being wary.

'I'm no stranger to the East Riding, brothers. I know this is the track to the ferry crossing and it's that I am making for.'

'Ferry's finished,' the terrier announced almost gleefully.

I glanced up at the sun in surprise. It was surely only mid-afternoon – not yet time for men to abandon their work for the day, especially after weeks of enforced idleness and empty purses because of the frozen rivers.

'Fell into that one, didn't you, *brother*?' the toad said with an unpleasant grin. 'Just given yourself away, haven't you? 'Cause if you did come from these parts, you'd know the ferry is at the bottom of the river.'

'But only recently, I'd wager. Otherwise, she would have been replaced by now. Bubwith depends on that crossing for its life-blood.'

The look of triumph melted from the toad's face. He grunted sourly, and began plodding back towards the small coppice of scrub and trees. He'd lost all interest in me, though I suspected he'd spread the word about my arrival soon enough.

The terrier hung back. 'Old ferry stopped running on the eve of the feast of Saint Nicholas. Come morning, she was stuck fast in the ice, couldn't haul her out. Heard her timbers cracking for days after, so everyone knew come the thaw she'd sink. But the river's in such a spate that they daren't risk using any of the smaller boats till waters go down. Be swept away or overturned, most like. That river's always a cantankerous mare, taken more lives than the King's axeman, but she's a foul temper on her now. I reckon she's getting her own back for being trapped so long by that shot-ice.'

'The horse ferry downriver at Breighton, is that working?'

He looked at me with a flicker of surprise. He was beginning to believe I did know my way round these parts after all.

'Aye, it's still afloat. Might have trouble reaching her, mind. The river's overtopped its banks 'tween here and yonder crossing. Road's under water. But with the river being this high, you'd best offer the ferryman more than the regular toll – summat for his own pocket, like.'

He tapped the side of his nose and gave me wink. The extra payment would clearly not be handed over to the ferryman's master. But I had no quarrel with that.

There was a sudden gust of wind and as my overlong hair and beard lifted, I saw the startled look as the terrier caught a glimpse of my throat. I yanked up the muffler that had loosened on the ride.

Glancing swiftly over his shoulder at his distant companion, who had resumed his wood chopping, the terrier came closer. Grasping Valentine's bridle, he stared up at me.

'You a dead man?' he murmured. 'You've a gallows' mark around your neck.'

'It's a firemark, is all, brother. I was cursed with it in my mother's belly.'

He didn't look convinced. 'I've heard you can cheat the gallows, feign death, if you've got friends to help you, and then when they've cut you down, you can vanish. 'Cause there's no one going to go searching for a walking corpse.'

'If a man's cut down quickly enough, he can sometimes be brought back from the dead,' I agreed.

I'd heard tales of men trying to cheat the noose by pushing a metal tube down their throats, or wearing a harness under the shirt to take the weight if the hangman could be bribed. The prisoners in Newgate often pinned their last desperate hope on such stories. But if FitzAlan ever carried out his threat, I'd be praying the noose would finish me, when the alternative was to be cut down alive, castrated and disembowelled before the axe finally fell. Strangling on the end of a rope was not a death any man would relish, but it might be considered a merciful end compared to some that the Crown and Church had devised.

With another swift glance behind him, the terrier leaned closer. 'You say you're bound for Bubwith? If a man needed help . . . shelter, he might find it in the church there, if he knew the signs to look for and the signs to leave. That's where the dead men go.'

He scurried off back to his companion, his dog scampering at his heels. I stared after him. He was taking a huge risk telling me. But I suspected a good many Catholic fugitives came through here to find a place to lie low or make their way to the unwatched coastal villages and a boat to safety. I shrugged the thought away. I was not here to do FitzAlan's bidding and hunt for conspirators – not this time, not until I was forced to when he summoned me again. I was pursuing another quarry. It was mine and mine alone.

I didn't know exactly where the turning was that led to the crossing opposite Breighton. But the direction of the terrier-man's gaze when he had spoken of the road confirmed that it lay ahead. So, I nudged Valentine to the pace and walked him briskly past the small coppice. Both the terrier and the toad kept their backs to me; only the little dog raised his head and cocked his ears. But when I looked back, the toad had paused and was watching me. Judging by his scowl, he didn't like what he saw.

I found a track branching off on the right, stone-lined and wide enough for carts. It more or less followed the path of the river. I could see glimpses of the 'cantankerous mare' now, surging thick and brown, almost boiling as it raced past, sweeping along a jumble of broken timbers, cracked branches and what might have been a dead sheep. The water had spilled over on to the meadows on either side, and only a few bushes and some willow scrub sticking up out of the flood marked the boundary between river and land.

In part, the track was higher than the pasture and far enough away from the edge of the flood to remain dry, but wherever there was a hollow, it was submerged and I could only guess at its route from where it emerged on the other side. My horse hesitated, unnerved by several geese flapping in front of him in the water.

I urged him forward. So far, he had lived up to his name, *Valentine* – which, if I remembered correctly what my old tutor, Father Waldegrave, had thrashed into me as a boy, meant 'strong and vigorous'. But the shifting stones beneath the horse's feet and the debris dashed against his legs by the current unsettled him and several times it seemed that he might veer off from the submerged road and stumble into the river itself. As soon as he caught sight of the track rising out of the flood ahead of him, he made a reckless dash for solid ground, where I let him stand and rest for a few minutes.

The sodden land rolled away on either side of the river, crushed flat by the weight of the vast expanse of leaden sky above. I felt myself plunging back into the desolation I had felt as a child growing up here. The day that old Lord Fairfax had flung me out on to the road, no longer a boy, but not yet a man, I had vowed that my boots would never wade through the filth of this Yorkshire mud again. And that was half a lifetime ago.

And I'd be a fool to return – I'd told myself that a dozen times while I'd been kicking my heels in growing frustration as I waited for the thaw to set in. Yet, the more time I had to think, the stronger the demon that possessed me grew.

Before I'd arrived in Battle, someone in the Abbey had already been cruelly and mercilessly blackmailed into watching every man there and reporting what they saw to London. I had assumed that the blackmailer was one of Robert Cecil's men, tasked, just as I had been by FitzAlan, to discover who was being smuggled in and out of the Abbey. The threats bore all the hallmarks of one of Cecil's ruthless intelligencers. But I had got it completely wrong. The desperate victim swore that the blackmailer was not a King's man, but rather 'someone who works against the King and Robert Cecil, someone who would see them both dead and the true faith restored to England'.

Then, back in London, in the very inn where I'd discovered the coded messages were being delivered, I saw him – Richard Fairfax, the boy I had grown up with, no longer a boy, but a man. A cub grows into a wolf, and a rat into a rat. And that rat had had me dismissed from Viscount Rowe's service, forcing me on to the streets. But even that had not satisfied him. I had no proof, but I was convinced he was responsible for my arrest on charges of sorcery, which had nearly seen me executed.

And the moment I'd set eyes on Richard in that inn, I had been certain his presence could not be a coincidence. He was the blackmailer: he had tormented his victim with the same ruthlessness as he had set out to destroy me. But what more was the little rat capable of? How far would Richard go to further his cause? Murder? Regicide? He was at the heart of the King's Court. I could not get near him, but wherever I turned, a handful of almost invisible threads seemed to be twisting around him, like a spider's web. And if he was the spider, I was beginning to feel like the fly.

I'd come close to killing him twice in London in a fit of anger, but in my cooler moments, I'd known that if I had, I'd have been hanged or worse, and that little turd was not worth dying for. As they say, though, 'ill blows the wind that profits no man', and the great freeze had brought one benefit to me at least – it had given me time to think. For I had learned something else in London on my return – my old tutor and Fairfax's chaplain, Waldegrave, was dead.

The news had left me numbed. Encountering Waldegrave again in Bristol had brought the resentment and anger at what he'd done to me surging back, when I had thought it long gone. I'd been just four years old when he had wrenched me from my mother, from the life I had been born into, and taken me into the Fairfax household to be raised as boyhood companion to Richard. Waldegrave had stripped me of my name, of my father's name. I knew nothing of my family, nor why Waldegrave had chosen me. He had kept silent all those years and now he had buried that secret in his own grave. I should have rejoiced at the death of that old priest; instead, I felt cheated.

But as I sat staring into the flames of the hearth fire in my London lodgings, while the ice crackled on the Thames outside, one remark Waldegrave had made when I'd first encountered him again resurfaced in my head – *If I had stayed, I might have prevented . . .* That was it; that was all. He'd been talking about the death of Richard's father, George Fairfax. I had long suspected that Richard had somehow been behind his father's untimely demise. Then it came to me as I sat there, warming my hands over the fire, that this was the very snare I needed, the trap that might yet catch the rat. If I could just find witnesses, proof that Richard had murdered his father, I might yet put him on the block where he belonged and rid the world of that vermin.

THE BREIGHTON FERRY was moored up on the opposite side of the river. Somewhere below the impenetrable brown water lay the staithe where customers would usually disembark. A few yards behind stood a small cottage, raised on wooden piles, so that even when the Derwent burst its banks, which it did most years, the ferryman and his family might sleep dry. A narrow walkway, also on stilts, led from the landing place to the cottage. The winter ice had not dealt kindly with it and even from a distance I could see it was sagging in places. But the rope by which the ferry was propelled still hung above the river and it looked sound enough.

A bell hung from a post on my side of the water and I rang it vigorously, but I had to make several more attempts before a man finally emerged from the door of the cottage and stood in the open doorway with his arms folded, staring at me across the swollen river. He turned his head, speaking to someone inside. Then he vanished back into the dark interior. For a few moments, I thought he was going to refuse to carry me. He could be summoned to court if he did. But given the condition of the river, he would likely be excused, unless whoever owned the revenue from the ferry was a friend of the judge or *was* the judge.

Eventually he re-emerged, pulling on a leather jerkin. A tall, tow-haired lad trailed after him, looking as though he'd sprung up like a seedling kept in the dark, for he was so spindly a stiff breeze might have bowled him over. They picked their way down the walkway, which rocked and sagged under the ferry-man's weight, and clambered into the flat-bottomed boat. Hand over hand, the ferryman pulled the rope through the two cleats mounted on the craft, and edged it out into the current. The river seized the boat at once and it was pushed downstream, the rope above it so taunt that it threatened to snap. But the lad, using a long pole, skilfully kept it on course.

Slowly, the ferry slid across on the rope until its square nose nudged against the submerged bank a few feet from me. The ferryman let go of the rope and flexed his gloved hands as he stared up at me, but he did not lower the end of the boat for me to board.

'Powerful big horse you got there. You be best leaving him here, unless you've a mind to swim him across.'

'He'll be steady enough on the boat. I'll see he keeps still.'

'Aye, but he's a heavy beast and with that current pullin', rope could snap and send us all careering downriver.'

'You carry carts that are heavier,' I told him firmly. As the terrier had warned, the ferryman was holding out for a larger sum, not that he dared demand it in case I reported him. But with the river so swollen, I couldn't really blame him. He'd earn it.

I gave him double the usual toll for a passenger and horse. Without a word, he stuffed the coins carefully away, then lowered the end of the boat. I splashed down into the floodwater and coaxed Valentine into the centre of the flat-bottomed craft.

'You mind you keep a sharp watch upriver, Dob,' the ferry-man called out as he grasped the rope. 'Anything weighty slamming into us will see us at the bottom.' He grunted as he made each pull on the rope, the current hammering against the wooden side.

The lad nodded, his face screwed up in anxious concentration as he used his pole to fend off anything being swept down towards us, as expertly as a master swordsman in a duel. I held Valentine's head hard against my shoulder as he shifted his hooves, trying to keep his balance.

By the time we felt the boat bump against the submerged bank, the ferryman's face was wet with sweat from the effort.

'Best wade him,' he said, glancing at the horse and then at the battered walkway. I needed no persuasion. I wasn't convinced it would even hold my weight, much less Valentine's.

I dragged and tugged the beast through the water and by the time we were level with the cottage, my breeches and riding cloak were soaked in icy water and I was squelching inside my boots. I had half the river in them and probably a few fish too.

The cottage door opened and a woman peered out, wiping her hands on her sacking apron. She looked inquiringly at the ferryman and jerked her head towards me. He nodded.

'There's a good fire inside and a bite to warm you, if you've a mind,' she said. 'Catch your death if you ride on soaked like that.'

I allowed the ferryman's lad, Dob, to take Valentine and tether him on a mound that stood clear of the water, then followed the woman inside. Steam was rising from a large iron pot hanging over the fire, which was burning cheerfully in the hearth. The room itself was dominated by a long rough table, with benches on either side. It was far bigger than even a good-sized family would need, for the ferryman and his wife added to their income by serving food and ale to those using the crossing. I dragged off my sodden cloak, which was dripping on to the boards, and the woman hung it near the fire. I tipped the muddy water out of my boots and padded across to the bench in my hose, leaving a trail of wet footprints.

The woman brought me a bowl of stewed turnip and tiny

river fish, still with their heads on, and watched me with the same anxious expression as her son as I dug my spoon in.

As her husband came in, she glanced up at him, wringing her hands. 'I've no bread to give him. Flour's all but gone till I can get to market. Wasn't expecting travellers.'

'A pottage as good as this has no need of bread,' I assured her. She offered me a grateful smile.

In truth, the broth was as thin as water, and the pottage tasted mostly of dried thyme and mud, but it was hot and I'd eaten far worse on the battlefield. If I'd been served this in Newgate gaol, I'd have thought it a banquet.

The ferryman slid on to bench opposite me and poured himself a measure of beer from the jug his wife had just set before me.

'Cupboard's pretty much bare after all these weeks of frost. Lass used the last of bacon back end of January. She's right, we've not had many wanting to cross since thaw, except those who live hereabouts and they don't need to sup with us.'

He was watching me closely. His son had edged back into the cottage and I was aware that he and his mother were eyeing me with not so much curiosity as apprehension. They would be well used to travellers, but a stranger arriving when the roads were little more than liquid mud and the rivers in full spate must either be a fool or have business that would not wait – King's business – and such men brought nothing but trouble to those who lived in these parts. I knew I had to offer some kind of explanation.

'I used to live hereabouts when I was a lad.'

'Oh aye, and where would that be, then?'

'I worked at the Fairfax Manor at Willitoft.'

That was not quite true, of course, but close enough. I had no intention of telling anyone the truth about my position in the household. 'You and Richard should behave like brothers to one another,' George Fairfax had told us sternly when, as small boys, he caught us punching each other. If bloody noses make blood-brothers, we were certainly that. But I wasn't about to lay claim to kinship, or explain to these good folk why I had been banished. Better that they believe I was one of the dozens of stable lads, farm-boys or scullions who'd been employed there over the years.

'Left there to seek my fortune in the city and I haven't been back for years. Has the manor changed much?'

'By the looks of that beast of yours, you've done alright for thee sen. But there's many that don't, as I keep telling the lad here when he mithers on about running off to London. He'll end up digging the shit out of other folks' privies to scrape a living, or summat worse. Isn't that right?'

I glanced at Dob, whose pale eyes looked at me beseechingly, hoping I would tell his father the streets of the city really were paved with gold. But I couldn't afford to annoy the ferryman and, besides, I could see at a glance that every trickster and thief in London would spot the lad as a freshly hatched pigeon as soon as he ambled through the gates.

'If you've got no trade, you'll starve in the city,' I told him. 'You've a great skill on the river, anyone can see that, but they won't let you work as a ferryman down there. The London watermen are a brutal lot. Their wherries pass down from father to son and any outsider trying to muscle in on their customers would be lucky to escape with only his hands smashed to pulp.'

The boy's mother pressed her fingers to her mouth, as though the mere thought of her son lost to that city was enough to make her weep. Dob lowered his gaze, looking sullen. I knew I hadn't convinced him. I wouldn't have been able to convince my younger self either. The young are always certain they will succeed, however many others they see fail.

But the ferryman nodded with satisfaction. He picked up a clay pipe, filled and lit it. The smoke smelled of coltsfoot, not tobacco. He sucked on the long stem before he was seized by a rattle of phlegmy coughs. He spat into the fire.

'So, Willitoft, is it? Aye, well, you'll find a good few changes at the manor. Not been the same since the old lord died.'

I feigned surprise. 'George Fairfax is dead?'

'Oh aye.' He glanced at his wife. 'Accident, it were. At least that's what they say.'

'Are there any who doubt it?'

'I hear tales. Folks talking among themselves. We don't bend our ears, do we, lass? But . . .' He paused, waving the stem of his pipe towards the walls. 'Only someone as deaf as an adder could miss what's being said at this table.'

'So, what did you hear?' I asked, trying to give the impression that the question was merely born of idle curiosity.

'Some of the servants who used to work at the manor came this way. Young Richard sent them packing even before his father was laid in his grave. I dare say you'd have known them, for they'd been serving there, man and boy, for decades. Years of loyal service they'd given to the old lord. Then suddenly no work, no roof over their heads and precious little hope of finding another at their age.'

'And they told you about this accident?'

'Whole of Bubwith parish knew there'd been a mishap the day his lordship was taken. Out riding, he was, his horse baulked at the wall and threw him. But the beast had jumped it a hundred times and it was so low a lady could have done as much on a palfrey. The servants all reckoned there was summat queer about that, summat amiss.'

''Appen it saw a viper in the stones or something affrighted him,' his wife said.

'Unless the horse has a mind to start speaking, we'll never know what it saw,' her husband said impatiently.

'Did the coroner question the servants?'

'Maybe he did, those that were still at the manor, anyroad, but they weren't about to stir up trouble for themselves. Who'd risk crying murder when their master's a noble, even one who was . . . ?'

The ferryman petered out, catching the anxious glance from his wife. He lowered his gaze and seemed to be entirely absorbed in the complex ritual of refilling his pipe. I knew he'd been about

to say *a Catholic*. But not even the most zealously Protestant
Justice of the Peace would let a servant escape severe punishment
for deliberately injuring his lord and master. It would be counted
as treason and they'd pay with their life. The fear of another
popular uprising, like the Newton Rebellion which had broken
out in Northamptonshire only a few months ago, had long
been an even greater threat in the minds of the justices than the
Catholics. Indeed, in Northamptonshire it had been a Catholic
landowner whose enclosures had been destroyed by the local
workers, but the King's men had ridden them down and fifty
rebels had been killed or executed before the day was over.

I could coax nothing more about the *accident* from the ferryman. I doubted he knew, anyway. But it was a blow to learn
that many of the old servants had left. It greatly diminished my
chances of finding a witness. But perhaps it would, after all,
work to my advantage, for there would be fewer left who might
recognise me. And I was relieved to learn from the ferryman's
grumbles about the loss of trade that Richard seldom, if ever,
visited the manor now that he was at the Royal Court. With their
master absent, there might be someone who could be persuaded
to talk, especially if they had reason to hate him, and if anyone
could give a servant cause to do that, it would be Richard. If
the ferryman was to be believed, he'd certainly antagonised the
villagers.

'Milks the manor dry for every drop he can squeeze out of
the land and tenancies, but leaves all the manor business to that
bastard of a high steward he's installed. *High* is the right title
for him an' all. High and mighty, the cock of the dung heap. He
wants to remember that the cock that crows loudest is the first
to get his head bit off by the fox.'

'Hush, Robert!' his wife said urgently, her eyes rolling in my
direction. She gave me a timid smile. 'He means nowt by it, sir.
Just his foolish way of talking.'

'We all rail against the cocks who lord it over us and we all
want to see them plucked and boiled. There's no harm in talk,

mistress,' I assured her. But I'd seen too many pay on the gallows for a careless word or a foolish threat. Still, I doubted the ferryman and his wife had too much to fear from this man of Richard, as long as they kept out of his way.

I paid them what they asked for the fish pottage and beer. More than it was worth, but still only half of what the London innkeepers would have charged, and the woman beamed her thanks.

Dob followed me out on the pretext of helping me mount Valentine. 'Ma's afeared that if I go, I'll not come back,' he said, though he seemed to be confiding this to Valentine rather than me. 'She says days are coming when Father will be too doddered to pull a laden ferry any more, and if I'm not here to take over . . . But I know can earn far more in the city and I'll send all my money back to Ma. They'll not be in want.'

'Watermen *can* earn more in cities such as London, but there are hundreds of men competing for the custom and what I told your father was true. They don't take kindly to outsiders stealing their trade.'

'But I don't want to be a ferryman here, forever going back and forth over the same little bit of water for the rest of my days like him.' He glanced back at the house and lowered his voice, drawing even closer to Valentine. 'Sometimes, I even think of cutting that rope and letting the river carry the ferry away with me on it. In a town there'd be other work besides ferrying. You found work right enough, didn't you?' He looked up at me for the first time, his mouth drooping, but his eyes burning with excitement.

'I've done many different things, lad, to keep my guts from sticking to my ribs. Even a spell on the battlefield – I saw men screaming as they were hacked to pieces, women too with their babes in their arms. I've travelled to France and beyond, worked and sweated my passage out, and paid with a jewel to voyage home. I've slept in ditches and stolen food that men have tossed to the hounds chained outside their doors. I've had some fine work too, sitting every night at a viscount's table, with silver buttons on my jerkin, eating food fit for a queen. But Dame Fortune plays with a man's livelihood as wantonly as she does with his dice. One throw and you're winning, with the next you've lost everything. My last job got me thrown into a stinking dungeon, chained in irons, and fed food not even a starving cat would've touched. There are many who long for what you have here, lad, and never gain half as much in their lives, though they labour day and night until they're half dead from exhaustion.'

The lad shook his head impatiently. And I realised that although I thought myself comparatively young – I was only around thirty-one or thirty-two years – to a youth half my age, I must seem like one of those old codgers wagging a finger and cautioning care, when all he wanted to do was gallop like the wind.

'But you've seen sights,' he said mulishly. 'Had adventures. I could come with you . . . as your servant . . . You could teach me . . . I'd not ask for wages, just vittles.'

'Come with me? To Willitoft?'

'When you go back to the city.'

'How do you know I won't stay here?'

''Cause no one ever does, not once they've been away.'

I wondered how many others the lad had begged to accompany; how many he'd watched leave and not return. I glanced back at the cottage to see his mother watching us anxiously. Sooner or later, Dob would run off. It was probably the day most mothers dreaded. The day I had walked away from the Fairfax's manor, no one had been sorry to see me go. George Fairfax had threatened to have me hanged if I set foot back across the Derwent, the first of many such threats I've received over the years. I have a gift for making enemies. But now, looking at that woman standing by the cottage wall, her reddened hands twisting her skirts, I wondered if my own mother had watched me with same dread when I was taken from her arms as a little boy. Had I looked back, trying to snatch one last glimpse of her?

Had she been waving or weeping? I couldn't remember, and the two men, George Fairfax and Waldegrave, who could have given me the answers were both dead. But I had crossed the Derwent. I was back.

Chapter Three

'Now here's a lad who'd bring a blush to any lass's cheeks, wouldn't he, Magota?' The two women giggled.

There was no mistaking they were sisters. Both had thick curls of hair the colour of oxblood falling from their caps, bushy eyebrows that met in a continuous line across their foreheads, round faces, red cheeks and eyes that twinkled with merriment. Their meaty arms and broad hands were folded across rounded bellies and their plump hams swelled out under their skirts. Magota was slightly shorter than Rosa, but it was hard to tell which might be the elder, for they both looked to be around forty.

'Not had new customers come to stay—' Rosa began.

'Since afore Christmastide,' Magota finished. 'Only had one man here while thaw set in.'

'But he got away,' they finished in unison and chuckled.

The inn was small, barely more than an alehouse, with what must have once been the family's bedchamber now divided into two for paying guests. But it boasted both a name, 'The Lusty Tup', and a sign in the form of a roughly carved wooden model of a well-endowed and rampant ram hanging over the entrance. In case the meaning was lost on the traveller, one of the painted cloths hanging from the walls of the bedchamber depicted sheep and shepherd disporting themselves in pastures by the river, the ram vigorously doing his duty by the ewes while the shepherd fondled a bare-legged girl beneath a tree.

The chamber was comfortably furnished with rush matting on the wooden floorboards, a bedstead with a deep feather pillow and well-bleached coarse linen sheets, two small chairs and a hutch chest whose back could be swung horizontally to form a table. A dark, steep and narrow staircase led directly up from the passageway below into the room, the only door being at the bottom. I noticed the door was furnished only with a latch and no lock, but there was a bolt on the outer side. The sisters' way of ensuring guests didn't sneak out without paying; at least I hoped that was the reason.

There was still an hour before sunset and though my bones ached from the saddle, I could not sit still in my chamber. A few people hurried up and down the main street, heads down against a wet wind. The tiny shopfronts beneath the signs of butchers, poulters and grocers were fastened shut. They had probably sold out of what little they still had earlier in the day, if they'd opened at all. Men and boys were labouring in workshops or yards, sawing and hammering, too anxious not to waste the last dregs of fading light to look up. Only an old man sitting on a stool in front of his door watched the street, while his fingers, unsupervised, mended a net. He grunted as I greeted him, but almost at once his eyes darted away from me, making it plain he did not want to talk.

I found my feet drawn back towards the swollen river. It had overtopped its banks but not flooded the village, seeping in only as far as the rise on which the church stood. On the opposite bank, though, it had spilled over, turning the land beyond into a lake. The water swirled thick and brown around the trunks of trees sticking up out of it. Two ducks squatted on one of the half-submerged branches, eyeing the river suspiciously as if not even they were willing to venture in. A sack spun past me. I thought I saw it wriggling, as if there was some living creature trapped inside, but in the grey light and writhing current, I couldn't be sure, and it was swept away and out of sight.

As I stared down into that swirling brown water, I was suddenly gripped by a realisation colder than the river itself. *Waldegrave was dead.* I had known for weeks, but it was only now, only here, that I seemed to fully grasp it.

Half my life I'd longed to hear those words, hating him so much that his death seemed the only way to free myself of the burning anger I felt. But over the years since I'd left Lord Fairfax's house as a boy of fifteen and walked away from all I had ever known, war and life had banked down that rage until it was nothing more than a smouldering ember, whose heat I could barely recall. And when I had finally encountered my tutor again fifteen years later, he was old and frail, and the anger in me that had briefly flared again at the sight of him had been doused by . . . by what? Pity? No, even as an old man he had not invited pity.

It had been two months now since the young acolyte had found me in London and given me the message that Waldegrave's corpse had been dragged out of the river, but that he had *not* died of drowning. Another *accident* that was not accidental. The message had not named him as Waldegrave, of course. *The Yena*: that is what it had said. It was the sobriquet the thieves at Bristol Castle had bestowed on him. Now the Yena, the beast that feasts upon corpses, was a corpse himself, murdered. Maybe the castle thieves had thought he'd betrayed them, or perhaps Robert Cecil's men had finally discovered his hiding place. He was, after all, a priest, a hunted man, and like rats, they do not want for enemies.

My boyhood prayers had finally been answered. My wish had been granted, and yet this did not bring the relief, the peace I had always thought it would. I stared down into the swirling icy river, so thick with mud a dozen corpses could be drifting below me unseen in that darkness. His death should have been the end. It should have been over, but it wasn't. Fairfax and Waldegrave were gone and I had returned. They were dead and I still lived. But for how long?

I turned away, deliberately fixing my gaze on the great square tower of grey stone that seemed to have been hacked from the granite sky above. But the spectre that was Waldegrave would not sink back into that river. This place, the Church of All Saints, had stood as the battle flag of the enemy. I had been raised in its menacing shadow. It had loomed over me as a child like the Tower of London stands as warning to any man who dares to rebel against the King. I'd been taught to believe it was the mouth of hell itself. George Fairfax and Waldegrave would no more have knelt to pray in there than they would have danced in a witches' coven.

Of course, as a man, I had attended services in other Protestant churches many times before when the law demanded it, for I had no love for either the Catholic or Protestant faith, and saw no point in suffering fines, imprisonment or worse for a religion to which I felt, at best, indifferent. But not this church. I could hear the voice of Waldegrave behind me forbidding me to enter; I could feel his iron fingers, cold as the grave on my neck, dragging me away. I marched up the path to the great door and turned the iron ring. I half expected it to be locked, but the door swung open silently and I stepped in.

Now that I was inside, I was almost disappointed. The Church of All Saints did not look in the least like the abode of the Devil. It looked sad, neglected. Bosses had fallen from the ceiling. The roof evidently leaked and rain had left damp patches high on the walls, green with slime. Wind funnelled through holes where segments of stained glass had fallen out. The lead lines had probably long been rotten and the savage cold of the last two months had hastened their decay. It was strange to see it, like remembering a deep chasm you feared to cross as boy, and returning as a man to discover it was no more than a shallow ditch.

I heard the scrape of shoes on a gritty floor. There was someone at the far end of the church. My hand flew to the hilt of my dagger beneath my cloak. An elderly woman stepped out from beneath the chancel archway. She started as she caught sight of me, and tugged the edge of the hood of her plain brown cloak deeper over her face. Then she slowly made her way down the aisle towards me, passing the wooden communion table. She seemed to have grown more infirm in a few paces, her limp more pronounced, her back more stooped, her head angled away from me so that I could see little more than a sallow cheek and a wisp of ashen grey hair that stood out vivid as a ray of moonlight in the half-light.

As she drew closer, her fingers grasped the side of the hood, pulling it almost like a mask across her face, but her eyes raked my clothes, as people do when they are searching for a badge of a sheriff's man or King's official.

'God give you a good night, mother.'

'And you, sir,' she mumbled with a small bob of her head. She shuffled past, then paused, still half turned away from me. A yellowish-brown patch of newer cloth had been stitched across the shoulders and hood, to reinforce her cloak against the rain and years of wear.

'If it's the records of baptism you be wanting, you'll find them in the parish chest, yonder corner. It's driest there, see, furthest from the window. It'll not be locked. Clerk doesn't like to be disturbed, so it saves him the trouble of fetching the key.'

More likely he was afraid of being questioned about them by officials checking to see if suspected Catholic families had brought their child to be baptised in the Protestant faith. It could mean a heavy fine or worse if they hadn't.

She limped towards the door, but even as I made my way up the aisle, I could sense her watching me.

I walked under the archway from which she had emerged into the chancel and wondered what she had been doing up there. If she'd been cleaning, she'd made a poor job of it, for the floor was covered in mouse and bird dung and the corners swathed with cobwebs. Another archway led from there into a small space, which must have once been a chantry chapel. You could see the scars where the stone altar had been smashed and removed. Now it was used to store parish chests and baskets containing assorted brushes, cleaning clothes and earthenware jars.

I had not come into the church to look at old books, but to shake off the clinging malaise of Waldegrave's ghost, for he'd never follow me in here. And yes, if I was forced to admit it, the boy in me wanted to thumb my nose at the old bastard. But the old woman's mention of records had suddenly raised a thought. Somewhere in that chest might be a record of my own birth, and the names of my parents.

They were long dead, that much I'd come to realise as a boy. Waldegrave had never tired of telling me to pray for their souls, or instructing me to give thanks for my benefactor, Lord Fairfax, who, in his Christian duty to widows and orphans, had charitably taken me in. Maybe my mother had already been dying when Waldegrave had removed me from her cottage, and she was buried somewhere in this churchyard. But it was no use searching for a grave. Village women were not granted stone tombs, just simple wooden crosses that rotted away even before the corpse beneath had become earth.

As the old woman had said, the great, banded oak chest was not locked. I eased open the lid and started lifting out the heavy leather-bound books, examining them one by one and replacing them, until I found the one covering the year in which I thought I had been born – *1576*. I might have been birthed a year earlier or a year later, but it couldn't have been more than that. It was one of the only two things I knew about myself, if you can call such a vague date knowledge, and the other was the name I dimly remembered hearing my mother call me – *Moke*, the pet name in those parts for *Matthew*. Was it my name, or had I heard her call some other boy that? I couldn't even be certain that it was my own mother's voice which echoed in my dreams. Perhaps, after all, it was another child's mother I'd heard calling down the years.

I hoped that if I saw a full name, I might instantly recognise it. I ran my finger down page after page of baptisms, squinting at the fading ink in the failing light. But nothing stirred any memory. My neck aching, I finally slammed the book shut without bothering to examine another year. I was annoyed with myself. If my parents were Catholics and, in all likelihood, they were – why else would Waldegrave have taken me to be raised in the Fairfax household? – then probably I'd never been brought here for baptism. I closed the chest and turned to go.

It was only then that a tiny flash of yellow caught my eye in the lacy stone tracery that arched over the small piscina set into the wall. It was where the priests would once have disposed of water used in the Mass, so that it drained away into the earth beneath the church and couldn't be used in casting spells or sold for cures – a relic of the old faith, long abandoned. There was now little light trickling through the window, but curiosity made me step closer just to see what it was – only a dried flower, a marigold, the stem pushed through one of the small holes in the carved stone, so that the flattened flower head sat like a tiny badge. Some child had probably poked it in there. An image suddenly flashed into my head of the old sewing maid in the Fairfax manor who always wore marigolds pinned to her gown when they were in season. *Mary's gold*, she called them, the flowers of grief. I'd not seen women dare to wear those for years.

Outside, twilight was thickening swiftly, and with it a steady beat of rain falling on the sodden churchyard and the flooded land beyond. I wrapped my cloak tighter around me and prepared to set off at as brisk a pace as the mud would allow, back to the Lusty Tup. As I turned at the end of the path, from the tail of my eye, I saw something move behind me. The old woman was slipping back in through the church door. She must have been standing outside in the rain all the time I'd been in there, watching and waiting.

IN TRUTH, THAT evening I'd have gladly sought my own company and eaten my supper alone in my chamber. Valentine, though a strong and handsome beast, was far more skittish and nervous than my accustomed horse, Diligence. I soon discovered he was liable to shy at the sight of a partridge flying up in front of him, or a woman shaking the dust from her broom at the cottage door, and I had to stay constantly alert to anything that might spook him and be ready to calm him. I hoped it was merely a sign that he was uneasy having a new rider and that we'd eventually settle into each other's stride.

Now I was longing to stretch my aching bones out on a soft bed. But Fairfax's death and Richard's part in it were gnawing at me like a tooth-worm. The fact that he had dismissed many of the servants before they could be questioned had only served to convince me that I was right: there was, as the ferryman had put it, 'summat queer about that, summat amiss'. I had to see what more I could glean from the local gossip. And strong ale loosens tongues better than any rack.

The Tup's parlour was built on several levels, so that if the river barged in through one door, it could be swiftly booted out through the other. Several men had already settled along the benches either side of the long narrow table, tucking into boiled mutton, which was well seasoned with dried herbs, but like the ferryman's wife, the sisters had evidently run out of flour, for there was no bread to eat with the meat, only a thick porridge of oats and dried beans. But it filled the belly. The beer was old. It would have been as strong as a double-brew, except that it had been watered down. But the locals weren't complaining and I felt sure no one would report the sisters, for every household was trying to stretch out whatever they had, for fear they would not be able to buy more in the coming weeks.

It seemed food, or the lack of it, was on everyone's mind. The giant wave which had destroyed so much farmland and livestock on the west coast the year before had been followed by the great freeze which had lasted for two months. What little grain had been stored had long been exhausted. The winter wheat crop was destroyed and the ground was so sodden after the thaw that the spring planting would be badly delayed.

'That thieving merchant was charging twice what he was last year and three quarters of that sack of white peas of his were mouldy. He'd put a layer of good 'uns on top. It was as well I dug down deep afore I parted with my coins. I told him to go try his luck in York. You could sell those city folk a three-legged horse if you told 'em you'd left t'other leg at the blacksmith's to get it shod.'

Hearty laughter rolled around the table. But as it died away and another man said grimly, 'Happen, all the horses in these parts will be three-legged ones soon, 'cause if things carry on the way they are, we'll be forced to eat the other.'

'The manor at Willitoft will have kept a good measure of grain in store,' I said, 'and the ferryman tells me Lord Fairfax is absent, so they must have some to spare.'

George Fairfax had always made sure that food from manor farms was sold at a fair price in the local markets, and there was always some kept back to distribute among the widowed mothers and the elderly who'd fallen on hard times.

All heads around the table turned towards me, and all were scowling.

'It's as plain as a pikestaff you've been *absent* yourself for a good few years, if that's what you think,' one man said. 'They've not sent so much as a sack of turnips to market since the shot-ice set in.'

'And there's men from this village, aye, and from Breighton and Gunby too, gone up to the manor to fetch a few measures of grain and hay to fill their bairns' bellies and feed their livestock, but the steward turned them all away. Wouldn't spare them so much as a split pea.'

'They weren't asking for charity, neither. They'd money to pay if the price were reet.'

Another gave a hollow laugh. 'If they had been asking for charity, he'd have set the dogs on them.'

'I'd like to feed *him* to the dogs, in small pieces, letting good grain rot in his barns while folks go hungry.'

'He'll not let it rot. You mark my words, he's too wily for that. He'll wait till folks are desperate, then he'll sell for ten times what it's worth.'

'And will that go into his own pocket or Lord Fairfax's coffers?' I asked.

'They'll both be well lined, you can be sure of that. We should march on Willitoft and empty those barns of theirs of every last grain and, when we're done, burn them to the ground.'

Several of the men around the table sank lower on to their benches, heads down as they muttered their approval. Others hushed the last speaker loudly, peering round anxiously at the other customers of the inn who were sitting at the small tables closer to the fire, playing cards or dice. That kind of wariness, like a yawn, is catching. I found myself scanning the parlour too, suddenly aware of a man sitting alone in the far corner of the parlour, his hand grasping the handle of his tankard as though it was a weapon. As I turned, our eyes met, though he swiftly looked away, apparently engrossed by the state of his mud-splattered boots. From the pattern of the stains on his breeches and his cloak, which he'd thrown over the side of the settle, he'd ridden to the inn, not walked. So, he didn't live in the village. I wondered if he too was staying in the Lusty Tup, but when Magota and Rosa came bustling to clear the platters and refill the tankards, I saw them both stare curiously at him and exchange glances with each other. Plainly neither knew him.

He was perhaps in his forties, with gaunt cheekbones and deep-set eyes, his pale skin drawn tight as a kid glove over a fleshless skull. His black hair was only just beginning to grey. It hung lank and straight, grazing a soft linen collar, but his black beard, which was short and trimmed to a sharp dagger point, had a stark white streak running straight down the middle of it. He was watching me again, this time making no secret of it. Was he one of FitzAlan's men? He couldn't be: FitzAlan believed I was still in London.

I drained my tankard and rose. The door behind me opened into a cross passage. One end led to the courtyard where Valentine was stabled; the other opened out on to the narrow street in front of the inn. I walked rapidly out into the street and retreated a short way up the road, sliding back into the darkness of a ginnel. Almost at once, I saw the door open and a figure emerge from the Tup and step into the street. As the light spilling from the passage-way briefly caught him, I recognised the man who had appeared to take an such an interest in me in the parlour. But he didn't glance up or down the street, as I might have expected if he was following me, but instead strode off purposefully in the opposite direction. Maybe he'd been watching all of us at that table; the talk had strayed into dangerous territory.

I'd barely taken a couple of steps from the ginnel when I heard the crunch of boots behind me and whirled around, drawing my dagger. Two men were behind me. One had his arm drawn back, his fist clenched. But my blade must have glinted in the light from the candle in the house opposite or he recognised the movement a man makes as he draws a knife, for he spread his fingers in a placatory gesture. I could see nothing of their faces in the dark street, but even in the darkness I could tell they both had the muscular bulk of men who'd spent their lives hefting barrels or wrestling oxen. I lowered my knife a little, but kept it plainly visible.

'Fine night for a walk, brothers.'

'B . . . best enjoy your walk while you still can,' the second man said. He forced out his words with some effort, and as he took a pace towards me, he staggered slightly; evidently the beer he'd been imbibing had not been watered.

'And what might prevent me from walking?'

'Hard to walk with your legs broken.' He giggled, nudging his companion, but his friend did not join in the laughter. Elbowing the drunken man aside, he raised his fist again, though keeping well out of my dagger's reach.

'What's your business here? Folks round here don't take kindly to strangers sticking their nebs in, trying to stir men up, then clattering to their masters in York or London. We know what happened in Newton, when decent folk rose up and tried

44

to defend their own rights to graze on common land. There, were you, feeding the King's men their names so they could round them up and hang them?'

'I'm not one of the King's men,' I said.

'Would say that,' the drunken man hiccupped, 'if . . . if'n he was.'

'I used to work at the manor as a lad, years ago. I remember the old lord there was a decent sort. But I heard today that he's dead. Killed in a riding accident, they say.'

'That's what they say, is it?' the more sober of the two sneered. 'Happen you best take care, then, hadn't you? We wouldn't want any more accidents in these parts, now, would we?'

Chapter Four

It was reckoned to be only two miles from Bubwith to Willitoft, and on a warm summer's day when the track was baked hard, it was an easy journey for horse, cart or a man on foot, for the land stretched flat, broken only by small coppices, the occasional hut and tiny cottage squatting between the fields of golden corn and contented sheep and cows grazing on rich green pasture and foraging among the tall reeds on the marshy ground where wild duck nested. At least, that's how I remembered it. But it wasn't what I saw when I set out from Bubwith late the following afternoon.

I had deliberately waited until an hour before sunset, not that you could see the sun behind the battlements of granite-grey cloud. And I had dressed with care, donning the finest clothes I had brought. I did not need to make my cloak and boots look travel-stained, though the scullion in the Lusty Tub had, at the insistence of Magota and Rosa, cleaned both. But the mud of the track had undone all his hard work. Once I was out of sight of the last of the cottages in Bubwith, I'd bound a cloth around my neck with a wad of wool beneath.

The great freeze had caused havoc on the track, dislodging stones and creating pits filled with liquid mud. Several times, I was obliged to dismount and lead Valentine, for fear he'd step down into one that was deeper than it looked and fall, breaking his leg and my neck. Pools of water gleamed dully in the bare earth of the fields, and sheep, lame with foot rot, extended scrawny necks to reach any green shoot that had not been blackened by the ice. Such sights I had seen often as I'd ridden from

London to the Ridings, but it was the change in the landscape that struck me. The huts and cottages I glimpsed across the fields and marshland looked abandoned. No smoke rose from their heaths. Doors were missing, thatch had slithered off and walls were crumbling. Fences and walls now divided fields which I was sure had once been wide-open common lands, where cattle and sheep owned by different cottagers had grazed together. It seemed that Richard's steward had deprived the local people of more than just the right to buy grain.

Fairfax Hall was shielded from those passing on the road and from the bitter winds of the lowlands by a row of crack willow, with thick, fissured trunks, and great bare limbs. Now that I saw them again, I could almost hear the loud retorts when the branches broke on those cold, dark winter's nights of my childhood. Through the leafless twigs, I glimpsed the grey limestone and dull red bricks of the manor walls, like the faces of prisoners peering out through the bars. Only the tops of the many chimneys stood clear above them. A spasm knotted my guts as I drew closer. I had faced armies on the battlefield, fire and bullets, and been afraid; only a fool or a liar says he isn't. But staring once again at that house, I felt the kind of primeval fear and loathing only a child can know.

I dismounted and kicked the mud with my boot until I uncovered a small sharp stone. Heaving up one of Valentine's great feet, I wedged it into the hoof, not hard enough to do any permanent damage, but to temporarily lame him. Then I led the horse down the track and across the small bridge over the ditch girdling the house, ready to turn and retreat if I saw anyone I recognised. I hoped that the ferryman had been right when he said that most of the long-standing servants had been dismissed. But even Richard would have had to keep some of the old hands on to ensure the smooth running of the manor and its lands. Trained servants and household officers were not easy to come by out in the remote reaches of Yorkshire, most preferring the towns and cities, where there were taverns, bear-baiting pits and playhouses in abundance.

The great door of the manor was opened by the porter, who, to my relief, I did not recognise. He looked to be in his forties and had evidently been chosen for his impressive height, emphasised by his slender frame. He wore, as most porters did in winter, a thick ankle-length robe against the cold.

His gaze darted from my clothes to Valentine and back, and he seemed at length to consider I was wealthy enough to warrant a small bow.

'Is your master, Lord Fairfax, at home? My name is Heyworth. Lord Fairfax will know it. He and my father had a long acquaintance in their youth, but my father's health has failed him these past years and he is unable to stir from his house. He wishes me to inquire after his lordship's own health and to invite him to call—'

'Your father, sir?' He studied my face, evidently trying to calculate how old I might be. 'Is it the old lord you wished to see, Master Heyworth? *George* Fairfax?'

'Yes, of course, what other master have you?' I said curtly.

'Forgive me, Master Heyworth, but the old lord is dead. His son, Richard Fairfax, is lord now. But he is in London at present, in attendance upon the King.'

I made as much play of appearing shocked as I could. 'I should have come sooner,' I groaned. 'My father asked me to when we first returned to England, but business prevented it. My father was so desperate to see him one last time and I have failed him.'

The porter regarded me anxiously. 'I will have the almoner bring you some wine.'

I hesitated, glancing up at the fading light and then at Valentine. 'I thank you, but I must make haste. This news is blow to me enough, but to make things worse my horse has lamed himself and I dare not risk injuring him further by riding. I'll have to walk him to the nearest inn. And this mud will not make for an easy journey. The fates seem to be conspiring against me today.'

'Please to enter, Master Heyworth. I'll call for a boy to see to your horse. I'm sure the young lord would bid you welcome if he was here, seeing as how your fathers were friends.'

I wouldn't wager on that, I thought grimly.

The Great Hall beyond the door seemed smaller and darker than I remembered it. A cold hand ran down my spine, as though I had walked through a ghost. The porter held a hasty whispered conversation with a man whose plump red cheeks, snub nose and close-shaven chin gave him the appearance of a giant baby, despite his grey hair. He introduced himself to me as the almoner and conducted me to a high-backed settle close to a merger wood fire dwarfed by the cavernous fireplace. Presently he returned with the promised wine and hovered nervously in front of me, his flingers fluttering over his chest.

'Where have you ridden from, Master Heyworth?' he asked in the apologetic tones of a man who neither wants to inquire nor be told the answer.

It was the question every man was obliged by law to ask of every stranger he encountered, in the bid to capture foreign spies and illegal priests infiltrating the country. If a man was suspicious of the reply, he was supposed to report the matter, even detain the stranger until he could be handed over to the authorities. But I knew that, like the two men I'd encountered chopping wood, anyone asking that question on this manor would be more concerned to discover if I was one of the King's men than a spy – was I hunter or hunted, predator or prey? It all depended on who asked the question.

It was just possible that word of a man making the ferry crossing in such treacherous conditions might have already reached the manor, so I did not risk lying about the road I had travelled on. 'From London. I'm bound for Scarborough, but my horse has gone lame.'

He nodded, stepped backwards and scuttled away. I knew he'd gone to consult with the steward as to whether I should be received as a guest or merely be allowed to rest a while in the hall with the servants. Though if what the ferryman had said about the steward was true, I might very well be kicked straight back out on the road.

The hall was deserted at that hour. Most of the servants would be preparing supper in the kitchens, dressing the table in the upper chamber, or checking the livestock before darkness. I stared around with a curious feeling of being caught up in a disquieting dream. Everything was still as I remembered it, yet all had changed. The plaster ceiling was still decorated with relief scenes of biblical characters, each oval tableau arranged like a fruit hanging from the plaster tree that spread across the ceiling, the trunk rising from the belly of a recumbent man. As a boy, I could never decide if he was supposed to be sleeping or, like one of the figures carved on top of the tombs of knights and lords, was dead. But now small pieces of the plaster, blackened with smoke, had fallen away in several places, so that the figures looked as though they had been nibbled by mice.

The dresser and the long servants' table at the far end still remained, and there were a few small pieces of pewter gleaming in the firelight, even one or two brightly coloured dishes on the sideboards, but there had once been many more. Maybe they had been stored away for safekeeping, only to be brought out when Richard was in residence.

A young man, wrapped around in a large canvas apron, had appeared and was clattering down trenchers, knives and spoons for the servants' supper. He worked on for a few minutes, whistling tunelessly to himself, then, catching sight of me, jerked upright and fell silent. He looked old enough to have been working here when old Fairfax had died, but I knew it would be a mistake to try to question him. Not here, not yet.

Footsteps sounded on the wide wooden staircase and I peered around the wings of the settle to see a man striding towards me, with the cherubic-faced almoner trailing in his wake. Like the porter, the steward was robed, but his gown was dark green with bands of scarlet and silver stitchwork down the front and around the cuffs, and he wore a broad belt with a large ornate silver buckle in the form of a stag's head. He was a sturdy man, though not fat, with sandy-coloured hair curling over his collar, and a spade-cut beard, slightly more ruddy than his hair. A seal dangled from a silver chain about his neck.

He gave a curt nod of his head. 'Master Heyworth? I have the honour of being Lord Fairfax's steward. My almoner has informed me of your arrival.'

His almoner? That word alone told me who he thought was lord of this manor.

'He tells me you are travelling to Scarborough from London. This is a strange road to take.'

'As I told the porter, it was my father who insisted I come here. I'm a shipping merchant and obliged to travel to Scarborough, from time to time, see my agent there. Knowing I travel through the Ridings, my father kept asking me to call here, but as you say, it is not on the way, and such a diversion adds days to my journey, so I have not been able to spare the time before. My father is old, he forgets how far it is.'

I deliberately prattled on to forestall any questions. 'You know how it is with the aged, their minds dwell increasingly on their youth, which seems but yesterday to them, while they cannot recall what they did the day before. And my poor father grows weaker – the physicians say he will not linger for many more weeks. That's why I came here. But now, to discover I am too late . . .' I shook my head sadly. 'That is a bitter blow and it will be to my father. I should have taken the trouble to call here when I last came to the Ridings before the great frost. Was that what brought about Lord Fairfax's death? The bitter cold of those weeks hastened the end of many of the frailer souls.'

'Lord Fairfax died six years ago in a riding accident.'

'So long ago? My father will be grieved to learn of it. But it seems I am absolved of the guilt of failing in my duty to him. My father and I were still in the Low Countries then.'

A glance flashed between the almoner and the steward. I knew what they were thinking. Either I was trusted enough by the Privy Council to be granted a licence to travel, which made me a good Protestant, unlikely to be corrupted by exposure to the Catholic faith, or I was living in exile or had fled there illegally, which made me a Catholic and a traitor.

'You have a house in London?' The steward asked cautiously. He was trying to discover if my property had been taken as forfeit to the Crown, which might suggest I was a Catholic.

I adopted a pained expression. 'Friends kindly allow me to lease their house. My father begged to return home to die in England.' I sighed. 'But it is . . . *inconvenient*, you understand. It is easier for me to manage my shipping business when I am abroad. But what can a dutiful son do except indulge the whims of his father? And perhaps it is to the good. I've had many problems of late with cargoes of coal from Newcastle. I fear my agent in Scarborough is being taken advantage of. He's not tough enough. For a business to prosper it requires a firm hand on the helm, isn't that right, Master Steward?'

'And when your father dies?'

'Then I shall take passage on one of my own ships. I find Europe suits me better.'

Another glance passed between the steward and the almoner, and the steward gave him a slight nod.

If Richard was somehow spinning the web of blackmail and treason that I had glimpsed in Battle Abbey, then he would surely have employed a steward with the same loyalties. He could not risk doing otherwise. I was certain I'd given the steward enough hints that I was of the old faith, and by claiming to have ships plying this coast, he might even believe that I could be of use to them, assuming he swallowed my story. But if I was wrong, if Richard had betrayed his father's faith, and the steward he had employed was not a Catholic, I had just put my head in the hangman's noose, for I had given him reason enough to send for the sheriff's men tonight.

The steward rubbed his hands. 'You will take supper at my table tonight, Master Heyworth, and I'll have a chamber prepared for you. The groom will attend to your horse and he'll discover the cause of its lameness, I'm sure. I am afraid the household is somewhat depleted. Lord Fairfax being much at Court, he does not entertain here, so we have no need for a full complement of indoor servants in his absence. But nevertheless, I trust you will find yourself better served here than at any inn.'

I DIDN'T FLATTER myself that I was being treated as a guest out of respect; rather that eating with the steward meant he could control who I talked to and what we talked about. Down in the Great Hall, I would be among servants who might be persuaded to gossip. I wondered what he was afraid they might say.

Supper in the Great Chamber upstairs was, as I had expected, a stilted affair. The steward had me seated next to him, with five of the senior officers of Fairfax's small estate ranged along either side of the table. The table linens were clean and well pressed. The pewterware and glasses gleamed, but even in here, the room seemed shabby, the candles few and there was none of the silver candlesticks or gilded mustard pots I remembered. A painted cloth depicting the finding of the Golden Fleece still covered one of the walls, yet I was sure that when I was a boy that had been a fine Flemish tapestry, not a painted cloth. Perhaps the passing years and tricks of the mind had given the house a grander aspect in my memory than it had ever truly had.

I shared a mess of dishes with the steward and found myself ravenous after the fare at the Lusty Tup. They had evidently hoarded grain as the ferryman suspected, for there were plenty of manchets of good wheaten bread, and there was a shoulder of mutton, salted beef, a custard, woodcock, and venison pastries. After Battle Abbey, where I had been obliged to play the servant, I might almost have enjoyed being waited on, but the atmosphere around the table was as cold as the winter ice had been. All of those entering glanced at me curiously, but the steward did not enlighten them. He was ensuring that none had reason to engage me in conversation. But I was aware of their suspicious and even hostile glances, though they always abruptly averted their gaze if I caught their eye.

One of the officers, in particular, kept staring at me. He was perhaps in his fifties and, to my disquiet, I thought I recognised him. I couldn't recall what his role had been when I was here sixteen years ago. Now he wore the badge of the office auditor, responsible for examining all the manor's accounts, the records of tithes collected, charges and fines imposed. I was sure he hadn't held such an elevated post back then. I tried to picture him, slimmer perhaps, fewer deep lines, more hair. He kept peering at me, frowning, as though he knew there was something familiar about me too, but he couldn't place me. I had to stop myself fiddling with the padded cloth wrapped around my neck to ensure it was in place. If he saw me touching my throat, that might just jolt his memory of a fifteen-year-old boy with a fire-mark around his neck.

The steward occasionally threw a question to me about my ship and cargoes, the routes they plied and ports they called at. But he was paying more attention to other conversations on the table, not joining in, but watching and listening. Not that there was much to hear. The officers spoke little, eating swiftly, making the occasional remarks about the state of the fields, foot rot in the sheep, the revenue still being lost with the ferry at Bubwith being at the bottom of the river.

Only when the subject of enclosing more of the common land was raised did an argument break out. It seemed that last year, newly built fences and walls around one patch of common grazing land had been torn down every night as soon as they were repaired in the day, and they had been obliged to set a guard on it. A couple of those at the table had the wisdom to realise that after the freeze and then the melt-water floods, if they were deprived of any more grazing land this year, the villagers and farmers might not vent their anger just on wood and stone. But the steward cut short any discussion by barking out the order for the table to be voided by the yeomen, even before some of those at the table had finished eating.

Linen towels, ewers and basins were swiftly brought to table for the rinsing of hands, before the steward rose, signalling for the others to leave. I wondered if supper was always eaten so swiftly. When I was a boy, it had seemed to take up half of the evening.

The steward ushered me towards a servant who had appeared in the doorway. 'My man will conduct you to your chamber, Master Heyworth. I regret I have duties to attend to, and of course, in Lord Fairfax's absence we can offer you no company in the Great Chamber. I dare say, if you have a long journey on the morrow you will wish to retire early. My yeoman will attend you. He will sleep in your chamber, should you require any service during the night.'

The yeoman seemed to have been selected for his size. He was perhaps in his mid-twenties, with the shoulders and muscles of a blacksmith. His black hair hung in lank curls to his collar and a dark matt of hair covered his arms down to his knuckles. The jerkin over his shirt strained at the buttons.

'That will not be necessary, Master Steward,' I told him firmly. 'I can manage quite well without a manservant to attend me. You said you have to run the manor with fewer servants while Lord Fairfax is away. I would not deprive you of another hand. You have shown generous hospitality by allowing me to rest here tonight.'

The steward gave a cold smile. 'But I insist, Master Heyworth, as would Lord Fairfax if he was here. And I would not want any report to reach his ears that the son of one of his father's great friends was not shown every courtesy.'

I silently cursed, knowing that this man would be my gaoler not my servant. I had only one chance to learn anything from the manor. I couldn't risk staying on, even if I could find an excuse that would satisfy the steward. The more the auditor saw of me, the greater the chances he'd remember.

The yeoman held the chamber stick, and by its light led me down the dark passageway, panelled in oak and green leather. At least, I remembered that was its colour; I couldn't actually see what it was now, for none of the candles on the sconces on the walls had been lit, though it was now dark outside. The chamber that Richard and I had shared as boys was along the passage leading the opposite way from the Great Chamber. I didn't know whether to be relieved or disappointed, but I had no desire to re-enter a chamber that had held so much misery for me.

The yeoman paused before the door of a room almost at the end of the corridor, flung it open and went before me to light a single candle on the wall, before setting down the chamber stick on a table in one corner. The room was small, but furnished with slightly more comfort than the chamber in the Battle Abbey where I'd been obliged to wait on the *gentlemen*. There was a high, narrow bed, a basin and ewer on a small side table and a chair of easement in case I needed to relieve myself in the night – I was not going to be able to use the excuse of slipping out to the jakes. A livery cupboard and several small paintings hung on the walls, though the light was too dingy to see what they depicted. The room smelled and felt musty, damp and cold.

My saddlebag had been brought up and to my annoyance, but not surprise, it had already been unpacked and no doubt searched thoroughly. Before setting out from Bubwith, I'd packed it carefully, knowing that it would be examined if I got this far. They had found the clean linens, shirt, nightshirt and, no doubt, the fake bills of sale and letters which I had concealed just enough to make them think they had *discovered* them.

I lifted the chamber stick and inspected the livery cupboard. It smelled of stale food and mouse piss, but the wine, bread, cheese and some pasties under the napkins looked fresh enough.

I turned to the yeoman. 'Before I retire, I must go to the stables to check on my mount. He was lame and I need to know if he will be fit enough to continue my journey on tomorrow.'

He looked doubtful. He'd plainly had orders to keep me in the bedchamber. 'You don't want to go breaking your leg in the dark; stones are as slape as butter in this rain. I'll send one of the lads.'

'And have him bring back some garbled message that tells me nothing? I'll be the judge of the whether the horse is fit to do the distance. I know the beast.'

He hesitated and I wondered if he was going to physically try to stop me, but whatever his orders, he must have realised he could hardly wrestle a guest to the ground.

'I'd best show the way, then,' he said uneasily.

'I can find my own way. You can fetch a warming pan to air that bed. I don't want to spend the next week suffering the torments of sciatica because the mattress is damp.'

'I warmed it my sen, a while back.'

'Then it'll be cold again by now,' I retorted. 'This chamber's as icy as a beggar's arse.' I rubbed my hands and nodded at him. 'Why don't you help yourself to some of that wine and meat pasties in the cupboard while I'm gone? Keep the cold out.'

I'd deliberately left the door of the cupboard open, so that the smell of fresh pastry and bread wafted out. He was almost drooling as his gaze strayed to it. 'Steward would rip out my gizzard if I ate a guest's livery.'

I laughed. 'I'll not tell him, if you don't. I've dined well tonight, and I'll want no more to eat before breakfast. But if you had to prepare this chamber, I'd wager you've only had time to snatch a bite or two at supper. No sense in letting meats go stale while you go hungry.'

I'd been obliged to forego half my supper to prepare bedchambers when I'd played the servant in Battle Abbey, so he had my sympathy; besides, I needed to keep him occupied.

He grinned his thanks. 'Best take the back stairs.' He opened the door, peering out into the passageway. 'See there. Far end. Turn hard to your right just before the casement, and there's a staircase takes you down to a door that leads out into a yard. Servants use it to empty the pisspots and the like. Meant to be locked after dark, but the porter never locks it this early. Archway at the back of the yard leads to the stables.'

I remembered that staircase. As a boy, I had used it many times to slip out. It was locked at dusk in those days. Waldegrave himself used to check on it. But after I'd begged the jester whom George Fairfax employed each Christmas to teach me how to charm a lock . . .

The yeoman held the chamber candle in the doorway until I had reached the end of the passageway. Though I was sure I could still have found it in the dark – I'd had enough practice.

The spiral staircase was even narrower than I remembered. On the other hand, I was much taller and broader than my fifteen-year-old former self and I had to trail one hand above my head as I groped my way down, to avoid braining myself on the treads above. The door was, as the yeoman had said, unlocked and I stepped out into the small enclosed yard beyond. It was in darkness, except for the candles in the casements of the house, which cast shafts of buttermilk light that barely touched the ground. The storerooms, dairy, washhouses and jakes which formed the other three walls of the yard were in darkness. No one glancing out of the house would be able to identify anyone standing outside, but all the same, I took care to keep to the shadows as I crossed the yard and slipped through the archway beyond.

A lantern hung above the open entrance to the row of stables, though it illuminated little more than the doorway itself. But before I had taken more than a pace, there was a deep snarling growl behind me. In a fury of savage barking, a huge dog leaped at me out of the darkness. I spun around, knife in hand, but the hound had been pulled short by the stout chain attached to the wall.

'Whist, Biter! Lie down.' A boy stumbled out of the stable block, holding up another lantern, and peered at me, yawning and rubbing his ear. He'd probably been asleep up in the hay loft. He was bow-legged and as thin as a whippet, and looked no older than eleven or twelve years, too young for what I needed.

The hound slunk back into the darkness, still growling.

'Fetch me the groom, lad,' I demanded. 'I need to see my horse, Valentine. He was brought here before supper, lame.'

The boy blinked at me, then nodded. 'Oh aye, the grey gelding. It was me that fetched him to the stables. But it were only a bit of cob wedged in his hoof that lamed him. He's as fit as a rope for a thief now. I washed the clart off his legs and belly, and gave him a good feed. I'll show you him, master.'

The boy was obviously hoping to be rewarded with a generous sum for his efforts.

'You've done well, lad. All the same, I'll speak a word to the groom,' I told him firmly.

A man appeared in another doorway on the opposite side of the yard, rubbing oil from his hands on a cloth. He was around eighteen: old enough to have been a stable lad six years ago, but too young to remember the youth that his master threw out ten years before that.

'I'm groom here, one of them, anyroad. What were you wanting, master?'

'My mount, the grey gelding, was brought in lame before supper. I've come to check on him. I'll be riding on tomorrow and I want to know if he's fit for the journey.'

'The lad'll show you.'

'I'll not risk ruining a good beast on the say-so of a boy, nor my own neck on these roads.'

The lad had opened his mouth to indignantly protest, but I forestalled him, addressing the groom. 'The horse has a tendency to a swelling of the knee on the right foreleg – an old injury.'

The groom took the lantern from the boy's hand and threw the cloth he was holding at his head, nodding towards the door he'd emerged from. 'Make yourself useful. Saddle wants polishing. It's been oiled up.'

The interior was dark and windowless, thick with the odour of horse sweat, dung and musty hay. The groom led the way up a line of tethered animals, who snorted and stamped their hooves, irritated by the light passing behind them, until we reached Valentine, where he hung the lantern on the wall. Having stroked the horse's nose, he began rubbing well-practised hands over every inch of him, feeling for any signs of injury.

'When the going's this clarty, it takes it out of a horse like this. I reckon he's more used to good stone roads than being up to his hocks in mud. A beast with hooves as broad as trenchers, that's what you want for these country lanes.'

'I usually stick to the main highway from London when I come north, but I turned aside to pay my respects to Lord Fairfax, only to learn that he's dead. God rest his soul. My poor father will take the news of his old friend's death badly, I fear.'

'Been dead these six years,' the groom said, continuing to check the horse. He was now running his hand down each of Valentine's legs.

'They told me Lord Fairfax died in a riding accident. I can't believe it; my father said he was a master horseman, the best. He must have fallen very heavily for it to have killed him. Was Lord Fairfax trying out a new horse?'

The groom glanced towards the open doorway, then studied the hoof he was supporting as he scraped at it with a pick. 'His favourite, same as always.' Valentine irritably jerked his foot. The groom released it and straightened up.

'So, were you working here then?' I asked.

He slowly wiped the pick with a cloth, studying it as if he was cleaning an exquisite jewel. 'Aye, I was. Just started my apprenticeship here. But I weren't allowed to touch the horses back then, especially not the master's beasts, too valuable. I were two years younger than the other stable lad. Mucking out stables and fetching water, that's what I did.'

'But I'd wager you know what happened, though. There must have been talk.'

'There was talk alright. Specially after the other stable lad died. I felt hard done by when I first come here, being given all the worse jobs and not being allowed to touch the horses when the other lad could. I knew I could handle them far better than him. I could ride better than half the grooms here even when I was in clouts. But after it happened, I reckon I was lucky, 'cause it could have been me dead instead of the other lad.'

'Dead? You mean he was also killed in the accident?' I knew that wasn't how the boy had died, but if I could just keep the groom talking, there was a chance I'd learn something more.

He kept his head bent, but his gaze darted again to the door. He leaned towards me, lowering his voice still further. 'The lad's death were no accident, no more than the old master's. The girth on his saddle broke, but when it were brought back here, it was clear it hadn't broken by its sen. It had been cut through part way, so as any sudden jerk would snap it. It's no secret, that, the story were in the broadsides far away as London, so they said.'

He rested his cheek against Valentine's neck, stroking his nose.

'The old lord's son said stable lad were to blame, 'cause it were his job to get the horse tacked up. He said even if he hadn't cut the girth himself, he must have noticed it when he buckled it up and he'd let Lord Fairfax ride to his death. Accused him of being paid to do it, or at the very least, look the other way. Lad went and hanged himself in the stables. Everyone said that proved he were guilty. They said he were afeared he'd be arrested for murder. And that were the end of it, as far as the justices were concerned.'

The groom glanced at up me, an expression of bewilderment on his young face. 'But what I can't fathom to this day is what made him cut that girth? What cause would he have to harm his lordship? I'd never heard the lad grumble more than anyone else if he got a telling-off and he'd been not beaten. And if he got paid to cut it, why did he hang around after? If he'd got a purse full of money, he could have bolted before Lord Fairfax even got thrown. 'Cause if he knew about that girth, he must have known he'd get the blame one way or t'other.'

He crouched, running his hands down Valentine's fetlock. 'And there's another thing. That girth held all the time Lord Fairfax was riding until the horse reared. He was a weighty man and, like you say, a good horseman. So, someone must have affrighted the horse to make it shy and rear, and the lad were back here in the stables.' He shrugged. 'But then so were everyone from the manor, so it couldn't have been anyone from here who did it.'

'Did what?'

We both looked round to see a figure standing in the doorway, cast into shadow by the lantern light outside. The groom released his grip on Valentine's fetlock, and swiftly removing his cap, gave a small bow. His face flushed at being caught gossiping.

'Master Auditor.'

I gave a silent groan.

'Gentleman wanted me to check his mount, make sure he were fit to ride on the morrow. It were only a stone got lodged.'

'I should have spotted that,' I said. 'But this infernal mud masks everything. You've a good horseman here, Master Auditor, and the stable lad, both. They're a credit to the manor.'

All the time we had been babbling away, the auditor had been picking his way along the line of stalls towards us. He stopped in the pool of light cast by the groom's lantern.

'I went to your chamber, Master Heyworth. The yeoman told me you were here. You should have sent him to inquire about your horse. There was no need for you to trouble yourself.'

'I know my horse and his weaknesses, Master Auditor. I wished to discuss his fitness with the groom tending him in person.'

The auditor was staring at my neck with its padding and cloth. 'You look to have a weakness yourself, Master Heyworth, I trust you weren't thrown and injured when your horse was lamed. Such falls can be fatal.'

I saw the groom stiffen. But the auditor appeared not to notice, for his gaze was still fixed on me.

'This?' I touched the cloth. 'I suffer with goitre. My physician advises me to keep it tightly bound, which he says in time will reduce the swelling.'

'I've heard if you bind a freshly skinned mouldywarp to it and leave it there till it rots the swelling will go,' the groom said. 'If you can stand the stink,' he added with a bark of laughter, which I suspected came more from relief that the subject had been turned.

'Then perhaps you should try that on your journey to Scarborough when you are riding *alone*,' the auditor said. 'I'll ask the bailiff to have one of his men kill you a mole, if you like.' He smiled faintly, but his tone was icy. 'If you have contented yourself over the health of your horse, allow me to escort you back to the house. It's dark and treacherous underfoot.'

I made a show of extracting a few coins from a stuffed purse and handing them to the groom. Then I followed the auditor back out of the stables. We walked in silence to the main door of the house. I was not to be allowed to slip back up the servants' stairs. But before we went in, he caught my arm, pulling me back into the darkness.

'You seem familiar to me, Master Heyworth. I cannot place you. But I will.'

'People say I look exactly like my father. If you were employed here in the time of George Fairfax, you will no doubt have seen my father in his younger days when he was a guest here, and see his image in me.'

The auditor slowly shook his head. 'It is not a man that I remember.' He massaged his throat thoughtfully. 'There is another cure I know for goitre, Master Heyworth. When men are hanged, sufferers pay the executioner to let them stroke the swelling on their necks with the dead man's hand before his corpse is cut down. As a boy, I used to wonder if a man with goitre was hanged, would his disfigurement vanish when he died, if it was touched with his own dead hand? Someday, I must put it to the test.' He led me back to the door and paused with his hand on the latch.

'I think you would do well to keep strictly to your own chamber tonight and leave as swiftly as you can as soon as dawn breaks. I wouldn't advise you to linger. A man's memory of something long forgotten is apt to return without warning.'

Chapter Five

HATFIELD FOREST, ESSEX

THE HOUND SPLASHED through the mire and shallow puddles towards the deeper pool beyond. The commotion flushed the heron yards before the dog reached it, as was intended. The bird's great wings flapped clumsily as it struggled to get airborne, then more gracefully as it gained height. It was ringing upwards in spirals towards the leaden clouds, as if it sensed the greatest danger lay not in the dog, but from a creature it could not see.

Robert Cecil stood motionless on a small grassy hillock, watching the bird's progress. Silhouetted against the silver-grey light, he appeared even smaller, and his back more crooked than usual, dwarfed by the great expanse of sky.

'You'll lose him if you tarry much longer, my lord,' a voice behind him cautioned.

Without taking his eyes off the heron, Cecil motioned the speaker to silence with his free hand. He stood for a few moments more, then he slipped the hood from the peregrine falcon on his gauntleted arm and allowed the bird to glimpse her quarry, before casting her off. The falcon took flight, speeding after the heron, circling upwards at a distance from it as though she had no interest in pursuing it. The peregrine's steel-blue plumage made her almost invisible against the clouds.

'We shall never make a falconer out of you, Northwood,' Cecil said, without taking his gaze from the falcon. 'You have no patience. Watch that bird. She does not attempt to attack until she knows she has positioned herself such that she can bring the heron down in one fatal strike.'

Jeremy Northwood scowled up at the sky. He was slight of build, with a mousy-brown beard and hair cut plainly, but not unfashionably, like his clothes. He was the kind of man you would not notice in a crowd, nor would you even be able to recall with certainty if he had been present at any gathering, which fitted him ideally for the role of one of the spymaster's many agents.

Northwood disliked hawking nearly as much as he disliked his paymaster. The old Queen had called Robert Cecil her 'little elf'; Northwood privately thought *malicious goblin* was nearer the mark. Not that he actually despised the Secretary of State, Lord Salisbury; on the contrary, he grudgingly admired Cecil for his ruthless rise to power, amassing a huge fortune as he climbed each rung. Who could not be in awe of the intellect, skill and cunning of a man who had achieved so much in spite of, or perhaps because of, the mockery he'd had to endure about his stature? But Northwood trusted him only as far as he trusted one of Cecil's beloved hawks. Those birds would accept food from your fingers as docilely as a lapdog, then, without any warning, could blind you with a single stab of their vicious beaks.

The falcon was directly above the heron now. If the heron realised she was there, it could do nothing to escape her. The bird of prey stooped, shooting down like a lightning bolt from the heavens, her outstretched talons slamming into the great bird's head with such force she stunned it. Binding to her helpless quarry, her claws locked into its flesh as the heron span and tumbled out of the sky, crashing to earth.

Cecil turned, grinning in triumph at Northwood before he and two servants set off to retrieve the kill and reward the killer.

Northwood watched with distaste as Cecil fed the peregrine a bloody titbit before hooding her. He thought, not for the first time, that it was entirely fitting that hawking should be Cecil's favourite sport – his only sport. He was as pitiless and twice as ruthless as any of his hunting birds. Look how he had destroyed

Essex, the boy his father had taken in to his house to be raised as a childhood companion to Cecil. Robert Devereux, Earl of Essex, was almost a brother to him, but he was everything Cecil was not: tall, handsome, well formed, a bold and dashing warrior. He had quickly become the old Queen's darling, her favourite. But Cecil had been watching and waiting. First, he had taken advantage of Essex's absence to manipulate all the offices which he had coveted away from him then he had ruined him by depriving him of the wine monopoly on which he depended; finally he'd had Essex convicted for treason by a jury Cecil himself had chosen. It had taken Robert Cecil four years of patient and merciless plotting to bring the Queen's favourite to the scaffold, and despite the warnings of his friends, Essex had not realised the depth of his adopted brother's treachery until it was too late – far too late.

Having stroked and petted the falcon, Cecil handed her to the servants to be returned to the mews. Then he picked his way back over the sodden ground towards Northwood. Lord Salisbury had chosen the rendezvous with care, Northwood thought, for now the servants had retreated, they were alone among the wide-open expanse of marsh pools and pasture in the hunting forest, where, even if anyone had been lurking among the distant leafless trees, they would not have been able to hear anything that passed between Cecil and his spy.

Cecil led the way to an open wooden shelter from where hunters could watch and wait for the wild ducks and geese to fly in without scaring them off. A few rough wooden benches had been arranged behind it, and Northwood was gratified to see that the servants had left baskets of wine and food. That was at least some compensation for him being summoned here, instead of to a comfortable chamber with a blazing fire. Cecil lowered himself on to one of the benches, and indicated to Northwood to take another. Cecil hated to talk standing, for it forced him to look up to most men and Northwood was no exception. He was more than a head taller than the Secretary of State.

Cecil drew off the thick, bloodstained gauntlets, and handed Northwood a flask and a small glass. He shook his head when Northwood offered the flask back to him. Northwood's eyebrows arched in surprise, for what he had assumed would be wine proved to be Huguenot brandy, devilishly strong and costly, though it certainly kept out the cold.

'So, what news have you brought me, Northwood?'

That was typical of the scheming little goblin. He always wanted to discover exactly what you knew first, before he'd come to the point of the meeting.

'The thefts from the churches and cathedrals have started up again,' Northwood said cautiously. You could never tell what Cecil already knew, whether he was testing one source against another.

'England has been plagued with disasters in these past two years.' Cecil waved his hand towards the puddles of glistening water lying on what, in good years, was firm grassland. 'Food is scarce: half the farmland in the west was ruined by the salt in the flood, thousands of cattle and sheep drowned or frozen, winter wheat wiped out by the frost, and the land now too sodden to be worked for weeks. It is only to be expected that the poor will turn to stealing.'

'There have been many thefts from houses, shops and warehouses – that's true, my lord. And there are always those who will break into the churches' alms boxes for a fistful of coins. But few men, even those who don't fear God or the law, would take church plate, paintings and treasures. They can't exchange those for bread and even the pawnbrokers rarely touch them, for they're too easily identified. Who would they sell them to? No, these thefts follow the same pattern as we saw before in the months leading up to the Gunpowder Treason, my lord. Catholic sympathisers stealing the valuables and spiriting them abroad to fund their plots. They claim the chalices and treasures belonged to the Catholic Church before the Reformation, so they are merely reclaiming what is theirs. Besides, they think it a good jest to use things stolen from the Church of England to bring about its destruction.'

'And the Jesuits will certainly not condemn that as a sin,' Cecil agreed. 'So, you too believe that an attack is imminent, one that requires a deal of money to fund it.'

'But this can hardly be news to you, my lord?' Northwood said shrewdly. 'I thought your intelligencers in the Low Countries told you when one of the English exiles so much as made water in a pisspot, and reported the colour and stench of that piss too.'

A frown creased Cecil's brow and clouded the large puppy eyes which in his youth had lent him an expression of guileless innocence that had served him well. 'It is interesting that you should speak of them, Northwood, for one of my informants in the Low Countries appears to be missing. I have received no reports from him for months and none of my intelligencers knows his whereabouts. Have any rumours reached your ears?'

His gaze darted to Northwood's face, and fastened on it.

'Missing, my lord?'

'*Missing* means he cannot be found,' Cecil said icily, 'either alive or *dead*. I repeat, have you heard any rumours?'

Cecil's tone left Northwood in no doubt that this was an accusation rather than a question. The agent shifted uncomfortably on the rough wooden perch, the sharp edge of which was now digging painfully into the back of his knees. Did Cecil suspect him of having known a man had vanished and not passing that information on to his master, or was he suggesting that Northwood had failed to discover something he should have learned?

'Perhaps, if I knew the name of the man whom you . . . are *concerned* about?' Northwood had been about to say *whom you have lost track of*, but it would not be wise to accuse Lord Salisbury of losing anyone.

'Anthony Copley. I trust you recall the name?'

Northwood nodded. 'Of course, my lord. It was the year the King came to the throne; Copley was one of the men who plotted to kidnap the King and hold him in the Tower until he agreed to the full toleration of Catholics and the removal of all Officers of State whom they held responsible for their plight.' *Particularly you, Cecil,* Northwood thought. *You were the man they most wanted thrown out, or better still, executed.*

At his trial, Copley had denounced his fellow conspirators, by whom he claimed to have been sorely misled. He'd made a flamboyant confession of his misguided involvement and had even written a letter swearing eternal loyalty to Cecil and the King, in that order. Then, having first been returned to the Tower with the other plotters, Copley had been removed to the Gatehouse, granted a pardon and had gone into exile. Little wonder that some agents and the underground broadside writers speculated that Cecil had used Copley as an *agent provocateur* from the beginning.

'Perhaps Copley tried to stir up more mischief and the English exiles saw through it,' Northwood said. 'They can't all be as beef-witted as Lord Cobham and George Brooke.'

He was baiting a bear and he knew it. But the tone in which Cecil had asked the question about the missing informant still rankled. He just couldn't resist the opportunity to remind Lord Salisbury that the kidnap plot had brought to light an even more deadly plot to kill the King. That had involved not only the disgraced Sir Walter Raleigh, but members of Cecil's own family, in the form of his brothers-in-law, Cobham and Brooke. To give the man his due, Cecil had shown no favouritism to his own kin. Quite the contrary: he had succeeded in getting both Cobham and Brooke sentenced to death with Raleigh. Cobham and Raleigh had been reprieved on the block, but Cecil had refused to intervene to get Brooke a reprieve. Was that out of justice or vengeance?

To Northwood's surprise, Cecil did not appear to be insulted by the jibe, though you could never be certain what he was storing up to avenge later.

But on this occasion, he merely nodded. 'That's why Cobham

will remain in the Tower, where his lunacy and foolishness can be contained. If the King had permitted him to go into exile, he'd probably have given such insult to his hosts he'd have had us at war with half the nations of Europe before the month was out. But Copley was different. He was intelligent and loyal, once he had been convinced of his past errors.'

'*Was*, my lord?'

'I suspect we may be speaking of a dead man, Northwood. Though not because, as you put it, he was "stirring up mischief". As we know, a man of great importance to the Catholic network was brought in by ship through Battle Abbey. It is likely that Copley discovered his identity and was silenced. I fear if he is found, it will be as a corpse. But no matter: if that particular thread of information has been severed, it is all the more important that a new thread is picked up here in England to track this threat. You must increase your surveillance, Northwood. I want to know every rumour, every whisper, however faint or far-fetched, as soon as you learn of it. Leave nothing out.'

His agent felt a sense of relief almost bordering on gratitude. For a few moments he had thought Cecil was on the verge of dispensing of his services. It wasn't just the loss of income and influence that had worried him, but what else Cecil might do to express his disappointment and displeasure. But it seemed he was safe, at least for now.

Cecil now poured himself some brandy from the flask, but did not offer any more to Northwood. The interview was concluded. Northwood rose and bowed.

'I will be diligent, my lord. Every scrap I can obtain, I will send to you without delay.' He bowed again and turned to go.

Cecil allowed him to take two paces before he said, 'One thing more. Are you acquainted with a young man called Oliver Fairfax? He is at Court with his cousin, Lord Richard Fairfax.'

'I know them by sight, my lord. I had heard you have your eye on young Oliver. But he is a mere boy. Surely, he can be of no use to you, or is he suspected?'

'Oliver is seventeen or thereabouts, and a green twig is more pliable than a mature one.'

Northwood shook his head, smiling. 'I swear one day I will find you in the birthing chamber, ready to catch them as they pop out of their dam's bellies and have them eavesdropping in their cradles.'

Cecil laughed. 'Why not? There would be much to be gleaned by an infant in his mother's bedchamber, if only I could teach one to talk. But to return to young Oliver. I want to know how loyal the youth is, how far he can be bent before he breaks. The day is coming when I may have need of his services.'

Chapter Six

DANIEL PURSGLOVE

A PALE SILVER SUN had crept over the horizon, its rays barely penetrating the cold grey mist that hung over the marshy fields. I had heeded the auditor's warning and ridden out at daybreak, much to the bemusement of the stableboy I'd roused from the hayloft. I could not be certain whether the auditor had remembered who I was, but I could not risk waiting to find out.

I reached the main track back to Bubwith. The mist was lighter here, almost blown away by a gathering breeze; but for that, I might not have glimpsed something moving in a grove of trees ahead of me in the corner of the field. Moments later, an elderly woman stepped out and set off in the direction of Bubwith. As Valentine passed the spot she had emerged from, I saw a narrow but well-worn path leading away from the track in the direction of Willitoft and the manor.

I had almost caught up with the woman, but she veered off the track again, cutting off the serpentine bend in the road, and vanished, though not before I had seen that brown hooded cloak with its patch of yellow-brown stitched to the shoulders. I glimpsed her again briefly as she crossed a piece of open ground before disappearing behind a clump of willow. If she had gone to the Fairfax manor in the hope of begging a small measure of grain, she had evidently been sent packing, for she was returning home empty-handed. But perhaps she hadn't gone there to fetch anything.

I urged Valentine forward, around the twist in the track, passing the opening to a couple of narrow paths cutting across the marshy ground and scrub. They were probably used by local villagers tending livestock on the commons. How long would that practice remain if Richard's bailiff was allowed to have his way and enclose ever more of the land? When I had ridden far enough along the track to be sure I was ahead of the old woman, I dismounted, and made a play of inspecting Valentine's hooves. The sodden ground must surely force her back to the main track.

I heard her limping up behind me and sensed her hesitate, then press on towards me. Her gown and the bottom of her cloak were stained and sodden. She was wearing wooden pattens tied over a pair of cracked leather shoes. But even these were clogged with mud and the small steps she was obliged to take to balance were evidently taking their toll, for she was breathing hard and pressing a hand to her hip, her lips bloodless and compressed against the pain.

'Good morrow, mother. You're abroad early.'

She stopped, clutching her cloak to her bowed body, with fingers as thin and fragile as a sparrow's foot. She peered up at me and after a few moments' scrutiny, she nodded to herself. 'You're the gentleman came to inspect the baptism records.'

'I'm not one of the King's inspectors. It was my own record I wanted to read, mother. I used to live in these parts.'

'That would explain summat.' Her stance became no less wary, but a little frown creased the soft wrinkles of her brow and she regarded me with interest.

'What? What does that explain?'

'The books. One from near the bottom was atop when I opened the chest. The King's men are usually after the bairns born this past year.'

'You've sharp eyes and a good memory, mother.'

'Aye, well I have to check, see, make sure all the books have been put back right and the lid shut tight. The King's men don't always bother, but the water leaks in there summat bad when it rains and if the books get spoiled and they canna read them, it'll be us as gets blame, not their own men.' Her fingers twitched as though they were going to make the sign of the cross to ward off that evil, but instead she clenched her hand. A spasm of pain contorted her face and she staggered, clutching her hip.

And you wanted to see who the King's man might have been checking up on, in case you could warn them.

'I'm heading back to Bubwith. Will you ride with me? It'll save your legs.'

She shook her head, taking a pace away, but the back of the high wooden patten caught on a stone beneath the mud and she toppled backwards. I caught her arm to keep her from falling.

'Come, mother. I swear on the Holy Virgin, I mean you no harm. But if you slip and break a leg, who's going to tend you?'

Her eyes flashed wide at my oath, but I was certain I had not mistaken what she was.

She nodded and allowed me to lift her up on the horse, so that she sat sideways behind the saddle. She was as light as a bag of chicken bones. I heaved myself up, and walked Valentine slowly on.

'Hold tight to me, mother!'

For a few minutes she said nothing, clinging on, trying to adjust to the motion.

'Did you find what you were looking for . . . in the chest?' she suddenly asked.

'No, mother, no record.'

'There was a good few in the past who didn't bring their bairns to that church for baptism and didn't suffer for it, not under the old Queen, not like now. There's a snide wind blowing in these parts now.'

What had the terrier-faced man said? *If a man needed help, he might find it in the church there, if he knew the signs to look for and the signs to leave. That's where the dead men go.*

I had not been mistaken as to who this woman was or what she did. We had the measure of each other now.

75

'I worked at the manor at Willitoft, when I was a boy,' I told her. 'I was hoping someone there might remember me. But they tell me many of the old servants left after the old lord died and the steward is not welcoming of strangers. Are there any of the old servants still in these parts? Be good to chew the cud over old times.'

'Most of them I grew up with are in the churchyard now. I go to talk to them most days, but they never answer.' She gave a sad chuckle. 'But you're still young. Your friends must still be alive.'

'Maybe, mother, but they're scattered to the four winds.'

She said little more until we came in sight of the first of the Bubwith cottages and asked me to let her down. I readily agreed. It would not help either of us to be seen together.

I dismounted and lifted her down. From a moment, her thin hand, cold as a grave stone, rested on mine and she grasped it as she wordlessly nodded her thanks. She had limped away a few paces when she stopped and took a step back. 'Old servants, you said. Was one, sent packing with the rest, but she was too old and her eyes grown too feeble from a lifetime of sewing to find new work. She finished up in the poorhouse in Holme, over yonder on Spalding Moor. I used to go see her a few years back, but can't walk so far now.'

My stomach lurched. Was it possible it was the same sewing woman I remembered? Once, when we were young boys, Richard had been taunting me about my firemark, telling the servants I should be exhibited in a fair, and she'd tried to console me. *That firemark on your throat, that's lucky, that is, means you'll never drown.* Funny how I'd clung on to that. Every time old Waldegrave told me I'd hang, I'd think, *but I'll never drown.* I realised I was smiling and the old woman was regarding me curiously.

'This sewing maid, mother, what's her name?

'Grissell, I calls her.'

I was sure that was it. But if I remembered her . . . I couldn't risk that a second time.

'You said her eyes were failing.'

'Aye, she could scarcely see her own hand. But she knows voices right enough and her wits are as sharp as one of her own needles. Leastways, they were. But who knows what the years have done to her since. They don't treat any of us kindly. If you go, tell her old Sybil was asking for her. Tell her . . . tell her I'll be waiting for her up there.' Sybil raised her hand to the heavens with a smile. 'If she's not gone there afore me.'

I REACHED THE village of Holme on the great desolation of marshland they call Spalding Moor in the early afternoon. A strange hill rises from the flat lands that surround it and from the distance the church that perches on top resembles an ancient fortress or castle, standing guard over the lands below. Not that there is much to guard, except a few sheep and the birds, calling unseen from the marsh pools hidden behind the brown sodden wreckage of last year's reeds and sedges. The track was raised above the land, but even so, after the ice and rain, it had fallen away in places and I was forced to dismount and lead Valentine round.

The poorhouse looked as miserable as its name suggested, but I had seen worse in the cities, where such places are usually to be found in the festering alleys and dark corners of the worst quarters. This house, which the parish had been obliged to provide for those too infirm or elderly to be put to work, was separated from neighbouring cottages by a snicket on one side and a small strip of garden on the other, where a few moth-eaten chickens scratched among some bare currant bushes, picking over the rotting remains of last year's cabbages and beans.

The door at the front of the house lay open, hanging drunkenly from its one remaining hinge; it was so warped it probably could not now be fitted back into the hole. The dark, damp passageway behind was used as a store and, by the smell of it, a midden. I skirted around broken pots, rusty pieces of metal and bulging sacks stinking of mildew, damp and piss.

The first door I passed was shut, but the second lay open. A man and elderly woman were sitting on either side of a small fire, in a tiny room crammed with three narrow beds and a battered table. The man, who looked as if he might be the old woman's son, was rocking back and forth, mumbling continuously and clawing at his hands, which were covered in grey, oozing bandages. The elderly woman peered out at me, a hopeful expression on her face which instantly died as she saw I was a stranger.

'God grant you a good day,' I said cheerfully. 'I am told that Goodwife Grissell lives here. Where can I find her?'

The woman didn't answer, still watching me warily. I took a pace into the room. I realised it had no casement, so the occupants were obliged to leave the door open during the day if they were not to sit in darkness. My approach caused the man to squeal like a frightened infant and the old woman grabbed one of the crutches that was leaning against her hard wooden chair, holding it as a weapon in front of her. Not wishing to distress them, I retreated back into the doorway.

'Grissell,' I repeated. 'She is almost blind. An elderly friend from Bubwith used to visit her, but she's too infirm to make the journey now, so I am come in her stead.'

It took several more attempts before the old woman pointed upwards. A wave of disappointment washed over me. The old sewing maid had, after all, beaten Sibyl to heaven.

'How long ago did she die?'

'Upstairs.' The man had stopped muttering to himself, and appeared to be addressing the table. 'Upstairs,' he shouted. 'Grissell's upstairs. Ma can't climb the stairs. I can. But she won't let me.' He sank back into his mumblings and scratching.

I made my way up the sagging staircase and walked along another passageway, passing more open doors. The inhabitants, infirm through age, maimed by life or crippled at birth, were lying under heaps of old blankets or huddled next to small smoking fires. Some greeted me cheerfully with a smile or a joke; others merely stared, their eyes dull and lifeless.

Like the others, Grissell's door was open. She was sitting on a rickety chair, a threadbare blanket over her knees, a woollen shawl pinned round her shoulders. In her lap was a pile of sheep's wool, which her fingers were busy working on a drop spindle. She turned her face towards me at the sound of my footfall, but her spinning never faltered.

The woman I remembered had been plump, with dimples in the knuckles of her hands which were then, as now, never still. Even back then her hair had been grey, which is why as a boy I'd thought of her as old, though she probably hadn't been more than forty or fifty. But now the fat had melted from her frame, leaving the skin sagging and loose, draped over the bones like wet washing. The whites of her unseeing eyes were an angry red, continually weeping, so that the lids had thick yellow crusts.

I told her Sibyl had sent me and she beamed a toothless smile, urging me to come in and sit awhile. There was nowhere to sit except on the corner of the bed, the lumpy straw of the mattress crunching beneath me each time I moved. For several minutes she chattered happily as questions tumbled out of her about her friend and other villagers she recalled. It was some time before I could work the conversation round to her time in Willitoft manor and the death of George Fairfax, but when I did, a great sadness suddenly engulfed her.

'Whole household was watching when they carried him back to the house. By the time they fetched the bier and men had set off to bring him home, the whole house knew. Those that weren't standing outside to wait for their coming were watching from the doors and casements. No one could bring themselves to do a peck of work, they were that worried.' She shook her head and for the first time laid down her spindle. 'I was standing at one of the casements upstairs as they carried him underneath. Could hear him, plain as day, still giving orders, refusing to admit how much pain he were in, being jolted over the track for a mile or more.'

It was a moment before I grasped what she had just said. 'Giving orders?' I broke in. 'Then he was still alive when they

brought him back? I thought the fall had killed him instantly.'
That's what the broadsides had reported.

'That's what we all feared at first. 'Cause all we knew is what the girl who found him said when she came running to the house to fetch help, and she was that frighted you couldn't get two words of sense out of her. But the fall didn't kill him. He still had all his wits about him when they brought him back. And he seemed right enough in his sen once he was lying in his own warm bed. Broken shoulder and a wrench to his back, but the leech said he'd recover from both in time.

'Master Richard tended his father his sen, sat up with him all night after the leech left. He was that fond of the old man. But then he came out of his father's bedchamber in the dark hour before dawn, said his father had asked for—' She suddenly stopped herself, her hand flying to her mouth.

'A priest?' I suggested. 'It's no secret Lord Fairfax was Catholic.'

She hesitated, picked up her spindle, and resumed her work. The motion seemed to calm her. It suddenly struck me how frightening the world must have become for her, when she could no longer see danger coming or flee from it.

'Master Richard rode off his sen to find such a one.' She spoke softly and I had to lean in to catch her words. 'He had to go all the way to York, there was none nearer then. But when the yeoman went in to serve the master his breakfast, he found him dead in his bed. Cold as charity. 'Course it was too late to stop Master Richard. Took them three days to get word to him.'

'Cold? What did the physician make of that?'

'The old lord was dead as a coffin nail – no one needed a leech to tell them that. As I recall, he did come calling a day or two later, but the master's corpse was sealed in the coffin by then. Must have done his innards a mischief or else hit his head and bled inside his skull. Can kill a man days after a blow, the leech said. One minute he can be talking, pert as a pie, the next he's gone.'

She sighed. Laying down her spindle again, she rubbed her eyes with her knuckles. It was hard to tell if the wetness on her cheeks was simply from the inflammation or were tears of grief.

''Course, his death was the death of us all, in a manner of speaking. Young master didn't let grass grow on his heels. His father wasn't even in the ground afore a whole pack of us found ourselves on the road. I had nowhere to go, save back to the place I was born, and if the parish hadn't taken me in, I'd have been as cold as the old master before the first winter was out. Old master said I was to have a place at the servants' hearth till my dying day, but young master – he's cut from a different cloth.'

'Do you think he could have had anything to do with his father's death?'

She looked startled, and finally shook her head. 'Nay, were an accident . . . but I'll tell you this for nowt. There was a death I reckon he did have a hand in.' She paused, as if making up her mind whether or not to continue. I kept silent.

'When the young master was growing up, there was another lad brought to live here, an orphan most likely, a ward of the master or a bastard bairn. There was lots of talk among the servants, though no one ever knew for sure. Went by the name of Daniel.'

I felt my breath quicken. Did she know? Had she guessed who I was? But she continued without a pause.

'Him and young Richard were raised as brothers. Not that they ever acted like brothers – at it tooth and claw from the moment they set eyes on each other, got no better as they got older. There was this lass in the village, both lads were sweet on her. They used to sneak out of the manor at night at different times to keep company with her. I saw them go sometimes from the casement – my old eyes were sharper back then, and I used to think to my sen, that'll end in tears. Mind you, I never imagined just how bad it would turn out.'

I could still picture her. Josiane, with blue-black hair and breath as sweet as peaches. At least that's how I remembered her, though the passing years had no doubt gilded her in my mind. But she was my first love and I was smitten, eaten up at the thought of Richard laying his sweaty hands on her. More so because I knew he'd never have looked at her twice, but for the fact that he knew I wanted her. It was a game to him, like snatching a toy or luring away a faithful hound.

Grissell shook her head sadly. 'Poor lass was found dead one night, throttled by a rope or some such, though they never found it. I'd seen Daniel creeping off earlier in the evening, but I said nowt to no one, 'cause I couldn't believe he'd had a hand in it. Aye, the lad had a wicked temper on him, especially when Richard needled him. Gave the young master a right good braying more than once, and got a worse one back from his tutor for doing it. If Daniel had murdered Richard, that wouldn't've surprised me one mite. But he'd not hurt anyone who couldn't stand up for themselves, not the lad I knew back then, anyroad.'

I sat, the blood pounding in my ears as the horrors of that day engulfed me again.

'But someone else must have seen Daniel stealing out that night and told the old master. He questioned both lads and from what I heard after, Richard told his father that Daniel was jealous 'cause the lass preferred him. He said she was always laughing at Daniel, taunting him 'cause he had this firemark about his neck, looked just like the mark of a noose. They reckon that's why he used a rope to kill her, make her look the same as him. Some said maybe he hadn't meant to kill her, just mark her with the cord to serve her for mocking him. Well, that's what the old master chose to believe.'

'What . . . what happened?'

'Daniel was turned out that same day. We all stood outside watching. Old master dragged the lad to the track and threw him down on to it. Told him that if he ever set foot back across the river again, he'd hang him with his own two hands from the highest tree on the manor. Paid off the girl's family to hush it up.

Daniel wasn't his flesh, but he'd been raised as if he were, so the shame on the family would have been the same.'

'Did all the servants believe Daniel was guilty?'

'Most, I reckon. But I caught the look on the young master's face when he came back to the house after Daniel was sent packing. A fox that's just bit the head off a chicken, that's what he put me in mind of, and I reckon I was right not to trust him. Look what he did to us before the old master was even laid in his grave. As the oldens used to say, "The fox may grow grey, but he'll never grow good."'

Chapter Seven

THE EDGES OF SWELLING grey clouds were gilded silver by the light slowly leeching from the sky. A clamour of rooks circled the trees in the graveyard of All Saints, cackling malevolently. They settled on the branches, then restlessly flapped up again, irritated by my presence. As soon as I was sure I was unobserved, at least by people, if not birds, I slipped in through the side door of the church

Inside it was already near darkness and the heavy silence was broken only by the caws of the rooks outside and the scratching of tiny claws on stone. My own footfalls echoed as I made my way through the chancel to what had once been a chantry chapel. There was as yet no sign of Sibyl, but I was sure she would come to check.

I crossed to the stone piscine. The dried marigold was still threaded through the tracery, but it had been moved to the opposite side, near the bottom. Was that a sign that someone had left a message for Sibyl to carry, or had she brought one back from Willitoft and left it here to be collected? I ran my fingers under the lacy arch and poked down the drainage hole in the bottom of the stone basin, exploring every inch where a message might be hidden. I don't know what I expected to find – another wyvern symbol?

Ever since I'd left Battle nearly three months ago, that winged beast had gnawed away inside me. I still couldn't fathom what connection the wyvern had to Spero Pettingar, the only one of the known gunpowder plotters to evade capture. But there was no reason to imagine that the conspirator had any links to this place, much less that I'd find the man himself hiding in Bubwith. If the piscine was being used to pass messages and Sibyl was the courier, then it was most likely that, just as the terrier-faced man had said, it was the means for ordinary Catholics fleeing from the law to get help.

I dragged my thoughts away from Pettingar and wyverns, to what had brought me to the Ridings. That bastard Richard!

It would be impossible to find any proof of his guilt after six years had passed. Even had there been any signs of poison or suffocation, those would have long rotted with the corpse. I had known that much before I set out, but I had hoped to find witnesses who might have seen someone tampering with the saddle or who had discovered what had caused Fairfax's horse to baulk at that wall. But even that hope had been dashed. The servant who'd found his master dead in his chamber and those who had prepared the body for burial were scattered to the four winds. The stableboy was dead. Richard had ensured no one remained who could be questioned, keeping only those who were loyal to him, like that auditor, whose current position was no doubt his reward for silence. There was nothing more I could discover here.

I had almost reached the door when it swung open and Sibyl shuffled in, a small horned lantern swinging perilously in her hand. She started as she caught sight of me, but swiftly closed the door behind us, raking the feeble light across the rows of dark empty pews.

'You come back to see those books again?'

'I came to find you,' I lied, 'to tell you I went to Holme and found Grissell. She still lives and she was eager for news of you.'

The old woman smiled. 'I told her I'd be walking through the gates of heaven afore her, but she always argued she'd be the first. How does she fare? Parish feeding her well enough?' She shot a dozen questions at me and I answered them as well as I could.

Then Sibyl lifted the lantern again, shining it on my face. She stepped closer to me, peering up at me. Then, she suddenly reached up, grasped the edge of the soft linen collar I was wearing and dragged it down, exposing the side of my neck. I snatched the collar from her hand, stepping backwards, cursing myself for having removed the padding and binding before I'd returned to the inn.

'Gallows mark,' Sibyl muttered. 'That first evening I saw you in here, I thought I saw summat, but I couldn't be sure. Mark of a dead man. That really why you come here, is it?' Her gaze momentarily slid towards the chancel and the old chantry chapel beyond. Did she think I'd come in to leave a message?

'It's only a firemark, Goodwife Sibyl. I was born with it.'

She jerked as though she'd been stung and hobbled to the nearest pew, clutching her hip and lowering herself painfully. 'Come closer.'

It was too late to try to conceal it from her now. I knelt down in front of her, lifting my beard, while Sibyl held the little lantern up so that the buttery light fell on the dark red mark which encircled my neck like a noose.

The old woman crossed herself, openly this time, and muttered something under her breath, warding off evil. Her crabbed hands were shaking.

I clambered to my feet. 'Do you recognise it, Goodwife Sibyl?'

'Died of the fever same month as my poor brother, Tom. A good many died that summer.' She heaved herself to her feet and shuffled towards the old chapel, mumbling to herself. 'Gallows curse, that's what she said . . . his punishment . . . Christ have mercy.' She repeatedly crossed herself as she spoke each phrase. I couldn't tell if she was praying or her wits were wandering.

I heard the creak of the chest lid being lifted and presently she hobbled back, a book tucked beneath her arm. She laid it on the pew, set the lantern down next to it, and eased herself back down till she was sitting again. 'Around about Feast of Assumption, that's when our Tom was taken. Most died around then. Sexton got sick his sen, and they couldn't keep the corpses till he was well again, too many little ones, too many graves to dig, so the bairns had to be laid in a common pit. But their names are in there. Fifteen-eighty, that was the year.'

She opened the book, wetting her finger as she slowly turned the pages, then stopped and peered closely, before thrusting it at me. 'Reckon you'll find it somewhere about there.'

I scanned the list of names; some had ages recorded next to them. The fever had taken many of the old and even more of the young.

'I helped a fair few babes into this world at one time. But I don't speak of it to most.' She glanced up at me, searching my face anxiously.

'You have my word that I'll tell no one.'

She nodded, briefly pressing her cold hand to mine by way of thanks. She had meant she wasn't licensed by the Church to be a midwife. Catholic women preferred to be delivered by those of their own faith, so that the baby wouldn't be baptised as a Protestant if it was at risk of dying, even though such women often lacked the knowledge of the licensed midwives and both mother and child could perish.

Sibyl tapped the open page. 'I delivered all three of your mam's sons, all Matthews.'

I knew it was the custom if a son died young to give the same Christian name to the next boy born after the death of the first, and to keep using the same name for each new child until it landed on a son that thrived.

'So, my mother had two sons before me and both died.'

'You were Elena's firstborn. The middle one didn't live but a month or two, and the last, Maw, she used to call him, he left these parts soon after your mother died, must be near on eight years now.'

'Then I can't be this woman's son nor the child you remember birthing, Goodwife Sibyl,' I said, as gently as I could. 'It was after all over thirty years ago and you must have delivered countless children in your time, too many to remember.'

'I grant you I don't always recollect a name told to me yes-terday, but those from thirty years ago stick fast in my old head like linnets in birdlime. And I could never forget that firemark. Your mother was convinced it were a curse on her. God marking you for her sin, but she blamed herself, not you. Wept for days after you died.'

'But as you can see, I am very much alive. I'm not a ghost.' I touched the paper-thin skin of her hand. She was cold, so cold that it seemed she was the one who was dead. 'I am sorry, Good-wife Sibyl, but I can't be the child who died.'

Sibyl pulled the book on to her lap and held up the lantern, running her fingers down the list. 'There it is, plain as day,' she said, jabbing her finger at the entry.

'Matthew Issott, died eighteenth August fifteen-eighty, aged four. You died on the feast of St Helen's, your mother's name day.'

Four years old: that was the age I thought I'd been when Father Waldegrave had brought me into Lord Fairfax's house. Richard and I were both the same age, at least that's what they'd always told me.

'And the man who fathered me and my brothers?'

'Aye, well now, they'd only be your half-brothers,' Sibyl said. 'Elena got wed to a mariner about a year after you died. He'd not long come to these parts, so it's certain he wasn't your father. But he couldn't settle to the land. Missed the sea and went back. She waited for him for years, but he never returned. They never do. She died not knowing if she was wife or widow.'

'Then who was my father?'

The old midwife craned her head round sideways to look at me. It was a while before she finally answered.

'Elena would never say. There's a good many have their first bairn before they're wed. Woman gets tupped before they seal the knot to make sure she can get in lamb. They don't make a secret of who the father is; the lads are proud to make it known . . . Unless he's already wed,' she added grimly.

'And you think that was the case with my mother?'

She shrugged.

'In villages there's usually some gossip,' I said. 'And any couple would find it hard to meet regularly without someone spotting them, or at least noticing that there was something between them at a harvest home or a local gathering. Did my mother have close friends, a sister, another woman she knew from girlhood she might have confided in or who might have guessed? If any of them are still alive, they—'

But Sibyl cut my questions off with a sad shake of her head. 'Your mam, she was of the faith . . . There's not many in the village would talk to her, because of it. Her hens got taken, worts too, or they were trampled into the mire. Dung thrown at her washing when it was left out to dry. Signs and curses painted on her door. It happened to us all over the years. Small things mostly, but it wears a body down in the end. And even though some felt sorry for her, they'd not want to be seen going in to her cottage or passing the time of day in the street in case they got the same or worse. I reckon that's why she took to the mariner, 'cause he was from outside the village.

'And the priest too. He was good to her, kept her strong in the faith, as he did all of us. He'd come over from the manor at Willitoft to hold Mass in secret outside the village. If you worked there as a lad, I dare say you remember him. Sometimes he'd visit folk in their homes after dark to hear confessions or shrive the dying. He used to visit Elena often, more than most of the others, not that she was sick, but he knew she was having a rough time of it, a woman all alone without kin.

'Come to think on it, I reckon if she told anyone who your father was, she'd have told him. Must have, mustn't she, when she made her confession? Not that he'd tell you, even if he's still alive. No priest would ever break the seal. But he never came back here again to Bubwith after the year of the fever, when you died. Another came in his stead, from York way. But when Elena was birthing you, she kept calling out the name of the priest from Willitoft. Pains were that bad, she thought she was dying. So, she wanted the priest to shrive her. I had to put a rag in her mouth to stop her crying out, case anyone passing in the street heard her. But thanks be to the Blessed Virgin, she lived.'

Her finger made a small sign of the cross, her hands buried in her lap. Then struggling to her feet and taking the book back from me, she limped off to replace it in the chest. She returned and stood leaning sideways and breathless against the back of the pew. She gave a grimace of pain as she seized my hand.

'There was a curse put on you in your mother's womb. I don't rightly know how you came to be alive, but I reckon that curse died with the bairn whose name is in that book. There's nowt left for you here. You'd best be gone and let your name rest in the graveyard with the other corpses.'

She didn't move, obviously wanting me to leave before she returned to the piscine; maybe she'd something to put in there. She waited until my hand was on the latch of the church door.

Then she called out softly. 'Take it from a relic like me, you go disturbing owd bones and you'll awaken demons you'll never be able to send back into the earth.'

I stepped out into the darkened churchyard. The rooks were quiet now. Woodsmoke from the scores of chimneys hung heavy in the damp night air. The distant barking of dogs, the trundle of handcart wheels over stones and some notes of music drifted towards me from the streets beyond, but inside the graveyard the loudest sound was the roar of the swollen river rushing unseen in darkness.

I stood, trying to take in what I had learned. *The priest from the manor at Willitoft used to visit Elena often, more than most of the others . . . if she told anyone who your father was, she'd have told him.* Yet after he had spirited me away, after all those in Bubwith had been told that I was dead, Waldegrave never returned to visit my mother again. Could he have been more than my mother's confessor, more than just my *spiritual* father? The thought filled me again with a rage that I had not felt so keenly since I was a boy. His savage cruelty had not broken me then, but neither could I forgive it. *I* was the sin in himself he could not absolve, the vice he could not flagellate from his flesh, though he tried, by God, he tried.

Waldegrave was dead. He was the man who might have fathered me and he was dead! And that knowledge only added bitterness to my rage. Had he thought of me as he was dying? Had he prayed for forgiveness for what he had done to me, or had he prayed to be absolved for the sin of having created me, for the living sin that was me to be wiped from the earth? Had he begged for mercy as they stabbed or battered him? Had he suffered? I had to know who had finally done what for years I had dreamed of doing, what I *should* have done. And I had to know why they had done it.

The rooks in the tree above flapped up with startled shrieks and I realised I was pounding my fist against one of the wooden crosses. I took a deep breath and started back in the direction of the Lusty Tup, forcing myself to suppress my anger as I had learned to do years before. I could not afford to brood about what Waldegrave might have been. I needed to think clearly, calmly.

There was nothing more I could learn in Bubwith. I'd be a fool to linger any longer. If word reached the manor that I was here, especially if others had glimpsed my firemark, that auditor would soon remember exactly who I was. George Fairfax might be dead, but even after all these years, Richard could find a way of getting me hanged for the murder of Josiane if he learned I'd returned, and I had little doubt he would be told. And FitzAlan would certainly do nothing to stop him.

I had come to the Ridings looking for evidence that Richard had killed his father, but Waldegrave had been killed on the other side of England in Bristol. Two deaths, two murders, six years apart. Yet, they suddenly seemed connected by one of those threads that kept leading back to Richard. Waldegrave had been forging travel papers for the men that Skinner had been paid to smuggle out of the realm, that much I knew. The messenger from the ship who had been found dead on the sands by the priests in Battle had come from Bristol, and he was carrying a letter for Smith, telling him the Yena had been fished out of the Avon. Why would anyone send Magdalen's chaplain news of someone found floating in the river unless the victim was already well known to Smith? He'd known about Waldegrave, probably months before, even received messages from him. His acolyte, Erasmus, had almost let slip as much – 'Father Smith speaks of Bristol. He has made inquiries there. He knows . . .' I was sure Erasmus had been about to name Waldegrave, before fear gagged him.

And then there was Richard, the blackmailer in the shadows, learning all that passed at Battle, all the news they received. If Richard had discovered that his old tutor and chaplain was hiding out in Bristol, he could easily have had him silenced. But why? Because Waldegrave was betraying the cause, or because Richard was? I'd been looking in the wrong place and at the wrong murder. It was Waldegrave's killer I needed to find; that was the blood trail that might yet lead straight to Richard.

I heard the snapping of twigs behind me, someone brushing against a bush. I whipped round, fully expecting to see Sibyl making her way home, but someone else was standing by the edge of the flood water. I couldn't make out more than a dark outline, but I was certain the figure was a man. He stood, not moving, then he slowly raised his hand, swept off his hat and bowed. I took a pace towards him and slipped on a patch of mud; I regained my balance swiftly, but not swiftly enough. When I looked again, he had vanished.

Chapter Eight

THE CREAK OF THE narrow stairs leading to my chamber jerked me instantly awake and propelled me on to my feet, dagger in hand. Outside the small casement, the sky was only just beginning to lighten. The footsteps reached the door, followed by a soft rapping and muffled giggles. I relaxed a little, slipping the knife back under the pillow. Magota didn't wait for a reply before she bustled into my chamber with a basket, closely followed by Rosa carrying a pitcher. They looked me up and down with undisguised interest, grinning at each other.

'Now where did you get to last evening, Master Heyworth?' Magota asked.

'Business to attend to, goodwife.'

'We know all about the kind of business occupies a handsome man of an evening, don't we?' Rosa said with a wink. 'Reckon we'll have to lock our door tonight, sister.' They both chuckled.

'He'll have a good appetite this morning, then,' Magota said, lifting a platter of cold brawn from her basket. But she had barely set it down before we were interrupted by the sound of raised voices and shouts from the street outside, rapidly followed by the sounds of running feet and the urgent tolling of a single bell.

With a unified cry of 'Lord defend us!' the sisters rushed to the casement and flung it open, squeezing their heads out together and yelling for an explanation from those tearing along below. By the sound of it, windows and doors were being opened all down the street as more voices joined in the clamour to learn what was afoot. But if anyone knew, their answering shouts were drowned out, for now the clamour of the church bells had also taken up the alarm.

While the sisters were occupied with the scene outside, I dressed hastily, slipping my dagger back into the sheath dangling from my belt, and by the time the pair had decided to go down to find out what was happening, I was already ahead of them on the stairs. Small knots of anxious people had gathered outside. The bells suddenly stopped ringing and the voices which had been raised in competition fell silent. Women peered down the street towards the church and river beyond.

'Whatever do you think is amiss, Master Heyworth?' Magota whispered behind me.

'Summat on fire? A flood?' Rosa breathed.

'I can't smell smoke and there hasn't been a storm in the last few days,' I assured her. But remembering Bristol just a year ago, when the giant wave had struck without warning, I knew the absence of a storm was no guarantee of safety, especially with the Derwent so swollen from the melt waters. 'I'll find out what's wrong. You'd both better stay here, where you have a good solid door.'

The sisters nodded gratefully, their usually merry faces sagging in fear.

I strode off in the direction I had seen men running. Glancing down one of the side streets that led to the church, I saw a crowd had gathered outside one of the cottages and hurried down to join the back of it. The cottage door was wide open and a watchman stood full square, a stout staff gripped in both hands to show he meant to crack the skull of anyone who attempted to enter.

A woman was standing in the doorway of a nearby house peering out, pale and wide-eyed with alarm. As I walked towards her, she tried to shut the door, but I caught it and held it open.

'What happened here, mistress?'

She shook her head, her hand pressed tightly over her mouth.

'Wicked! Wicked!' The words burst out between her fingers as though she could no longer contain them.

'You must have been frightened out of your wits.' Something had clearly terrified her and she was visibly trembling.

'I knew summat was wrong when there was no smoke from her chimney . . . Always up afore sunrise . . . I thought she might have taken ill or had a fall . . . at her age . . . can't be too careful.'

'So, you went inside to see if she needed help?' I prompted.

She nodded vigorously. 'As soon as I saw everything tossed about, overturned . . . I knew it wasn't just a tumble she taken.'

'And did you find her?'

She nodded miserably. 'She was behind the table. Not even her own mam would have known her, save by her old kirtle . . . Face all purple and swollen up . . . hanged or strangled, I reckon . . . rope-mark deep in her neck. But that wasn't the worst of it.' She screwed her eyes shut, trying to obliterate the image that had reared up in front of her. 'Her hands, her poor hands . . . skinned they were, like . . . like a hare for the pot, and all the bones in them broke . . . smashed to splinters . . . her tongue ripped out, lying right there in her lap . . . reckon they must have used the tongs from her own hearth to do it, 'cause they were dropped beside her.'

She pressed her fist hard to her temples.

'I'll never be able to close my eyes again, I swear I won't. What if whoever did this comes back to this street and attacks someone else? The constable reckons it must be thieves, but I mean, what cause would thieves have to do that to a frail old woman? Besides, what did poor Sibyl have that would be worth the stealing? She'd already sold anything that was worth owt to keep body and soul together. Even her mam's wedding ring had to go this winter and she'd been keeping that safe to pay for her funeral.' She flinched, staring at me aghast. 'Who's going to bury the poor soul now? It'll be a pauper's grave for her and that's what she dreaded most.'

But I was barely listening, for one word had leaped at me from the torrent of her distress. 'Did you say your neighbour was called Sibyl? Are there others of that name in the village?'

'None as I know. She was named for her mam.' She stared at me suspiciously. Shock had loosened her tongue, but she suddenly seemed to realise that she was talking to a stranger. 'Why are you mithering me? I don't recall setting eyes on you before. You're not from Bubwith! You're one of the sheriff's men! I can't tell you anything. I saw nothing and I heard nothing!' She slammed the door shut and I heard her brace it from the other side.

The knot of men around the door of the cottage had swollen as the news spread. Voices which had been muttering in awed and shocked tones in the presence of death were now raised, demanding to know who had murdered the old woman and just what the constable intended to do about it. It seemed members of the watch had been dispatched to the ferry to find out if anyone had crossed to the other side and to ensure no one else did. The constable was trying to commandeer men to march to the crossroads outside the village and stop anyone trying to leave by road. But the villagers were melting away. Few, it seemed, had the stomach to confront whoever had killed with such savagery. Some protested that they were not going to leave their own wives and mothers alone with a ruthless murderer roaming loose, while others argued it was better to let the killer escape. Let him go off to torment another village instead of trapping him inside Bubwith where, like a cornered beast, he'd surely be provoked into striking again.

I hurried back to the Tup and sought my chamber. That gentle old soul had not deserved this – no woman of her age deserved this, though I could think of a few men I'd be more than willing to beat to death at that moment. I was certain Sibyl's murder had not been the work of thieves, or even of a madman. The crushing of her hands had all the hallmarks of the pursuivants, vicious little rat-turds like Richard Topcliffe, hired to execute the arrest warrants issued by the Privy Council to seize known priests and traitors and to extract a confession of guilt, by torture if need be. Sibyl would not herself have been the quarry, but if it was known she carried messages, she might well have been questioned, not by Topcliffe, of course, who was too well known to pass unnoticed in these parts. But there were plenty of others, greedy for money and power, who enjoyed inflicting pain.

I didn't know what the poor soul had been forced to blurt out in her agony, who she might have named. In their delirium of pain and their desperation to put an end to it, victims often babbled any name that surfaced in their fevered mind, guilty or innocent. And my name, spoken perhaps only an hour or two earlier, might well have been one of them.

But a pursuivant would not risk his real quarry escaping, not once word of Sibyl's murder spread. I gambled that if the old woman had told him where to find the person he sought, he would already be on his way there. Willitoft manor, was that where he was headed? Sibyl had been returning from that direction when I'd seen her on the road and there was nothing there except the manor and the cottages of its landsmen. I couldn't believe Richard would risk his life and property to save a priest or anyone else from the gallows; quite the opposite, he'd look to turn a profit by selling the hangman the rope. Yet someone in that manor might. It would not be the first time that servants or farm workers had hidden fugitives without their master's knowledge, especially if he were absent for months.

I had intended to start out on the long ride to Bristol straight after breakfast, but I had no desire to spend the day being questioned by Bubwith men blocking the roads with pitchforks and axes, assuming the hapless constable had actually found anyone brave enough. Better to keep to my chamber until they had convinced themselves that the killer had already slipped beyond their grasp. My growling stomach reminded me I had not yet eaten and the brawn was still on the table..

But I had taken only a single mouthful when there was an explosion of voices in the passageway below. Boots pounded up the narrow wooden staircase leading to my chamber and I had time to do no more than draw my dagger before my chamber door was flung open and four men burst into the small room. The petty constable leading the way in front was almost driven on to the point of my blade by the men storming in close on his heels.

'Hold hard there,' the constable ordered. 'Drop that knife, else you'll find yourself in a worse trouble for threatening the King's peace.'

'I threaten no one's peace, but when armed men barge into a man's chamber without the courtesy of asking for admittance, especially when there's been a murder, you can hardly chide a man for being wary.'

'See, he admits he knows all about the murder,' one of the men at the back jeered.

'Is there anyone in Bubwith who doesn't?' I snapped. 'What brings you to my door?'

'Murder, that's what. You were seen talking to old Sibyl after dark last night.'

'In the church,' another added, certain this detail was proof of my guilt.

'Aye, and then you followed her home and throttled her to death.'

'And why would I do that?'

The constable shrugged. 'That's for the justices to find out. My duty is to arrest felons and see they're kept safely locked up until they're delivered for trial and hanging.' He slapped his iron-tipped cudgel against his palm. 'Now, you drop that dagger, unless you want to die here.' He must have seen me glance towards the tiny casement, for he chuckled mirthlessly. 'Not even a bairn in clouts could get through that. And in case you're thinking of fighting your way out, there's a dozen more men at the foot of those stairs, all of them armed and all itching for the chance to chop you into cat-collop for what you did to that poor owd biddy.'

The men behind him grunted their affirmation and added a few more threats of their own. I could have fought my way through the men in the chamber, but judging by the shouts out in the street, any Bubwith man who could swing an axe or lift a scythe was massing outside, baying for my blood. I tossed the knife on to the bed, and the constable grabbed my shoulder, while a watchman seized my other arm. I offered no resistance as they bound my hands behind me, which clearly annoyed them. The constable insisted on leading the way down the stairs, no doubt wanting to be seen to have captured a desperate cutthroat. It meant that, thankfully, those coming behind couldn't shove me down it headfirst, a sport the Newgate gaolers had perfected.

The passageway was crowded with men brandishing whatever tools they had snatched up, and the howls redoubled as they caught sight of me. They surged towards me, but the constable and watch pushed them back.

'My responsibility is to see him delivered in good order,' the constable bellowed. 'Don't want him cheating the hangman by dying afore we can watch him dancing on the gallows tree.'

The mob reluctantly let us through, grumbling like sulky children cheated of their sport, but those within reach couldn't resist landing a few punches or savage blows with their staves on my back and shoulders as I was dragged past. I glanced towards the parlour casement. Magota and Rosa stood side by side, clinging to each other, staring at me in horror and disbelief.

As I was marched down the street, children began to scoop up handfuls of dung and mud from the road and hurl it towards me, laughing and jeering as my guards yelled at them, for they were getting the worst of it. Being in the centre of the knot of men, I was largely shielded from the missiles.

We halted in front of a small hexagonal stone building. The stout, studded oak door was furnished with a small hatch that could be opened from the outside, just wide enough to inspect the prisoner or pass in his dole of bread and water. Hampered by his reluctance to relinquish his grip on either my arm or his cudgel, it took some time for the constable to unhook the iron ring chained to his waist and select the key to the gaol from the two that dangled on it. Eventually the door swung open and he shoved me in, sending me crashing against the wall on the other side. Fearing that, like a wild cat, I'd immediately spring back out again, he slammed the door quickly and I heard the key rasp in the lock. Shouts and bellows from the other side told me exactly what they hoped the justices would do to me, before the voices faded as they tramped away. A rattle of stones and dull thuds of sticks beat against the oak door, children probably, but they quickly tired of the game and they too ran off.

I found myself standing in a tiny circular cell in semi-darkness, not wide enough at any point for the average man to lie full length without pulling his knees up. The only light came from slits at the top of the conical roof, too high and too narrow to offer any hope of escape, but wide enough to allow a cold wind to whistle in and no doubt the rain too, judging by the puddles on the stone-slab floor. A small heap of wet and rotting straw lay against one wall and there was a shit pail on the other side, which judging by the stench had not been emptied since the last guest had occupied this chamber. The only other furniture was a couple of iron rings embedded in the floor and wall, from which rusty fetters dangled. At least the constable had not thought to use those . . . yet. I crouched down and sawed the bindings that still fastened my hands behind me against the jagged edge of the metal. As soon as they broke, I stood up, massaging the life back into my arms and flexing my back, which was beginning to stiffen and throbbing where fists and sticks had struck it.

I still could not quite believe what had happened. It was natural enough to accuse a stranger of such a crime: no one would be willing to believe that one of their own neighbours, or worst still, a relative had committed such a vicious murder. But surely someone in the village must have known or at least suspected what Sibyl was doing? The terrier-faced man at the ferry obviously knew the church was being used to leave messages. But clearly no one wanted to admit that was why Sibyl had been killed; unless, of course, they thought I was a pursuivant.

In the gloom of that cell, I pictured the corpse of the old woman I had talked to only hours before. The face I had seen, now purple and swollen ... the hands. I could still feel the fragile bird-like touch of her fingers on my own hand. She was dead, with a rope around her neck – the gallows mark.

If what she had told me was true, she was the woman who had brought me into the world, the first person who had ever seen me and held me. And I hadn't even asked her what kind of woman my mother had been; what she had looked like; whether there was anything in my face that resembled hers. I had been too preoccupied by the revelation that I was supposedly dead. And I might well be dead soon. I had no way to prove my innocence, any more than I had all those years ago when they'd found Josiane. I had escaped the hangman's noose then, but if whoever had killed Sibyl needed a scapegoat, I had no hope of evading it this time. Old Waldegrave was at this minute boasting to God and the Devil that he'd been right all along when he'd predicted that I'd end my days on the gallows.

I was convinced they wouldn't leave me in Bubwith for long. They'd send word to York today, but given the state of the roads, with luck it would be tomorrow or the next day before the locked wagon would arrive in which I'd be carried to the city, there to be thrown into a crowded cell to await judgement at the assizes. FitzAlan had given me the chance to walk out of the hellhole of Newgate. Now, little more than a year later, I was back in gaol. I couldn't hope he'd rescue me a second time, even if I could bribe a gaoler to get word to him. He'd probably regard it as just punishment for having defied his orders to stay in London.

I touched the heavy purse that FitzAlan had given me that I'd hidden beneath my shirt. The petty constable had been so keen to have me safely locked up, he hadn't searched me, but I couldn't count on that to last, certainly not once I reached York. If the gaolers were anything like those in Newgate, they'd turn a prisoner inside out, looking for anything of value they could take from him.

There was nothing to be done until nightfall except sit and wait. From time to time, I heard stones rattle against the walls and door, and yells of *murderer* and worse, but since I made no response, they soon wandered off. They evidently had posted no guard, for the walls were so thick and the door so stout, no one could have ever broken out. Only the pigeons squabbling and shitting through the slits in the roof kept me company. A thick pall of clouds hid any trace of the sun and time seemed to pass as slowly as a funeral procession. My stomach growled, reminding me that it had received only a single mouthful of brawn since that morning – possibly my last. If I was taken to York, I certainly wouldn't be tasting meat or ale again.

Chapter Nine

THE GREY LIGHT above me was dissolving into darkness, but the street outside had fallen quiet. Most would be sitting down to supper at this hour; the only thought on their minds would be filling their bellies.

I pulled out the thin spike I always carried in a pocket sewn into my shirt and set to work on the lock. It took a while. The mechanism was large and stiff, and it had been some months since I'd last had occasion to practise the art of lock charming, but eventually it yielded. I eased the door open a crack and listened for passing footsteps. Voices and the sounds of clanking vessels drifted down the street from a nearby alehouse. I slipped out. The street was, as I'd hoped deserted, so I risked a few precious moments relocking the door. If the watch were satisfied it was still secure, it would buy me a little more time.

The door of the alehouse ahead of me opened and two men stepped out. Keeping to the centre of the street to avoid the candlelight spilling from the casements on either side, I walked towards the pair at a steady pace, mumbling a greeting. They barely glanced my way, and neither did the woman who hurried by as I turned the corner. I carried on past the Lusty Tup. Judging by the noise, the parlour was full, which meant Magota and Rosa would be kept busy. By the sound of it, half the village had turned up there, hungry for any morsel the sisters might let slip about the ruthless killer they had so lately sheltered beneath their roof. At least I'd brought them good business.

I glanced up at the chamber I had occupied. There was no light shining from the casement, but it would be foolish to risk climbing those stairs to collect my spare clothes. I could too easily become trapped. Besides, the room had probably been searched and all I'd left there already removed by the sisters or the constable. I skirted around the inn until I came to the entrance to the courtyard and the small stable. Lanterns burned on the walls, but their light did no more than dimly illuminate the doorway. To my relief, though, I could just make out Valentine still in his stall, tethered next to two other horses. I could not risk taking any of the tack outside to examine it, so I grabbed what felt like mine from the wall and began to saddle up Valentine. He recognised me, but the other two horses were plainly unnerved at a stranger moving around them in the darkness, which in turn made Valentine agitated, and I was forced to waste precious time soothing them.

The door at the back of the Tup opened and a shaft of light darted across the courtyard. I froze. Footsteps were clacking across the yard, coming towards the stables. The sound stopped. Whoever had been moving was standing still, listening. A woman appeared in the doorway, silhouetted against the light from the lantern on the opposite wall. Her face was in shadow, but I caught a smell of roasted meat fat, and from the outline guessed it was one of the two sisters.

She glanced behind her, then moved swiftly inside. She hadn't brought a lantern and, as I had done, was feeling her way down towards where I was standing, behind Valentine. As soon as she touched the horse, she'd realise he'd been saddled and she'd start yelling, bringing all the men drinking inside charging out. I'd be dead before I ever got to a trial. The woman reached my horse, and was feeling her way along his flank as I stepped swiftly up behind her. I grabbed her arm, clamping my hand across her mouth from behind. I felt the jolt of shock through her body, and pressed hard to smother her scream.

'I won't hurt you, goodwife, but you must not make a sound. Swear you'll keep silent and I'll take my hand away.'

She hesitated, then nodded as vigorously as she could manage with me gripping her jaw. I slowly eased the pressure on her mouth, ready to clamp it back instantly, but she made no attempt to scream.

'I swear I did not kill Sibyl,' I murmured close to her ear. 'I had no reason to do so. But I will not get a fair trial. Those who did kill her will see to that. I just want the chance to get away. Let me take my horse and, I promise, you will never see me again. You can tell them tomorrow that Valentine was stolen during the night. They'll believe that.'

Magota turned towards me, her eyes shining in the faint glow of the lanterns in the courtyard. 'I told Rosa you'd come for him, Master Heyworth. I said, he's clever as a cat, that one. He'll find a way. So, we packed your saddlebag ready, at least what that constable didn't take for himself. You'll find it in yon corner. And we put a wrap of meat and cheese in there. I warrant they've not given you a bite to eat. Heard one of them say you was to starve till you begged for pigswill. And don't you fret none, our Rosa'll see to it there's a good din inside to cover the sound of the hooves.'

'But I thought you'd told the constable I'd not come back for supper last night?'

'Now whyever would we do a thing like that, Master Heyworth? We'd not give that crook-pated bladder the time of day. He harasses us from morn to night, accusing our customers of playing at cards when they ought not, or disturbing the King's peace when they're just making merry. And everyone knows he's simply after free beer or a bribe, so as he'll look the other way. Thieving toad! Anyroad, we've spent all our lives serving men and we can tell the decent ones from the vicious bastards, just like a shepherd can tell a hound he can trust from a sheep-killer. We knew you weren't the kind of man as would do that to a poor old—' Her words were severed by the sudden urgent clanging of the church bell.

'They've discovered I've escaped!'

'Aye, that they have, and they'll come straight here looking for you. Mount up! Rosa will stall them.'

I grabbed the bag and swung into the saddle, hoping I'd tightened it properly, and ducked low as Magota unfastened the tether and led the horse out. Raised voices and the sound of overturning benches were clattering out from the inn, suggesting that some of the watch might already be trying to force their way in.

Magota flung open a small gate at the back of the yard. 'Down the ginnel. Cross the field at the end, then you'll be clear of the village.' She seized my hand and planted a hard, lingering kiss on it. 'There'll always be a warmed bed in the Lusty Tup for a man as comely as you, Master Heyworth. Uz and my sister share everything, so mind you keep your strength up.' She chuckled, slapped Valentine on the rump and strode back towards the courtyard, where no doubt she intended to make the crook-pate's life as difficult as possible.

The ginnel was dark and narrow, just wide enough for a horse and rider, but I couldn't push Valentine as swiftly as I would have liked, for he was wading through several inches of liquid mud and, from the stench of it, the contents of many piss pails and slop buckets. As I had discovered at the river, Valentine became nervous when his footing wasn't sound. I coaxed him along, trying to keep him calm and not let him sense my urgency. Behind me came the shouts and bellows of the constable and his men as they burst out into the courtyard.

I urged Valentine forward, but he was stubbornly resisting. There wasn't enough space for me to dismount and squeeze round to lead him; all I could do was try to calm him and keep him moving. I saw something ahead of me, a man walking past the end of the passageway. Then a shout went up as he caught sight of me. He stood full square in the entrance, blocking my escape, yelling to those behind me in the Tup that he had me trapped. They were making too much noise to hear him, but that wouldn't last, and I had nothing to fight with. Valentine had stopped dead. I forced myself to sit still, knowing there was only one way out of this.

Then the gate behind me was dragged open. Light from the flaming torches that the men carried gushed out into the ginnel, and with it an explosion of movement and yells. It was what I had been waiting for. Unnerved by the threat behind him, Valentine reared and shot forward. I stooped low in the saddle, urging him to speed. In his panic, he forgot what was beneath his feet as he thundered and splashed towards the figure blocking his way ahead. The man held his nerve for a few paces, but as we reached him, he threw himself out of the path of the trampling hooves. We cannoned out into the open field. I knew the bellows and yells of the men running behind us would be enough to bring half the village out on to the streets, but I didn't waste time looking back as we charged across the field into the darkness beyond.

Chapter Ten

THE PALACE OF PLACENTIA, GREENWICH, LONDON

ROBERT CECIL HAD NOT even reached the door when the screaming began. One of the oarsmen from the tilt boat had offered his arm for support walking on the long wooden jetty, for rain was shafting down in silver arrows, creating tiny explosions of water on the Thames and making the wooden boards as slippery as fish guts. The boatman had just turned back towards the great river when they heard the shriek.

'God's cods, what is that? Begging your pardon, my lord,' the waterman added hastily.

The cries coming from the upper storey of the King's apartments were becoming ever more shrill. Cecil overlooked the curse; he could hardly blame the startled boatman. Those screeches certainly did not sound human.

'Some wild bird or beast captured in the New World,' Cecil suggested doubtfully, 'intended to join the lions and leopards at the Tower.'

James was constantly expanding his menagerie of savage animals, who were pitted together in his experiments to determine which might prove the stronger or more cunning. It was never a spectacle that Cecil enjoyed watching. Even James's own son and heir, Prince Henry, detested it, though in the hunt he was as fearless and able as his father, perhaps even more so, though he was still only fourteen.

'If that's a beast, it's not one I fancy meeting on a dark night,' the waterman muttered. 'I hope they've got it well caged, for your sake, my lord. Wouldn't want you to be its supper.'

But almost at once, shouts and bellowed orders ricocheted through the building in front of them. The waterman shook his head and retreated as swiftly as he could back to the safety of the boat. The river might have its dangers, but at least out on the water you were safe from strange beasts and even stranger Scottish kings.

The guard standing to one side of the door glanced anxiously upward and, taking a firmer grip of his halberd, turned sideways, holding the gleaming axe-blade firmly in both hands, prepared to strike should danger burst upon him from either inside or out.

Cecil whirled around at the noise of the pounding feet behind him on the path and the rasp of swords being dragged from their sheaths as the Gentlemen Pensioners, the King's personal bodyguards, thundered straight towards him. A flying elbow caught Cecil in the ribs as they ran past. He staggered backwards, his leather satchel knocked out from beneath his arm, but the guard didn't even turn to see if he was unharmed, much less pick up the fallen case.

On any other occasion, the Secretary of State would have demanded that the man be disciplined and ordered to make a full apology, but even he could see that the guard's offence to him was nothing to what might be occurring inside. He retrieved his case from a puddle and brushed the water from it. Small knots of servants and of courtiers were gathering along the riverbank, or peering out from doorways and casements, though none were venturing inside. After some moments' hesitation, Cecil made for the door through which the guards had just vanished. The unearthly shrieks had subsided into wails and noisy sobs, and though no less alarming than before, the sound was now recognisably human.

Bracing himself, Cecil strode inside, pushing past several Gentlemen of the Bedchamber, and mounted the stairs. Even in his anxiety, he was acutely aware of the men standing below watching his awkward ascent. His twisted back was stiffer than ever this morning, and he knew all the jests that were murmured behind it, but today the whispers below were not about him.

A young maidservant was being escorted towards a back staircase by two guards who gripped her on either side by her upper arms. She was weeping, and her cries were becoming louder again, turning into the shrieks Cecil had heard earlier. One of the men shook her, bidding her to hold her peace, and when that had no effect, he let go of her long enough to slap her hard across the back of her head. Her cap tumbled to the floor, and a long plait of auburn hair snaked down her back. The guards marched her on. She was shaking and still weeping, but more quietly.

Two Gentlemen Pensioners stood before the door to the King's bedchamber and his attiring room. As Cecil approached, they shot out their arms, slanting their gilded halberds into a cross, blocking the way.

'Is His Majesty . . . injured?' It had been on the tip of Cecil's tongue to say *dead*. But even to utter such a thought aloud would be treason.

A warning glance flicked between the two men before one of them cleared his throat. 'His Majesty is unharmed. But no one is to enter until the rooms have been thoroughly searched.'

Being barred from the royal bedchamber was nothing new. Cecil had rarely been admitted into that private sanctum since he had engineered James's accession to the throne of England. The Scottish courtiers and the King's favourites, of whom the handsome and muscular Robert Carr was still cock of the dung heap, had between them ensured that few, if any, Englishmen were admitted to the rooms where the Scots alone had the private ear of the King. And Cecil had set off for the palace that morning fully expecting to have his meeting with James in one of the public rooms below, until the maid's screams had drawn him up here.

'Why are the rooms being searched at this early hour?'

Again, that fleeting glance passed between the guards, before their eyes flicked back to attention, staring straight ahead, over Cecil's head, which only stoked the small man's irritation.

'Ordered not to spread rumours, my lord,' the guard said.

Cecil was sure he caught the flicker of an insolent grin on the other man's face, but decided to ignore it. 'At least that is one order you seem to have understood. Let us hope you exercise the same diligence in protecting the King's person.' He turned on his heel and stalked away.

ONCE CECIL HAD descended to the public rooms, he had little trouble in locating James. Visitors and members of the Court alike were milling around in the antechamber, but it appeared that James was not in the mood to receive any of them, though they could plainly hear him through the closed door.

'Get that great clumsy gowk out of my sight!'

The door was flung open and a page-boy hurried out, his face scarlet, closely followed by a Gentleman Usher, whose expression said that whatever abuse the lad had taken from the King, he was about to receive a great deal worse. Without waiting to be announced, Cecil whisked through the door, his cloak almost getting trapped in it as the two servants inside hurriedly closed it.

James was limping up and down the long gallery, pausing to peer behind the tapestries on the walls and poking his stick beneath the chests. Catching sight of his Secretary of State, he lashed out at a finely carved oak cabinet.

'I gave instructions no one was to be admitted. Will no one heed a word I say? When a king gives an order, it will be obeyed.'

Cecil sensed the agitation of the two servants standing behind him, plainly uncertain if James meant them to expel the Secretary of State as they had the unfortunate page.

Cecil bowed. 'Sire, I heard the commotion. It was evident to me that something had transpired and if it was another attack on Your Majesty, I would be failing in my duty if I did not investigate.'

'Aye, your duty. Well, it seems ye have failed, my little beagle. Plainly there are things afoot in this palace your informants have neglected to tell you about. It would appear your spider's web of intelligencers has holes in it, holes through which venomous worms can freely crawl.'

Cecil's mind was racing. Northwood's reports of the church thefts had confirmed that something major and well organised was being planned, but it could not be unfolding this soon, not if those involved were still trying to find the money to finance it, and they would certainly not recruit some half-witted serving wench to carry it out. But there were a dozen threats a month made by madmen or fools intending to kidnap or murder the King, most wanting to slaughter James because they believed he was 'the Beast' spoken of in the Book of Revelation or a were-wolf in disguise. One man, who was now chained up in Bedlam, had claimed God had told him that if he killed the King the plague would vanish, never to return. But a madman might well succeed where the gunpowder plotters had failed, for not even Cecil's vast network could possibly keep watch on every lunatic or fanatic in the realm.

'That woman the guards were taking away, did she try to attack you, Sire?'

James glanced down the length of the hall towards the two servants standing by the door.

'Out, the pair of ye! And see that no one comes in, do ye hear? No one! Else I'll be using your arseholes as candle prickets, do ye ken?'

James clambered up on to the dais and threw himself down into the ornate chair which had been positioned so that he could conduct audiences well out of touching distance. With only the two of them remaining in this great long hall, it was hardly necessary for James to seat himself up there, but Cecil knew he was determined to make the point that he was Sovereign and

King. All the same, it necessitated James to beckon Cecil to come closer, if all that passed between them was not to be heard by those crowded in the antechamber beyond the door.

'The wee woman was screaming out of fear, most likely. The foul thing was hidden beneath the manchets in the basket brought for me to breakfast.'

'What thing, Sire?'

'A waxen image of a man with a crown pushed down around its neck, being strangled by it,' James gabbled impatiently. 'Come, man, you'll recall that Agnes Simpson and the witches of North Berwick confessed to making wax poppets in my image and melting them with fire to raise that storm at sea which had me near drowned.'

'Was there any hurt done to this mannikin you found, Sire?'

'I'd call a crown around a man's neck to choke him hurt enough, wouldn't you, Lord Salisbury, or do you think that a trivial matter?' His long grimy fingers were massaging his throat as though it pained him, but Cecil was sure he was not aware of the gesture.

'But if this *object* was intended to cause injury, wouldn't the witch who fashioned it keep it, so that she could destroy it as Agnes Simpson did?'

'I dinnae doubt that was her intention. But someone else made sure I got wind of it.'

'Or someone put it there to alarm you?' Cecil suggested, carefully avoiding the word *frighten*. 'The woman who was screaming, was she the one who discovered the mannikin beneath the bread?' Even as he asked the question, Cecil realised that was unlikely: female servants did not usually enter the royal bedchamber, even to perform the most menial of tasks.

'I'm told she was the one who took the manchets from the ovens and arranged them in the basket. She covered it with the linen cloth, brought it up with the other servants who were fetching the meats and fish. All the dishes were handed to my yeomen to bring into the chamber and the whole gaggle of the servants watched as they are obliged to till the door was closed on them, so there is none other that could have put that foul thing in there except that woman.'

'Does she admit it?'

'Not yet!' James said sullenly. 'She started screeching like a wild cat when the thing was shown to her. Couldn't get a word out of her. But she'll be made to talk.'

And long before they finished persuading her, she'd be agreeing that her mother was a black cat and she'd flown on her distaff to kiss the Devil's arse, Ceil thought. But all the same, someone had put that wretched doll in that bread basket. Anyone with malice enough to do that could have poisoned the bread just as easily, but if poisoning was the ultimate intention, only a fool would alert James beforehand.

It seemed far more likely their purpose was simply to unnerve James – and it had succeeded. Maybe the malevolent trick was revenge for some humiliation the King had offered them, a cruel joke he'd made at their expense – he made plenty of those – or a favour he'd shown someone else that they'd expected to receive. But that suggested the culprit was much closer to James than a serving maid: someone in his own bedchamber; someone he trusted. And the question was – had they concluded their game of spite, or were they just getting started?

Chapter Eleven

BRISTOL

DANIEL PURSGLOVE

'I'LL MURDER YOU, you little maggot! Seize him! Don't let him through, you useless cod-wits!'

But it was too late. The urchin had slipped through the wedge of people, carts and wagons crowded in front of Lawford's Gate like an eel and before the guards even realised what was happening, he'd dodged around them. He paused, and turned, grinning impudently and brandishing the stolen sack above his head, then vanished out into the city beyond. He was probably one of Skinner's band – a bunch of cutpurses and thieves who occupied the ruined castle. Since King James owned the castle, the Bristol authorities could not set foot inside, so Skinner and his gang were free to terrorise the city, taking whatever they pleased and thumbing their noses at the guards from the safety of their lair. I'd had more than one encounter with Skinner, and I wasn't anxious to renew my acquittance just yet, not least because he'd given orders to his rats to kill me and they'd take great pleasure in doing that.

The man on the cart next to me was still swearing and cursing, both at the young thief who had stolen the sack from among the cages of poultry and baskets of eggs on his cart, and the guards who'd failed to catch him, but who were, as he vociferously complained, stopping decent law-abiding folks earning their bread, by searching their wagons and asking clay-brained questions, when they should have been catching the real villains. 'If they hadn't kept us here, I'd have never got robbed!' he groused. 'I reckon half of them are in league with the castle rats, jamming folks in this crowd of carts like ducks in a fowler's trap, so that those thieves can help themselves to whatever they fancy.'

'Is there always such a crowd at this gate?' I asked. I'd last been in Bristol a year ago, just after the great flood, and most people were trying to leave the city then, not enter it.

'It's worse since the thaw. There wasn't many could get their loads shifted while the roads were covered in ice, so they've been making up for it since. And then there's them.' The poulter jerked his head towards a group of beggars squeezing between the horses and carts, their hands and faces wrapped in filthy bandages, lifting alms bowls up to the riders or thrusting them in the faces of those on foot. A gaunt-faced woman edged towards us, a tiny, wizened goblin of a baby slung across her shrivelled breasts. The poulter raised his whip menacingly and she spat at him, jerking her fist in the fig sign, but took care to stay out of his range.

'Bristol's already got more than its fair share of beggars and vagabonds, what with the maimed sailors being dumped here when they're no more use to the sea captains, and a constant gaggle of morts left behind in the city with brats in their bellies once the ships have sailed. But with food being so short, there's swarms of mumpers making for Bristol from the villages and byways round about, thinking there'll be richer pickings in a city. But these last two days the queues have been worse than usual. The guards are looking for someone. There's a handsome price on his head, by all accounts. Think he might be making for a ship to flee these shores. Every man on the gates is hoping he'll be the one to claim the prize for the felon's capture. You wait and see; they'll be searching my cages next in case he's hiding under one of my hens.'

I stiffened, but tried not to betray my disquiet. 'What's this man wanted for?'

The poulter shrugged morosely. 'Murder or treason, I dare say. It's always one or the other, or both, aint it? There are broad-sides pasted up round the city, with a woodcut of his face, but you can't recognise anyone from those. Looks like half the men in Bristol, if you ask me. Could even be you.' He peered at me sideways. 'You're not a wanted man, are you?'

'Not even by my wife,' I said with an exaggerated sigh, which at least brought a smile to his gloomy face.

I briefly contemplated riding around the city and entering by another road, but I knew that all of the approaches would be watched, if the reward posted was high enough. The city's guards would take no chances on a lucrative bounty slipping past them. And I could hardly back out of this throng without drawing unwanted attention to myself. I was sure I was not the man they were hunting. The murder of an old crone in a piss-poor village would hardly merit a manhunt this far from York or the Ridings. But all same, the poulter was right, these woodcuts portraits were so vague that they resembled every second person in the country, and innocent men were often seized in error. I had no desire to be held prisoner while they checked where I had spent these past weeks.

Carts and wagons, men on horseback and pedlars pushing handcarts edged slowly towards the gates. Tempers frayed as the afternoon wore on; insults and fists flew if someone thought they were being edged aside by someone behind them. Cartwheels locked with wagons, restless horses stamped on the feet of pack-men and all the while, ever more traffic joined the throng from behind, each new arrival demanding to know what was causing the delay.

Then finally the poulter was impatiently beckoned forward to have his load searched, and one of the guards imperiously gestured to the space beside him beneath the archway gate and ordered me to dismount. The sky was grey and heavy as yesterday's porridge, and the wide archway blocked out what little daylight filtered down into the city. He peered at me, thrusting his face close to mine in an effort to see me more clearly, his breath stinking of raw onions and strong tobacco. 'Where are you from?'

'London,' I said. It was a gamble – the wanted man could easily be from there – but it was safer to name a large anonymous city than some small hamlet where all strangers stood out. Then before he could object that this was not the London road, I added, 'But I'd business which took me to Gloucester on the way here.'

'Oh aye, and what business would that be?'

I was sorely tempted to say *my own,* for the guard had unfastened the strap of one of the saddlebags and was rummaging through under linens and hose, dropping a shirt carelessly into the mud. But the poulter, who had been telling the guards that they couldn't catch a cold, much less a thief, was getting the worst of it. They were taking a malicious delight in searching his cart as minutely if they were looking for stowaway spiders instead of fugitives.

'I work in the law,' I said vaguely. 'Wills and estates can take much untangling when a man has businesses in several cities.'

'Thumbs in a dozen plum pies,' the guard said. 'I know the sort. And you'll find no shortage of those in Bristol.'

I pulled a face. 'I know it. The lawyers take their fat fees, but the tedium of combing through piles of old ledgers falls to us ill-used and underpaid clerks. I dare say it's the same for you. The sheriff and the city fathers sit by roaring fires and dream up their orders, while you have to freeze your cods off in this gateway carrying them out.'

The young guard had stopped riffling through my bags, and was nodding in agreement. 'And they don't have to listen to the threats and curses that rabble hurl at us from dawn till dusk.'

'There'll be more than curses being hurled at you, you idle scut.' An older guard had detached himself from the group searching the poulter's cages and sacks. 'Have you questioned this man?' He peered at me, then pulled out a sheet of paper folded over his belt. He glanced down at the woodcut, then up at me again. 'Are you blind?' he demanded of his helpless junior. 'Can't you see the likeness?' They held the paper between them, their heads bobbing up and down as they looked from the broadside to me.

I stared intently at the poulter's cart and before long they both followed my gaze. 'He's a lucky man,' I murmured to myself, but ensuring it was just loud enough for them to hear.

'Don't reckon he'd agree with you, he's been bellyaching that he's just been robbed.'

'But the thief didn't spot that egg. He'd have made off with it for certain if he had.'

'Couldn't have been that hungry, then,' said the older guard.

I took a step towards the cart and lifted the egg from the nest of straw, nodding to show my suspicions had been confirmed. I placed it in the hand of the young guard. 'Feel the weight of that?'

He jiggled it up and down. 'Feels same as any other, bit heavier. Double yolker, maybe.'

'This one is far more than that,' I breathed. Taking it from him, I cracked it on the cartwheel, pulled the two halves apart and held them out to him. There, nestling in the golden yolk, was a silver shilling. The guard, whistling in amazement, snatched it out, wiped the slime on his breeches, then bit it to ensure it was genuine. He held it up to the others, who were peering at him in dumb amazement.

'How the devil did it get into that egg?' the older guard asked.

'Chickens will peck at anything shiny,' I assured him. 'Comes out in the egg. Saw a hen lay a gold ring once. If those hens chanced on a dropped purse or scratched up a buried hoard . . .'

I didn't need to finish. The guards were already seizing the eggs from the basket. As the travellers waiting in the throng relayed the discovery to those behind them, men and women surged forward to ransack the cart. I felt a pang of guilt about the hapless poulter, who was trying in vain to beat back the hands grabbing at his baskets, but I couldn't afford too much remorse. Tugging my horse forward, I headed out through the archway into the city, and, pretending not to have heard the belated order to wait, I swung into the saddle as swiftly as I could and trotted briskly away.

Tempted as I was to return to the Salt Cat, where I had lodged when I'd come to Bristol a year ago, I couldn't take the risk. Mistress Crugge was not known for her discretion and if Caleb Crugge was still organising the cockfights in his cellar where the band of castle rats plied their trade, then word would quickly get back to their leader, Skinner, that I had returned. I intended to confront him, but only when I was ready. I didn't relish the prospect of him creeping into my chamber as I lay sleeping, or his henchmen trapping me in some deserted alley, and ending up, as Waldegrave had done, floating lifeless in the Avon. As I'd been once warned, Skinner had not acquired his nickname by flaying rabbits.

I headed over the bridge to the south of the city, and Redcliffe Backs. At the time of my last sojourn, this area had been battered by some of the worst of the flooding: entire walls had collapsed, streets had been strewn with broken ships' timbers and jagged metal. Cellars and undercrofts had been full of stinking water, and workshops and dwellings were buried beneath mud and slime, peppered with rotting fish, drowned rats and human corpses.

Now along the quayside, the river mud and silt had largely been dug from the streets and those buildings which could be salvaged had been shored up and rebuilt. Patches stood out starkly on walls like newly healed scars on skin. But between some of the houses and yards, rubble-filled gaps still remained, like broken teeth, where the owners could not afford to rebuild or were dead, dragged out to sea by the wave or crushed beneath their own roofs. These derelict sites were not deserted, though, for scattered among them were fires and makeshift shelters fashioned from broken spars and old sailcloth.

The freeze had dealt a further blow to the battered city and though the river was flowing freely now, wherries and other crafts that had not been taken out in time lay embedded in the steep glutinous mud banks, squeezed and crushed by the ice. But the air was filled with the cacophony of banging and sawing, shouted orders and the clang of metal. Barrels rumbled as they were rolled across stone, and gulls shrieked on the roofs above. The salty wind carried a witch's soup of stenches – hot tar, sawdust and fish, seasoned with tobacco, spices, woodsmoke and whale oil.

But just a street or so further into the city, around St Thomas's church, it was a different story. This was the home of the wealthy cloth merchants with their tall, three-storey houses and grounds filled with little orchards and knot gardens. The damage here had evidently been swiftly repaired and there were no beggars huddling around stinking fires in these streets.

I found a small inn, the Three Choughs, on a row of houses and craftsmen's shops along Redcliffe Street, on the opposite side to those houses occupied by the merchants. The inn, like other buildings in the row, backed on to the warehouses and chandlers' workshops along the quay, and the chamber to which the grim-faced Goodwife Barfoot led me was a narrow room, with a casement so high up in the wall that it could only be reached by a ladder. The yard behind it must have been occupied by a barrel-maker or some such, judging by the hammering and sawing.

Goodwife Barfoot nodded to the wall. 'The lazy sots down tools as soon as the light goes. So, you needn't fear you'll hear their noise after dark, Master Issott.'

I could not use the name I had gone by before in Bristol – *Daniel Pursglove*. I'd had a strange compulsion to don the name my mother had bequeathed me, like wearing the ring of a dead parent or their cloak. I had nothing of hers to touch, except that name.

Goodwife Barfoot, a widow, was a short woman of about fifty years, thin as a weasel, with sharp, inquisitive eyes darting everywhere. Every movement she made seemed at twice the speed of any other person, her fingers constantly adjusting anything within reach, whether it needed it or not. Even as she spoke to me, her hands were twitching the cover of the narrow bed and turning the pitcher and basin on the chest.

Though I had already paid for a week in advance, she moved restlessly about the small chamber, slyly glancing towards me out of the corner of her eye. She was waiting for something more.

'I will not detain you longer, Goodwife Barfoot.'

She hesitated and then addressed the chair she was straightening. 'I'm obliged to ask where you're from and where you are bound, Master Issott, being so near the wharf. The King's men been coming in every night this past week asking questions about my customers who lodge here and if I'm not able to tell them . . .'

I repeated what I had told the watch at the gate, assuring her that as soon as my business was concluded, I would be returning to London. 'Do you know who the King's men are searching for? The watch at the gate seemed to be expecting someone to try to steal into Bristol.'

She looked at me again with that sideways darting glance. 'I reckon they are, though they don't say. The King's men ask questions by the barrelful, but won't give you so much as a drop of an answer in return. Rude, I call it. Words cost nothing. And if they want their questions answered, then they'd best learn to be civil or they'll find us all turning as blind and dumb as the statues on High Cross.'

I longed to rest, but as soon as she had scurried away, I made my way back out on to the street, searching for one of the broadsides pasted up on a wall. I avoided the market places and churches, remembering that the Jesuit, Oswald Tesimond, one of those accused of the Gunpowder Treason, had been arrested in London when he stopped to read a description of himself on a broadside pasted up in the street.

Many walls had an assortment of broadsides stuck or nailed to them, some so old that only fragments remained, others newer. Some heralded ships that would soon be putting into port with spices, wine, oil and all manner of cargoes for sale; others recounted scurrilous gossip from the King's Court or months-old news from the colony of Jamestown in Virginia. They had, in places, been overlaid by radical tracts or religious invectives denouncing sin, the world and the Devil in his many human guises. There was no woodcut image of a wanted man on any of them.

Then I finally spotted a face leaping out from among the printed words. Judging by the ragged edges where the wind had teased it and the rain crinkled it, the broadside had been up there for a couple of days, but it was not bleached and faded.

I strolled past the wooden post on which it was nailed, turned the corner into the next road, and after a few minutes spent closely examining a tailor's shop, I retraced my steps, disappointing the young apprentice who'd been trying to encourage me in with smiles and gestures. As I walked past the broadside for the second time, I swiftly jerked it from the post, stuffing it into my shirt, and continued to walk briskly on.

I hurried back to the Three Choughs. My room was now so gloomy, I was obliged to light the stinking whale-oil lamp I found outside in the passageway, the night-candles for the chamber sticks having not yet been supplied. Plainly Goodwife Barfoot wanted to ensure her customers did not squander an inch of wax before she deemed it absolutely necessary. I held the torn paper close to the flame and read.

A barbarous traitor and vicious murderer is lately absconded from Newgate gaol. He is judged to be above thirty years old. To be of stature tall, broad-shouldered and upright with a soldier's gait. Black-hair and beard which he is accustomed to wear overlong. His complexion brown, his nose straight and narrow, flaring somewhat at the nostrils, high cheeks. His lips may be thought pleasing in their fullness. In his speech he can ape both a lord and a common man at will. He passes by diverse false names, most recent Daniel Lyrypine, Father Montague, John Willitoft and Joseph Pursglove.

Be it therefore known, the King's most excellent Majesty doth straitly command and charge all Sheriffs, Justices of the Peace, Mayors, Bailiffs, Constables and all and every other of His Highness's Officers, within the realm of England, that they make diligent search and inquiry for said malicious person.

The face staring out of the woodcut portrait with its thick untrimmed beard, long hair and wild eyes resembled a Cornish mariner, newly ransomed from one of the Turkish slave ships. The poulter had been right: the portrait was so crudely drawn that it might have been any man between the ages of twenty and sixty in Bristol. Even the description might fit dozens, even hundreds, of men in the city. There was no mention of any distinguishing mark that would have immediately identified the felon to anyone who seized him, such as a mole on the cheek, a scar on the hand, or . . . a firemark around the neck. Nothing in the physical description or portrait marked it out as me alone. I could have simply laughed it away, had it not been for those names.

I had used none of them in the form in which they were printed, but each one seemed to point directly to me. *Daniel* – the first name listed, *Pursglove* – the last. *Willitoft*, where I had been raised, *Montague's* estates at Battle where I had been spying for FitzAlan only three months before. And then there was Newgate gaol. I had not escaped, but I had vanished, with the assistance of my patron, Charles FitzAlan, the most powerful man in the kingdom. Had he discovered that I'd ignored his orders not to leave London?

But what of the word *murderer*? Was that simply a wild accusation to turn me into a wolf's head, an outlaw who could be killed on sight with impunity? Did it allude to Sibyl's murder or to the strangled girl whose death had had me banished from the manor all those years ago, or another . . . ? A face swam in front of my eyes, hair soaked with scarlet blood. I pushed it away. Someone knew I was in Bristol, someone who also knew a great deal about me. This was a threat, more dangerous and sinister than if I'd found a noose hanging in my room. And I knew neither who it had come from nor why.

Chapter Twelve

IF THE BROADSIDE was an attempt to warn me off searching for the truth about why Waldegrave had been killed, then whoever had written it did not know me well. It only served to convince me that there was a truth to be uncovered that ran far deeper than the death of an old man. I was determined to find out who'd murdered him and what he had been mixed up in to get himself killed, and whether that truth led back to Richard . . . But I sensed I didn't have much time. If whoever had posted that warning realised it hadn't frightened me off, then they were liable to go further, maybe even ensure that I joined Waldegrave in the river.

I needed to search Waldegrave's lodgings. That attic room might have a dozen hiding places beneath floorboards or in the roof where the old priest could have slipped anything he didn't want the authorities to find, knowing that they might come for him at any time. As soon as breakfast was over and the streets were crowded enough for me to pass unnoticed in the throng, I made for the old tithe barn.

Unlike many of the buildings in Bristol which, since the flood, had been repaired or patched, the barn where Waldegrave had once lived looked even worse than when I'd last seen it. The winter freeze had deepened the cracks in the stone walls and created fresh ones. The great double doors set into one side, through which laden wagons had passed decades before, were even more rotten than I remembered. Assorted pieces of wood and rusty iron had been nailed or braced across the holes in a vain attempt to repel the weather and vermin, both the animal and human kind.

Dagger ready in my hand, I walked around the building and pushed the sagging side door. It was as dark as the Devil's crotch inside, but the walls of the passageway were so close together my shoulders grazed them on either side, so that even without light I could hardly lose my way. The eye-watering stench from the nearby privy had, if anything, grown worse; I could discern not only human and feline piss and shit but a new odour – rotting flesh. By dint of banging into the wall, I found the rickety stair rail, now so broken it was likely to give way if a rat so much as touched it, and I cautiously mounted the sagging steps.

I could still hear the old man's voice warning me – *Ten steps. But take care, the eighth is almost cracked through.*

I had hoped to find the room empty and abandoned. I couldn't imagine many desperate enough to set up home in that shit-hole, but as I reached the door at the top I heard a woman's voice, brittle with age. She was muttering in a continuous stream, though who-ever she was talking to was either ignoring her or couldn't get a word in. I rapped. There was instant silence. Whoever was inside had frozen, not daring to move.

Then the door opened a chink, and a filthy claw slithered through it. 'Payment first. Sixpence it is, to do whatever you fancy.'

I dropped two pennies into her palm and she withdrew the hand to examine the coin. She muttered what might have been a complaint or a curse; the coins vanished and she grudgingly pulled the door wider. The room, tucked in directly under the eaves of the barn, looked even more miserable than it had in Waldegrave's time. Streaks of green slime on the walls marked where the rain had oozed in and several gaps in the roof were filled with oddments of wood stuffed in place with rags. The old priest's hutch table was gone; instead, a mouldering straw pallet lay on the boards close to a brazier, the mattress heaped with an assortment of threadbare, ragged blankets and shawls. There were no longer any books on the shelves that hung on ropes from the beams. They'd been replaced by bundles wrapped in cloth, a few jars, some evil-smelling blackened herbs and slender faggots of dried fish. A thin curtain screened off the end of chamber.

The old woman was watching me. She was clad in a faded red gown hanging so loose it might have fitted a woman twice her girth and cut down to her naval, so that her pendulous dugs swung bare. Her long grey hair was pushed up into a greasy cap. But the deep, open sores on forehead and breasts suggested she was a victim of the Great Pox. Father Waldegrave's ghost would be shrieking in torment if he could see the jar of mercury ointment now sitting on the shelf where, just a year ago, crumbling tomes about the Immaculate Conception or the Blessed Sacraments had been placed.

'Mother, I wanted—' I began, but she held a hand up to forestall me and shuffled towards the curtain at the back of the room.

'Here, I got just what you want, what every gentleman wants.' She poked her head behind the cloth and mumbled something I couldn't catch. Then she reached her claws inside and dragged out a young girl with tousled mouse-brown hair. The child was naked save for a lace ruff around her little neck, which must once have been white, but was now grey and torn. She was probably around ten or eleven years old. Her ribs stood out starkly, like the beams of the river boats crushed by the winter ice. Some kind of scarlet stain had been smeared on her lips and cheeks to redden them, but her elfin face was dominated by huge hazel eyes that stared at a point somewhere behind me, as lifeless as a butchered calf. The old woman, who was still gripping her wrist, gave it a little shake, trying to animate the child. The girl obediently struck what must have been meant to be a winsome pose.

'Pretty creature, ain't she? And as willing as they come. She'll do anything you fancy. Cost you sixpence,' the bawd said firmly, 'but for some things I charge extra. She's new to this, an innocent. Doesn't always understand what a gentleman wants straight off, but you tell me and I'll see she does it.'

'I don't want the child . . . or you either,' I added swiftly, seeing her eyes flash with interest.

The bawd glared at me. 'Then what have you come here for, wasting my time?' Her head jerked up angrily. 'By rights I should charge you anyway, 'cause some men are more than willing to pay just to look.'

'You've already had two pennies from me,' I reminded her

'And you needn't think you'll be getting them back,' she retorted.

'I'll pay you your full sixpence, if you let the child go back there and sleep. All I ask in return is a little information.'

She had loosened her grip on the girl's arm. The child looked bewildered, as if she thought I was demanding some new trick from her which she didn't understand, but when the old woman gestured towards the curtain, she scurried back behind it.

The bawd shuffled closer, her expression now one of deep suspicion. 'You want to know about one of my customers, that it? 'Cause I warn you now, they don't tell me their names and I don't ask. But I might remember something, if you was to refresh my memory.' She held out her dirty hand again in expectation.

'This man was not one of your customers. He lived in this room a year ago, during the great flood. Do you remember that?'

'Aye,' Her face suddenly lost its crafty look. 'Some of the stewhouses down near the wharf vanished, like the sea had opened its great mouth and swallowed them whole. Most of the women were still sleeping at that hour. I knew a good many of them, being in the same profession. I was working for Mother Kitty back then.'

I knew that stewhouse. It stood near the castle wall, marked with the sign of the rose above the door, though it was certainly not a house of romance. 'How came you to leave there? Her house escaped the flood, didn't it?'

She gestured helplessly towards the weeping red lesion on her face. 'Couldn't hide these no longer. Customers were afraid. Wouldn't touch me. And Mother Kitty wouldn't even let me stay on as a serving wench, said it put her customers off when they saw me. Like as not, I'd have been found frozen in the ice this winter, if Skinner hadn't put me in here and given me the girl to break in. He takes the money we earn and leaves us a few pennies for food and the like.'

'How often does he collect from you?'

'He doesn't come himself. Sends his mort, Joan, or her daughter. But if we haven't taken enough . . . that's why I have to have your sixpence, see. If someone saw you come in . . . It'll get back to him. It always does.'

So, Skinner still had the place watched. I wondered if it was the same beggar who had been here watching the comings and goings in Waldegrave's time. 'I'll give you your sixpence. More if you can help me.'

She nodded, a desperate yet greedy expression on her face.

'The man who lived here during the flood. Old Ambrose . . .'

That's what Skinner's watchdog had called Waldegrave. He'd also called him the Yena, 'on account of him having such a fancy for cadavers'. But I thought it wiser not to mention that particular nickname yet.

'. . . Did you know him?'

'He was gone afore I moved in here.'

'Gone?'

She evaded my eyes. 'I heard he fell into the river . . . drowned.'

'Did Skinner tell you that?'

Her eyes darted back to me, scared. 'Skinner didn't tell me nothing, except that the old man had gone.'

'Has anyone come asking for him?'

She shook her head. 'Why would they? Everyone knows he drowned,' she said with a certainty in her tone and gaze that made me believe her. 'You're the first . . .' She frowned, her eyes narrowing suspiciously. 'So, why are you asking?'

'I wanted to know what happened to his things, his books. Were they still here when you moved in?'

Again, her gaze darted away. 'Some.'

I waited, watching her shuffle.

'What's it to you?' she finally demanded, with an anger plainly born of guilt.

'Ambrose was . . . my kin.' Somehow, speaking the words aloud had turned the suspicion into a reality from which I could never now retreat.

'How was I to know he had family?' the bawd said querulously. 'Laid in a pauper's grave. No one come to mourn him. If you was kin, you should have seen him treated better. Anyhow, there was only a few books here when I came. Chucked over there, they were, all in a heap.'

'No chest or table . . . papers?'

She shrugged. 'I reckon there must have been a few bits, 'cause I'd seen the marks on the floor where they'd stood. Maybe he'd sold them to keep body and soul together afore he died. Could be that's how he ended up in the river – nothing left to sell, so he . . .' She drew a finger across her own throat, glaring at me reproachfully.

The thought that Waldegrave could have taken his own life had not even crossed my mind. *A man was found dead in Bristol. His corpse was dragged out of the river, but he did not die of drowning.* Those were the words Erasmus had remembered seeing in the letter. I had taken it to mean Waldegrave had been murdered before he had been dumped in the river. And it was unthinkable for any priest to commit suicide believing, as they do, that he would be damned for eternity. Waldegrave would never have done it from despair or the misery of hunger. But guilt? Guilt that he had betrayed his faith, his God, or might do so if he could not withstand torture? Waldegrave was old and frail, but surely he would have realised that his fragility would mercifully shorten his suffering, not prolong it, and besides, I couldn't imagine him ever shrinking from pain. He had been murdered; I could not conceive of anything else.

The bawd was watching me anxiously.

'The rumours that you heard about Ambrose's death . . . are they certain he drowned?'

'There's always talk, you know how it is. Maybe he fell, hit his head, tumbled in. Who knows?'

'I'd wager Skinner does. There isn't much that goes on in Bristol he doesn't know about, because he has his grubby little thumb in most of it, isn't that so?'

She shrank back, her gaze darting to the door.

'I know you are frightened of him, mother, and you've good reason to be. So, I'll not press you.' I pulled sixpence from the small purse at my belt and held it up. 'But tell me this. Have you heard any gossip that Skinner or his men were involved in this *drowning*?'

The woman's unblinking gaze had fastened on the coin like a hound's eye on a piece of meat. She hesitated. 'There's always talk and Skinner don't mind it, if it keeps folks afeared of him.'

I could get nothing more from her. I finally surrendered the coin, which vanished as swiftly as my two pennies.

'One last thing, mother – those books that were thrown into the corner. Where are they?'

A mulish expression settled once more on her face. 'How was I to know he had any kin to claim them? Besides they were torn, covers missing, hardly worth a flea's fart.'

'But you got a few pence for them.' I held my hand up, seeing she was about to deny it. 'I don't want to know what you got for them and I'm not here to claim them. Just tell me who you sold them to. I suppose Skinner took the valuable ones.' By law, books were only supposed to be owned by men with property, but that was hardly likely to trouble the castle rats.

'Maybe he took the furniture if there was any left, pots and such like if they were worth the selling,' she said cautiously. 'But not the books. He'd not touch those. Books can get you hanged or worse. And if you can't read so good, you don't know if it's a hanging book.' She nodded towards the empty corner, as though she could still see the treacherous volumes lurking there.

'Skinner said to burn those, cook our supper on them. But if they're books of spells, then demons or curses could have come flying out to take revenge, like when you burn a wax poppet. I couldn't get a wink of sleep with them lying next to me, thinking about what evil magic might be lurking in those words. So, I sold them to Jackdaw, passed the curse on to him and serves him right, the old muckworm. But if there were any books left here that were worth the stealing, it weren't Skinner who filched them, you can be sure on that.'

Chapter Thirteen

A SINGLE WHALE-OIL LANTERN burned in the darkened courtyard of the Salt Cat inn. The landlord, Caleb Crugge, had always been a pinchpenny and the puddle of mustard light illuminated little more than the door which opened out into the courtyard from the parlour. But this time I was glad of the cloak of shadows. I edged towards the stables, hoping that Mistress Crugge had not, after all, persuaded her husband to buy a dog. But the stable was empty: even the sturdy little horse Crugge kept for pulling the cart was gone. It had evidently been a hard winter. Remembering Mistress Crugge's experiment with seals-head brawn, I hoped the unfortunate horse hadn't found its way into one of her pies.

The door of the parlour opened and the pungent stench of strong tobacco and sour ale rolled out with a babble of voices. A man tottered out, making for the jakes, but seemed to think it wasn't worth the trouble walking all the way across the yard and stopped in the doorless entrance to the stables. I retreated deeper inside. He cocked his head, distracted by the scuffling noise, but evidently decided that that it was only rats in the soiled straw. He pissed through the doorway, then backed out and lurched back towards the parlour.

The door opened again, and this time a small figure trotted out, a teetering stack of bowls in his arms. Someone inside must have called to him, for he turned in the doorway to yell a reply and the light from the parlour fell on his face. It was Myles, the young lad I had befriended the last time I was in Bristol. It had been a year since I'd seen him. His clothes were no longer rags and his wild hair had been chopped and even combed so that the curls neatly grazed his collar.

He scampered nimbly across the courtyard, sidestepping a puddle without even glancing down. No doubt he crossed the yard so often every day that even in the dark he knew how to avoid every stone and hole. I didn't want to alarm him by stepping out and grabbing him. The pile of bowls would crash to the ground if I did. But as soon he came close enough, I called out softly.

He halted, staring around.

'Myles, don't be scared. It me, Master Pursglove, remember?'

'I'm not scared of nothing,' he said defiantly, taking a hasty step away from the stable doorway while at the same time trying to look in.

I stepped out into the courtyard. 'You ran errands for me last year.'

He peered up and after a moment or two his face slit into a wide grin. 'Master Pursglove! You still got old Diligence?' He peered around me, looking for the horse.

'Had to leave him behind.'

'You staying here again?' He jerked his chin towards the little chamber at the top of the outside staircase which I had once occupied.

'No, I came here to look for you. I need—'

The door to the parlour opened and Mistress Crugge's massive breasts and belly hove into view, followed by the rest of her. 'You wool-gathering again, boy? There's customers in there dying of thirst. Shift yourself, you useless sprat, else I'll have you cleaning every pot and pan in that kitchen till dawn and back.'

The door slammed shut and Myles grinned up at me. 'She doesn't mean it. That's just her way. Soft as sleech really. You wait till I tell her you've come back.'

I grabbed his shoulder. 'No, Myles. Don't tell the Crugges or anyone. I don't want them to know I'm back in Bristol. Our secret!' I held up a coin.

He nodded, beaming, evidently wanting to grab it, but his hands were full. I tucked it into the top of his boot. Myles couldn't read, but the Crugges could and they revelled in gossip, especially if murder was involved. It would be halfway round Bristol before morning that they'd had a murderer in their inn if they thought I was the wanted man in that broadside, and they might just recognise the name *Pursglove*.

'You best get about your work before she comes looking for you. Can you get away tonight after the Salt Cat closes?'

''Course I can. Easy,' he said proudly. 'No one can keep me in unless I want to stay.'

'Where would be a good place to meet, somewhere Skinner's men don't go?'

Myles thought for a moment. 'The Racks behind Temple Church. There's no cloth left there to dry after dark in winter.'

So, nothing for Skinner's men to steal, then. Myles knows them well.

'Gates are locked, so you'll have to climb in through the fence There's a loose board at the back, where a big tree hides you from the city wall. But I reckon you'll be too fat to get through. Gorebelly like you might have to climb over.'

He laughed as I lightly cuffed him for his impudence. I'd missed the little urchin.

ALTHOUGH THE WEAVERS' work had long finished for the day, candles and lanterns shone from the upper storeys of their houses along Temple Street. Voices raised in quarrels or laughter threaded through the wails of infants, the clatter of pots and the discordant notes of a clumsily played lute. In the street, skeletal dogs and cats scavenged for scraps, growling and hissing at one another, and a man whose legs were severed at the knee, sleeping in one of the workshop doorways, shied a stone at a hound that cocked its leg on him, then closed his eyes again.

I found the high gate towards the end of the street between two of the weavers' houses. It was, as Myles had predicted, locked and probably braced too on the other side. I dismissed any idea of charming it. The gate was lit up by torches on either side and was plainly visible from the houses opposite. I continued to the end of the street and turned, walking along beside the city wall. On the other side of the road, a high fence protected the large field with its rows of tenters on which the newly woven cloth was stretched. Following the fence around the corner, I finally saw the old tree Myles had told me about. Its trunk and branches were certainly thick enough to block the view of the fence behind from guards up on the city wall.

I discovered the loose post, which gave sufficiently for a reed-thin lad like Myles to wriggle through. But he was right: I was not going to get in that way. The tree offered more than screening, though. I scrambled up into the branches and edged along until I was crouching above the field, freezing each time the moon slid out from behind the clouds. I jumped down, narrowly avoiding impaling myself on the lethal barbs jutting up from the tenter racks.

In contrast to Temple Street, the field was dark as ink, and eerily silent. As the moon emerged again, it glinted off the wooden racks and the steel hooks, making them look like an army of pikemen standing in line, waiting for the order to advance. I called softly, but there was no reply. The voices of the watch at the city gate drifted through the night, challenging any man trying to slip through. I had little fear that they would see me in the pitch-black field, but even so, I kept behind the tree, in case the moon suddenly emerged again.

I had almost given up when the fence creaked and the smudge of a figure slipped through. We sat together on the wet grass.

'Mistress and master are in abed,' he announced cheerfully. 'I heard her snoring. And she gave him poppy juice for his toothache, so as he won't disturb her by groaning and tossing all night.'

'I'm pleased to see you're still working at the Salt Cat. They treating you well, then?'

'Old Ma Crugge, she nags me and him from morn to night, but like he says, she's not a bad old hen really.'

There was affection in his tone when he spoke of Mistress Crugge now, the way a young man might laugh about a mother who frets too much about him.

'What you been doing with yourself, Master Pursglove?'

'Long story, Myles. I'll tell you another time, but I don't want to keep you away from the Cat for long.' The later he was out on the streets, the more likely it was he'd run into the castle rats. 'I came back to Bristol to learn what happened to old Ambrose, the Yena.'

Myles drew his knees up to his chest, sinking his head on to them. Though I couldn't see them clearly, I knew his fists had clenched.

'You used to take messages for him. Did you go on doing that after you started working at the Cat?'

'Sometimes,' he muttered. 'He's old. Had to look out for him. Took him a bit of food now and then. I owed him. He used to share his supper with me, afore I went to Salt Cat. Always said he wasn't hungry, so I should eat it, but I reckon he was just saying that.'

'He's not in his lodgings now.'

'That's 'cause he's dead,' Myles said. 'Everyone knows that. Dragged his body out of the river.'

'Do you know who killed him?'

Myles shook his head, his chin still resting on his knees.

'Is there someone you think might have done it? Maybe you heard people talking about it.'

'Didn't hear nothing.'

'I believe you,' I assured him.

I didn't, not for a moment, but I'd only just walked back into his life after a year away; I could hardly expect him to confide in me straight away. He had lived long enough on the streets to know what happened to those who informed on thieves and murderers. He had every reason to be wary.

'But that wasn't really what I wanted to ask you,' I continued. 'A friend of mine had something stolen. It's not valuable, but it belonged to their father and they miss it. I wanted to buy it back for them. Someone told me it might have been sold on to a man by the name of Jackdaw. I was sure you'd know where I could find him. There's not a street or shop in Bristol you don't know.' I hoped I wasn't spreading the flattery on too thickly.

He brightened at once, only too eager to get off the subject of the old man's death. "Course I do, but it's not easy to find if you don't know the city. Could show you, if you like. Wouldn't cost you much.'

'Oh, I knew it would cost me,' I said, giving a heavy mock sigh. 'Doesn't it always?'

He chuckled. 'Best go there in the afternoon. There's others that do business with Jackdaw mornings and evenings.'

Skinner's rats, no doubt. Getting rid of what they'd stolen hours before.

'Can you get away from the Cat then?'

'Ma Crugge usually sends me on errands afore the men start coming for their supper. I'll show you where it is then . . . but I'll not come in with you. Best if he doesn't see me.'

As WE SET OUT the following afternoon, I suspected, from the grin on his face, Myles was guiding me via a far more tortuous route to Jackdaw's shop than was necessary, to ensure I paid him well for his trouble. But the street that we eventually reached proved to be a narrow, twisting row of shops and workshops, where the overhanging upper storeys were so close to those on the opposite side that women could chatter to each other across the small gap as though they were sitting either side of their own hearth.

Even though it was still mid-afternoon, the workshops beneath were already in twilight and it was hard to distinguish anything on the ground. Several times I came close to stumbling into the open gully that ran down the middle, over topping with stagnant water and filth. Mustard-yellow candle flames glimmered deep inside the shops behind the tiny panes of thick glass. The listless goldfinches, linnets and canaries in the cages that hung outside a bird-seller's shop seemed to think it was night, and were roosting, hunched on perches or squatting at the bottom of their cages, their feathers fluffed up in the chill breeze. A small boy in the open doorway, seeing me glancing up at the birds, darted out, stick in hand to knock against the cages and stir the bedraggled creatures into twittering.

'We've talking parrots inside, sir. One that'll tell your lady how pretty she looks.'

'He doesn't want none of your mangy sparrows,' Myles told him.

The small boy thumbed his nose at him as he continued to call after me. 'We've a parrot that curses the Pope and the Devil!'

Myles stopped, looking anxiously round for any sign of Skinner's rats, then gestured further down the street. 'That one, the sign of the mermaid.'

He held out his hand, grinning as I dropped a coin into it. I feigned a cuff at his head and he dodged it, as I knew he would, and ran off, laughing.

The carved mermaid dangled from a chain suspended from a pole above the door. Her huge, rounded breasts and nipples were painted bright pink and scarlet, and the serpent's tail which curled over her back was poison green. Her lips, also scarlet, were parted, showing a row of wickedly pointed shark's teeth.

The door was shut, but a gleam of candlelight rippling in the depths beyond the casement revealed that that they might be open for business. I glanced up and down the road one last time and stepped swiftly inside.

The room was narrow but long, vanishing into a dark archway at the back. A battered table squatted near the door, piled with ledgers and an assortment of small wooden boxes of various sizes. The upper parts of the walls were lined with shelves, and below them were heaped dusty chairs, chests and small cupboards. Every flat surface was crammed with more boxes, earthenware jars and a bewildering array of objects that mariners and travellers had brought back from their voyages: skulls of monkeys and large cats with savage fangs; the statue of a woman with eight arms; pots decorated with exotic birds and flowers; dried Jenny Hanivers and curved daggers. The beams above were strung with copper jugs, Turkish scimitars and a long, twisted horn, which any shopkeeper would doubtless claim was a unicorn horn.

I had seen many similar things on the stalls of London, newly arrived from the boats, but they had been beautiful and bright, still smelling of spices, tar and the salt-sea. These were dulled, dusty and broken, the handles of the daggers missing pieces of inlay, the pots dented or cracked. And between them were piled the pathetic possessions of those who had never ventured outside the city, much less to the New World – battered ewers and prickets, spoons and boots.

I didn't notice the man at first, for he appeared silent as a wraith, seeming to materialise out of the darkness itself, his short robe cut from the shadows. His moon face had the unhealthy pallor of old parchment, and the narrow dung-coloured beard that projected from the bottom of his chin resembled a goat's horn. But what he lacked in colour in his person or clothes, he had made up for in an assortment of gaudy brooches, silver chains and keys that dangled from various parts of his robe and swung from the leather belt around his waist, which was studded with slithers of bone carved into animals, fish and naked human figures. I wondered how long he'd been watching me, and braced myself in case he too thought I resembled the wanted man on the broadside. But he seemed more interested in my clothes and boots than my face, no doubt trying to calculate how much money he might squeeze out of me.

'What does the gentleman wish?' His voice was like a boy's on the cusp of breaking, yet I would have taken him to have been around fifty years of age. He swept a pudgy hand around his shop. 'Not everything can be displayed, but it can be found. Oh, yes, it can certainly be found.'

Although the shelves and floor were crammed, I suspected it wasn't lack of space that prevented certain items from being displayed.

'I'm in search of books.'

He regarded me warily, as well he might. Skinner had been right about books: danger lurked between their pages, and scuttled among their words. They could all too easily be stacked into gallows' steps or turned into kindling to fuel a martyr's pyre. The shopkeeper was torn between caution and not wanting to lose a customer.

'Books?' He shook his head. 'Those who I buy from can scarcely read their own names, much less a book. Now if you want something to while away the hours, a gentleman has just brought in a fine fuddling cup. Pour your wine into one cup and it will vanish and reappear in another. When your friends have had a few ales, bring this out and you'll be splitting your sides watching them gawp in astonishment.' He turned towards one of the shelves.

'Not on this occasion. Books, Master Jackdaw, books.'

He started slightly as I spoke the name the bawd had given me.

'I've not seen you before. Who sent you?' He took a step behind the table. His hand slipped beneath it and I saw the muscles tighten. He'd grasped a weapon of some kind, a cudgel probably. His voice might be that of a boy's, but I was willing to bet he knew how to defend himself.

'A woman marked with the Great Pox came to sell you some books she'd found.'

'Half the women who sell to me have the pox,' he said sourly. 'Same tale from all the doxies – they say they found their treasures in the street. If London streets are paved with gold, then the streets of Bristol are paved with rings and brooches, if you believe them.'

'But they don't find books in the purses they lift from their customers. These were left in the woman's lodgings by the previous tenant. Not worth much, I should think. She says they were torn.'

'Then what do you want with them?'

'The man who left them behind borrowed some of them from a friend of mine who is anxious to have them returned. I will buy them, of course, if they should prove to be among those you have.'

'*Anxious?*'

'If his mark is found in them . . .' I was taking a gamble, but I was certain that Jackdaw dealt in enough forbidden items not to risk reporting anything to the authorities. He would not want his premises searched.

A pale, slug-like tongue slithered out of his mouth and licked his lips. 'And the titles of these books?'

'He did not confide that. But I will recognise his mark if I see it. I ask only that you allow me to look through the books she sold you. I will pay for the *inconvenience*, whether I find it or not. Just to put my friend's mind at rest, you understand.'

Jackdaw seemed to be considering the matter, then held out a pudgy paw. 'A trifle in advance,' he said. 'I'm taking a risk trusting you.'

'As am I,' I said quietly, as I pressed a coin into the moist palm. *And as the old proverb says – Trust is the mother of deceit.*

Jackdaw beckoned to me to follow him under the archway and through a small parlour smelling of stale tobacco. It was set with tables and chairs, and probably served as an illicit gaming house, though there was no sign of dice, cards or boards at this hour. He paused to light a fresh chamber candle, and, selecting one of the many keys that hung from his belt, he unlocked a low door. Stepping aside, he handed me the candle.

'Try the chest with the serpent eating its tail. You'll need this.'
He unhooked one of the smaller keys pinned to his robe. 'Leave
the door ajar. I don't want to risk you getting locked in.'

The windowless room was narrow, and, like the shop, lined
with chests below and shelves above stacked with boxes. Sacks
dangled from the low beams. But none of the merchandise in this
storeroom had been left out on display. I was relieved that Jackdaw wasn't intending to lock me in the small, crammed space,
but I knew this wasn't out of concern for me. He wanted to keep
watch on what I was doing. Pity, I'd have liked to have delved
into some of those boxes. But I edged along until I came to an
old and cracked chest. An ancient alchemists' symbol of a serpent
swallowing its own tail was carved into the top, and judging by
the remains of other marks, now half obliterated, it had once
been decorated with more dangerous magical symbols too. Not
a chest you'd want to leave in plain view in a shop window.

Jackdaw was perching on one of the chairs in the small parlour, from where he could see directly into the storeroom. I set
the candle down on a neighbouring chest and made a play of
struggling with the key and lock. I didn't want him to suspect
that I could have opened that chest or any other in his shop
without using his keys. I heaved the lid and at once the perfume
of old books wafted out – a miasma of damp paper, decaying
leather and dust. Some volumes were bound and in good order.
I did not waste time on those. The books I'd seen before in
Waldegrave's lodgings had all been ravaged by mould, worm and
rats, long before whoever had ransacked his chamber had laid
their ungentle hands upon them.

I examined the books with missing covers. Their title pages
had been torn out so that it was not immediately obvious what
they were about or who had written them. But I was not interested in the books themselves, only in what might be concealed
in them or anything that had been written in the margins. Bindings were good hiding places for papers, but since those were

missing, I resorted to flicking through the pages, looking for any signs that sheets had been added. I held up any page I thought looked promising to the heat of the candle, in case messages had been written in citrus juice or glimmers of light might reveal pinpricks made above or below certain letters.

But I found nothing, and if Waldegrave had made annotations in the margins of any of the volumes, those books had been taken away by whoever had searched that room before Skinner. I lifted out the last of the volumes and flicked through them. Again, I found no notes or any markings. I was just on the point of returning them to the chest, when my fingernail snagged on a small, hard fragment of something stuck to one of the pages. It looked like a piece of old parchment, but though it was flat, the surface was far too rough to write on.

With my back to Jackdaw, I tilted the page into the puddle of yellow light. A brown stain, about the length and width of my spread hand, showed faintly in the candlelight. The shape was indented into the paper. I turned the page and discovered that several of the pages before it and after it were also marked with the same outline, where something had been pressed inside the book. Aware that Jackdaw was watching me, I tossed the volume back into the chest, feigning disappointment. Laying another of the books carefully aside, I replaced the others and locked the chest, but not before I had covertly retrieved the one that really interested me and tucked it beneath the other.

'Find your friend's mark, did you?'

I nodded, thinking that would satisfy him, and began to haggle for the worthless volumes, arguing that the books were so damaged they were only fit for arse-wipes.

'But that's not the worth of them to you, is it?' He tapped his stubby nose. 'Silence and safety, can't put a price on those.'

'But you evidently can and do,' I said, handing over what he demanded before stowing the books in the pocket inside my cloak. I walked towards the door. Then, when I was sure he had relaxed, I whirled around, knocking over the table, scattering the coins and pinning him against his shelves with my knife at his throat.

'Silence and safety, Jackdaw. That's what I've just brought from you,' I growled. 'So, if one word of our transaction reaches the castle, I'll be back for recompense and I won't be collecting it in coin. Do we understand each other?'

I marched out, allowing him to watch me walk down the narrow street and out of sight, before doubling back to a point where I could see anyone entering or leaving his shop. But he did not make any attempt to rush out and find Skinner. I hoped my threat had worked, but I couldn't be sure. He could still send a message to the castle at any time and I couldn't watch for ever. I set off back to the Three Choughs.

Though the light was draining from the sky, the pounding of metal and sawing of wood had not yet abated by the time I reached my room. But the parsimonious Goodwife Barfoot had finally supplied fresh candles and I lit one to examine the books, turning straight to the page in which the brittle fragment had been stuck. The book itself, the life of King Arthur, was unremarkable, with nothing to alarm either Church or Crown. It was what had once been placed inside it that intrigued me. The indentation was irregular, deeper in some parts than others, indicating the object had been of an uneven thickness. In the bottom left-hand corner, the paper was pricked a score of times, the pricks making a rough arc, but to the depth of several sheets, so if it was a code, I couldn't fathom how it might work.

I prised off the brown fragment, turning it over and over. It was brittle, almost translucent. And it was only as I pictured Jackdaw's shop that I suddenly realised what I might be holding. But why would Waldegrave, of all people, have kept one of these? It wouldn't have been of any interest to one of Cecil's men, but if the Jackdaw had found it in the book, he'd have removed it to sell it. No need to hide that away. I certainly couldn't risk questioning him, though.

The sweet smell of steam from a bubbling cooking pot was edging into the room, reminding me that I was starving. Laying the books aside, I hurried down to the parlour.

Supper proved to be boiled mallard, well seasoned with pepper and ginger, but the few pieces of turnips floating in the broth had been blackened by the ice, and with so little bread to sop it up, the meal certainly didn't fill the belly. Still, after the great freeze, many in the city did not have even that much. I reminded myself that my fellow prisoners in Newgate would have sold their souls to the Devil for a mouthful of duck, however tough and stringy.

The parlour was shaped like a horseshoe, wrapping itself around a cavernous hearth, which appeared bigger than it was because the fire which had been set in it was so small. The wood, which had been chopped from old boat timbers, spat and popped, the flames crackling blue from the salt. There were maybe a score of men eating or drinking in the room. I had tucked myself into the far end of one of the arms, where I could watch the door to the street and had an escape route to the stairs close behind me.

I'd seen him come in, but I hadn't seen his face. He was enveloped in a travelling cloak and I caught only a glimpse, my view blocked by the lad who was setting my supper and a flagon in front of me. He must have gone to sit in the other arm of the parlour, for I had finished my supper before I saw him again. He was bending down towards the fire, holding a taper in the flames to light a pipe of tobacco. As he straightened up, he looked intently at me. He had known all along I was there. And as my gaze meet his, as it had once before in the parlour of another inn, I was jolted into recognition. The gaunt cheekbones and deep-set eyes, pale skin drawn tight over a fleshless skull, the long, lank black hair and the short dagger-point black beard with the white flash running through it.

It was the same man I'd seen in the Lusty Tup in the Ridings. He stood in front of the fire, sucking on the long stem of the pipe until a tiny red glow appeared in the bowl and a stream of dark smoke slithered from his mouth, coiling around his face like a black viper. All the time he was staring at me, his face devoid of any expression. Then he turned and vanished back into the other arm of the parlour.

I grabbed the serving lad as he slouched back towards the kitchen. 'The man behind the hearth over there. Beard like a badger's snout, black and white. Is he a regular customer?'

The boy looked mystified.

'Have you seen him before?'

The lad wove his way through the benches, peering into the part of the parlour I couldn't see.

After an age, he ambled back. 'Not seen that beard in here before. We get our regulars, then we get others just passing through, like you. Mostly come for the ships. That why you're here, is it, you waiting on a ship?'

Knowing the guards were looking for the mystery fugitive trying to board a ship, I thought it safest to repeat the same story I had told the watch at the gate. But the lad was clearly unimpressed by the mention of estates and wills. No one had ever left him anything in their will and in all likelihood they never would.

'Is the beard with anyone or is he drinking alone?'

'Alone, I reckon.' The boy suddenly looked suspicious. 'Why are you asking?'

'I think he's the man who sold me a horse at a fair a while back. Beast went as lame as a one-legged goose before I'd even ridden a mile.'

The lad grinned, showing several broken teeth. 'I'd not buy a jar of elbow-grease from him. He looks just like the Devil in a play I saw. But if you reckon to get even with your fists, you best do it out in the street – the mistress won't stand for brawling in her inn. Last time she made the guards take all of them to the lockup, even two men who'd done nothing except stand aside.'

'I won't tackle him in here,' I assured him with a smile.

But I would find time to have a little talk with Badger-beard. I couldn't believe that the same man had turned up in both inns by chance. Yet if he was following me, he was certainly not trying to keep out of sight. On the contrary, he was going out of his way to make sure I knew it.

Chapter Fourteen

THE CLATTER AND SHOUTS of the parlour being cleared of customers for the night woke me as I knew it would, and wrapping myself in my cloak, I slipped down the stairs and through the door just as the last of the drinkers were leaving. I followed them as they weaved and shouted their way up the dark street towards the wharf. Several times, I drew back into the doorways and waited, watching the street in front and behind me. Once, I thought I saw movement at the far end of the street caught in the pale ghost of light from a candle in an upper casement. But the light dissolved into darkness before it could reach the muddy ground. Dagger drawn, I started back towards where I thought I'd seen it, but the spot was empty except for a rat trotting along on its own business. It stopped abruptly when it saw me and scurried under a gate into a yard, where, judging by the barks, snarls and shrieks that followed, it ran straight into the jaws of a dog.

When I encountered the watch on the bridge, I staggered a little, blinking in the lantern light and beaming like an imbecile, just enough to make them believe I was merry, but not enough to get me locked up. They let me pass, shaking their heads and grumbling that they wished they'd been able to spend the night in the tavern.

As soon as I was out of sight of them, I looked around for a small lit lantern. Most of the householders who hadn't already been relieved of their yard lanterns by Skinner's band, wisely kept them inside their casements, though that only gave the castle thieves more cover by darkening the streets still further. I finally spotted one hanging above a privy door, but as soon as I crept inside the yard, I realised from the creaks and grunts emanating from the privy that someone was inside, maybe even two people. Even occupied as they were, they'd surely notice if the light shining in through the hole at the top of the door disappeared. I grabbed a mud-rake and wedged it up against the latch, so that it could not be depressed, then snatched the lantern, and thrust it under my cloak. The startled cry of a girl, the angry muttering of a man, and the violent rattle of a shaken door followed me as I hurried out of the courtyard.

The street leading to Jackdaw's shop had only a torch burning at either end, sending oily yellow and red light flickering over the stinking black water in the gulley. A few lamps glowed in the upper casements, but since they overhung the street, no light penetrated the street below, which was as dark as a tunnel. I edged along the row of shops, pausing to glance behind me several times. If Badger-beard was planning to stage an ambush, this would be the perfect place.

Jackdaw's shop was in darkness. I hoped he didn't own a dog. The door, I felt sure, would be braced on the inside. The wooden shutters across the casement were sturdy and thick, with broad metal bars fastened by a stout padlock. I pulled out the slender metal spike I carried and inserted it in the padlock. After a moment or two the lock yielded and I eased open the shutters, listening for any sound from inside. All was quiet.

The next task was to prise away the soft lead which held one of the little panes of thick glass in place, so that I could insert the same spike and flick up the latch. That was so quickly accomplished it might even have won the admiration of Skinner and his castle rats. I glanced round to ensure the street was still deserted before I eased myself through, stepping down on to one of the chests. I pulled the shutters back behind me to hide the lantern light from anyone passing. It was a risk that a glow might be seen, but the shop was so crammed, I knew I'd send a dozen things clattering on to the flags if I took even a single step in the dark.

I swept the lantern across the shelves. The many-armed dancing women and the animal skulls took on new and sinister shapes, seeming to come alive, stirring and snarling, as the lantern sent ripples of light and shadow crawling across yellowed bone and metal. Then the lantern caught what I was searching for – five, maybe six of them, stiff and brown, in some parts almost translucent like old parchment. Jenny Hanivers, the sea-creatures that had been shaped, cut, twisted and dried to resemble mummified demons or basilisks. I could see at once that three of them were too large to have been inside the book. Two of the imp-like creatures were around three feet long. The third, which resembled the evil-looking mermaid sign that hung above the shop, had sharply pointed, rigid breast-like appendages which could not have been shut in the book. I examined the two smaller ones and reached for the fragment I'd found, intending to try to match it to the dried creatures.

There was a distant creak, then another and another. Someone was creeping down a staircase behind the archway at the back of the shop. I stuffed the two Jenny Hanivers into the pocket inside my cloak, and, sacrificing silence for speed, grabbed several small items from the shelves as I passed. Scrambling back up on to the chest, I pushed the shutters wide and scrambled through.

Something flashed over my head and a small axe thwacked into the edge of a beam on the overhang of the opposite house. It was a skilful throw and it had come within an inch of embedding itself into my skull. Jackdaw's high-pitched voice bellowed curses and threats, among which I heard Skinner's name. I tore down the street, only slowing when I turned the corner, so that I would not attract attention. Jackdaw didn't follow me; nor, I suspected, would he summon the watch. But Skinner would learn soon enough that there was a thief operating outside his gang, and he would not ignore that.

The courtyard from where I'd stolen the lantern was a seething cauldron of shouts and curses. A matronly woman in a nightgown was belabouring a man and a younger girl with an iron frying pan. The girl was attempting to hide behind the man, but he was more concerned with protecting himself from the blows. Neighbours, roused by the commotion, were leaning out of upper casements, adding their own bellows of protest. I grinned as I slipped past unnoticed.

As soon as I'd regained the safety of my chamber, I examined the stolen items. A small pewter box, which was empty, and two necklaces – one of many multicoloured beads with a small enamelled charm that resembled a blue eye, the other a silvery chain hung with tiny carved fish and birds. I set them aside. The two Jenny Hanivers were a little battered, having been stuffed in my cloak so hastily. From the texture of the dried skin it seemed they'd both been fashioned from skates or some other flat fish, but they'd been cut and tied to resemble creatures of legend. The first was a small grinning demon with red stones inserted for its eyes, bat wings, and a whip-like devil's tail. It was brittle and several fragments had broken from the edges, but as soon as I laid it on the stained indentation in the book of King Arthur, I knew this couldn't be the one.

The other fitted perfectly, though, and when I replaced the broken fragment which had been stuck to the page, there was no doubt in my mind that this was the Jenny Haniver that had been inside the book. If the intention had been to keep it or transport it inside the book, then I would have expected a hole to have been hollowed out for the fragile object. But this appeared to have been thrust in hastily, as though to conceal it from someone arriving unexpectedly. And with a chill, I suddenly understood why.

This creature was not intended to be a fake demon or one of the legendary sea monks; it had been fashioned to resemble a wyvern, with two wings, two forelegs and a body tapering into a long tail covered in sharp little spines. It was those spines that had made the arc of pinprick holes through the pages in the book. The wyvern's teeth were bared, and the two polished stones, inserted above the mouth to make its eyes, shone like liquid tar in the candlelight.

I reached into the pocket sewn inside my shirt and pulled out a small iron disc that I had *borrowed* from Battle Abbey. It bore the same image – a two-legged dragon with a serpent's tail. Spero Pettingar's mark! Had he sent this wyvern to Waldegrave as a death threat? Was this proof that Waldegrave had died at his hands, or had the old priest been protecting Pettingar all along? And not just protecting him, but helping him to evade Robert Cecil's clutches?

Last time I'd been in Bristol, I'd become convinced that Waldegrave had been forging documents for Skinner, providing false identities and fake permits to travel in and out of the port. If anyone could have smuggled the gunpowder plotter out of the country, Skinner and Waldegrave together could have managed it. But if Waldegrave had supported the conspirators' cause, he would have kept their secret even on the rack: Pettingar would have had no need to kill him to ensure his silence. If Richard was bent on destroying his father's cause, though, and had learned that Waldegrave was in Bristol, he would also know who could arrange for him to die. Any man, woman or child in the city could have told him that. Skinner would betray anyone and any cause for a price and swear on his mother's grave that another had done it. It was Skinner's men who had murdered Walde- grave, whether or not the king rat had been there to watch his minions throw the old man into the river. And now it was time to settle that score.

Chapter Fifteen

LONDON

A THICK BLANKET of fog oozed up over the city as dusk crept in. It rose like marsh gas from the open sewers and reeking cellars, and from the slug-grey river itself. Conjured by the bat-winged demons who haunt the night, it rolled upwards to engulf the city, enveloping the severed heads of the traitors impaled on their spikes on London Bridge, affording them the shrouds that man never would. The fret sucked up the coal smoke from the chimneys of houses, from the braziers of watchmen, from the furnaces, laundries and smoke houses, and from the wood fires of the beggars who had no hearths to call home. The mist gathered in all the stinks and smells emanating from cooking pots and cesspits, from the slaughter markets of Smithfield and the ale vats of the brewing houses, until it become a sulphuric, yellow miasma that chilled the bones and burned the lungs.

A linkboy trotted along the street ahead of the black gelding and its rider, for the lights from the torches and lanterns that burned on the walls of the houses glowed deep inside the smothering brimstone, illuminating nothing, but turning the swirls of fog into wraiths to mock the living. The linkboy's own blazing torch illuminated little more, but he knew these streets as intimately as he knew the tenement where he slept in daylight hours. He paused only now and again to hold the flames close to a door, checking that the mist had not led him astray like the trickster it was. Finally, he called up to the figure seated astride the horse, wrapped deep inside a heavy cloak. They turned through an archway into a small courtyard. The lad held the bridle while the rider swung down easily from the saddle on to a mounting block, then handed the reins to a stable lad, reluctantly dragged from his fire by the new arrival.

A servant, who had heard the iron horse shoes in the yard, swiftly opened the door at the soft rapping. He knew the agreed pattern of the knock that he was to listen out for, and as soon as the visitor stepped across the threshold, he locked and bolted the door again. The hallway was in near darkness, but though the servant could not have distinguished the visitor from Lucifer himself in the gloom, he nevertheless made a point of averting his face to ensure that the nocturnal visitors knew they were not being studied. Holding the chamber candle low, so that only his own countenance was lit, the manservant passed ahead of the visitor and led the way to a small withdrawing room, bowing as he turned away at the door. What he had not seen, he could not speak of. In his master's employ, he had always followed that rule. Wise men have neither eyes nor ears.

The door opened almost silently behind Sir Christopher Veldon. But he had heard the creak of the two sets of footfalls outside, and he had already crumpled the letter in his hand and tossed it into the heart of the fire blazing in the hearth. Veldon leaned forward over the blaze, his hand resting on the overmantel and his head bowed, staring into the flames, watching the paper flare and writhe in the fire before collapsing into ash.

Cimex closed the door as softly as she had opened it and plucked off the heavy leather gauntlets, dropping them into the chair. Veldon did not need to look up to know who had entered. The strong, sweet, musky perfume that Cimex always favoured when she was in this guise billowed across the small chamber as she swept off her travelling cloak and dropped it beside the gloves.

'Burning a message you do not wish should be read by other eyes?' Her tone was sharp. 'Did it contain something I should know?'

'From my brother, Gabriel, m'lady. He writes in cypher, but that in itself would be grounds to condemn us both even if they could not decipher it . . . *especially* if they could not.'

Cimex said nothing, and her silence demanded an explanation more effectively than her words ever could.

Veldon sighed. Pulling himself upright, he poured Flemish brandy into two glasses, handing one to her. She had seated herself in one of the chairs. He continued to stand, too restless tonight to settle. He watched her sip from the glass. She was elegantly attired in black breeches, doublet and jerkin slashed with ruby silk. Her dark copper hair was piled up under a plumed hat, leaving a man's long lovelock trailing down over her shoulder. A single teardrop emerald earring hung from one ear, as was the fashion adopted by most of the wealthier young men in London. It glistened like liquid poison in the candlelight. Usually, the sight of her would have aroused a burning appetite in Veldon, one that, regretfully, had to be satiated by some obliging youth, but tonight not even the sight of those legs stirred anything in him.

'Gabriel wrote to tell me he has been forced to move to Ingleton in the West Riding to escape the attentions of magistrates in York and his neighbours, m'lady.'

Cimex lifted her chin. The earring danced and flashed. 'At least he is at liberty. I recall that the last time we spoke of him he was imprisoned in York Castle. Those Puritan magistrates appointed to North Riding—'

'Thomas Holby and Stephen Proctor, pursuivants as well as magistrates,' Veldon cut in, his voice dripping with venom. 'They loathe and resent Lord Sheffield for having been appointed Lord President at York in spite of him having a Catholic wife. My brother's a friend of Sheffield. They can't punish Sheffield, so they are picking off his friends one by one.'

Veldon tossed back the glass, swallowing the remains of the brandy in one gulp. Cimex had rarely seen him in such a savage mood. Whatever was boiling away beneath the surface, to the world and even to Cimex, Veldon usually presented the image of a bored man of wealth and breeding, whose only passions were horses, food and sex, and in these three he demanded infinite variety. The dark humour that gripped him now was a dangerous one. Anger made men act rashly, and this was a time for careful planning and concealment, not for action.

'If I recall, your brother was not imprisoned for long in the castle, Sir Christopher. As you say, it is Lord Sheffield those Puritans really want to punish.'

'It was long enough for his neighbours to have driven all his livestock to market and sold them. I was obliged to send a purse to a friend so that he could buy them back for Gabriel. Otherwise, he'd have returned to nothing but empty fields and stables.'

Veldon poured himself another measure of brandy and for once didn't even glance across to see if her glass needed refilling. 'Even when my brother is at home, his neighbours, tenants and the villagers use his lands like their own gardens, poaching his game, stealing his sheep, pigs, cutting down his timber. More than once they robbed his house quite openly and they know he cannot take them to court, because if he will not take the King's Oath, he cannot swear out an oath against them. All he could do was fight them off, with the help of those of his servants who were willing to remain to defend him.

'But even then, one of his own tenants, whose sons he had driven off when they were trying to steal his sheep, lay in wait for Gabriel outside his gates and attacked him with a cudgel tipped with an iron spike. He swore he meant to kill him. Gabriel took a blow to his arm, which broke the bone, but thankfully his horse managed to carry him through the gates to safety. It may be Lord Sheffield that Holby and Proctor want to see executed on the quartering block, but it is my brother and those like him, who merely want to live quietly in peace, who will be hounded into their graves.' Veldon rose again, his gaze on the jug of brandy.

Cimex was swifter. Taking the glass from his hand, she refilled it, but ensured that his measure was much smaller than those he'd poured himself. When Veldon was in company, he could hold his drink far better than most, but in her experience, when a man was already choleric and brooding, strong drink was apt to plunge him even deeper into the pit so deep he could drown in it.

'If your brother has left his manor, the York magistrates cannot serve him with another summons for recusancy, and if he cannot be served in person, he cannot be fined or worse.'

'Until it begins again in the next place,' Veldon snapped. 'I would see Holby and Proctor and all men like them in chains, and by God's strength, I *shall* see them there. And Gabriel will witness it, I swear, before my blood is cold.'

Cimex's gaze darted towards the fire. No trace remained of the burned paper, but if a coded letter could be received it could also be sent.

'Nevertheless, Sir Christopher, I think it expedient your young brother remains in the Ridings, and is not tempted by anyone to venture further afield, say to London. The wrong done to your brother will be avenged, but not by him, not yet.'

Veldon's grip on the glass stem tightened so hard she thought he might snap it in two.

'Our circle is closed, Sir Christopher. Remember that. It cannot admit another. If a snare is opened too wide, then it fails to tighten in time to catch the prey. And each new link in a chain is a link that might fail – and if it does, the whole chain will be broken.'

Only the crackling of flames broke the silence in the small chamber, a silence which hung heavy with menace. Veldon took another gulp of his brandy, then tossed the dregs into the fire. There was a great hiss and roar as the spirits caught light, sending a sheet of blue flame flashing up into the dark chimney above.

'The snare will not be stretched by me, m'lady, for my brother's sake, to protect him if nothing else. But are you still so sure that your little hound will perform as required? You speak of the chain, but it is Daniel who is the untested link. A man who is willing to give his life for his convictions has a fire that will drive him to the end, even if he finds himself standing alone. But a man who is blackmailed into doing what he has no inclination to do cannot be trusted to see it through. *He* is your weakness, m'lady. He is the break in the snare. And that man is not even in London now.'

'But he will be, Sir Christopher. I have seen to that. Though he does not know it, he will be. And he will do what is required of him. *Blackmail*, as you so delicately put it, will be the whip that guides him, but in the end, he will do it, not because he is driven, but because in his heart he will come to realise it must be done.'

Chapter Sixteen

BRISTOL

DANIEL PURSGLOVE

THE CARVED RED ROSE above the door of Mother Kitty's stew-house had suffered during the great freeze. The scarlet paint was peeling and the open lips of the wooden flower had cracked, but those who came in search of pleasure after dark would neither notice nor care. I had arrived early, just as the light was leeching from the sky, ahead, I hoped, of most of Mother Kitty's regular customers. The house was tall and narrow, but I knew from my last visit it extended deceptively far back, with many tiny rooms squeezed into every nook and cranny.

I was relieved when a familiar, wizened old face peered out of the grille in the door in answer to my knock.

'Early to bed, eager to rise, is it, master?' She cackled at her own joke. 'The early bird catches the worm, but he'll have to wait if he wants to catch a girl. They'll still be preening them-selves.' Her voice was even more cracked than before. She'd had a hard winter.

'Still guarding your little chicks, Magpie?'

She pressed her wrinkled cheek against the iron grille, peering at me with one sloe-black eye. 'You've been here before. Not one of our regulars, though, and not a sailor.'

I lifted my beard by way of answer.

'I know that firemark. For all that my back's crook, my eyes are still as sharp as a ship's spike, and my wits too. Never forget a face, especially not one as comely as yours. But if you're looking to speak to Mother Kitty again, you're out of luck. She'll not be back till late.'

'It was you I wanted, Magpie.'

The old woman gave a coquettish giggle. 'If you'd come here twenty years back, I'd have gobbled you up. Could have shown you tricks these young girls haven't even dreamed of.'

'I wager you still could, Magpie,' I laughed. 'But that's not what I've come for.' I edged closer to the door, holding up a coin. 'Is Skinner here?'

'Bit early for him.'

'But he is expected?' I pressed

'Maybe.' She darted an uneasy glance behind her, fearing he might already be standing there in the shadows.

I pushed the coin through the grille and she snatched at it. 'Let me into the chamber he uses . . . so that I can wait for him,' I added quickly, in case she thought I shared the same proclivities as that little ferret.

'He wouldn't like it.' She looked and sounded scared. 'And nor would Mother Kitty. You come back in an hour and if he's here, I'll ask him if he wants to see you.'

'I want to surprise him.'

'I don't reckon Skinner likes surprises.'

I held up the two necklaces I'd stolen from the shop, dangling them in front of the grille so that they clinked. 'One to take me in; the other is yours after I come out, provided you haven't tipped him off first.'

Her grubby paw shot out and tried to grab the necklaces, but I snatched them out of her reach. 'Is it a bargain, Magpie?'

She hesitated, then seemed to make up her mind. The key grated in the lock and she pulled the door wide enough for me to slip through before she softly and swiftly locked it again.

Magpie cast a greedy look towards my hands, but I had already made the necklaces disappear and they would remain out of sight until I was sure she would do what I asked. She had shrunk in the year since I'd seen her and the demure servant's gown hung even looser than it had before. But her earlobes were still dragged down by the heavy earrings and the number of glass bead and bone necklaces around her withered neck had multiplied; many more and it would snap like a flower stem from the weight. Still she wavered.

'I know the secret route between this house and the castle. Skinner showed it to me. I'm sure neither he nor Mother Kitty would like me to tell the sheriff how he's coming and going.'

The old woman glowered at me, and then without a word turned and stomped along the passageway, her necklaces jangling furiously. The chatter of female voices filtered out from behind the doors we passed as the girls prepared for their night's work.

Magpie paused in front of the narrow door I remembered from before and tugged it open to reveal a staircase directly behind, almost as vertical as an upright ladder.

'I can't promise he'll come. Doesn't always, not if he's got other business to tend to.' She held out her dirt-encrusted hand.

I pulled out the necklace of carved beasts, wagering that it was the other one she'd covert more. I kept a firm hold of it as I held it out. 'I want your word that you will not tell Skinner he has a visitor.'

'I swear on my ma's grave,' she said sullenly.

'Do you know where that is?'

She shrugged. 'Never even knew her name. But I was born under a bush, same as everyone.' A cackle of laughter broke from her. 'And I can still swear on her grave, 'cause it stands to reason she must be dead by now, given I'm not far off it.'

I released the necklace. 'The other after I've spoken to Skinner.'

She nodded. 'But you'd better not start any trouble, or Mother Kitty will finish it. She's half the men in this city in her pocket, given what she could tell about them, so she'll soon find a way to get even if you get Skinner riled.'

Darkness enveloped the staircase as she closed the door. Once again, I had to feel my way up. But at least this time I knew what lay above me. I couldn't recall the number of steps, so reached up above me to ensure I didn't crack my skull on the trapdoor above.

A pool of oily yellow light trickled down from above as I lifted the trapdoor. I tensed. Perhaps Magpie had lied to me and Skinner was already up there.

I drew my dagger and rushed the last few steps, throwing back the trapdoor as hard as I could. But the tiny chamber was deserted, though Skinner was clearly expected: a lantern had been lit ready and a cold roasted pullet laid on the small table, together with a flagon of wine. The stained blankets heaped on the pallet on the floor, stinking of rancid fat and semen, looked even fouler than before. The only other furniture in the chamber was a battered wooden chair.

I moved the curtain concealing the door that led to the passageway to the castle. It was locked. Skinner held the key. I could have opened it, but that would put him on his guard. There was nothing now to do except close the trapdoor and wait.

THE ROOM WAS windowless and there was no way of knowing how much time had elapsed, but I knew it must be well past sunset. Night had come creeping over the city and the stewhouse was now open for business, for I heard a door opening in one of the chambers below, the murmur of voices, the creak of bed ropes and a grunting like a pig foraging in mud. This was what entertained Skinner. I glanced down at the four round spyholes in the floor, covered with plugs of wood and iron rings to lift them out. Skinner liked to watch and he paid well for it, if Magpie was to be believed.

The animal noises rising up from beneath the floor distracted me from the sound I was listening out for, but I heard it just in time: the groan of wood beyond the curtained door, the squeak of the key in the lock. I drew back against the wall. The door opened and a hand reached through to push the heavy curtain aside, the yellow fingernails as thick and long as the claws on chickens' feet.

Skinner clambered up into the chamber. He had his back to me, but from behind he looked even more like a ragged crow than before, his untrimmed black beard and long black hair were wilder than ever. His attention was fixed on the roasted pullet but the lure of food did not overcome his instinct for caution and he paused to lock the door. I grabbed him from behind. Pressing my dagger across his throat, I wrenched his hand up his back.

'Don't so much as squeal, Skinner. I'm inching for an excuse to slice through your miserable windpipe.'

'You'll not . . . get out of here alive . . . if you do,' he croaked, flinching back so far from the sharp blade he could scarcely get the words out.

I dragged him over to the chair and forced him to sit down, just out of reach of his meal. Moving the dagger so that the point dug between his shoulder blades, I ordered him to pull out his knife and drop it on the floor.

'Me? A knife? I'm an old man, unarmed. What would I need a knife here for?'

'To cut your meat?'

'Oh, that . . . couldn't harm a strong man like you with that even if I wanted to, not sharp enough to cut the leg off a spider.'

He pulled out the knife dangling in plain sight from the battered sheath in his belt and dropped it on the floor. He was right: it was nothing more than a short, blunt and bent knife, only good for paring fruit.

I pushed the point of my dagger through his clothes until a jerk and yelp told me I had drawn blood.

'The other knife, Skinner,' I growled.

He hesitated and I pushed the blade in another half-inch.

'Alright! Give a man a chance.' He sat rigid as he struggled to reach inside his shirt without moving his back. Finally, he withdrew the razor-sharp flesher's knife I'd seen him use before. 'I'm old, I get a mite forgetful sometimes,' he whined. 'You can't hold that against me.'

In a flash, the knife was in his left hand and he jerked round, slashing furiously at my face. I rammed my fist into the side of his head, sending both him and the chair crashing into the wall. I stamped hard on his arm, grinding down on the bone until his clawed fingers opened and the knife clattered on to the wooden boards. With a kick, I sent it spinning across the floor and into the far corner. Skinner pushed himself up until he was sitting on the floor, propped against the wall, alternately rubbing his arm and his head. He glowered up at me, a trickle of blood crawling from his thin nostril.

'Brother Pursglove – I heard you were still alive.' His tone suddenly changed and he attempted what he must have thought was a disarming smile. 'Look, there's no cause for things to get unfriendly. It was all a misunderstanding. I only meant for Runt to show you the way out. He's a bit slow-witted, is the Runt.'

'I've not come looking for you because you tried to kill me, Skinner, but because you *did* kill the Yena. You murdered that defenceless old man and kicked his body into the river, or more likely you put out his eyes and stood there laughing while he groped about in agony, until finally he blundered over the edge into the water. Isn't that how your rats amuse themselves? Wagering on how long it will take a man to drown? So, do you fancy laying bets on how long it will take you to die, Skinner? Because I promise I do not intend to make it quick.'

I picked up his knife, pulled the chair over to the table and sat down on it, holding my own dagger pointed towards him.

But the expression that darted across his face wasn't one of fear, more of curiosity. 'You weren't in these parts when they fished the body out, so who was it told you about the Yena?'

'Come now, Skinner, are you admitting there is someone passing on information from Bristol who isn't in your pay? It would seem you are losing your influence.'

He regarded me for some time before he answered. 'There's one thing I will admit: always curious, I was, as to why the Yena protected you. He told my men we were not to touch so much as a curly little hair on your handsome head, else he wouldn't help us again.'

'It didn't stop you though, did it?' I said savagely. 'Was that why you killed him, because he wouldn't forge the papers you needed any more, or did someone pay you to do it?'

'You're so sharp you could shave a flea. Worked out what our little arrangement was all by yourself, did you? 'Cause I don't reckon he'll have told you.'

'And I worked out that you killed him.'

Skinner held up a yellow claw. 'Ahh, now see, that's where you're wrong. Not as clever as you thought, are you? We never touched him. What would be the sense in killing the goose that lays the golden eggs?'

'Then who? Who murdered the old man? Who ordered his killing?'

'You've not answered my question yet, not very civil of you, that isn't. And while we're about it, you can toss me a leg of that roasted pullet over there. I'm famished.'

'If you have any hope of leaving this room alive, you'd better convince me you had nothing to do with the old man's murder.' I held up a key and had the satisfaction of seeing the look of shock on Skinner's face as his hand flew to his hip and he realised his key was missing. 'I can make things vanish from pockets as easily as any of your nips. You've trapped yourself in here by locking the door to the castle, because I've bolted the trapdoor to Mother Kitty's. So, neither the Runt nor any of your lickers will be able to save you.' I held up my dagger, testing the sharpness of the point with my own thumb.

'Maybe not,' he muttered sullenly, 'but they'll see to it you'll not leave Bristol alive.'

I tore a leg off the pullet and ate the meat slowly, watching a thin stream of brown saliva trickle from the corner of Skinner's mouth into his matted black beard.

'Like you say, if my men had done it, they'd have flicked his eyes out and made him walk into the river. Me, well, I dare say you know what my touchmark is.' He jerked his head towards the flesher's knife now lying on the table. 'But I saw his corpse after they fished him out. Hands crushed to pulp, like they'd been in a vice, and his tongue torn out.'

An icy surge flooded my bowels. Sibyl! Those were the same injuries that had been inflicted on that poor old woman in Bubwith.

'Runt's tongue was cut out.'

'Aye, but not by me. That was done to him under the hag's reign. Sedition, that's what he was accused of. But he hasn't brains. If he spoke out against old Queen Bess, it was words some other bastard put in his mouth.' He looked up at me slyly. 'As for the hands, I reckon you'd know more about the men who enjoy that pleasure than me.'

I knew only too well who he meant: pursuivants, men like Richard Topcliffe. God knows, as my tutor. Waldegrave had inflicted pain enough on me as a boy, but the thought of the agony he must have endured for hours made the bile rise in my throat. Had he told them what they wanted before they ripped out his tongue? And what was it they had wanted of him? What had he known?

Skinner was watching me closely, but I didn't reply.

'You've still not told me why the Yena was looking out for you,' he finally said. 'See, I thought at first you might have been one of that Robert Cecil's scum yourself, seeing as how you'd come from London and you were asking questions. Crossed my mind that if he was a friend of yours, the Yena might be double-crossing us. But I don't reckon he'd have risked trying to protect you if that was his game. They'd throw any of their own to the sharks without losing a wink of sleep. No, there was something else between you two, something I can't fathom.'

When Elena was birthing you, she kept calling out the name of the priest from Willitoft.

'It scarcely matters now, does it, Skinner? The Yena is dead.'

Skinner laughed. 'Ahh, did I not tell you? See, that comes of me being near faint with hunger. At my age it's apt to make a man forgetful. Now, if you was to toss me the other leg of that bird and pour me a cup of that wine, I reckon it would all come flooding back to me.'

'What would?' I demanded.

'That important thing I forgot to tell you.'

I jabbed the dagger towards him and he flung his hands up in a gesture of surrender.

'No call for that! There you go again, threatening a poor old man, when all you have to do is ask nicely and save us both a deal of trouble. See, if I starts to scream, they'll have my men standing ready on the other side of both those doors before you can say, "Curse all kings." They'll chop you down the moment you to try to set foot outside this chamber, so you see we're both trapped. No option but to trust each other.'

'"Trust not in a new friend or an old enemy." Isn't that what they say, Skinner? And which one are you today?'

He laughed. He was a cunning old fox, I had to give him that, but he had a point. I tore the other leg from the pullet and tossed it towards him. He reached up and deftly caught it in mid-air.

He tore the flesh off with his teeth, swallowing in hungry gulps, then gnawed on the bone till there was little left but splinters. He sucked his long fingers and stared pointedly at the rest of the carcass. The skin on his long bony nose shone, blue-black as a raven, against the corpse-pallor of his cheeks.

'Trust, Skinner, remember. You've had your leg. You'll get the rest of the bird when you tell me.'

He gave a twisted grin. 'But I've still not got my wine.' He put his hand to his throat. 'Can't expect a man to speak when his gullet's as dry as coals in a furnace.'

I poured the wine and stood holding the beaker over his head, taunting him.

'The corpse, they fished out of the river,' he said, finally. 'The sheriff's men put it on a handcart and dragged it in front of

Stephen's Church. Made anyone who was passing look at it, and hauled along a good many men as wasn't passing and made them look too. Said they needed to see if any could name the dead man, but I reckon they wanted half the city to see what had been done to him, as a warning.'

'Isn't that what you usually do, Skinner? Make sure the whole city knows what you've done to anyone who crosses you, just as a warning?' I said savagely.

The thought that half of Bristol had gawped at the old priest's mutilated remains sickened me. The sheriff's men would have made quite certain he was displayed naked, however he'd been clad when he went into the water. I had seen the naked corpses of executed men and bloody corpses stripped of everything on the battlefield, and barely registered the fact, but suddenly Waldegrave's humiliation was my own.

I found myself lowering the cup. Skinner grabbed it and drank deeply from it. He laid it down, wiping his mouth with his sleeve.

'So, who identified him?' I couldn't imagine anyone foolish enough to claim acquaintanceship with a man the pursuivants had just tortured to death.

'I dare say you'll remember Joan? Relieved you of your purse, if I recall . . .'

'Your mort, Joan? Why would she help the sheriff's men?'

''Cause she was paid to. Joan can't resist a purse, no more than Magpie can resist a bright shiny necklace. She was paid to tell the sheriff's men that it was old Ambrose, a priest in hiding, who went by the nickname the Yena. They hung a notice round his neck saying who he was and left the body there till sunset.'

'Do you know where they buried the body?' At least I could mark the grave.

'I dare say they took it to the laystall outside the city, where the gong farmers dump the shit from the jakes. That's where they take the gallows carrion, if their families don't buy them back. Corpses rot down in Bristol's shit and they spread it on the fields. So, we end up eating hanged men in our bread. Now that's a thought to give you a good appetite.' He sniggered.

I must have looked as murderous as I felt, for he instantly became serious and leaned forward.

'Thing is, though, I said Joan was paid to say the dead man was the Yena. But he wasn't.'

It took me a moment or two to register what he'd said. 'Are you . . . are you telling me the dead man they pulled out of the river wasn't Ambrose? Is she sure?'

Skinner nodded. 'She knows the Yena as well as I do. He did a lot of work for us. She's certain it wasn't him and so am I. Saw that corpse with my own eyes and it was nothing like Ambrose. A good twenty years younger, for a start. I've no notion who the poor bastard was, don't reckon anyone knew. None of my lads at the castle recognised him and they all took a good squint on the sly. But someone wanted everyone to think it was the Yena, someone as could pay handsomely.'

'Who paid Joan?'

Skinner laughed. 'Hardly likely to introduce himself, was he? And you know Joan, she's not one to ask any questions if the purse is heavy enough, which it was, even though she'd lightened it before handing it over to me, like she always does if she thinks she can get away with it. Besides, she reckons she was doing old Ambrose a good turn. If whoever killed that poor gudgeon was after the Yena and thought he'd got him, they'd not be hunting for him any more, would they?'

My head was reeling. If this little weasel was speaking the truth, then I had fallen for a lie fed to me by that young acolyte Erasmus. But though I didn't trust either of the men further than I could hurl a millstone, I trusted Skinner least of all. I didn't like being played for a fool.

I lunged at him, pinning him back against the wall by his scrawny throat, the point of my dagger so close to his eyeball that if he so much as coughed, he'd lose it.

'You're a liar, Skinner. Waldegrave is dead and you're just

spinning me this tale to get out of this chamber with your cods intact. If Waldegrave is alive, then where is he now? Because I know he's not in that rat's nest he used to live in.'

Skinner was straining as far away from the blade as he could, but with his head already jammed against a solid wall, he had nowhere to go. I pressed harder on his windpipe, taking a malicious pleasure in hearing him choke. His face was puce and his eyes were screwed shut. His fingers clutched my wrist, trying to drag my hand from his throat, but I felt his cold grip weakening. Just another little squeeze, that's all it would take to finish the piece of rat-shit, once and for all. And I'd be doing the whole of Bristol a great service if I did.

I eased my grip just a little and felt him take a huge, shuddering gulp of air. I pressed my face close to his ear. 'You are going to tell me the truth for once in your miserable life, Skinner, because if you don't, I'm going to start with the trick your men enjoy. I'm going to cut your eyes out and then I'll work down the rest of your stinking carcass, fingers first, or shall I make it your cods? You won't be able to see where I'm aiming at until you feel the knife go in. And you can scream all you like. It might bring your henchmen running, but by the time they break in here your reign will be over. And I think they might even thank me for that, for there's bound to be some of them who are itching to take your place as king of the rats.'

Skinner held up his hands. 'No . . . lies . . . I swear.' His eyes were still screwed shut. I pressed hard on his throat again, just long enough to be sure he knew I meant it, then released my grip and stepped back.

'Is the Yena dead?'

Skinner rubbed his bruised throat, glowering at me resentfully. 'Might be, might not be.'

He ducked away as I lunged at him again. 'Look! It's the honest truth. I don't know. All I can tell you for certain is that it wasn't him they fished out of the river. I saw the Yena two days before they found the floater. But I never saw him again after that, nor has anyone from the castle, and there's not a corner of the city nor an inn that my lads don't go scavenging in.'

'Thieving, you mean.'

Skinner shrugged. 'I went to his lodgings same as you did. Someone had ransacked them. His table and cooking pots, all that was still there, but thrown about, like someone had taken the place apart. Papers were all gone, but I don't know if he took them and bolted, or if they were pinched by whoever searched the loft. Maybe whoever took them took him an' all.'

'You sold what furniture was left there, I take it?'

'Obvious that he wasn't coming back to fetch it. No sense in it going to waste.'

'And his books?'

'I never touch books,' Skinner said, almost shuddering, and for a moment I thought he was going to cross himself. 'But I tell you this much, someone did. 'Cause most were gone and what was left was thrown in a heap in the corner. Old Ambrose would never have done that. Treated them as tender as a mother nursing a new-born babe.'

'There's just one thing you haven't explained, Skinner. When I was last in Bristol, there was a man who kept watch on the Yena's lodgings.' I could hardly forget him; I'd last seen him sitting astride a pile of rubble, turning human vertebrae into a gruesome rattle. 'He always sees who comes and who goes, and I'd wager he reports it all to you. He must have told you when Ambrose left and who searched his lodging.'

Skinner grimaced. 'Used to see, you mean. They found him stuffed down the jakes where the Yena lived, the day after that corpse was fished out of the river. Reckon he'd been dead best part of a week, though it's hard to tell if you've been lying head-down a shit-hole and the rats have been feasting on you. But I'll tell you one thing. He didn't throw himself down that hole. His throat had been cut, and not by me.'

Chapter Seventeen

'I'VE BEEN WAITING for you,' I said, stepping in behind Myles and gripping his shoulder.

He stiffened, ready to wriggle from my grip and run – old instincts kicking in – but relaxed and flashed me his impish grin as he realised who held him. He was hefting a small sack over his shoulder. He'd being carrying one the first time I'd seen him, except that had been full of looted treasures he'd found in the flooded city; this time it looked like a sack of something bloody, and I wondered what unfortunate creature might be about to be made into another of Mistress Crugge's infamous pressed brawns.

'You find what you were looking for at Jackdaw's?' he asked cheerfully.

I nodded, then seeing his hopeful expression, added swiftly, 'But you've had all you're going to get for guiding me there. Come on.' I turned him around and steered him away from the Salt Cat.

'She'll be waiting,' he protested, half turning back.

'You hungry?'

His eyes lit up. He was always hungry, though I knew from the way his skeletal frame had filled out that he was well fed at the Salt Cat. Strangely, though, his plumper cheeks and chubby hands made him look even younger than he had a year ago when he'd been a starving street urchin.

I had waited at the corner of the street for more than an hour, watching for his return. Ever since I had walked away from

Mother Kitty's and from Skinner, who regretfully I'd thought it wise to leave alive, one thought had been buzzing round and round in my head. *If* Skinner was telling the truth, and I would not have wagered a dead cat on that, then not only had Erasmus lied to me, but Myles too. The lad had thieved things when he lived on the street – what urchin hadn't – but I'd always trusted him and believed he had trusted me. I'd never known him to lie to me before, especially not about something so serious, and I couldn't understand why. Had he too been paid, like Joan? But if so, by whom and why?

I steered Myles towards a pieman I'd heard shouting his wares from a few streets away. I bought a couple of marrow-bone turnovers, and led him into the ruins of what had once been a workshop. Having driven off a stray dog that came sniffing, attracted by the smell of pastries or Myles's bloody sack, we squatted side by side on the remains of a broken wall to eat.

In the old days, he'd have been so hungry, he'd have almost choked himself cramming the turnover down before it could be snatched from him. Now, though he still gobbled his food as fast as a hound, he did manage to pause halfway through and glance up at me.

'You got another job for me? Remember that time you had to search those lodgings, and you wanted me to keep the landlady busy so she wouldn't catch you?' He chuckled. 'Kept her busy alright, didn't I? We was good together, wasn't we? Do you need me to do it again?'

'Not this time.'

He looked disappointed, but turned his attention back to the remains of his turnover. I waited until he'd finished licking the sauce off his fingers.

'Myles, what happened to old Ambrose?'

He jerked as if he'd been stung. 'Told you afore! He's dead, isn't he? They pulled his corpse out the river.'

'But did you actually see them pull it out? Did you see Ambrose's body?'

''Course I did.' He shrank into a ball, his shoulders hunched, but I couldn't tell if it was misery or fear that was making him retreat.

'But if you did see the corpse, then you know it wasn't the Yena.'

His head shot up and he stared at me. 'He's dead,' he repeated stubbornly.

'Myles, Ambrose asked you once to look out for me and you did. You probably saved my life. Don't you think he'd want you to tell me if he's still alive?'

Silence. Either he was too frightened to speak or he had been sworn to keep a secret. I knew from my own boyhood that lads will keep a pact they've sworn more loyally and stubbornly than the most fanatical of religious martyrs.

'Let me tell you what I know. A body was fished out of the river, a man who'd been badly hurt before he was killed. Some-one paid Castle Joan to say it was Ambrose, when she and all of Skinner's men knew it wasn't. Now, that means Ambrose is hiding somewhere, either in the city or he's left Bristol and gone to a new town. Did the Yena tell you to say he was dead?'

'He didn't tell me nothing!' There was anger and hurt in his tone. 'I wouldn't have told anyone. He knows he could trust me. I went to his lodgings to give him some mutton I'd saved, I took it specially, just for him, 'cause I knew he'd be hungry. But all his things were gone. Skinner was there. He said the Yena was dead.'

'So, you didn't see the body yourself.'

Myles squirmed. 'When I got down to the church, they'd taken it away. But I wouldn't have been scared to look at the corpse. I've seen hundreds of them!'

'But no matter what Skinner told you, I think you know that the Yena is alive. How do you know?'

Myles straightened his back, his face turned away from me and his arms folded defiantly. He wanted me to know that all the instruments of torture in the Tower would not make him talk.

'You know that you can trust me, lad, just like Ambrose trusted me. We're both his friends. Wherever he is, perhaps I can find him and help him. He could be in trouble. He could be starving.'

There was a long silence, but I knew that if I pushed him too hard, he would stubbornly refuse to tell me anything. I would have done the same as a boy.

The cries of the pieman drifted towards us, more distant now. Somewhere a dog was whining.

'There's a place,' Myles said finally. 'A secret place. The Yena used to send me there to hide messages and things, and I had to look to see if there were any letters or anything to fetch back to him. After . . . Skinner told me he was dead, I went there a few times, in case someone had left a message for him. Someone who didn't know he was dead. I thought . . . sometimes they left money, see. It wasn't stealing, 'cause it would be no use to him if he was dead!' he added fiercely.

'No, and there would be no sense leaving it there. He'd want you to have it. Did you find anything?'

He shook his head. 'No money, but there was a letter, a letter from the Yena. He must be alive, mustn't he, if he left a letter after everyone said he'd drowned?'

'How can you be sure it was from him?' I asked. 'Maybe it was a letter someone was sending to him. You said that happened sometimes.'

'It had his mark on it. No one else draws it like that.'

'Draws what?'

Myles hesitated, unable to find a name for it. 'A beast . . . like a snake except it had wings.'

A bubble of excitement welled up in me. 'Could it have been a wyvern?'

'What's that?' he asked, genuinely puzzled.

'A dragon.'

'I think . . . sort of,' the boy said cautiously. 'A kind of dragon.'

'Myles, the letter. Do you know what happened to it? Is it still in this secret place? It's important. I must know.'

The lad drew his knees up higher and buried his face in them, hugging his legs. His voice was so quiet and muffled that when he did finally speak again, I had to strain to catch the words.

'Took it . . . Angry 'cause he didn't tell me he was going away. So, I took it to pay him back.'

'What did you do with it? Tear it up?'

'No,' he said in small voice. 'Hid it. Hid it at the Salt Cat. I felt bad after, 'cause he trusted me and I haven't ever let him down, not ever! And I was going to put it back, but I got scared, 'cause I thought he'd know I'd taken it when the person he was sending it to came looking and there was nothing there. They'd know it was me, and they might be waiting to catch me, so I never went back.'

'Myles, do you still have that letter?'

He nodded, his expression wretched. Guilt was eating him alive. That was why he'd lied to me. I should have known it wasn't because of any threats. He'd too much spirit for that.

'Why don't you give it to me? I'll take charge of it and see that it reaches the person it's meant for.'

Relief flooded his face. He'd probably been too scared to destroy it, but equally terrified it might be found at the Salt Cat. It had become a cursed object for him.

The chimes of a church clock made him spring to his feet and snatch up the sack. 'Ma Crugge wants this to cook for the customers' supper. She'll skin me alive if I'm late.'

'The letter!' I urged.

'I'll give it you tonight, after the Cat shuts. Same place as before. Racks behind Temple Church.'

As he turned to go, something small and yellow fell from his jerkin. I picked it up. 'Myles, where did you get this?'

He stopped and twisted round. 'Saw it on the steps in the yard as I was going out, the ones that go up to the room you used to have at the Cat. I'll give it to Ma Crugge when I get back. Keep her sweet. Have to do that with women, don't you?' he added with a wink, as if he was already a man of the world.

He took a pace back and grabbed his gift from my hand. It was a little dried flower – a marigold.

Chapter Eighteen

SOUTHWARK, LONDON

'WE SHOULD LEAVE, Richard. It grows late,' Oliver murmured in his cousin's ear.

Richard Fairfax was seated at the gambling table with three men, Oliver standing uneasily behind him. Richard ignored him. The small gambling house was crowded with men huddled around similar tables, unable to wrench their eyes from the cards, dice or checkered boards. Bare-breasted girls and comely lads sidled between the tables, refilling cups from flagons of illegal double beer or smuggled sack. The customers dropped coins into the outstretched palms without even glancing up. A few of the older women stood around the walls directing newcomers to tables where they might join a game, while burly men with faces as scarred as fighting dogs and muscles forged hard as steel from hefting cargoes lounged against barrels, ready to step in at the first sign of a brawl. The owners paid them to ensure that any heads that needed to be broken were hauled outside to be dealt with before the fight spread. Oliver's gaze kept straying back to them. He'd been taught to dual by an expert and was sure, in spite of his youth, he could take on almost any man at Court in a sword fight, even the bastard Scots, but these men wouldn't fight with swords; they didn't need to.

Richard had been in a foul mood ever since he'd received the letter from his High Steward at Willitoft that afternoon. Oliver had watched his face darken as he'd read and reread it, before tearing it into shreds with balled fists and hurling the mess into the fire.

'I'll see that prick-louse flogged to the bone and hanged from the highest gallows in the land!'

'Your steward?' Oliver had asked. 'What's he done?'

'No, you frog-wit. Daniel, who else? It seems he had the audacity to return to the Ridings and trick his way into Willitoft manor. The Devil knows what he wanted in there. I imagine he thought there would be valuables lying around that he remembered from his childhood and intended to steal them. Well, he'd have been sorely disappointed in that. The steward didn't realise who he was until he'd gone. Then . . . *then*, would you believe it, he murdered an old woman in Bubwith. They actually arrested him for it too. But that blockhead of a constable let him walk out of the lockup before he could be dragged off to York.'

'Murder? Why? Was he trying to rob her?'

'I don't know,' Richard had stormed. 'Lost his temper, because he couldn't manage to steal anything from me? It wouldn't be the first time he's killed an innocent woman in one of his rages and the Devil knows how many more he might have murdered. And those numbskulls just let him walk away!'

Richard had brooded and seethed for the rest of the day until Sir Christopher Veldon suggested they take a tilt boat upriver from the Palace of Placentia.

'What you need, my churlish friend, is an evening at the tables to sweeten your temper, and I know just the place.'

As was his habit, Veldon had put an arm around Oliver's shoulder. 'Bring your young coz along too, Richard. It's high time we continued his education, otherwise he'll be at the mercy of every pigeon-plucker in the city, and we can't have him losing any more of his family's fortune, can we?'

But Veldon had separated from Richard and Oliver as soon as they were admitted into the illicit gaming house and now Oliver couldn't see him anywhere, though it was hard to distinguish any man's face through the dense fog of tobacco smoke that filled the room. For once, he wouldn't have minded feeling Veldon's arm on his shoulder. At least Veldon could usually manage to handle Richard when he was in his cups, and right now Oliver needed someone to do that.

Richard had won the first game of Hazard, which had considerably improved his temper, but if anything, that and the liberal quantities of sack he was swigging after each throw of the dice had cast him into a dangerous euphoria. He'd won a little more, but lost every game since and had wagered ever-higher stakes, convinced his luck must change.

Oliver had caught the glances exchanged between two of the other players and was certain they were somehow cheating, though he could not see how they were doing it. Oliver was no coward – he'd got himself in trouble more than once at Court for losing his temper and being first to draw a sword or knife – but even he realised that to challenge cheaters in a place like this would start more trouble than either he or Richard could handle.

The two dice rolled again, and Richard stared at them as they came to rest in the centre of the table. He let out a loud groan, and sank his head into his hands. One of the men raised a hand. clicking his fingers and motioning to the girl who was wiggling towards them between the tables to refill Richard's cup.

Oliver put a hand on his cousin's arm as he reached for the cup. 'Richard, we should go. Veldon will be waiting with the tilt boat.'

Richard flung off the restraint, catching Oliver hard in the chest as he lashed out, making the lad stagger back. He had not been winded by the blow – his padded jerkin deflected most of the force – but the grins on the faces of the men at the table were injury enough.

Richard took a swig from the cup, spilling a little as he slammed it back on the table. 'Let Veldon wait. Serves him right . . . deserves to be kept waiting. His idea to come.' He flicked his hand at Oliver as if he was swatting away a fly. 'You go . . . if you want to. Go play "goosy" with the ladies . . . if you can't afford a li . . . little wager.'

The men at the table laughed. Oliver felt his face burn and, seething with fury, stalked towards the doors. He didn't know if Veldon had already left or was playing cards somewhere else; either way, he didn't care. Richard could stay here all night and lose every penny he had if that's what he wanted.

But before he reached the door, a man stepped in front of him. 'I wouldn't leave Lord Fairfax in their company, Master Oliver.'

At the mention of his name, Oliver stared at him, trying to place him. He looked vaguely familiar, like someone you see daily on the river or in the street without ever knowing who they are – average height, brown beard and hair, plainly clad; nothing to distinguish him from a dozen other men.

'It's his choice,' Oliver replied sullenly. 'I've tried to persuade him to leave, but he's determined to play. Everyone can see he's being cheated.'

'Not everyone by any means, Master Oliver, otherwise those tricksters wouldn't make such good profits for the owners of this dicing house. You did well to spot them. You have a keen eye.'

The admiration in the stranger's face convinced Oliver that, for once, he wasn't being mocked.

'You saw that man palming the regular dice, and sliding his own pair out of his sleeve?'

Oliver nodded, trying to look as if that's exactly what he had seen.

'His pair,' the man continued, 'doesn't have the complete set of numbers. Same numbers on two faces. The other man's dice are loaded. They work as a team. If a customer challenges them, they're dragged out before they cause trouble and taken to a dark corner where they're convinced to leave quietly or else.' He jerked his head towards a broken-nosed bear of a man leaning against the wall. 'And something tells me your cousin is not going to leave quietly.'

Oliver again stared at the stranger, who clearly knew both him and Richard. But though he struggled to think, he simply couldn't recall the man's name. Oliver had been at Court for almost a year now, and one of the many lessons he'd rapidly had to learn was that nobles and officers tended to take it as a great insult if they were not instantly recognised, especially by those they considered their inferiors. It was safer not to ask.

The man was still speaking. 'They spotted the reckless mood Lord Fairfax was in the moment he entered, which is why he was selected for that table. He behaves like someone determined to vent his frustration, whatever the cost. I'd wager he's received bad news, am I right?'

Oliver sighed, rolling his eyes. 'Absolutely right, sir. A letter from his estates in Yorkshire – it's put him in the foulest humour ever since.'

'Your poor cousin must have received grievous tidings,' the man said, his voice and expression full of sympathy. 'Was it a fire at his manor? Cattle murrain? I could suggest someone who might loan him money if that would help. He'll not win what he needs in here, I'm afraid.'

'It wasn't—' Oliver began, but an arm slid around his shoulder. He gave a start, and automatically tried to pull away, but the grip was too firm. He glanced sidewise at Veldon's red-gold beard and corpulent belly.

'Northwood,' Veldon drawled. 'I hope you haven't been trying to lead young Oliver astray. Lord Fairfax is most protective of his cousin.' As always, Veldon sounded as if the person he was addressing amused him. But the arm around Oliver was tense, the fingers pressing hard into his shoulder.

'On the contrary, Sir Christopher.' Northwood offered a small bow. 'We were trying to devise a plan to extricate Lord Fairfax from the clutches of the gaming-house tricksters without any broken noses or smashed fingers.'

'I'm sure his little coz and I between us can manage to persuade him it's time to seek his own bed. We wouldn't want him waking up in one of theirs, now, would we?' Veldon gestured towards two serving girls and a lad who were giggling together nearby. 'I hear the Great Pox is worse than usual after the freeze. Nothing else to do except warm each other's arses, isn't that so, Northwood?'

'I bow to your superior experience of such matters, Sir Christopher.'

Veldon laughed. Both men inclined their heads courteously to each other, smiling politely, and Northwood retreated through the door, disappearing in the cloud of smoke that swirled around him in the sudden draught, like an imp vanishing on the stage of a playhouse.

Veldon's grip on Oliver slackened, but his smile had turned instantly to a frown. 'What did Northwood want?'

'He thought I shouldn't leave Richard alone with those cheats. He knew how they worked.'

'He was asking you about the news Richard had received. What did you tell him?'

'Nothing!' Oliver retorted, flushing. 'I don't discuss my cousin's private correspondence with strangers or anyone.' *What business was it of Veldon's what they had discussed?*

'Quite right too, my lad. You keep it that way.'

Veldon glanced over at Richard, who was evidently about to lay another wager. 'We'd better remove your dear cousin, before they strip him to his cods.' He gripped Oliver's shoulder again and this time met his eyes. 'Stay well away from Northwood, and don't accept any favours from him. If he approaches you again, be very careful what you say. If you have to throw him off, babble like a lovesick swain about some wench you're besotted with.'

Oliver had never heard him use that tone before. 'Why, Sir Christopher? Who is Northwood anyway?'

'No one, just a shadow. But when you see the shadow, you know someone of substance is casting it.'

Chapter Nineteen

BRISTOL

DANIEL PURSGLOVE

THE NIGHT WAS, if anything, darker than the previous time I'd met Myles in the weavers' field. I had loosened some additional fence posts near the overhanging tree and with an effort I was able to squeeze through, which was easier than climbing the branches, though an ominous ripping sound warned me I'd torn my cloak. I settled myself in front of the tenter where Myles and I had talked before. A damp, misty rain was falling, the kind that clings to your clothes, soaking them.

I had arrived at our meeting place earlier than I needed to, unable to contain my impatience. I had no idea what the letter might hold, but if the boy was caught handing me a message from a priest, both our lives would be forfeit. That dried marigold had reminded me just how dangerous playing the messenger could be and I was unnerved by where Myles had found it. Was it simply a coincidence, a flower fallen from an innocent posy or from a bundle of dried strewing herbs, or were my old lodgings being used by someone fleeing Cecil's men? There were probably a dozen of them hiding out in Bristol, waiting for ships, and a dozen pursuivants on their trail. Either way, I had been reluctant to leave my chamber for the rest of the evening, in case I was spotted by one of Skinner's men or Badger-beard. He hadn't shown himself to me since that night in the Three Choughs, but he was probably still in the city somewhere. If he was one of FitzAlan's men, I did not want him following me here.

Ever since Myles had confirmed that Waldegrave's death had been faked, I'd been tossed like a ship with a smashed rudder between relief that he still lived, and anger and humiliation that I had been taken in by his deception. 'He didn't tell me nothing!' Myles had blurted out, hurt and angry. The boy in me wanted to scream out the same. I had almost allowed myself to grieve for that malicious devil. I'd come to seek his murderer, avenge his death. I knew exactly how Myles had felt – betrayed. But I couldn't afford to give way to anger, not again, not this time. I wouldn't allow him that victory.

And I had learned one thing by coming here: Waldegrave was not simply forging documents for Skinner or the Catholic network. He was tangled as inexorably in this web of treason and deception as Richard, but were they on the same side or deadly enemies? Someone had gone to a great deal of trouble to help the old priest vanish, someone ruthless enough to brutally take another's man life, to create a sacrificial lamb to save Waldegrave.

Smith's acolyte, Erasmus, had fed me the news that Yena was dead. Had he done so innocently, believing what he told me, or had he known the truth and deliberately set out to deceive me? If the latter, on whose orders? Who wanted me and others to think the Yena was dead? Waldegrave himself? When I had last been in Bristol, he'd ordered me to bury my questions here and *leave them to rot among these bones*. He'd insisted I must leave the city. But I had not left; I had not buried my questions among the rotting corpses of Bristol. And I certainly wouldn't now.

The wyvern, Spero Pettingar's mark, had turned up at Battle Abbey, then in the form of a Jenny Haniver in Waldegrave's book, and now on a letter the old man had sent. And Myles had said it was not the first time. Waldegrave had used that mark before. That letter was vital: it could hold the clue to unravelling the whole Gordian knot. Where was that boy? If he had changed his mind about bringing it, I'd wring his neck.

I peered across the dark field of racks on which the weavers stretched their cloth to dry in the summer, standing as stark as the ribs of a skeleton in a gibbet cage. Beyond were the gardens of the houses. Small shards of candlelight in the upper chambers blinked like signal lights as the breeze tossed the bare branches of fruit trees across them. Torches and a brazier, burning beneath the city wall gate, bathed the archway in a dark red flickering glow, silhouetting the watchmen so that they looked like imps guarding the mouth of hell.

I turned to look once more at the backs of the distant houses where one by one lights were being extinguished in the casements as families settled to sleep. It was only then that I noticed one of the racks in the field seemed to have something hanging from it. I peered through the misty rain and darkness. A section of cloth that some careless apprentice had neglected to bring inside? He'd suffer for it when that was discovered. But it was too short and narrow for that; a bolt of newly woven cloth usually covered many yards of the rails. A piece of sacking blown in the wind and caught on the hooks, maybe? Curiosity as ever got the better of me. I heaved myself up and edged towards it.

Even as the shape resolved itself, and I realised what I was staring at, a voice in my head was telling me I was mistaken. It was too small. I had witnessed such sights before, but this must be a fake, a Jenny Haniver. It couldn't be . . .

The small body was dangling, suspended by the back of its jerkin on one of the tenterhooks, as you might hang up a robe in a bedchamber. The arms were stretched out in a cruciform, each slender wrist impaled on the steel spikes. The head lolled forward on the chest. Only the edges of his wet clothes stirred in the breeze. Until I touched the hand, part of me was still insisting this must be a scarecrow, hung there to keep the birds from soiling the cloth. But the hand, though lifeless, was flesh, warm and slippery with blood. I gently lifted the head, not wanting to see what I already knew. The open eyes, wide with pain and terror, glistened in the dark. The grotesquely swollen face was wet from rain or tears. I felt the deep indentation in the skin where a rope had cut into the neck.

I cradled Myles's head against my chest, cursing man and God and most of all myself. I had thought that Sibyl had been killed because she was carrying messages for those helping Catholics to safety. But not Myles, not him too! They didn't need to do this. They didn't need to do it!

I suddenly couldn't bear to leave him hanging a moment longer. He was far beyond help, yet to leave him impaled in that obscene mockery felt like one more betrayal. I grasped one arm to ease the wrist off the savage steel hook, but the point had been thrust between the two bones. The only way to release him was to lift him up. Though he was a small lad, I was struggling to hoist the limp body with one arm and detach him with the other . . .

'There he is! Watch said he's snatched a boy! Catch him afore he does the child a mischief!'

Across the far side of the field, the gate between the houses had been opened. Men, some carrying flaming torches, were pouring in through the gap, fanning out into a long line as they advanced. They were yelling and pointing towards where I stood. I had no choice but to let Myles's body drop again. Keeping low, I darted towards the tree that marked the gap in the back fence. But before I reached it, red and orange torchlight began to fill the alley behind it and there came the thunder of pounding footsteps as men lumbered down to cut off my escape.

The watchmen were already hurrying along the top of the city wall, peering down and shouting to those below. There was only one way left for me to run, up the long field towards Temple Church. I dodged between the tenters, keeping low and trusting that in the darkness the poles would disguise my form. The two waves of red and orange light were creeping closer to each other as those approaching from the gate penetrated deeper into the field. Those behind the fence on the opposite side thrust their torches over it, sweeping them back and forth, combing the rows of racks. I headed towards the dark corner and the great bulk of the church with its leaning tower.

I did not need to look back to know when they discovered Myles's body. A roar of outrage and anger exploded in the field. They were starting to spread out now, quartering like scent-hounds, peering into the ditches and up into the branches of the trees. They had seen me standing where they had discovered the body. My form would only have been a dim outline at that distance, but it was probably enough to have given them an idea of my height and bulk. My hands and my shirt were soaked in Myles's blood. If they caught me in the field, I wouldn't live long enough to come to trial.

I found the wall that separated the churchyard from the weavers' field and crouched low beneath it, listening. If I'd been hunting a man trapped in the field, I would have ordered men to surround it on all four sides. Either they had left this side unguarded, or more likely they had not yet reached this end. I might only have minutes.

But the commotion in the field had roused those living in the cluster of houses around the church. Lights were appearing in the upper casements; doors and windows opened as men in nightshirts leaned out, craning around to see what might be afoot. Even at the risk of being seen, I couldn't remain any longer. I took a few paces back and ran at the wall, leaping up to get a handhold on the top, then heaved myself up and tumbled over, crashing on to the ground below. I thought I heard some-one shout from one of the nearby cottages. I scrambled up, and bending low, scuttled towards the church as heavy boots pounded up the lane leading to the river.

I crept round to the small side door of the church. A yew tree growing close to it gave me enough cover to pick the lock, which was as well, for it was rusty and stiff and my fingers were sticky. I was probably leaving a gory trail everywhere I went, which would be as visible as a fireship come daylight, but I hoped

I would be gone by then. I locked the door behind me and stood still in the icy silence, breathing hard.

A flickering red glow from the torches outside was just visible through some of the windows, but it was not bright enough to light the interior. I edged deeper into the church, blundering into the sharp corners of tombs and tables. The muffled shouts and cries told me the search was coming closer. They'd swept the far end of the field where poor Myles's body hung and were moving towards the church, no doubt spread across from fence to fence to flush everything in their path.

My first thought had been to make for the bell tower, where I could climb up and watch what was happening below, but they might well use those bells to sound the alarm, if they thought they had lost me. I desperately searched for another hiding place. If the weaver in the cottage had seen a figure scrambling over the wall, they would search the church thoroughly.

I stumbled against another chest-like tomb. I'd first met Myles when he was hiding in a graveyard tomb, but that had been smashed open at the side. These were sealed and one man alone couldn't hope to move the lid. I groped along the wall towards the chancel until I felt a gap and the stone steps of a narrow spiral staircase. I knew that the stairs would once have led to a rood loft above the chancel. The loft would have been removed years before, but the stone steps leading up to it, built into the wall, could not be so easily obliterated. I had to turn sideways to squeeze up them until I arrived at a small wooden door at the top. Not even a glimmer of the orange torchlight that was flickering across the windows penetrated the shaft. In complete darkness, I was still groping for a latch when the voices reached me. The men were right outside the church.

Shouts and snapped orders rang out, and then came the rattle of the great door and the grating of the key. The door crashed open, swiftly followed by the echo of many heavy boots. Even though I had climbed into what felt like the pinnacle of a spiral shell, a faint glow of the torch flames was now visible below me at the bottom of the stairs.

An officer's voice bounced off the walls. 'I want every inch of this place searched, even the rat holes – especially the rat holes! A good citizen, a man who had his wits about him, told the watch he'd spotted that felon who's on the run from Newgate, said he saw him dragging a little lad into the Racks. If those idle blockheads had shifted their arses sooner and got the word out, we might have caught the louse before he killed the boy. But I reckon they'll have to double the reward for this Daniel Lyrypine now, whether he's taken alive or dead, and I favour *dead*. You've seen what that vicious sod has done to an innocent lad. He won't come quietly and the murdering bastard has killed before. He's cornered and desperate. So, be on your guard and get him before he gets you.'

I heard the men scatter, the clang of metal on stone as they jabbed the spikes of their halberds into dark recesses and slashed at shadows with their swords. It would only be a matter of time before they searched the rood stairs. I felt again for the latch and this time I found it. If they looked up and saw the door opening high above their heads I was finished. I might be anyway if there was nothing but a drop on to hard stone waiting for me on the other side. I cautiously pulled open the door. It creaked with disuse, but it was drowned out by the noise the men were making below, clattering and banging, all the while jeering and yelling for me to give myself up.

From high above, the floor of the church appeared to be on fire as the men circled around below, sweeping the flaming torches in front of them. Their light showed me what I had dreaded; even the beams which would have supported the rood loft were gone. I was trapped. I had no means of getting down except by those stairs. I cursed my own stupidity. If I'd stayed in the churchyard there might have been a chance of slipping by them, but there was no way out now.

Two men were advancing towards the chancel. They had left that till last; even in the Protestant faith all laymen seem to have a strange reluctance to trespass into that sanctuary. I had to go back down. If they caught me up here in the open doorway, they'd only have to push and I'd be lying smashed and helpless on the stone floor below.

But as I turned, I caught sight of something on the opposite side of the church: a flat slab of stone jutting from the wall, the top of a column. I glanced down. There was its twin, just to the left of the door. No wider than a foot and a half square, it was evidently where the main beam of the rood loft had been supported.

'Anyone looked up here?' a voice called out from the bottom of the stairs.

I stepped sideways on to the slab, dragging the door shut as I did so, and found myself balancing on a ledge, staring down into the chancel below like the statue of a saint. There was nothing to hold on to except the latch of the door. Torchlight rippled far below me. The whole building seemed to be rocking, though I knew it couldn't be. I fixed my gaze on the dark cavern above me, but still the pillar beneath me seemed to be swaying.

I heard the scrape of grit on stone as a pair of boots ascended the staircase. He was mounting the steps exceedingly slowly, no doubt fearing a ruthless killer was lurking above him, out of sight, preparing to strike. If he opened the door, I would lose my only handhold. I tensed, ready to release my grip the moment he touched it.

He was on the other side of it. I could hear his breath rasping from the climb, the leather of his jerkin creaking, a metallic clang as his blade knocked against the stone.

'Stairs are clear!' he yelled. 'There's the old rood-loft door, though.'

'Leads nowhere, so he'll not be through there, will he, you beef-wit, unless he can change himself into a bat?'

'More likely a demon,' the man on the stairs muttered to himself. He cursed the tight space as he endeavoured to turn around. Then he stumbled, crashing against the door, which juddered violently, almost jolting the latch from my hand. I grabbed on again, rocking perilously, pressing my back as hard as I could against the solid wall behind.

The men had gathered almost directly below me, their blades and helmets glinting and winking in the flickering light. The smoke from their torches rose upwards, circling my feet and spiralling around my legs. My eyes were beginning to water in the stinging, acrid stench and my throat burned. I was going to cough and I couldn't even move my hand to try to suppress it, for fear that someone would glimpse the movement. I clamped my tongue between my teeth, biting hard, hoping pain would stop it, willing them to leave.

The church door was flung open and a young lad appeared, breathless and panting.

'Watch on Redcliffe Gate . . . reckon they've spotted him . . . You're to go there to help search along the wharf.'

'Aye, well we know he's not in the church. Must have crossed the graveyard, then gone straight out into Temple Street when halfwit Digby here was looking the other way.'

There was a vehement denial from one man, but the others were already plodding out. One by one the torches vanished. Then came a thundering crash as the great door was shut, plunging the church into darkness. I dared not move a muscle. It had been dark before, but after staring down into the torch-light, I now felt as though I'd been struck blind. I'd have to try to unlatch the door, push it open and judge the step across the yawning gap into the doorway. If I pushed the door too wide, I'd lose my grip on the latch. If I held on to the latch, I'd risk pulling the door closed with my weight as I stepped across, which would send me plunging into the black abyss below.

Unable to see anything, I felt as though I was pitching forward. Only the hard wall against my back convinced me I was still upright. I eased my dagger out of its sheath, gripping the latch as firmly as I could with a hand that was slick with blood and sweat, then lunged sideways, striking the dagger with all the force I could muster into the wood of the door. I was dangling in mid-air, my full weight suspended from my arms.

For what seemed like an age I hung there, knowing any sudden movement as I scrambled over the edge could wrench the dagger loose. The knife tipped, jerking downwards; my fingers were sliding down the hilt. It was now or never. I swung one foot up and wedged it in the partially opened door, then propelled myself forward. My head crashed into the stone wall and my knees collided painfully with the steps as something clattered far below me. Dazed, I rolled over. I was alive – for now. I felt for my dagger in the door, but found only the splintered hole it had made. That was what I'd heard fall below.

I groped my way down the stairs, lurching against the walls, dizzy from where my head had struck the stone. I wasted a few minutes feeling over the cold floor for my knife, but I knew I could search all night and miss it by inches. I had to get out of the city before dawn broke. Groping my way along the wall, I limped towards the small door through which I'd entered, stumbling over steps and colliding painfully with the edges of tables and tombs. Several times the lights of torches briefly glowed beyond the church windows as heavy boots lumbered by and shouts rang out. Finally, my fingers encountered warm wood instead of cold stone. I charmed the lock – that at least I could do blindfolded – then eased the door open a few inches and stood listening, closing it swiftly as I heard shouts and running feet.

When I opened it again, the churchyard was still and silent. At the far end of the field a circle of flames marked where men were laying Myles's broken body on a bier. There was every chance they'd bring his corpse back into the church to rest there until the coroner and jury were summoned in the morning. I couldn't risk going out into Temple Street, and there were rows of cottages between the graveyard and the lane behind the church.

There was only one way left to me: I would have to cross to the top of the weavers' field and make for the river on the opposite side. I crept along beneath the graveyard wall until I found a headstone close enough to it to use as a foothold. I slithered over the wall, landing in a clumsy heap beneath, and lay still, waiting for a shout of alarm, but none came.

I glanced down the rows of tenters. A solemn procession was setting off, pacing slowly towards the gate. One man led the way, his torch held high, smoke glowing red and orange trailing out behind over those following like a pennant. Behind him, four men carried the bier, which was covered by a cloak. Two men could easily have borne the weight of that body, but no doubt they all wanted to boast of their role. It would make a good tale for their drinking companions in the taverns tomorrow. I suddenly wondered if anyone yet knew the identity of the mutilated boy. The Crugges were probably asleep in bed in the Salt Cat, not even realising that Myles was missing. How would they learn of his fate?

I was in no doubt that whoever had murdered Myles and sent the guards to the Racks to catch me would also have taken Waldegrave's letter. But they could have easily taken that from a boy his size without killing him. What else had they tried to make Myles tell them? He would have held out as bravely as he could, but I had to assume his murderer now knew all Myles could tell them about Waldegrave, including that he was still alive. But for how much longer? The method of the torture and killing of Sibyl and now Myles had all the hallmarks of Robert Cecil's pursuivants. If I had been mistaken and Badger-beard was not one of FitzAlan's men, but one of Cecil's, then I had led him straight to Myles.

As soon as the solemn procession had passed through the gate leading out of the field, I ran for the fence opposite, keeping low in the shadows. There were no obvious gaps: the weavers kept the fence in good repair for fear of thieves stealing the cloth they'd left to dry. Bent double, I scuttled along the length of it until I reached the old tree, my leg muscles protesting violently at the strange gait. I was tempted to push straight through the loosened posts, but I forced myself to crouch and listen. The alley behind the fence lay in darkness, and the only voices were those drifting down from the city gate.

I barged through, breaking another post, and hurried up to where a short alley led down to the river. All of the gates and roads out of Bristol would already be guarded. The broadsides had speculated that the felon Daniel Lyrypine or Joseph Pursglove would be attempting to board a ship to take him out of England. If the sheriff's men believed that, they would concentrate their search on the two wharfs to the west, from where boats were towed down to Pill and then continued under sail downriver to the Bristol estuary. But if I could find a boat along this stretch of the Avon and row upstream, I might escape the city unnoticed.

I reached the riverbank unchallenged and risked a glance behind me. At the other end of the lane, orange lights and black shadows flickered above the cottages from the many torches moving back and forth along the wharf. Distant shrieks, like a flock of gulls, drifted towards me on the wind. I slipped between the long expanse of a ropewalk and the riverbank. The water twisted black, racing into the city. The ruby glow from the kilns of a brickworks on the opposite side burned deep within the river's heart. There were few boats moored along this stretch, and they were on the opposite bank. I crept further along, acutely aware that my search was taking me ever closer to the round tower on the city wall that guarded the river, cutting off the path along the riverbank.

Then, just beyond a small clump of scrub willow, I saw the glow of a small fire and smelled woodsmoke mingled with frying fish. A man squatted with his back to me, digging the point of his knife into a pan and deftly transferring the hot morsels to his mouth. His small boat lay moored next to him on the bank. A square of sailcloth, fixed like a tent over the prow, marked where he was intending to sleep. Several wicker cages in the back of the small craft suggested that he'd brought live poultry or wild birds from the country to sell at the city market in the morning. I couldn't risk asking him to carry me out of Bristol at this hour, whatever price I offered. Even if he hadn't heard they were searching for a dangerous murderer, he was bound to be suspicious of anyone trying to steal out of the city in the middle of the night.

My knife was gone. I couldn't even threaten him. I glanced up at the menacing tower of the city wall. In the light of the brazier and torches on the top, I could see three, maybe four, men, but they were all peering out in the direction of the Red-cliffe wharf. I crept forward. The man was picking every last scrap of flesh from the bones of the fish, determined not to miss a single shred. My belt was round his neck before he could even cry out. As I pulled backwards, he did what everyone instinctively does, attempted to get his fingers between the leather and his throat, leaning forward, resisting the pull, which only made my task easier. He tried to call out, but only managed a feeble croaking noise. He was starting to weaken, his body limp and heavy, and his hands fell away, but before he lost consciousness, I suddenly released the belt and kneed him in the back. His own momentum did the rest and he plunged headfirst into the river with a great splash. He gave a faint cry, struggling frantically, and finally managed to grab the gunwale of the boat, but I'd already cast off and scrambled aboard. I prised his fingers loose and heard another cry as the current seized him, sweeping him down towards the bridge with its many archways. I hoped he'd be able to catch hold of something and clamber out. He did not deserve to die.

I positioned the oars and shoved the skiff away from the bank. I was dimly aware of shouts from the tower. The splash must have drawn the attention of the guards and a boat moving on the river at this hour was bound to arouse suspicion. I had my back to them as I rowed towards the city wall, and I kept my head low. A waterman who spends his life on the river is accustomed to rowing against the current, but I had not had occasion to row a boat for several years and while the art of it returned easily enough, the strength did not. For every three strokes that took me forward, the current pushed me back two. It seemed to take an age to draw close to the city wall and tower, and all the while the shouts and orders to stop and pull on to the bank were growing more distinct and threatening.

Watchmen had raced down from the top of the tower and were running towards the water's edge. One held a torch that blazed out behind him in the darkness. Flames glinted on the steel blades of halberds and metal boathooks. As they neared the river, one of the men began whirling a spiked grappling hook on the end of a rope. He let it fly. It arced through the air towards the boat, and I dug in with one of the oars, causing the skiff to jerk sideways. It rocked violently, almost capsizing, but the hook splashed harmlessly into the river, just inches from the bow.

I reached the tower wall where it jutted out into the river, blocking the path. The watchmen in the tower above were leaning over, their orders and yells for me to stop redoubling as I rowed beneath them. I kept the skiff as close to the wall of the tower as I dared, so that I would be screened from their sight, at least for as long as it took to row past. Though my arms were beginning to protest, I couldn't afford to rest even for a single stroke, knowing I'd be swept straight back downriver towards those waiting hooks and grappling irons. I bent to the oars with all my remaining strength and the skiff slid forward to the far side of the tower. I was out of the city. I knew that beyond the wall, cottages gradually gave way to fields and pasture, and with luck, forests, where I could lie low for a few hours. The tension in my chest eased just a little.

There was a loud retort and flash of light from the tower. Something flew past my head and hit the water. Even as I realised it was a musket ball, a second cannoned towards me, smashing through the side of the skiff. A splinter of exploding wood pierced the back of my hand with the force of an arrow. Hot blood ran down my wrist as I grabbed at the oar I had dropped. I lost precious moments getting back into the stroke, pulling with all the strength I could muster on the oars, trying to keep my grip on them, though my fingers on the injured hand were numb. There were two more flashes up in the tower as the red-hot balls shot into the skiff, one slamming into the wicker cages. A duck shrieked, and all of them began to flap and hiss. If all the men up there had fired, they would need time to reload. A few more strokes and I'd be out of range. But I was losing my hold on the oar. I risked letting go long enough to wipe the blood off, and pulled again. Another crack echoed from the tower. The musket ball hit the water a foot behind the skiff, sending up a plume of spray. Either he was not a good marksman, or I was pulling out of range.

I kept going, though my right stroke was rapidly becoming much weaker than my left and I had to ease up on that side too, otherwise I would start going round in circles. Another shot rang out, so close I felt the whistle of the air against my ear. The current was dragging me back towards the tower, and I suddenly realised it wasn't just my weakened rowing that was slowing me: the whole skiff was become harder to move. Water was streaming in. One of the earlier shots had punched a hole just on the waterline. Enough water had trickled through it to drag the craft deeper and now it was gushing through the hole.

I dared not stop rowing to bail, even if I could have found something to use. The ducks and geese were frantic, trying to escape. I dropped the oars and plunged on to my stomach in the water at the bottom of the skiff. Wriggling forward, I flipped open as many of the cages as I could reach. The birds scrambled out, in a frenzy of flapping wings and outstretched beaks, struggling out of the sinking boat. Under cover of the commotion, I took a gulp of air and slithered into the river. As the icy black water closed over my head, the current seized me and sent me spinning back towards the tower.

Chapter Twenty

I STAYED UNDERWATER until my lungs were on fire, all the time trying to kick out upstream and towards the far bank. My head felt as if it would explode and I was forced to the surface to gulp air. The lanterns and torches in the tower gleamed gold and red on the black water. Downriver I glimpsed what I thought must be the prow of the skiff jutting up. It surfaced briefly in the pool of light before the river swallowed it. Ducks, geese, bobbing cages and the assorted possessions of the unfortunate waterman were sailing past the watchmen. Flashes exploded in the darkness, the bangs and cracks echoing off the walls as the guards fired into the flotsam, obviously thinking I was among it, sending the birds squawking and flapping over the surface. Taking another great gulp of air, I plunged my face into the water. Gleaming wet skin would be too easily seen if the light from the torches struck it.

It took several more attempts before I was finally able to grasp the thin branches of a leafless willow dipping low to the river and drag myself out of the current. I clung to the branches in the freezing water. I could see clearly the lights of the tower behind me and the glow from the brick kilns on the other side, but I had managed to emerge upstream of both, and guessed that I was now on the edge of what they called the King's marshes. For one absurd moment, I found myself wondering whether King James even knew these marshes existed.

The icy breeze, though not strong, sliced like a sharpened knife across my wet hair and skin. But now that I had stopped swimming, I was aware not only of the throbbing and numbness of my hand, but of muscles that suddenly seemed drained of every last drop of strength. Darkness would hide me as long as it lasted, but dawn must break and then, when they did not find my corpse downstream, the hunt would start in earnest. Grabbing at any handhold I could, I edged along the bank, searching for a way up. Several times, I grabbed at some rotting vegetation, only for it to come away as I heaved on it. Finally, I found the roots of a tree. If it was dead, I'd probably bring the whole mass sliding into the river on top of me, but I was too chilled and weak to search further. I heaved on it and after several attempts, finally managed to crawl out, impaling the shaft of wood from the boat even deeper into my hand in the process.

The thaw had left wide pools of gleaming black water across the marsh and great expanses of mud soft enough to sink into – *sleech*, young Myles had called it. Guilt and grief surged up inside me again as his voice echoed in my head. I hoped the boy would be treated better in death than he had been in life.

I stumbled, slid and squelched across a short stretch of marsh to reach a narrow, raised track that ran parallel to the river. It was muddy and the winter's ice and meltwater had left gaping holes in it, but for the most part it was firmer than the marsh and I could make swifter progress. I was shivering violently now in the cold wind, my boots sodden and my clothes clinging to me. I had to find shelter soon or I'd succumb to cold and exhaustion, but there seemed no chance of that until I was clear of the marsh. I could see little around me except the paler stones of the track, but the darkness was not silent. Through the roar of the river came the rustling of old reeds and the shrieks and cries of alarm as somewhere the unseen creatures of the night fought for survival. I searched for lights that might reveal a cottage, looking for the faint smoky glow from the top of a chimney or the pinpoint of a fire warming a traveller or waterman, but if there was anyone living out on the marshes, the candles would have long been extinguished at this hour and fires banked down for the night.

The raw wind had numbed my reasoning along with my bones, so it took longer than it should have done to become aware that there were new sounds in the darkness – the ring of iron on stones, the squelch of hooves in mud, the creak of leather. Two mounted men were picking their way along the narrow track behind me. They were some way off and I could barely distinguish their outlines, even against the distant glow from the city wall. Darkness would cover me for a few more yards, but not once they got closer, and I couldn't outrun them. There was no time to look for any kind of hiding place. I slithered down the side of the path and found myself knee-deep in a marsh pool. I dropped to my knees, pressing hard against the bank of the track. My face down, my hands beneath the mud, I waited.

'Waste of time searching this stretch. He's lost his boat. Where's he going to get another? And even if he did, he'd not get further upriver than the first weir. So, what'd be the point?'

'But maybe he don't know that, if he don't come from here. So, if he's got himself another skiff, the sergeant reckons he'll be forced to ditch it at the weir or let it float back down. Either way, if we find a boat adrift, we'll know which way he's headed.'

'I can tell thee now, he's headed out to sea, that's what. That rump-fed coxcomb of a sergeant needs to leave the thinking to men who was born and bred in these parts, not march in here thinking he can . . .' Their voices become indistinct as they urged the horses on down the track.

I dragged myself upright, so cold now I couldn't even feel how far the marsh-pool water came up my legs. I knew that I daren't risk scrambling straight back up on to the track. Now that I was behind them, my outline would be visible against the lights of the city if they glanced back. But the man-at-arms was right: I had no idea how far upriver the weir was that they were making for, and if I waited until they were far enough away to risk the track again, I could very well run straight into them as they returned. *Think! Think! You can't stay here!* But I couldn't think. My mind was as frozen as my body.

I tried to move, but my feet had sunk into the mud and were held fast. I sank back on to my knees in a vain attempt to spread my weight, with some vague idea that I could swim or pull myself forward. But I couldn't think how to manage it, what to do with my arms. The water, which had been so cold, now felt almost warm. I could stay here, sleep . . . if I could just sleep, just for an hour or two . . . I could work it out . . .

Someone seized me by the shoulder and jerked me upright. Before I'd even consciously registered the grip, I struck out with my left hand, while reaching for my dagger with the other. The end of the sliver of wood embedded in my hand caught in my cloak, making me gasp in pain, even as my fogged brain remembered I had no dagger.

'Easy, lad! I'm not the one you has to fear, I reckon.'

I tried to turn to face the man, but I was trapped like a sparrow in birdlime.

The man extended a hand. 'Here, I'll pull, you heave. Get one leg free and up on that tussock. I reckon t'other will follow.'

It seemed to take an age before I was finally out of the sucking mud, falling rather than climbing on to the tussock of grass.

'You could have sunk up to your ears in that.' I could see little of my rescuer except that he appeared to be a man of some bulk. 'Looking for you, were they? Saw you take a dive off that track to avoid them.'

'I slipped . . . in the dark.'

'If you say so, but I reckon they'll be headed back this way soon.'

I tried to move and almost fell back into the pool.

He grabbed my arm. 'I've seen new-born lambs steadier on their feet than you. Come on, you'd best come home with me.' He gave a low grunt as I tried to pull away. 'I don't reckon you've much choice. Else you'll either have to let the sheriff's men take you or drown on the marshes. You're betwixt the Devil and damnation, lad.'

I let him heave my arm over his neck and we set off. He

seemed to be able to find a path between the sheets of water where there was none, twisting and turning between the mounds of rotting reeds, the expanses of stinking mud and the tangle of rivulets that oozed from them. I eventually realised that his progress was helped by what seemed to be a framework of wood strapped to the soles of his boots, like those that farmers fasten to horses' hooves.

I could scarcely put one leg in front of the other, and only his arm held me upright. I had no sense of how long we had been walking in the darkness. My eyes closed. I was aware of nothing except the numbing cold.

'SOON HAVE YOU warm, lad.'

I was sitting on a high-backed chair inside a small wooden cabin. A figure bent over a peat fire in the stone hearth, stirring it to life. There was no other light, but by its glow, I could make out a table and a second chair drawn close to the hearth. A narrow plank bed was wedged hard against one wall, from which hung what seemed to be an assortment of tools, but they were too much in the shadows to distinguish. I could see little of my rescuer either. He had pulled off a heavy sheepskin coat, which had made him appear bulkier than he was. His hair and beard were close-cropped, but ragged, as though he had hacked away at them himself with a knife. But in the firelight, it was hard to make out his age, though his swollen knuckles as he gripped the poker and his voice suggested a man in his fifties or sixties.

'Best strip off those clothes, before you catch your death.'

I made a poor fist of trying to unfasten my sodden cloak, which was clinging to me like second skin. He helped me off with it from behind, reluctant to show his face or see mine. I let him take off my jerkin too, and hang that near the fire to steam. The river had washed out much of Myles's blood and the marsh mud had disguised the rest. I refused to allow him to remove my breeches, shirt or boots. What money and possessions I still had were in pockets sewn inside my shirt and if I had to run again, I had no intention of leaving those, or my boots, behind. He didn't argue, but tossed me a blanket smelling of tar and marsh mud.

He turned his attention to a small iron cooking pot which he hung over the fire, stirring it until it began to steam. He ladled some of the contents into a beaker and thrust it at me, retreating to the shadows with his own measure. It was a broth, the kind that country folk never completely finish, simply adding whatever they find each day, and stewing the whole mess up again, fish and fowl, herbs and roots. And it was all the better for it. I drank it gratefully, though even that did not warm me. The blood in my veins had turned to ice.

'That hand of yours will want seeing to.'

I could see only the glitter of his eyes in the red light of the peat fire. I glanced down. The pain had been numbed by the cold water, but now in the heat I was aware of the throbbing. A jagged shaft of wood about half an inch wide had been driven through the back of my hand by the musket shot and part of it was now sticking out of the palm. Each time I tried to flex the hand, blood trickled out. I couldn't feel two of my fingers.

My rescuer heaved himself up, replacing my beaker and his own back on the shelf, unwashed. He peered over my shoulder at my hand.

'That's a splinter and a half, that is. Be beyond the power of even a fox-tongue poultice to draw that out.'

'I'll have to pull it out.' I tried to grasp the end, but my fingers were clumsy and I couldn't get a firm enough grip.

'Wait!' The man laid a hand on my shoulder. 'Snap it off and you'll be in a worse fix.'

He crossed to the back wall and the row of tools and snares hanging there, then returned with a pair of pincers, the kind carpenters use to pull out nails. He dragged my arm across a stool, wedging his knee down hard on my wrist and clamping the pincers around the end of the shaft of wood, and pulled smoothly, but agonisingly slowly.

I clamped my jaw hard tight, feeling the beads of sweat popping out on my forehead, then hot blood was gushing down my fingers and splashing on to the beaten earth floor. He bound my hand tightly in some old rags, then sat back, watching my face.

'That feels better out than in, I'll wager.'

'I have much to thank you for, brother. May I know the name of my rescuer?'

'*Brother* will serve us both well in these times. And I'll not ask yours, nor what those men wanted of you. A man who doesn't know the truth can't be made a liar by denying it.' He rose and pulled his sheepskin coat on. 'You'll be needing to snatch what rest you can in the dregs of this here night.' He jerked his head towards the bed. 'There's enough stew in that pot for you to have another bite before you leave, but you'd best slip off just as soon as there's light enough to tell a bush from a barrel. They'll likely have men combing these marshes soon after sun-up. When you leave the hut, look for the peeled withies stuck in the ground about a hand high. Stay close and keep them always on your right; they'll lead you off the marsh to a stand of trees on higher ground, and from there you'll see the road.'

He lifted a heavy leather curtain that hung across the door, ensuring it was back in place before he opened the door. Then I heard it close behind him. It seemed my rescuer had reason enough to be cautious, even before he'd come to my aid.

I staggered across to the bed: a thin straw-filled mattress laid upon planks, but covered by a sheepskin which softened and warmed it, with a couple of threadbare blankets for the sleeper to wrap himself in. I knew before I lay down that the sheepskin was full of fleas, but I no longer cared. I lay in the red-tinged darkness, shivering, knowing he was right: I had to snatch what sleep I could in what little night remained. But I could not. My hand was throbbing and swelling so swiftly that I could no longer bend any of the fingers. It was a bitter irony that all those weeks I'd lain fettered in Newgate gaol, my only preoccupation had been the thought of losing my hands on the executioner's block. I'd actually found myself praying then that they'd hang me instead, for even that end seemed preferable to the lifetime of misery and humiliation which stretched ahead of me. FitzAlan's intervention had spared me that fate, but if this wound festered . . . .

'HE'S BURNING UP!'

'Aye, it's why I fetched you. Poison from his hand, I reckon, but he can't stay here. They'll find him for sure.'

I was listening to the voices, but they were distant, distorted, as though my head was beneath water. Their words made no sense. I didn't know who they were talking about. I wasn't burning. I was cold, so cold. Faces swarmed at me. I remembered them from long ago, but they wouldn't keep still long enough for me to recognise them. They kept changing, twisting and re-forming into different shapes like blood dripping into a lake.

'You'll have to let me dress the wound before he's moved. It must be widened to stop the flesh healing too quickly and closing over. It needs to mend from the inside outwards. And it will have to be dressed with ointment to draw a laudable pus and keep it green, else he will lose the hand, and more than likely his life too.'

'There's no time!'

'Then why did you drag me from my bed? You should dump him in one of the marsh pools – at least he'll die quickly. You want a physician, so healing takes time, or are you like those other fools? You think because I'm a Jew I just wave my hand, recite a few magic words and he leaps up and walks out of here?'

I was burning. The blanket was suffocating me. I couldn't get it off. It was sticking to my skin, twisting itself round my legs and arms, heavy as chains. I fought it, tearing it away, but it wouldn't let go of me.

'Hold him down. I can't cut the flesh while he's thrashing about.'

They were stretching my arm over the executioner's block.

The crowd was roaring in my ears. The blade flashed down to separate flesh from bone, muscle from sinew.

'Keep him still or I'll have his hand off!'

Hot blood running down my arm. The child's blood, soaking into my shirt as I lift him. His blood scalds my skin. But his skin's cold, so cold. He is silent. I can't feel his breath, but he must still live if he bleeds. He must live! Have to wrap up him, keep him warm. Have to get him away from here, but there are others, so many. I'm walking on them. Hands reach up, clutching at my legs like brambles. All around me the cries, screams, moans, sobs and dying whimpers pound my ears. 'A mháthair! A mháthair!' I can't help them. There are too many of them. I have to save this one, don't you see? This one. He bleeds, so he must be alive. Where are you taking him?

'Where are you taking him? No, don't tell me – it's better I do not know. There, that is all I can do for him. You'll have to change the tent in the wound each time it swells with suppurate. I'll leave you some bundles of flax. When you pull the old one out, push the next into the flesh as tightly as you can, so that the foul air can't reach it.'

'Help me lift him on to the sledge. The fever's boiling his brains. We'll have to rope him down tight all round to keep him still. I'll cover him with sedges and drag him. They'll not risk riding their horses into the mire to search the sledge leastways, I pray they don't.'

'I shall be praying too. Maybe *HaShem* will have ears for one of us, who knows? But this is the end of what I will do for this man. Do not send for me again. Every day of my life, I give thanks for an old priest who forged the papers to help my brother and his family escape from the Inquisition, but the debt has been paid many times over, you understand? Tell them this. Tell Spero.'

'The debt is not paid. Why do you think I am hiding him? Because once you are in debt to Spero, it can never be repaid. You'd best remember that.'

Chapter Twenty-one

I WOKE WITH A START as something dropped on to my face. It wriggled over my cheek and down my neck. I raised my hand to dash it away, suddenly aware that my palm was covered and bound. I couldn't clench my fist, and the pain of trying made me desist. I flicked away the creature with my other hand – a worm, by the feel of it. I could see nothing, not even a glimmer of light. Was it day or night? I'd woken before into this, at least I thought I had. Other times, I'd thought I was back in the Hole in Newgate gaol. Was I now a prisoner in another dungeon?

I clawed at my chest with my unbound hand, then suddenly my arms, legs, every inch of skin was itching madly, covered in small lumps. I must have felt it before, I knew I had, but it had seemed a long way off from me, not my body. Now the fleas were driving me mad.

I tried to heave myself upright. I wasn't chained, but I couldn't stand; there was only enough space above me to sit up. I couldn't feel anything on either side of me, just empty space. I could only touch the wet, cold earth beneath me, and the wooden boards just above my head.

Somewhere a door closed with a loud echo and heavy boots grated on dirt. I tensed, reaching for my knife, only then recalling that it was lost and suddenly remembering *where* I had lost it. The footsteps stopped and a blade of fire cut through the darkness above me. It widened, and I found myself momentarily turning away from the blinding light. Someone blocked it, peering down at me, but he was just a blur. He knelt awkwardly and dangled a lantern over me, sweeping the light across my face as I covered my eyes.

'Now that's a sight I feared I'd not see. You sitting up.' The lantern vanished and he extended a meaty arm into the hole. 'Here, give me your hand and let's have you out of there.'

Even with my rescuer's help, it took a while before I could haul myself out through the trapdoor in the floor. I was unable to put any weight on my injured hand to lever myself up, and as soon as I stood up in the hole, it felt as though my bones had been replaced with marsh mud.

The man I knew only as *brother* helped me to sit on a plank laid over two trestles. He set a leather bottle and some chunks of smoked eel next to me. I was in a barn. A small cart and a sledge stacked with peats stood by the wide door and a few farm tools dangled from the walls.

The floor of the barn was beaten earth. The open trapdoor revealed that the small hole excavated beneath had been re-inforced with wooden planks, but when the hatch was in place, and straw had been kicked back over it, it would be hard to spot.

I greedily gulped sour ale from the bottle. I had a raging thirst, which even a barrelful of beer wouldn't quench. I shook my head at the eel – that would only make it worse.

'Let's take a look at that hand of yours, then.'

'How long have I been down there?'

He shrugged as he unbound the wound. 'Three nights, maybe four. I don't bother to keep count of the days. Mostly by myself out on the marshes fishing and fowling, and the sun comes up and goes down same as it's always done. Makes no difference to me what day of the week it is, nor month of the year, not since my wife and young uns got took by the flood.'

I winced as he plucked at the wad of flax stuffed deep into a long wound in the back of my hand. The gash was straighter and longer than I had remembered. The physician must have opened it with a knife. My rescuer sniffed at the flax, then thrust the yellow-stained bundle under my nose. 'Stank worse than rotting fish guts before, but I reckon that's clean enough now.'

He was right: the wound was not suppurating and the edges of the cut, though tender, were not inflamed.

'The Jew has some concoction of his own, but I reckon this does well enough. My old ma's old recipe. Everyone on the marshes used to swear by Ma's ointment.'

He handed me a small earthenware jar. It smelled foul, but then every ointment I'd ever encountered did. Most apothecaries seemed to the follow the principle that the worse it stank, the more powerful its effect. 'What's in it?'

For the first time I heard the man chuckle, a deep belly-laugh. He tapped the side of his nose. 'My ma used to say every piss-prophet in Bristol would pay a fortune for the recipe, but she'd not sell. Reckoned the fairy folk gave it to her and she'd be struck blind and lame if she ever told the secret.'

He was suddenly grave again. 'Now that your fever has broke, you'd best be on your way. I'll guide you as far as the Bath road, but you'll have to make shift for yourself from there. They'll have watchers posted, so you'll have to come up with a good tale.' He studied me critically. 'Those clothes of yours look like you dragged them off a scarecrow. But I've none better to give you, so I reckon the best plan is to make you look worse. Bandage that jaw and neck of yours to start with. That noose-mark round your throat makes you stand out and you don't want to be putting any ideas about gallows in their heads. And we'll swaddle your foot, to draw attention from your hand. You can use this here crutch I made. It's rough, but they'll expect a beggar to have none better.'

'I'm grateful, brother. I owe you my life. But all the same, I'm curious to know why you'd take such risks to help a stranger. When I was sick, I remember you saying something to the physician about a debt.'

'Reckon you must have dreamed that. You were vlothering all sorts when the fever was on you.' He wasn't looking at me, busying himself with rubbing dirt from the floor into some already filthy rags.

'The debt you owe to *Spero*,' I persisted. 'The physician spoke his name.'

Just for a moment he seemed to freeze, but in the flickering yellow lantern light it was hard to be sure, much less read his expression.

He shook his head. 'Like I say, fever boils men's wits. One time you were thrashing around 'cause you thought that hole was full of snakes. Had to tie you down and put a gag in your mouth in case anyone passed this way and heard you.'

'But you still haven't told me why you've taken such risks to hide me. Is it anything to do with this?'

I fumbled in the pocket sewn inside my shirt and dug out the little iron disc I'd stolen from Battle, embossed with the sign of the wyvern. I passed it to him. He stared at it, but he did not hold it up to the light to study it. I was sure it was already familiar to him. For a long time he said nothing, then handed it back.

'I'd help anyone the sheriff's men were hunting, like I'd help a wounded dog. But when you passed out cold in the hut, I did a bit of searching. Not to steal, mind.' He swiftly raised his hand in denial. 'But you might have been a thief yourself, carrying the crown jewels or like, and I'd no wish to be hanged alongside you. Saw that.' He nodded to the disc of metal. 'Knew then you must be one of them, or leastways working for them. Maybe a messenger.'

I had to choose my next question carefully. 'So, you also work for them . . . for the faith, brother?'

He shook his head. 'I work for no man, nor no faith neither. I've had enough trouble come knocking unbidden to my door in my life. That's why I took to working out here alone on the marshes.'

'I don't blame you,' I told him. I took the filthy bandages he handed me and began to wrap my neck and head, my gestures made clumsy by my stiff hand. 'I heard the physician mention a forger, a priest . . . I knew one such in Bristol; they called him the Yena.'

'Did you now?' He glanced at me sideways beneath his bushy brows. 'Find all manner of men in the city – forgers, smugglers, thieves. Like I say, I keep to the marshes and my own company. Stay out of the city, safer that way.'

'But you recognised the sign when you found it on me. Spero's sign. I hope he hasn't brought misfortunate to your door.'

He was silent for a moment. 'There's always those who need to find their way in and out of that city without the guards knowing. Always have been, always will be, I reckon. I see things on the river. I see figures crossing the marsh. But after the flood, when I first took to living out here alone, a man come to see me, and I was warned. Warned that sometimes I should turn my back, stare into the fire and remember what crosses behind me is only shadows, nothing but shadows.

'He told me which night to turn my back. But I reckon it was a test to see if I'd let slip anything, 'cause they didn't move anyone out on that night. They were watching to see if the King's men came a-searching, and I reckon if they'd got even a sniff of a guard in these parts, I'd have found myself lying at the bottom of one of those marsh pools, whether or not I'd opened my mouth.'

He grimaced. 'And at first, they don't ask much of you, except that you look the other way. They paid me well enough and said they'd make sure no harm came to me. Later they told me how to send word if I ever found a man injured or in trouble. See, that's how they work. They suck you down into the sleech and you sink deeper into it, little by little, till you can't pull yourself out, and you realise you're up to your neck in it. You can't give them away without hanging yourself too. Is that how it was for you?'

I nodded.

'Still,' he shrugged, 'if they succeed, I reckon England will be a better place for all of us, when the wyvern's waving over us, instead of those mangy lions. The lion was never an English beast.'

'You think we'll have much longer to wait?' I asked casually.

'Reckoning it's starting, don't you?' he said.

'So, you've heard that too, have you?'

He edged closer. 'When river and marshes froze solid, before Christmastide, there was three men who left the city after dark. Managed to find a way out past the guards on the gates. Don't know how, but any man who does that is anxious not to be questioned. They took shelter in my fowling hut where I first took you. I came back to find them in there, like someone had tipped them the wink. One of the three was an old man, suffering badly in that cold. I reckon the way they must have got out hadn't been easy and he needed to rest. They were to be met by a gee-hoe just before dawn, maybe hide beneath the load the driver was carrying, but they needed to get the old man warm and feed him before setting off. They paid me to leave them to it, look the other way. But I heard enough to know they were making for London. One of them said every man needed to take up his position and be ready, because the Serpent was coiling and it was ready to strike.'

Chapter Twenty-two

THE PALACE OF PLACENTIA, GREENWICH, LONDON

'WAIT HERE AND don't move. When His Majesty enters, you kneel and keep your head bowed. Do not rise till he gives you leave. Do not speak unless he first asks you a question, and never turn your back to the King.'

The apothecary nodded, twisting his hat nervously round and round in hands that were already slick with sweat. The small antechamber was as cold as a crypt, but even so his shirt, the best one he possessed, was clinging damply to his back. He was a neat, thin man, barely in his forties, though his hair was already more grey than brown. The constant busy little motions of his hands and the manner he had of nibbling rapidly at his food, always anxious to be done and back at work, had caused his apprentice to dub him *the squirrel*, out of his hearing, of course.

His wife, Susanna, had done her best with his clothes, brushing his brown ankle-length gown, normally reserved for his guild dinners, with a linen cloth and trying to freshen his whitest ruff with hot irons. But there had not been time to summon a barber to trim his hair or beard. While Peter Frilleck had been hurriedly changing out of his workaday jerkin and doublet, the messenger who had brought the summons to his door had been waiting impatiently in their tiny parlour, ready to rush him into the tilt boat which would take them downriver to Greenwich.

The summons had conveyed nothing about why Frilleck had been ordered to the palace, and if the messenger knew, he refused to say. But his hand had rested pointedly on his sword hilt, making it plain that this was not an invitation Master Frilleck could decline, and he had sternly warned Susanna that no one was to be told where her husband had gone, not even the apprentice who was minding the shop. Master Frilleck would be returning the same evening. That, the messenger had curtly informed her, was all she needed to know, and his tone suggested she should consider herself fortunate to be told that much.

The tilt boat had been large enough only for two or three passengers, but it boasted the royal crest painted on its stern and bow, and a canopy which was open in front but closed at the back and sides to shield the occupants not only from wind and rain, but also from the curious eyes of the other river traffic. The apothecary might almost have luxuriated in the plump cushions and fur wrap to put across his knees, had he not glimpsed the bleak walls of the Tower of London looming over the little boat, and the blackened heads of traitors gazing sightless from the great bridge, reminding him of the fate that awaited those who fell foul of the law.

The antechamber in which he now found himself abandoned did nothing to allay his fears. It was narrow and dark, the wooden shutters on the casements closed and locked. Candles burned in sconces on either side of the room, but there was not much to see except a few worn and faded tapestries on the walls, depicting scenes from some ancient Greek or Roman legend in which terrified crowds were being massacred. The only furniture was a single chair and table, on which stood a globe of the world. The room smelled as damp and musty as a cellar, or a prison cell.

Peter Frilleck's brain began once more to rake through each and every possibility that might conceivably have brought him to this point. Had he inadvertently sold physic to a foreign spy? He had sold his ointments and distillations to foreigners; of course he had, there were many in a port such as London. How could he have known if one of them was an enemy agent? Maybe someone had died from drinking a syrup he had made, or one of his neighbours had accused him of blasphemy or sedition? Might a rival apothecary have been whispering that he'd stolen corpses from graveyards to make his *mummy*?

No, he was being foolish, letting his fears get the better of him. You weren't brought to a royal palace if you were accused of a crime; you'd be summoned to appear before the magistrates or thrown into Newgate gaol. Susanna was right, he was about to be rewarded for his skills; that must be it. He had made a physic for someone the King favoured and it had cured them. The King had brought him here to thank him, maybe even more, perhaps to offer him a post in his own household.

Frilleck tucked his crumpled cloth hat into his belt, knelt down, and practised getting up, trying to rise gracefully but almost falling flat on his face, for he'd knelt on the folds of his gown. He wished now he hadn't let his wife persuade him to wear it; he was much more at ease with the jerkin and breeches he wore most days. He tried again and, as he finally lumbered to his feet, he noticed for the first time that there were two doors into the chamber, one of which was behind him. *Never turn your back to the King.* Suppose His Majesty came in through that door and he was facing the wrong way?

Fear surged up in him again and he glanced round for something with which to distract himself. The sword-wielding men in the tapestries only made him more nervous, so he forced himself to stare at the globe on the table, its lands floating in vast seas through which an assortment of fish, leviathans and sea serpents swam among ships in full sail. That, at least, offered no threat. Frilleck moved closer, spinning the globe on its stand, slowly at first, then faster and faster, chuckling as the movement made the sea serpents appear to be thrashing as though they'd come to life.

'It amuses you, does it, to have the world in your hand, Master Frilleck?'

The apothecary spun round and only just managed to catch the globe before it crashed down on to the wooden boards, snagged by the sleeve of his gown. A man was ducking into the chamber, not from one of the two entrances the apothecary had seen, but from a door concealed behind one of the tapestries, which fell back into place as he limped forward.

Frilleck had only glimpsed the King once in a procession and he'd been so far away that he would not have been able to distinguish James from his own brother in this gloom. He knew the King had weak legs, though, and seeing a man leaning on a stick, the apothecary took no chances and dropped hastily to his knees, forgetting, until it was too late, to ensure he had not trapped his gown beneath him.

The King limped past him and sank down in the only chair, his sword sheath clanging against the wood. Frilleck at least held on to his wits long enough to realise that although he had been asked a question, it was not the kind to which His Majesty expected an answer, even if he had been able to think of one. The apothecary was left kneeling side-on to the King's chair, totally uncertain as to whether he should attempt to swivel around to face James. He realised that it might appear that he was trying to rise without permission, so he stayed where he was, keeping his head bowed so low, his beard was crushed against the stiff ruff.

'Searching for woodworm on those boards, are ye? On your feet, man. You canna see what I want to show you from there.'

Frilleck was obliged to clutch the leg of the table in order to rise and free his gown. He turned and faced the chair. He tried to study the man seated there, while keeping his head respectfully bowed. The King was clad in a russet and green doublet and hose. His hair was cropped much shorter than most men's in London. The position of the candle heightened the puffy bulges beneath the royal eyes, but even allowing for the unflattering light, the King looked hag-ridden, though Frilleck would not have dared to whisper as much to anyone, not even Susanna.

Kings are accustomed to be stared at and for a long while James said nothing, then suddenly broke the heavy silence. 'I am told ye are an apothecary and member of the guild.'

'Ye . . . s.' Frilleck's mouth was as dry as week-old bread and the word came out as a croak. He tried again. 'I . . . I am, if it please you, Your Majesty.'

'I'll wait until I see the results before I tell you if I'm pleased or nay.'

'Results?' The apothecary clapped his fingers to his lips, too late to stop the question escaping, but James showed no obvious sign of anger.

'You have a fair reputation for preparing the recipes the physicians give you accurately and, unlike some, I'm told you don't start changing them to suit your fancy or adulterating your physic with cheaper ingredients. They tell me you are discreet, too, keep your customers' business to yourself.'

Up to the word *discreet*, Frilleck had found himself swelling a little with pride, daring to hope that Susanna had been right all along. But in his experience, when a man used the word *discreet*, it meant he was seeking a remedy for some ailment he was too embarrassed to have known abroad. Mostly that was piles or a swelling or shrivelling of a man's cods, or a cock that stubbornly refused to rise, or even – Frilleck swallowed hard at the thought – a dose of the Great Pox. But surely the King had his own physicians who would prescribe for such things and have the remedy prepared by the royal apothecary?

James reached inside his doublet and drew out a piece of paper folded several times. He thrust it out towards Frilleck.

'Take it, man, I'm not holding this to swat flies.'

The apothecary hastily stepped forward and took it, bowing several times in such rapid succession he looked like a bird searching for worms. Frilleck clutched the paper, not understanding what was expected of him.

'Read it, then!' James snapped. 'Unless you've eyes in your fingers. Take it to the light, if it helps ye see better.'

The apothecary unfolded it, conscious of his sweaty palms. He stepped closer to one of the pairs of candles burning on the walls and angled the paper to catch the light. It was a list of some thirty or forty ingredients with quantities and other instructions added beside some of them: 'bruised . . . seethed in wine . . . distilled.'

'The ingredients are all familiar to you?' the King demanded.

The apothecary ran his finger down the list. *Saffron, ginger, cinnamon, honey.* Half the goodwives in London had those in their kitchens. *Opium, myrrh, beaver castoreum* and *mummy from a hanged male corpse, the felon to be no more than five and twenty years of age* – these he stocked in his shop and he could picture exactly where the jars were on the shelves. *Bistort, sea squills* and the *roasted copper* he did not as a rule keep in his stores, but he knew merchants who could supply such things. *Viper flesh – fresh*; he had viper skins, of course, powdered dried flesh, but not the fresh meat. That would be more difficult at this season of the year, but he was sure that the lad who fetched in herbs and other things from the country could oblige.

'I know all of these, Your Majesty. Some I have and some I can obtain, but there are a great many things on this list. I must know what each of the preparations are that I am to make from all of these and what conditions they are to be used to treat. If I could speak to the physician who examined the patient . . .'

'Your King is both physician and patient. You are to make me a theriac, an antidote to all forms of poison. I have studied the writings of the Greeks and Roman medici and the physicians of Salerno, and I have devised my own theriac from the ingredients that they employed, adding some ingredients of my own invention which I have discovered in other works on poisons.'

Frilleck gaped at him. 'But, Your Majesty, it is forbidden for anyone in London to make a theriac except for the one apothecary who has been appointed to prepare it by the Guild of Grocers. I would never be permitted to work as apothecary again if I broke that rule, and worse, I'd likely be imprisoned. Flogged!

Branded! My shop . . . my house . . . I would lose everything. Your Majesty, I assure you theriac bought from the Guild of Grocers is wholesome and made with the utmost care, using only the finest ingredients. They would supply any quantity Your Majesty desires.'

'I have it, but so do the poison-makers. They know what it contains and therefore they know what poisons will evade it. This is why I have devised my own, Master Frilleck, and I am granting you the honour of making it.'

'Your Majesty, I am deeply honoured, of course, and if there is anything else Your Majesty requires, I should of course be delighted to oblige, but I cannot . . . it is forbidden,' he repeated helplessly.

James slapped the arm of his chair, causing the apothecary to start violently. 'Do you think the Grocers' Guild or the City Fathers may dictate the law to the King? They may forbid whatever they wish to the commons, but they will *not* forbid it to their King, nor those he commands. *I* grant you permission to make it. And you will divulge the ingredients to no one. You will tell no one what you are preparing or who you are preparing it for. Here!' James unhooked a small leather purse from his girdle and tossed it towards the apothecary.

With the paper still grasped in his trembling hands, Frilleck failed to catch it and it fell to the boards with a loud metal clang. He bent to retrieve it, but he was so terrified, the act of bending almost caused him to vomit at the King's feet.

'That should be sufficient to pay for all that is on that list, Master Frilleck, and for your time and trouble. You will furnish me with the cost of each item and where you obtained it, so that I may be certain you have not neglected to add anything in that recipe. You'll make no copy of it nor show to any, and you'll return that paper to me as soon as you are done. Do not look so alarmed, Master Frilleck. Think of the glory you will receive when this theriac proves as efficacious as I am certain it will; then all the world will be clamouring for it and you will be the one apothecary who knows its secret. They will make you Master of the Guild of Grocers before this year is out. Now go, begin your work.'

Frilleck's frightened eyes opened even wider. 'But, Your Majesty, I –'

'It will be done, Master Frilleck. It will be done.'

Chapter Twenty-three

SHOREDITCH, LONDON

DANIEL PURSGLOVE

'YOU KNOW EVERY HOLE and rat-infested corner of this city, Titus,' I said. 'So where would a man with "forbidden appetites" – a man with uncontrollable desires that not even the street whores will indulge – go to find "creatures of the night" like himself?'

I was trying to recall the exact words the young acolyte Erasmus had used about himself the day he'd given me the message that Waldegrave was dead. If he had deliberately lied to me, then I was determined to find out who had ordered him to do it. If Waldegrave was in London, they would have him well hidden and, besides, not even the rack would make him talk. Erasmus, on the other hand, would be far more easily broken. And I would really relish doing the breaking, after the month of hell I'd endured since I'd first set out from London.

Titus drained the dregs of his tankard and set it down on the table of the inn with the hopeful air of a man who expects it to be refilled. In the old days, when I'd been entertaining on the streets of London with my sleights-of-hand tricks, we'd have rolled dice to wager who was going to pay for the flagon of March beer to be refilled, but I'd seen him appraising my clothes with a practised eye as we sat down, working out to an inch of thread how much each item was worth.

Titus prided himself on knowing where to find anything in London and how much to charge for it. He didn't have a profession as such, certainly not employment with any master, but he lived on his wits, discerning with more skill than any fairground fortune-teller what a stranger most desired and making he sure he helped them to find it, for a price. He haunted the roads into London by day, and by night the inns where those new to the city might lodge, always ready to make himself indispensable.

'Sounds like you're after the kind of sport the Hunting Lodge has to offer. But you don't look like one of those, Danni. You sure you want to get yourself in there? They can play rough if they think you're a peach.'

'You know I'm not, Titus.'

'I know it, but they don't. And like I say, I wouldn't have took you for a man who was interested in the things they get up to. Not, you understand, that I *know* what entertainments they indulge in.' He flashed me a wide-eyed look of feigned innocence. 'But it always pays to know where to find such things, for gentlemen and ladies who want to pass the time and have money enough to pay for it.'

Titus was a minikin of a man, with the protuberant brown eyes of a friendly spaniel and a range of expressions that any actor would envy, able to assume the gravid demeanour of a lawyer or the excitement of a student hell-bent on tasting all the forbidden fruits in the city – whatever he gauged might most impress his victims. But now, he was regarding me with a look that, if I didn't know him better, I might have read as genuine concern.

'I hear you landed yourself in Newgate, Danni. That was a mercy, because it could have been the gallows.' He glanced pointedly at the high collar concealing my firemark. 'You're a marked man, Danni. You want to stay clear of trouble, not go looking for it.'

'I'm not looking for trouble. Just an old acquaintance of mine.'

'Half those in gaol, and in the Tower too, are in there because of who they were acquainted with. If you get your beard trimmed by a barber who cuts the hair of a man accused of sedition, or if your sister is wedded to a man whose cousin is arrested for treason, you'll find the King's men storming into your chamber in the dead of night to take you too. I knew a woman who was accused as a witch, all because she borrowed a measure of flour from an old biddy who had a toad living under her flowerpot.'

I laughed. 'That sounds like one of the tales you spin for the cabbages who come up from the country to make their fortune in the great city. And I've not been that long away from London.'

Titus grinned. 'Maybe that last one is, but all the same, you were here when they hanged Guy Fawkes and his crew, and we all know a good many went to the block over that plot, only because of who they were *acquainted* with, for nothing else could be proved against them.'

'Then I'm surprised you allowed yourself to be seen with a dangerous felon like me.'

'Too late,' Titus said cheerfully. 'Any who knows you, knows we shared more than a few flagons in the past.' He lowered his voice and leaned forward over the narrow table. 'A man came asking me questions about those . . . *tricks* of yours, trying to get me to swear I'd seen you conjure a demon in your lodgings, or failing that, that I'd seen the signs you chalked on the floor or heard you muttering Hebrew incantations. It's my betting he'd have settled for a whiff of sulphur and maybe the odd black cock feather if that'd been all I could manage. Offered me a handsome purse too, which incidentally I turned down. And I tell you, I've only done that once before in my life and that was when an alchemist wanted me to find him a freshly killed corpse, only he didn't want no gallows carrion, if you get my drift. But like I told him,' Titus added, in a theatrically affronted tone, 'I have my principles.'

'Did the man who wanted you to testify against me have a name?'

'Men who come calling in the middle of the night don't have names, no more than rats do. He was trying to pass himself off as a hired man, swathed in a plain black cloak and old hat, but he had a costly sword under that cloak. And I saw a bit of his face in the lamplight. About your age, I'd reckon. Flaxen beard trimmed sharp to a point and eyes as green as sour apples and twice as sharp.' Titus was studying me closely. 'I wager you know the name of this particular bilge rat.'

Oh, I knew alright! So, it *was* Richard who'd had me arrested. By God's bones, I'd make him pay for that and everything else he'd done. But as a man in Newgate once told me, *revenge may wait a hundred years and still have its milk teeth.* Richard was tangled in this Spero affair as deeply as Waldegrave, though on which side I couldn't as yet fathom. But I would. The players were converging on London. The Serpent was coiling and it was ready to strike. But where and when? *Reckoning it's starting, don't you?* the old marsh man had said. If he was right, then time was swiftly running out.

Titus had positioned himself on the corner of two narrow streets, where he might watch people coming and going from both directions. I walked purposefully down the street, not looking at him until I'd taken a step past him.

'I've a great thirst for huffcap,' I said. 'A friend said I might find some hereabouts.'

'That right, is it? And would that be all you have a thirst for?'

'A swig or two of that gives a man an insatiable craving for salt and spice in his meats. It's an itch he must scratch at any price.'

Titus lowered his voice to a murmur 'You sure about this, are you? 'Cause you could come out with a lot worse than scratches, that's if you come out at all.'

'I'll take my chances.'

Titus grunted and peeled himself off the wall. Without a backward glance, he ambled around the corner ahead of me and started down a narrow street, crowded with two- and three-storey wooden houses, squashed in between older buildings, with dark little shops, inns and gloomy workshops. Rats scampered over the open sewers blocked by the waste thrown out from kitchens and workshops, and children and old women squatted by the foul water, picking out filthy rags and soup bones or anything else that they could sort and sell.

A gaggle of bare-breasted doxies, a couple of them scarcely more than children, leaned out of upper-floor windows, smoking pipes and calling out ribald jokes and invitations to men and lads below. If they were ignored, they pitched balls of dried mud at the offenders' heads or backs, laughing when the balls burst as they struck, showering their victims with dirt. But they did not call out or pelt Titus, who was strolling languidly ahead of me like a Court gallant, his chin raised, looking about him as though he was taking his morning exercise in the gardens of a palace. He turned and glanced back towards me, before leading the way between two houses, down a dark passageway that was so narrow my shoulders brushed the walls on either side.

The passageway disgorged into a narrow courtyard, surrounded by high walls. A door was set into the wall at the end, and to one side of it, stone steps vanished into the darkness below. Titus rapped on the door and a small hatch opened. I glimpsed the shadow of someone standing behind it. There was a murmured exchange before the hatch shut and then he turned back to me.

'They want to know if your taste is for spice?' Titus held one hand out towards the door. 'Or salt?' He pointed with the other hand down the stairs.

He was standing motionless with both arms extended, his head cocked. For a horrible moment in the stygian gloom of that courtyard, the image of young Myles's crucified corpse suddenly rose before my eyes.

'I don't often have to ask,' Titus said. 'I can usually tell just by looking what a customer fancies.' He lowered his arms. 'Knock and heaven shall be opened unto thee.'

Titus held out his hand again, and I made a show of pressing a coin into it. He swept off his hat and gave an extravagant actor's bow, whispering, 'Keep a clear head.' He flashed me an anxious glance, before strolling back along the passageway.

Which would Erasmus choose – up or down?

I descended the stone steps and rapped on the stout door at the bottom. Evidently, I'd been watched ever since I'd arrived, for the door opened almost at once, revealing a second door in the form of a heavy iron grille. A lamp was thrust towards me, but the person holding it was standing in the darkness behind it. There was a grunt, and the metal door too was pulled open. I stepped inside, around the person with the lamp. Behind me, I heard the grate of a key turning.

'This way, if you please.'

A heavy curtain was lifted long enough for me to duck beneath and I found myself in a low barrel-vaulted chamber, dimly lit by a few candles burning on the walls, which sent long shadows slithering over the rough stone walls. A dense haze of smoke hung in the fetid air, smelling of tobacco, but of something sweeter too. There were about a dozen or so people, who all turned briefly to look at me as I entered. They were clustered in groups of two or three, reclining on low benches covered with an assortment of cushions and carpets, with small tables set conveniently close at hand, furnished with flagons, platters of meats and pipes.

The walls seemed to be decorated with grotesque masks and the skulls of wolves, lions, bears and mastiffs, though they were hard to make out in the dim light and drifting smoke. Half a dozen Jenny Hanivers were stretched over the ceiling, moulded into the form of demons, some almost four feet in length with hideous snarling faces and whip-like tails barbed with thorns; none, though, resembled wyverns. There were also, I noticed with disquiet, several blackened and mummified human hands. Stuffed snakes coiled around the legs of the benches and hung down from the beams. Their mouths were frozen wide to reveal curved fangs poised to strike, and their polished stone eyes glittered red, green and black in the candlelight.

A curtain twitched on the far side of the chamber and a man ducked in, clad in a long black robe. A close-fitting cap of viper skin was pulled tight over his ears, the flaps tied beneath his many chins, making the pale rolls of flesh bulge out. He beckoned me towards an unoccupied bench in the far corner and set a beaker and flagon down on the table beside it, and poured a measure of thick black liquid into the beaker. I sniffed it and he nodded conspiratorially, waiting until I'd taken a sip. It was huffcap, alright: double-double beer, sweet as malmsey wine and twice as strong. The brewing of it was, of course, strictly forbidden. I feigned appreciation and he winked as he slid the coins I'd proffered into a bag beneath his robe. He had no eyelashes, nor eyebrows, nor even a trace of stubble.

'When you have drunk sufficient, you have only to lift that curtain and Jaculus will be ready to discover the nature of the other pleasures you seek. There is no thirst that cannot be quenched, at a price.'

'Tonight, I am waiting for a friend to join me.'

'Ahh! Then you will give Jaculus double the pleasure.'

From somewhere under his robe, he produced a second beaker with a flourish and set it down next to the flagon. Then with a bow he backed a few paces away from me, like a courtier leaving the presence of royalty, and vanished behind the curtain.

I took another sip of the huffcap and tried to look as if I was relishing this forbidden fruit. I was aware that people in the room were watching me, no doubt wondering what my secret vice was, and I was sure there would be hidden eyes too, observing all of us closely. But I could not afford to drink too much. Titus was right, this was not the kind of place where you ought to allow your wits to get fuddled.

From time to time, the leather curtain to the chamber of delights beyond would be briefly lifted aside and people would slip in or out, mostly men, sometimes women, though it was hard always to be sure, for several wore voluminous cloaks and masks. Muffled shrieks and screams of pain or pleasure, or both, occasionally punctuated the murmur of low voices in the chamber, but no one in the room even glanced up, occupied with the serious business of drinking, eating, caressing each other, or lolling back on the cushioned benches, mouths slack, eyes glassy, staring at phantasms. I had seen men grow glazed like this before in Ireland, not with drink, but from opium made there from the white marsh poppy. That was the strange, sweet odour twisting through the purple-grey eddies of tobacco smoke.

I found myself growing drowsy, though I had drunk little of the huffcap. The curtain to the outside door opened and a woman entered, dressed in breeches and blue silk hose. A half-cloak hung from one shoulder, and the fingers and thumbs on both hands glittered with thick gold and silver rings. Her nose and cheeks were hidden behind a black mask decorated with silver thread. Perhaps it was simply to conceal her identity, but as she crossed the chamber and vanished beneath the leather curtain, I realised it might also hide the ravages of the Great Pox. As the curtain dropped back into place, I saw someone standing in the shadows on the far side of the chamber. It was a boy, his arms held wide, his hands oozing blood. He was looking down at the ground, but he slowly raised his head to stare at me. His head jerked backwards, like the head of a slain beast and I saw the deep rope-burn around his throat.

I stifled a cry as I leaped to my feet, overturning the small table and sending flagon and tankards crashing to the floor, the dark liquid flowing across the flags. The phantasm had vanished. Part of my mind told me it had never been there, that it was opium smoke that had conjured it, but I had no wish to see it again, or worse. I had to get out.

I blundered towards the curtain that led to the door. I had just lifted it and entered the passageway when the door at the far end was opened by the porter, who stepped aside as a man entered. It was dark, and the newcomer's attention was diverted by the porter. He'd taken a couple paces towards me when he stopped. The passage was narrow, and we could not pass each other unless one of us retreated. I could see nothing of the face below the long hood, but I recognised those long bony fingers and knobbly wrists.

'Erasmus?'

He jumped like a startled deer and for a moment I thought he would bolt, but he stood there, rocking on the balls of his feet.

'Daniel, what . . . ?'

'Waiting for you, that's what.' I stepped forward, seizing his arm. 'We need to talk . . . but not here,' I added swiftly. Gripping him firmly by the elbow, I steered him back towards the door.

The porter extended a meaty arm across the door. 'Leaving without what you came for, master?' He glared pointedly down at my fingers clamped around Erasmus's thin arm. ''Cause if you'd rather stay here with us . . .' His hand slid to the hilt of a knife in his belt, as did mine.

Erasmus seemed to shrink further into himself, looking even more like a nervous greyhound than he had when I'd first encountered him posing as one of Lady Montague's servants in Battle Abbey. 'He's a friend,' he muttered. 'I'll go with him.'

The porter still looked unconvinced, but finally lowered his arm and unlocked the door. He was still watching us intently as I propelled Erasmus down the alleyway. Fearing the porter might have sent someone to follow us, I didn't risk taking him back to my lodgings; instead, I pulled Erasmus into the parlour of the first tavern we came to, making for the corner.

We sat in silence as a weary-looking serving girl set two tankards of small ale in front of us and retreated. The weak ale was a relief to me after the sweet, strong beer and even Erasmus gulped it gratefully, his Adam's apple sliding up and down in his scrawny throat. He had not looked at me since we'd entered, and fixed his gaze on a sticky dark puddle on the rough wooden table with the intensity of a man studying a particularly difficult passage in theology. In Battle Abbey, he had been determined to be ordained as a Catholic priest. I wondered if he'd even opened a psalter since he'd arrived in London.

I leaned forward and he flinched away, as though he thought I was about to hit him.

'When we last met, you told me the Yena was dead, murdered. His corpse pulled from a river in Bristol.'

Erasmus raised his head. 'I didn't say *murdered*. I didn't say anything.'

Now that I could see him properly, he looked, if that were possible, worse than at our last encounter. His face was even more sallow and drawn. He was a man who had known hunger. But it was the eyes that were the most changed. They had looked fearful before; now they were haunted, sunk into dark pits, a large red clot of blood staining the white of one of them.

He averted his gaze again. 'I only wrote down what I could remember of the message, the one that came to Battle from Bristol,' he said, his tone as sulky and defensive as a small boy's. Erasmus's shoulders hunched till they were almost touching his ears. 'Only told you what I'd seen.'

'Or what you'd been paid to tell me?'

'I was never paid!' Then, aware that his voice had risen shrilly, he glanced anxiously about him. 'Never,' he muttered.

'Threatened, then?'

He shook his head. 'Not threatened . . . not then.' He suddenly leaned towards me. 'I saw the message, the one Father Santi had given to Father Smith in the library, that he'd taken from the corpse. At least I saw part of it, not all, but I did see those words.'

'And you believed it was genuine?'

'Why should I not? Father Smith had spoken the name before when he was talking about you. He said you were known to the Yena.'

'Do you know if he ever received a message from the Yena about me?'

'I don't *know* exactly, but he must have, mustn't he? I told you he was trying to find out about you, trying to see if you were who you said you were. He checked up on everyone, especially the priests.'

'When Smith received the message saying the Yena was dead, did he seem pleased, or angry?'

'He was . . .' Erasmus appeared to consider the word carefully. 'Anxious. What he read had set him on edge, but whether the cause was the news of the Yena's death or something else in the letter, I cannot swear. The man who was to be brought in on the next ship, that seemed to occupy him more. But . . .' He held up his hand to forestall me. 'Don't ask me who that was. I swear I do not know.'

I slid the metal token embossed with the wyvern from my shirt and held it out in my palm, under the level of the table. 'This sign, have you seen it before?'

Erasmus stared at it for a long time, his brow furrowed. He slowly nodded. 'I've seen that sign, but I'm sure it was not like that, not on a medal.'

'Did you see it in the library at Battle Abbey, on one of the messages, perhaps on a wax seal?'

'Not the library and not a seal. Somewhere else . . . Anyway, what's its significance? It's a dragon, isn't it?'

'Of sorts,' I told him. 'It's a wyvern, a venomous snake with two legs, and its lethal poison lies in the barbed tail.'

He studied it again.

'Try to recall where you saw it at Battle Abbey, Erasmus. Try hard – many lives may depend on it.'

He glanced up at me, fear in his eyes. 'I don't want to get involved. I've left all that behind me!' His voice had grown shrill again and several of the other drinkers in the tavern turned their heads. He seemed to realise as much and lowered his voice, leaning forward and whispering urgently. 'I have my own demons to fight. I have done all I can to repay you. Now, please, just leave me alone.'

'I will, Erasmus. I have no wish to drag you back into this.'

And I meant it. Lady Montague's chaplain, Richard Smith, had delivered a harsh but all too true assessment of his erstwhile acolyte, describing him as a weak man who could not control his own emotions or actions. 'Erasmus will get himself into trouble,' Smith had declared, like a judge passing sentence. 'He will be arrested and when he is, he will talk . . .'

'I *will* leave you in peace, Erasmus. All I ask is that you try to remember where you saw some creature like this and what form it took.'

He held the token, rubbing his fingers over the embossed surface, his eyes tightly shut, like a fortune-teller summoning spirits. This was no act. He was earnestly trying his best.

Finally, he gave a sigh and his eyes flashed open. 'I remember now. It was in the chamber in which we both served, where the Fath—' With a frightened glance around to see if he'd been overheard, he corrected himself swiftly. 'Where the *gentlemen* slept. But it was before you came to the Abbey that I saw it, maybe a week or so before. As I was turning one of the mattresses, my foot knocked against something under the bed and I heard it skid against the wainscotting, so I delved under the bed and picked it up. It was a wooden spoon, a chrism spoon, one of those that are hinged, so that the handle folds down as a lid. I think it must have been pulled out of one of the chests with some clothes and it dropped to the floor. When the spoon was closed, it was shaped like an egg, so it might easily have rolled beneath the bed when it fell. I opened it, and that's where I saw this beast.' He jerked his chin at the wyvern medal in his hand. 'The creature was carved on the underside of the lid. I thought the theme of the spoon must be Christ crushing the serpent or the dragon beneath his heel. I expected to see Christ-in-glory carved in the bowl of the spoon, so that when the spoon was open, His feet would be standing on the beast's back. That's how it usually is, isn't it?' He fell silent, still staring at the metal disc in his hand.

'So, what *was* carved in the bowl?' I prompted.

'Flames. A great fire with a crowd of people burning alive, men, women and children, and in the centre one figure larger than the rest, a man who wore a crown. Hell! It was the flames of hell and this creature' – he thrust the medal back into my hands – 'must be the image of the Great Beast, of the Devil himself.' He shuddered. 'A strange theme for a chrism spoon. To use such a utensil in baptism, one that depicts Satan and hell instead of the glory of Christ, seems almost like laying a curse upon the poor infant.'

'If hell is what the spoon depicted,' I said cautiously.

'What else could it signify? I examined it closely. There was no saint or any other image on it.' Erasmus seemed genuinely perplexed. I was certain then, if I had not been before, that the wyvern held no significance for him.

'Whose chest did the spoon come from, Erasmus?'

'As I said, when the spoon was folded up, the outside was smooth and polished, it rolled easily. It could have fallen from the robe of anyone in the chamber, or out of any of the chests. I placed it on Fath— Master Santi's bed, because I found it under that one. But as you know, Holt's and Bray's beds were on either side of his. When I came back to put newly baked manchets in the livery cupboard an hour later, it was gone. And so was all the wine in the livery. I had to fetch another flagon and the way Steward Brathwayt railed at me, you'd think he'd paid for the wine from his own purse. He accused me of drinking it and threatened to report me to Master Smith. So, I remember that day only too clearly.' He lifted his tankard and drained it, his Adam's apple slithering rapidly up and down his throat. It was like watching a snake swallow a bucket of frogs.

'Who had been in the chamber before you returned with the manchets?'

'How should I know? It was empty when I returned. One of them must have seen the spoon and hidden it again. But I couldn't tell you who. Anyway,' he said, with irritation, gesturing to the wyvern medal as I slipped it back inside my shirt. 'Why are you so interested in that?' Then almost in the same breath, he held up a hand, turning his face away. 'No, don't tell me. I don't want to end up like your friend the Yena.'

Chapter Twenty-four

THE STREETS OF LONDON are never silent, not even in the darkest hours before dawn. Dogs howl, cats yowl, babies bawl, men reel drunkenly home from illicit gaming dens, while others, equally bleary-eyed, stagger from their beds towards their day's work. Every now and then, a cart trundles beneath the shuttered casements of those still sleeping – gong farmers taking stinking barrels of shit to the laystalls outside the city, and death carts collecting corpses.

Nonetheless, I had chosen this time in the hope that I would more easily spot anyone following me than on a jostling daytime street. Besides, it had taken the best part of the day to discover where Titus was currently lodging. I didn't want to risk meeting him in an inn or on the street again. He was inclined to get annoyed if he was interrupted when he'd spotted a potential mark he might latch on to, and who could blame him? It was his livelihood.

The house was tall and narrow. The oily mustard light from the lantern on the opposite side of the street revealed that the shutters of the lower windows had been ripped away and that the holes left by missing panes of glass had been stuffed with rags. The windows higher up had fared better, but the wall bulged outward so markedly that I was surprised it had not already collapsed. In places, chunks of plaster had fallen away, exposing the lathes below.

The door at the bottom was unlocked and I inched my way up the dark staircase, listening to the snores and creaks from behind the doors. I cursed as I collided with what felt like a broken chair and stumbled back against an overflowing pail of slops, splashing my hose. The door to what I'd been told was Titus's lodging was also unlocked and I eased it open. A dull red glow from the fire revealed that most of the room was taken up by a bed, the blankets heaped over two slumbering figures. Titus and his latest woman, I presumed. I eased myself down into a decidedly rickety chair next to the fire, preparing to wait until one or both of them stirred.

The shriek woke me from the doze into which I'd fallen. A dirty grey light was oozing between the slats of the shutters, and the woman was sitting up in bed, the blankets pulled up to her chin. She was staring at me and pummelling Titus into wakefulness. Despite her shriek, he had barely moved.

'Leave me be, woman,' he mumbled.

She shook him more violently. 'Wake up! There's a man by the fire!'

'If it's one of your spirits risen from the grave, tell him to go back down and play with his maggots, unless he's brought a sack of gold with him.'

'I'm no spirit, Titus,' I said softly, 'at least not for a while yet, I hope. A mere mortal.'

Titus fought to untangle himself from the blankets and sat up. 'God's arse, Danni, you've frightened Zeffy here into thinking she really has seen a demon.'

'My name is Zephora,' the woman said archly, 'and I *do* see Avery and he talks to me. And I see other spirits too.'

Titus laughed. 'That's what she tells her customers anyway. Make yourself useful, O mighty Zephora, and pour us some ale, unless you fancy conjuring your Avery to fetch it.' He gave a shove, sending her tumbling. She got her own back by clinging tightly to the blankets as she fell, pulling them off the bed and leaving Titus naked and shivering.

Zephora scrambled up off the boards and padded to the fire, wrapping the blanket tighter beneath her armpits as she poked it into life, adding a few more coals. She was a small, pretty creature, with a tangle of loose hair tumbling over her bare shoulders, dyed a vivid shade of saffron. As she handed me a beaker of sour ale, she gave me a sweet smile, and it was only then I realised that one of her eyes was sightless, the whole eye a bluish milky white.

Titus, evidently realising that he wasn't going to get his blanket back, began to dress, for in spite of the fire the chamber was as cold and draughty as a kennel. He hurled questions at me over his hairy shoulder.

'What do you mean by turning up here in the middle of the night? What do you want? Have you got yourself into more trouble? And anyway, how did you find me?'

'It took some effort,' I told him. 'I hear you left your last lodging in a bit of a hurry. The landlord's after your blood, by the way. But your friends know where to find you.'

'Aye, they do, and that's not a comforting thought.'

'They wouldn't give you away. All of them owe money to someone.'

'It's not my landlord I'm afraid of, Danni.' He sat down on the end of the bed, taking the beaker of ale that Zephora handed to him and paying her with a kiss. She retreated to the bed with her own beaker, lying legs drawn up, propped against the pillows with the blanket bunched up around her.

'Who are you afraid of, then?'

He ignored the question. 'What brings you here, Danni? Didn't you find anything to satisfy you at the Hunting Lodge?'

'I found the person I was looking for there. But there's another man I need to find and quickly. And I'd stake my life on that being the very last place he'd frequent, or any other bawdy house for that matter.'

'You can stake your life and all your limbs too, if you've a mind to,' Titus said sourly. 'You do it often enough, but I want to keep mine firmly attached. I know you of old, Danni, if you're looking for this man and he doesn't want to be found then I'll wager a pound to a penny he's big trouble, and that's just what he'll bring to anyone who goes around asking questions about him.'

Outside, the sky was bleaching and the pale light filtering through the broken shutters finally penetrated the corners of the chamber. There were no cooking pots or cupboards that might contain food. Whatever the pair of them ate, they must have to buy in the inns or from the street sellers, paying for it with what they could daily earn on the streets. I knew from experience that was a precarious existence. I drained my beaker and upturned it on the floor. Then I placed a small stack of coins on the top, deliberately letting each one clink as it dropped. Zephora rocked forward on to her knees, peering over the bed to get a better look.

'Put it away,' Titus said. 'Money's no good to a corpse. Two pennies to stick on the eyes and another on the tongue for luck, that's all the dead need. It doesn't buy you your life.'

'It buys some decent suppers, though, and a good gown,' Zephora said, pouting.

Titus rolled his eyes. 'Now see what you've done. She'll be nagging worse than a flock of scolds if I don't take it.'

I grinned. 'This man is most likely to have come through the gate you watch, Titus, from Bristol. He'll have arrived here around Christmastide when there was still the great freeze. So, there wouldn't have been the usual crowds pouring in. He's old, frail, probably travelling with two other younger men. Not many travelling far on the roads in that ice, especially the elderly, so he'd stand out. Sparse white hair and white brows like thorn bushes and he has a twitch he tries to hide, affects the left side of his face, his eye and mouth mostly.'

'Half the ancient codgers in London match that description, and when that great freeze had its hold on us, people went about muffled up. You could only see their eyes and sometimes not even that. Couldn't tell man from maid, much less if they were young or old.'

I cast about, trying to think of something that might distinguish Waldegrave from any other frail old man. 'His staff . . . he carries a staff with a carved eagle's head on the top. It's large and sturdy enough for him to be able to use the curved beak as a hook to snag a piece of flotsam or a rope.' I was seeing again the dark, water-filled tunnel where I'd watched him do just that. 'At his age, he wouldn't get far in the ice without it.'

'Could have sold it and bought himself another if he didn't want to be recognised, and most of your acquittances don't,' Titus said morosely, though I detected a flicker of something stirring in his memory at the mention of that staff.

'So does this carrion crow of yours have a name?'

'Several, though he's probably not using any of them here.' I hesitated, then plunged in. 'Those who know him . . . and trust him . . . call him the Yena.'

There was a sharp cry from the bed and we both glanced towards Zephora. Her knees were drawn up to her chin. She was clutching the edge of the blanket, pressing it to her mouth and staring wide-eyed over it, like a child woken from a nightmare.

'It was a yena stone that some old crone sold her,' Titus explained, with a sigh. 'Told her to put it under her tongue, so she could see the future clearer. Now she thinks she sees spirits swinging from the beams and hobgoblins dancing under the bed.'

'She didn't *sell* it to me,' Zephora said indignantly. 'It was the one she'd used since she was a girl. She said she was going to die soon, and knew I had the gift, so she wanted to pass it on to me.'

'She demanded you give her a shilling for it, what's that if it's not selling?' Titus retorted.

'I had to give her silver to protect her from the spirits taking revenge on her for telling me the secret.'

Titus shook his head in fond exasperation. 'If you ask me, it's you they've taken revenge on.' He turned back to me. 'Keeps waking me up yelling that a yena is coming for her.'

'I see this huge beast in a graveyard at night – it's digging up a corpse and eating it. I try to back away, but it hears me and turns its head. One of its eyes glows, but the other is a great black hole. It drops the corpse it's got clamped between its jaws and starts padding towards me. It knows I've got the stone from its eye and it wants it back. I try to throw the stone to it, but when I look down, its eye is in my palm, staring up at me. It's stuck inside my hand and I can't fling it away.' She was almost sobbing as she recalled the nightmare.

'Then your dream can't be about a yena,' I assured her. 'You said it turns its head to look at you, and a yena can't turn its head except by reversing its body, because its spine is rigid – one long, solid bone.'

'There, you see?' Titus said. 'If anyone knows about beasts and the like, Danni does. Read more books than the greatest scholar in the land.'

It was a pity Waldegrave wasn't here in this chamber to listen to that testimonial about his erstwhile pupil.

'But have you heard that name spoken in London?' I persisted.

Titus shook his head.

'You could ask around, though.'

'And will this *asking* see me fished out of the Thames some dark night?'

I didn't answer, but extracted the wyvern medal from my shirt. 'One last question, Titus, have you come across anyone carrying this sign? Maybe not a talisman like this, but on a ring, perhaps, or drawn in a message?'

He took it from my hand and crossed the few paces to the casement, peering at the medal as he held it up in one of the thin shafts of light. He shook his head.

'Kind of beast you might see carved in an old church. You can find mermaids and winged lions and all kinds of strange creatures in those. I could have seen it on some nobleman's shield when he was riding in one of Scottish Jemmy's royal processions. But can't say as I recall seeing anyone carry it.' He crossed to the bed and held it out to Zephora. 'You seen this?'

She cupped it in both hands, staring at it, then closed her eyes, letting her head fall back. With a cry, she dropped the medal on to the bed as though it was suddenly too hot to touch.

'I see a serpent – a serpent biting its own tail,' she croaked.

'Danni's not one of your pigeons,' Titus said, grimacing at me. 'He's seen more tricks than any man in London, performed most of them himself.' He scooped the disc from the bed and handed it back to me. 'Pay her no heed. She's gulled so many turnip-heads up from the country these past months, she's starting to believe her own mummery. You want to watch it, Zeffy. You start to believe this spirit of yours is real and you'll find yourself dancing on the gallows. And I tell you this much, that Avery of yours won't be flying down to rescue you. You ask Danni here. He came within a squawk of being hanged himself.'

But Zephora wasn't listening. She was staring at me, and the terror I saw in her eyes was only too real.

Chapter Twenty-five

TITUS WAS ANXIOUS THAT I did not leave his lodgings by the way I had come in, fearing that I might have been followed. As he pointed out, no one wants to be known as the friend of a man once accused of sorcery. There was a door leading to a wash-house and kitchen at the back of the building, and a wall, which he assured me was easily scaled. He'd no doubt had occasion to use this route himself, or at least he had ensured he was familiar with it, should the need arise.

The rickety door was at the far end of a long dingy passage-way at the bottom of the stairs, stinking of boiled cabbage and stale piss. I groped along the dark narrow space, stumbling over broken crocks and heaps of rubbish that had been abandoned there. I had almost reached the end before one of the heaps squealed as I stumbled over it. Pushing open the door to let in a little light, I glanced down, expecting to see a cat, and found myself staring at two filthy faces with wild tangled hair and huge eyes, peeping up at me from under an old blanket on the floor. The two little girls clutched each other but did not move. This was evidently their bed. I dropped a coin on to the ragged blanket and put my fingers to my lips, nodding towards the open door. They both nodded solemnly. I suspected they were well used to keeping silent about who came and went this way, in exchange for a coin or a bite of food. Children are as good as cats at finding ways to survive on the streets. With a sudden jolt of pain, I thought of young Myles and turned abruptly away, closing the door behind me as I left.

I scrambled over the wall and across several other yards until I found an alley that led back towards the street, dodging a furiously barking dog. The occupants of the various lodging houses who had curiously glanced my way said nothing, and some even deliberately turned away, determined to have seen nothing either.

Once I regained the street, I walked back past Titus's lodging house towards a young lad selling oyster chewets from a tray. I bought several, and hunkered down in an archway to eat them, keeping watch on the doorway of the lodging house. The pastry was hard and full of husks, and the filling was all oysters, with no dried fruit to flavour them. Even in a port such as London with her many ships bringing in spices and rare delicacies, it was set to be a hungry season for the commons, after the freeze and thaw.

The door opened several times as other tenants from the house stepped out to begin their day. Finally, Titus emerged. He peered suspiciously around him, but, as most people do, only scrutinised the faces of those people who were walking or standing, looking over the heads of the beggars and others squatting on the ground. He hurried away. I didn't trouble to follow him. If he found Waldegrave, I'd learn of it soon enough.

It was almost an hour later when Zephora came out. She was dressed now in skirts of plain dark green, but from the glimpse I saw before she pulled her cloak tighter, her bodice was an altogether more elaborate affair. Canary yellow, embroidered with faded and frayed patterns in blue and red, probably bought from a vendor of second-hand clothes, if it hadn't been stolen. When new, it would have been something a wealthy merchant's wife might have worn. Her saffron hair was piled up beneath a dark hood. She too scanned left and right, then hurried out into the street. I waited until there were a few people between us, then stood up and followed her.

From behind, clad in her dark cloak and hood, she was hard to pick out from many of the other women going about their business that cold morning. The streets of Southwark were bustling with goodwives and ladies of the night alike, making for shops and market stalls, men hurrying towards the river to hail wherries, rumbling handcarts, skittish horses and even a long wagon carrying a cage with a young bear inside. The bear was throwing itself from side to side in alarm at the noise and bustle, reaching out through the bars with long claws to swipe at anything or anyone that came close. Several times I was forced to quicken my pace and move closer than I would have liked to Zephora, to make sure I didn't lose sight of her. But finally, she slipped out of the crowded streets and, turning away from the river, emerged into an area of small, run-down cottages bordering a little piece of open land on which pigs, chickens and a tethered goat were foraging.

Lifting her skirts clear of the dirt, she picked her away across a patch of churned-up mud to one of the cottages. The door was opened by a bent old woman with a long pipe clamped between her gums. She nodded, evidently expecting her visitor, and shuffled back inside with Zephora following. I found myself a spot on the opposite side of the open ground, from where I could watch anyone approaching or leaving the cottage, hidden by the side of an old cart.

As the morning wore on, I found myself wishing I'd brought some ale with me: the dry, salty chewets had given me a raging thirst. I'd been forced to arm myself with a stick to poke away the snuffling pigs who periodically wandered too close, apparently convinced that my boots might prove a more appetising dish than midden filth. Mizzle began to fall, the kind that clings to cloth and hair and soaks as badly as any downpour.

Just when I had almost given up, I heard the sound of hooves on the stones. A horse and rider were approaching the cottage. Though the figure was riding astride, clad in wide breeches, it was unmistakably a woman. She wore a dark riding cloak and her chestnut hair, caught up in a silver fret, was half covered by a small black hat; a muffler covered the lower half of her face. Her clothing might simply have been a defence against the inclement weather, but it also disguised her, so that it was impossible to see her features. She reminded me of the women who had attended the illicit Mass at Battle Abbey, and though this cottage couldn't contain a hidden chapel, I was sure that what took place inside was equally dangerous.

The new arrival was admitted by the same elderly woman who had welcomed Zephora. She ushered the woman inside, then firmly closed the door. I circled around the cottage, staying at a distance so that I would not be seen by any of the women if they happened to glance out. But the shutters on the two tiny casements were closed and solid, and the only door appeared to be at the front. Anyone lurking near it in an attempt to eaves-drop would be plainly visible. Besides, although I was curious about what was passing between them, it was Zephora I wanted to speak with.

The woman remained for maybe an hour or so, then the door opened again and she came out alone, darting nervous glances around. She led the horse to a block set against the cottage wall to remount, then trotted swiftly away, heading towards the river. When Zephora did not emerge at once, I began to fear that she was waiting for another customer and I would be stuck there all day. The sight of the pigs slurping from the muddy puddles only made me more thirsty. Driving off one particularly persistent brute, I almost missed the moment when the door opened a crack and Zephora slipped out. I waited until she was turning into the narrow alleyway, heading back the way she had come, and then I strode after her. She started violently as she caught sight of me and her face flushed.

'This is a happy meeting,' I said cheerfully. 'I'm dying of thirst. Will you share a flagon with me and perhaps a bite or two?'

She shook her head. 'I'm going to the market. There is so little to buy since the freeze – if I don't get there quickly there'll be nothing left.'

'I suspect you've already left it too late,' I told her gravely, as though I believed her. 'Most of the goodwives are on their way home now or already cooking what they bought. And this is a strange route to take to the market from your lodgings.' She backed away from me, panic in her face, but I seized her elbow, on the pretext of steadying her on the slippery stones.

'I seem to recall there was an inn somewhere down the next street. If we go now, before men come seeking their dinner, we might be in luck.'

Again she tried to pull away, but I tightened my grip and did not release her until we were sitting in the corner of the tavern. The walls and low ceiling were black with tarry smoke from the pipes and the fire, and the small fragments of thick glass in the casements were also coated with it. Even on a bright summer's day, it would still have been as dark as a ship's bilges. The far corners were occupied by men sitting alone. These crouching spiders only betrayed their presence when they moved. A few others sat in twos and threes, leaning over the tables, muttering to each other. They glanced towards us as we entered, but seemed just as anxious not to be seen. Two bare-breasted doxies moved among them; one edged hopefully in my direction, then, catching sight of Zephora, nodded and backed away. I thought I caught a flash of recognition between the two of them.

A burly man set two beakers and a flagon between us. Zephora lowered her head as he approached. He studied her, but it was impossible to read his expression in that thick gloom. 'Vittles?'

I nodded and presently a skinny lad set two platters of Poor Jack, some coarse bread and a large dish of mustard on our table. I groaned: salt fish was not what I needed, but all the wilier innkeepers knew it made the customers drink more.

Zephora didn't seem to mind and attacked the dish as though she'd been presented with the finest roasted goose. Finally, when she could not eat any more, I refilled her beaker, and leaning over, grasped her wrist.

'Tell me about the Serpent, Zephora.'

She lifted her chin. 'I can't remember anything I say when Avery speaks through me.'

'Naturally, but the spirit didn't tell you about the Serpent. You heard about that in the old woman's cottage. She was the crone who gave you the yena stone.'

I didn't know any of this for certain. But I knew if I asked her questions, she would refuse to tell me anything. This way I might goad her into an answer.

'What if she was? Not against the law to give someone an old stone for a keepsake.'

'But is against the law to summon spirits. Titus was right, it is the quickest way to the gallows. And you'll count the noose as a mercy, after the agonies they'll inflict on you to extract a confession, because however readily you confess, they will always want more. It makes no difference if you really have the gift of second sight or if you're merely gulling your customers into believing it.'

She rose, but I jerked her back down, shaking my head at the innkeeper. He'd seen her attempt to leave, but I imagine it was a familiar sight in that establishment, and he was not about to intervene.

I leaned forward, lowering my voice still further. 'Tell me what you heard about the Serpent. I'll pay you well, and I will keep silent. If not . . .' I left the threat dangling.

She searched my face. Her blind eye gazed unblinkingly at me, like the eyes of the dead in that long-ago lake of blood. But she said nothing.

'I know the Serpent is preparing to strike, and it will strike soon,' I said. 'Those involved have been making their way to London. They are gathering here because they will strike here.' I pulled her hand beneath the table and wrapped her fingers around a small leather drawstring purse, making sure she felt the weight of it before I drew it out of her grasp. 'Now tell me what more you know.'

She gazed around her, then seemed to make up her mind. Her head lowered, she murmured so softly I had to lean in until our heads were almost touching to catch her words.

'There is a lady comes to ask questions of Avery. The first time, it was to find something valuable that had been stolen . . .'

'And he told her where to find it,' I finished. It was an ancient fortune-teller trick to lure in wealthy customers. The old crone or Zephora herself doubtless knew who had stolen it and had shared any money the lady had paid them for its return with the thief.

'Then Mary told the lady Avery could help her get with child. The spirit taught her the charms to say and the auspicious nights when she should lure her husband to her bed and what herbs to put beneath the mattress. And he gave her a girdle of stag's fur to wear beneath her shift.'

'And Mary explained what fine gifts this woman should leave for the spirits, so that they'd bless her efforts?' I suggested.

'Mary's old. She's no kin. How else is she to keep body and soul together?' Zephora said defiantly.

'And she gives you a share of these *gifts*?'

'So, what if she does? I earn it.'

I nodded. 'You do, and you'll get no quarrel from me. We all have to make a living. But tell me about the Serpent.'

Zephora glanced around her again, uneasily. 'Last week, when she came, she was different, agitated . . . afeared of something. She said that she wanted to know if her husband was in danger, if he might be arrested . . . or even killed. She wanted me to ask Avery to protect him, give her a charm or something that would keep her husband safe. Well, Mary didn't want to go on when she heard that. She told the lady I couldn't summon Avery, and said he wouldn't come to her, because she'd offended the spirits and made them angry. Mary told her she wasn't to come to the cottage again. At that the lady got even more upset, wailing that the spirits would take revenge on her husband.

'I tried to calm her; she was weeping fit to fill the Thames and so out of her wits, I was afraid that if someone saw her leaving in such a state, they might think we'd robbed her. And if her husband had seen her like that, he was bound to ask what ailed her and she'd blurt out the whole tale. He didn't know, see, and he'd likely have fetched the constable, if he thought we'd taken money from her.

'I thought maybe if I could get her talking, she might settle herself. So, I asked her who'd want to harm her husband. I mean if he'd got himself into a spot of bother, owed money on the cards or wagering on the cockfights, Titus might know someone who could frighten the lickers off. But she said something strange . . . said it wasn't who wanted to harm *him*, but who *he* wanted to harm. Couldn't make head nor tail of that, so I asked her what she meant. She said she'd heard her husband talking late one night. It was the night that Avery had told her she must sleep with him if she wanted to get with child. He told her that her husband had to dip his awl at a certain hour of the moon, so she went to his bedchamber, but it was empty and she went looking for him. She heard voices and she was curious because it was the middle of the night. She heard them talking about a serpent . . . in London, like you said. "The serpent's head had reached London and all was ready."'

'Zephora, when you looked at that talisman this morning you said you saw "a serpent biting its own tail". Are those the words this lady heard or did she see it drawn somewhere, on a message in her husband's chamber, perhaps?'

Zephora shook her head. 'I don't reckon she said that exactly. But it was what her words put me in mind of, 'cause Mary has that scratched on her wall behind a curtain, a serpent swallowing its own tail. She's lots of signs scratched there. She says the spirits tell her which one to draw, and sometimes we use them when we're making out to the customers that we're summoning Avery. Some of them like to see the signs, helps them to believe, see?'

'The wyvern, the dragon creature that was on the medal. Is that also one of the signs Mary scratched on her wall?'

Zephora looked puzzled. 'Is that what it was?' She fleetingly touched her blind eye. 'Didn't see it full on. I took it for a serpent. That's why it scared me, 'cause of what the lady said.'

'What made her think that her husband was in danger of being arrested? What is the Serpent here to do, did she tell you that?'

'Kill the fox and his cubs, that's what she said. That's the words they used before, wasn't it, in the Gunpowder Treason? I heard someone reading all about it from one of those broadsides when they hanged and quartered them that did it. Now there's others that mean to try again. They're going to kill the King, that's what it means, doesn't it? They're going to kill the King.'

Chapter Twenty-six

As soon as I left Zephora, I returned to the inn where I was lodging. The hours of sleep I had sacrificed to corner Titus before dawn had finally caught up with me and my limbs felt wooden, but I wasn't sure that sleep would come. My head was buzzing like a nest of wasps, trying to piece together what I had learned from Zephora and from the old man on the marsh.

'Wait, sir!'

I turned on the stairs leading up to my room to see one of the serving maids standing at the bottom. She laid down the empty platters she was carrying and delved down the front of her gown, fishing out a folded paper.

'Gentleman said I was to give you this, sir, soon as you returned.'

'None of my acquaintances knows I am staying here,' I told her. 'It must be meant for one of your other customers.' I had deliberately chosen an inn where I wasn't known. I did not want FitzAlan summoning me, not until I was ready.

'Your pardon, sir, but he said I was to give it to a Master Issott.'

My stomach lurched. My mother's name! I had abandoned it when I left Bristol, in case it had become linked to Myles's death.

'He described you too,' the girl continued cheerfully, holding out the letter. 'So as I couldn't make a mistake if I forgot the name. He mentioned your . . .' She made a vague gesture towards her own neck.

I hadn't mentioned the name *Issott* to Titus, nor had I told him where I was lodging, though he was resourceful enough to have discovered it. But even if he could write, I couldn't imagine he'd risk committing any message to me to paper.

I took the letter and handed the girl a coin, though doubtless she had already been paid for her trouble. Someone shouted from somewhere beyond the passageway. The girl swiftly collected her platters and before I could ask her anything more, she hurried away.

I trudged up to my room and sank on to the bed to read what she'd handed me. The letter was secured with wax, but no seal mark had been pressed into it. The message was simple.

'Jaculus has news of your friend. Descend the stairs at the ninth bell tonight, and ask for him.'

This could only have come from Erasmus. He had delivered news in a note like this before. Did that mean he had discovered something about Waldegrave, the man he knew as the Yena? I was disturbed that Erasmus not only knew the name I had used in Bristol, but where I was lodging. I had not mentioned either to him. But coming so soon after what I had learned that afternoon, I could not afford to ignore the invitation.

I was sure that Zephora was right: there was to be another attempt on the King's life. I was also convinced that whoever had been brought into Battle on that ship was the 'serpent's head' who she had heard the woman talking about. He was gathering a circle of conspirators around him, like those who had been assembled for the Gunpowder Treason. Zephora had mistaken the image of the wyvern for a serpent, and I had heard others call that two-legged dragon *a winged serpent*. I was certain now that what I had taken to be a wyvern was in fact a serpent. And the head of that serpent was Spero Pettingar, the gunpowder conspirator who had evaded capture and vanished. So who had been his agent in Battle Abbey?

Erasmus had told me he'd placed the chrism spoon carved with the winged serpent on Santi's bed, and when he returned to replenish the livery cupboard, the spoon had gone. Three men had shared that chamber. They posed as gentlemen, guests of

Lady Magdalen, but all three were priests, ordained on the Continent and smuggled into England to strengthen the resolve of Catholics and, if they could, convert others to the faith. I'd had to serve them, under Erasmus, who had assigned to me all the delightful tasks he didn't relish, like emptying the holy pisspots and shit pans.

The youngest of the three priests, Henry Holt, I had judged to be in his thirties. He had a pale, youthful face, in startling contrast to his hair, which was already as white as that of a man three times his age. George Bray, the second of them, resembled a rather plump bat, with protruding ears that stuck out through fluffy wisps of tawny hair, a pursed mouth, snub nose and dull brown eyes, monstrously magnified behind the thick glass of a pair of spectacles. The third man was Julian Santi, tall, olive-skinned, with a black beard cut into a sharp spike. He had a manner as cold and calculating as an assassin's. If I had to wager a purse on any of those three being involved with Spero Pettingar, I would not have hesitated to lay the bet on him.

But something Erasmus had said was niggling at me. When he'd returned to the chamber to place freshly baked manchets in the livery cupboard, he'd found that the wine flagon had been drained. Santi had been ascetic in his habits, drinking little wine even at supper. In contrast, I'd caught Bray raiding the livery on several occasions. He could empty it of food and wine more thoroughly than a plague of rats. He'd once even asked me to inveigle some of the better wine from the yeoman of the cellar for him. But if Bray had been in there drinking the cupboard dry, it did not preclude Holt or Santi having come in before or after him. Indeed, if Bray had had food or drink on his mind, he wouldn't have noticed if the legendary gold reliquary of the Battle Abbey was sitting on the bed, much less a small wooden egg.

All I knew for certain was that one of those three men was somehow involved with Pettingar, and Santi still seemed the most likely. But if the conspirators were gathering then Santi might already be in London. And that would be easy enough to arrange, for most priests smuggled into England passed through safe houses in London. Was Waldegrave now among them? The Serpents were gathering, but how soon would they strike?

I HURRIED THROUGH the dark streets, keeping under the overhang of the shops and houses. Heavy rain was falling, pouring in torrents from the roofs of the wooden buildings and gushing into the open sewers of the streets, sweeping cabbage stalks and horse dung along like boats on the Thames. In many places, the sewers overflowed, filling the road with a foul soup. The rain had driven most people inside, leaving the streets to rats, bedraggled dogs and vagrants, who grumbled and shuffled in doorways, pulling ragged cloaks and sacking round their shoulders. The prostitutes who were usually slouching in the archways or draped on the wooden stairs leading to their garrets were plying their trade inside and the watchmen were keeping close to their braziers, reasoning that the footpads would not bother hunting tonight if their quarry had gone to ground, and the drunks would soon sober themselves up after an icy drenching.

The narrow passage between the two houses was so dark that I might have walked straight past, but for the glow of a lantern light in the courtyard at the far end. As I turned into the alley, I nearly collided with a man who was hurrying towards me, holding the edge of his cloak across his face. I backed out of the passage to allow him to pass. He turned slightly as he stepped out into the street, bowing his thanks, and I glimpsed the flash of metal beneath his raised cloak, an elegant silver beaker hanging from a chain on his belt. The Hunting Lodge had wealthy customers, but then they catered for expensive tastes.

The courtyard at the end of the passageway was deserted and I groped down the stairs, slippery as soap from the liquid mud cascading over it, and splashed through the cold puddle that had formed at the bottom.

When the shuttered grille opened on the other side of the stout door, I uttered just one word – *Jaculus*. Whoever opened the door, as on the first occasion, stood concealed in the shadows, holding a lantern at an angle that revealed only his hand, the fingers covered in coarse black hair. It was not the hand of the man who had admitted me before.

'You know the way?' he growled, thrusting the light out into the passageway.

The fangs of a great bear skull above the leather curtain at the far end glowed white in the lantern flame. I ducked under the curtain and into the room in which I'd previously waited for Erasmus. The air was choked with fumes from pipes, beer, fried meat and the cloyingly sweet odour of opium I'd detected before. Ignoring the faces that turned to peer at me through the smoke, I strode towards the leather curtain on the far wall, lifted it aside and went in.

I found myself in a long arched tunnel set with heavy doors. I couldn't see how far it extended, for the place where I was standing was illuminated by a huge, circular brass oil lamp suspended on a chain from the vaulted ceiling, with seven or eight tiny flames flicking around the edge.

'Pleasure or pain? Or is pain your pleasure?' a voice sang out mockingly behind me. I wheeled around. A man was sitting cross-legged on top of a chest, perched on a heap of animal skins, a platter of pickled pigs' ears and trotters balanced between his thighs. A mask of silvery fur covered the top part of his face, extending over his head like a cap. A long bushy tail, like that of a huge cat, swung down from the mask behind his head, swishing as he moved. The tiny gold flames of the oil lamp were reflected in the glittering dark eyes peering out through the mask of fur. The man himself was beardless and his bare chest and arms were smooth and glistening with oil. His breeches were black and cut tight to his body. He wore no hose, only a pair of shiny black leather slippers.

'Jaculus?'

'I am he or she or it, master or servant, man or beast, which-ever is your pleasure.' He gave a snorting laugh.

'I've received a note saying you have news of a friend of mine.'

'And what manner of friend would that be – mare or stallion, or maybe a gelding?' He made a crude gesture towards his own crotch, with another irritating snigger.

'The note was delivered to Master Issott. It may have been sent by a man I know as Erasmus.'

Jaculus set the platter aside and sprang from the pile of skins. 'Ahh!' he said delightedly. 'Why didn't you say so at once? Your friend awaits you, my lord.' He swept out an arm and made a deep bow, his backbone almost folding in half. 'This way, if you please, and you will be pleased. I see to it that all of my patrons are.'

He led the way along the tunnel, not seeming to need any light to guide him. From what little I could see, every door looked identical. But he paused before one.

'Anything can be brought to your chamber . . . or anyone, my lord. Whatever your wishes . . . even the *darkest* wishes can be granted for a price.' He bowed again and as he straightened up, held out his hand for the coins that I already knew I would be obliged to press into it. As, he took them, he squeezed my hand and gave another of his sniggers. His fingers were unpleasantly hot and moist. He grinned, his eyes deep within the fur mask staring unblinkingly into mine, as though he was trying to see which demon might be lurking inside me. Then he retreated back up the tunnel.

I wasn't quite sure what Erasmus might be doing inside. I hoped he was merely sitting and waiting for me, but knowing the man's nervous disposition, I knocked, not wishing to startle him. There was no answer, but the door looked so stout it was likely he hadn't heard. I lifted the latch and pushed it open. The chamber was in darkness except for a single candle, burning on a pricket shaped like the claw of a bird of prey, which had been set on a stool by the door. The light was just sufficient to show the outline of a bed or bench at the far end of the long narrow room and a hump upon it. Erasmus had evidently fallen asleep while he waited. The stench of what smelled like an overflowing shit pail filled the room. If Jaculus wanted to please me, the first thing he could do would be to empty that.

I turned to close the heavy door before waking Erasmus. The back of the thick wood was lined with cloth and padded, though somewhere I could hear the drip of rain on stone.

'Erasmus.'

There was no answer. He was solidly asleep.

I lifted the bird-claw pricket, holding it so that the light fell on my face and he'd be able to recognise me if he was startled out of a dream. I called out again, louder this time. Still, he didn't stir. I strode to the bed, fully intending to tip him off the mattress and kick him awake. It wasn't until I had almost reached it that my mind finally made sense of what I was looking at, caught now in the pool of yellow light.

Erasmus lay on his back, his face grotesquely swollen, his blood-filled eyes wide with terror, staring sightlessly at the ceiling. The skin of his bloody hands had been removed, like someone might rip off a pair of gloves. White splinters of bone protruded through the mangled flesh, but his hands had been crossed over his chest in a mockery of a corpse respectfully laid to rest in a coffin. His mouth was wide open, stuffed with a cloth, and a purple rope mark was etched deep into the neck, above that prominent Adam's apple. In the suffocating silence, the steady drip, drip of rain on stone sounded louder than ever. But then I realised it wasn't rain: it was piss, dripping from the edge of the sodden sheet on to the flagstone floor. The stench of his evacuated bowels choked the air.

I strode to the door, resisting the urge to fling it wide. Instead, I opened it as silently as I could, closed it behind me, and marched towards the pool of light cast by the oil lamp.

Jaculus was once more perched cross-legged on his pile of animal pelts, sucking the meat from the bones of one of the pigs' trotters as the glistening juice ran down his chin.

He caught sight of me and grinned. 'Thought of a game you'd like to play already with your friend? What can I—'

I charged at him, punching him so hard he tumbled from his perch and slammed against the wall. He slithered down it and crumpled on to the floor, lying among the scattered pigs' feet and ears. Blood trickled from his mouth and mingled with the sauce on his chin. I seized him by the neck, dragging him into a sitting position, pinning him by the throat to the wall.

'Why? Why did you kill him? What was it, a game that went too far? One of your customers fancied some real sport, did he?'

Jaculus tried to shake his head, his blood spattering over my fist. 'Killed? Who . . . who's killed?' he mumbled.

'You know who! Erasmus, or whatever you called him! Was he the *someone* you brought to the chamber for one of your customers, someone too weak to fight back?'

Jaculus's face was turning purple. He feebly clawed at my hands and I realised I was very close to choking him to death. I eased the pressure on the throat just enough to let him snatch a deep, gasping breath.

'Don't know anything . . . can't be dead . . . he was alone . . . w . . . waiting for you.'

I hauled him to his feet. His animal mask had slipped sideways, covering one eye, and I dragged it off. A large, vivid letter 'B' had been seared into his forehead and both his ears were missing: he'd endured at least two, if not three, sessions in the pillory. On any other occasion, I might have felt pity for him, but not now. I dragged him down the tunnel, but I couldn't remember which door Erasmus lay behind. I stopped and pushed Jaculus hard against the wall.

'Look for yourself, you bastard, and then swear to me you didn't have a hand in this!'

I released him and watched him stumble back down the tunnel until he reached a door and unlatched it. I followed him in, half expecting he would deliberately choose an empty room, but as he lifted the candle and the light washed over the room, I saw again Erasmus lying on the soiled, bloody sheet. Jaculus uttered a small cry, more of pain than horror, and a convulsion seized his whole body. He turned towards me, the whites of his eyes almost luminous in the darkened chamber, but before either of us could speak, the door opened and two figures burst in. Fearing an ambush, a dagger was in my hand and my back pressed to the wall before the door closed again.

I saw small flashes in the dim light and realised they were coming from the silver thread on a half-mask on the smaller of the two, and from her many rings. I was sure it was the same woman I'd seen dressed in breeches the night I'd waited for Erasmus. She seized the candle from Jaculus and, taking a step forward, raised it to illuminate the scene. The man behind her groaned and cursed, but no sound escaped her. She stood regarding the bed calmly.

She turned to the man. 'Bring the box and see that he is removed swiftly. You know where to dispose of him. I want him swimming far downstream before dawn. And this chamber must be cleaned. It reeks.'

He grunted and I now saw it was the man in the black robe and cap who had served me beer two days before. He turned for the door, but I pushed in front of him, blocking his way, but addressing the woman

'You will not dump his body in the Thames like a dead dog! At the least he deserves a decent burial. He was a . . .' I stopped myself.

'And how will you explain his injuries to a vicar, much less to a constable when that vicar summons him?' the woman said calmly. 'Leave his disposal to us. We've had patrons whose hearts have burst in the height of passion or who in their excitement have inflicted fatal wounds on others. My servants are well practised in dealing with unfortunate accidents.'

'Does that look like an accident to you?' I demanded. 'Can anyone skin a man's hands and crush them to pulp by accident?'

She shrugged. 'Some men do not know when to stop. They don't *want* to stop. But no matter, the corpses wash out to sea, and if by some misfortune they are snagged by a wherryman or beached on the mudflats, they are never traced back here. Most of the wherrymen just prise them loose and let them sink or float away. Raising the dead is never a wise thing to do in this city. So, you need have no fear. You will not be made to pay for your night's entertainment, except by us, of course. Jaculus will be happy to tell you what you owe for the disposal.'

'You cannot believe that *I* killed him,' I growled. 'Look at him. A man can be throttled swiftly enough, but it takes a good deal of time to do that to a man's hands.' I rounded on Jaculus. 'You know exactly how long I was in here before I came out to tackle you. Tell your mistress.'

Jaculus regarded me reproachfully, pointedly massaging his jaw. His mouth had stopped bleeding, but the bruise on his chin was swelling.

'Tell her!'

'He wasn't in here more than a minute or two,' he conceded grudgingly. 'I'd hardly taken a bite of supper before he ruined it.' He seemed more aggrieved about that than his battered face.

'Then your friend had obviously enjoyed company before you arrived,' the woman said. 'Was it one of our regulars, Jaculus?'

'We've entertained the gentleman I showed into this room a few times before. But when I left him in here, he was alone. And that' – Jaculus gestured towards the bed without looking at it – 'is not him. He's not the man I brought in here tonight. That one is a regular customer, though. Well, he used to be. Not likely to be coming back now, is he?' He gave a little chuckle. 'But I didn't see him come into the Hunting Lodge tonight.'

'You're lying. I told you I was looking for Erasmus,' I said, 'and you said he was waiting for me in here.'

'The man I showed in here said a Master Issott would come at nine of the clock and he'd give the name *Erasmus*. I thought it was a password. Lots of our gentlemen use them when they're expecting company. I thought it was him you were coming to see, not that one.' Again, he gestured vaguely in the direction of the bed.

'Did you leave the cellar tonight, Jaculus?' the woman said, her tone crackling with ice.

The light was too dim to read her servant's expression, but there was a moment's hesitation. 'I'd never leave my post, m'lady. You know that. Never, I swear it.'

'Then did someone bring you the dish of pigs' ears and trotters?' I asked.

The slap echoed off the stone walls like a musket shot and Jaculus yelped, falling to his knees as the woman rained more blows on his head. He made no attempt to defend himself. He probably knew from experience it was better to let her vent her displeasure. I suspected that any punishment meted out after her initial rage had cooled was likely to be far worse. She kicked him away and sent him sprawling to the ground, where he wisely remained.

'The man who told you Master Issott would come asking and would give you the name Erasmus. What did he look like?' I asked.

'No names, no faces,' Jaculus chanted.

'He's just tortured and murdered a man!' I snarled, coming close to kicking him myself.

'If you want to take revenge for your friend, that's your business,' the woman said, 'but you will get no help from my servants. As I told you, accidents happen and the watch know better than to come sniffing round here. Some of our patrons are powerful men and women. Their reach is long – extremely long, Master Issott.'

The man in the black robe gave a little bow. 'I greatly fear, sir, that it would bring nothing but calamity down upon your distinguished head, were you to report this trifling matter. For, were I to be questioned by the justices, I would be obliged to tell them I saw you myself with your friend the other night. And if I was under oath, in all conscience I would be obliged to mention he appeared to be afraid of you. Most reluctant to go off with you, but it seems he dared not refuse. And Jaculus would have to tell them you were the only one who was with this unfortunate gentleman tonight. It would break my heart to see you hanged for this incident, dangling on the gallows for all the world to mock at, and your handsome face, all hideously swollen and purple. Look at him, sir, not a pretty sight, is it? We don't want you to end up looking like that now, do we?'

From his place on the floor, still sprawled at the woman's feet, Jaculus sniggered.

As she held the candle over the mutilated body, forcing me to look at it again, I caught a glint of something yellow tucked into the flayed hands crossed over his chest. The edges of the petals were stained with blood, but even at a distance I knew what it was – a single dried marigold.

'You will learn nothing from us,' the woman said, lowering the candle, 'and you would do well to forget your friend ever existed. Never bait lions, Master Issott, unless you wish to be their next meal.'

Chapter Twenty-seven

SALISBURY HOUSE, THE STRAND, LONDON

ROBERT CECIL, seated at his supper table, was not really listening to the chatter of his guests, particularly the lady seated next to him, who seemed intent on describing the speech, costume and gesture of each of the actors in the King's Men's most recent play. It had been tedious enough when Cecil had been forced to endure it himself, at James's command, but this woman's muddled recital made it seem even worse than he remembered. He should have had her seated far down the hall with the masque designer, Inigo Jones, and the playwright, Ben Jonson; then the three of them could have bored each other to death.

Although all the candles in the Great Hall had been lit, the room was so long it was almost impossible to distinguish who was sitting at the lower tables, or even at the ends of his own table, though he could hear Sir Christopher Veldon's infuriating drawl and the simpering giggles of the woman he was flirting with. At least the silver and glassware glittered and sparkled reassuringly, proof they had been thoroughly polished, even if it was too dark to inspect them properly. Cecil sipped his wine and found himself staring fixedly at the glass ewer in the form of a boat, an exquisite piece of Venetian craftsmanship which he had only recently been gifted. But he realised it was not the glasswork that held his attention, but the reflection of the tiny candle flames in it, which he could not tear his gaze from. God's bones, he must be more weary than he thought.

He dragged his gaze away and glanced pointedly at the side table where his carver was, with slow and painstaking precision, slicing up the goose, the breast of mutton and the ribs of roast beef. Cecil knew his impatient stare would not be seen, of course, not in this light, but courtesy demanded that he did not interrupt the prattling of his guest to bark instructions to a servant. Carving was a work of art that should not be rushed, but tonight Cecil was barely able to contain his frustration. He was itching to retire to his office, where a satchel of papers awaited his attention as Secretary of State, in addition to the other, far more interesting, correspondence which he trusted might also be waiting for him, from his intelligencers and agents scattered throughout the realm and far beyond.

The sewer checked that the linen arming towel was still neatly folded over his right shoulder and tucked in place beneath the girdle under his left arm, then took up the first of the dishes containing the goose, paused to bow his head in the centre of the room, and approached Cecil at a slow and solemn pace. He inclined his head again to his master, before laying the dish in front of him. He was followed by a servant bearing the sorrel sauce. The sewer repeated his procession to collect the beef from the carver and deliver that to the high table with its dish of vinegar sauce, then finally the mutton, to be served with gallandine sauce. Pastries and custard tarts also appeared, placed between Cecil and his guest.

Cecil had sat down to dine with little appetite, but as the smell of the meats and sauces wafted over the table, he found his stomach growling. The beef and goose were closest to the lady and she was already laying slices of them on her plate. Cecil helped himself to the mutton, and uncovered the thick bread sauce. Steam rose from it, fragrant with ginger, cinnamon and wine. He ladled it on to his plate, turning as he did so to the lady, to acknowledge the compliment she had just paid him over the excellent fare. All eyes were upon Cecil. No one could eat until he had taken the first bite, and aware that his guests were probably now as hungry as he was, he turned back to his plate and lifted his knife. He dropped it at once with a cry, scrambling to his feet in such haste that the chair he'd been sitting on fell backwards with a crash.

'How dare you serve meat like this to my guests? It is bloody, crawling with maggots!'

There were gasps and cries from some of the guests and officers in his household as they peered down at the meat that had been set in the messes before them, some even holding their platters up to the candlelight or sniffing at them.

The sewer and carver ran towards the high table, ignoring the courtesies of the bows they should have made when approaching it. Reaching it at the same time, they seized the dish of mutton slices, wrestling it between them as they both pressed to examine it.

'How could you not have noticed?' Cecil demanded.

But the two men were now staring at the platter in utter bewilderment. The sewer released the dish to the carver and lifted Cecil's own plate, on which were three slices of mutton and the rapidly cooling gallandine sauce. He seized one of the candles and held it close to the meat.

'My lord, I beg . . . but the mutton is wholesome . . . well roasted and there are no worms in it, nothing.'

Cecil stared back down at his plate and then at the dish of mutton. The sewer was right. The meat was perfectly cooked, and there was no sign of maggots or indeed anything else crawling on it.

A servant had righted the chair, and Cecil sank back down on to it with an uneasy laugh. 'Archbishop Bancroft once told me I see spies and traitors under every bed in England. If he were here, he would no doubt accuse me of seeing them on my plate now too.'

Nervous laughter rippled among his guests.

'I dare say one of the household is playing a jest upon you, Lord Salisbury,' Veldon called out. 'I saw such a joke played once at the Christmas feast of the late Queen. Unseen by all of us, the jester sprinkled pieces of dried catgut on to the hot meats of one of the guests and once the pieces had soaked and heated, they began wriggling about like worms.'

The laughter from the guests was louder than the account of the trick warranted. Cecil smiled and nodded, urging everyone to eat. Studied conversation and peals of unnatural merriment rang out among the guests, determined to show that their host's outburst had not troubled them in the least. At the side table, the carver and sewer were whispering anxiously together. The guests might be able to shrug it off, but the servants knew the matter was far from over. Their master would not let this go unpunished.

'IT MIGHT HAVE BEEN a trick with catgut or something similar, my lord, as your guest Sir Christopher Veldon remarked,' Inigo Jones ventured uneasily.

The small chamber to which he'd been shown after dinner was warm and inviting after the draughty hall, perhaps a little too warm and stifling, for Jones was perched uncomfortably on the edge of the chair, the thick strands of his unruly brown hair clinging damply to his forehead. He kept tugging at his soft linen collar, streaked with greasy stains where he had fingered it a hundred times already that evening. The glasses of wine Lord Salisbury had unexpectedly invited him to share were being poured by no less a person than Cecil's steward. After the events at dinner, he would trust none of the other servants to wait on his master.

'You would know about such tricks, of course, Master Jones,' Cecil said. 'You are the master of illusion and this was mere child's play compared to those you've created when staging the King's masques – conjuring oceans with rolling waves on dry land, thunder roaring and the sun blazing out in the middle of the night.'

A look of horror replaced the perpetually anxious expression on Inigo Jones's face. 'My lord, I swear I had no part—'

Cecil waved a hand, cutting him off. 'You are not accused of tonight's mischief, Master Jones. But someone will be,' he added darkly. 'If catgut could be scattered so easily on a dish intended for my table, then so could poison.'

'I will personally question every member of the kitchen staff and yeoman waiters, my lord,' Cecil's steward assured him with a bow.

'See that you do,' Cecil snapped. 'Someone must have seen something.'

But the truth was, he wasn't at all sure now that he had seen anything himself, real or fake. The night before, he had retired late. Realising that he had read the same passage three times without taking in a word of it, he'd surrendered to what his body was urging and climbed the stairs to his bedchamber. The passageway was dark, most of the lights had been safely extinguished for the night, and he had used only a chamber candle to light his way. He had been almost at his door when he saw another light approaching him. But he couldn't see who was holding it. Assuming it to be a servant, but guessing the man could no more see who was walking towards him than he could, Lord Salisbury had made some comment to alert him, expecting the servant to greet him respectfully and stand aside, but the flame had not wavered. He'd called out again as he walked towards the light. Then, to his horror, he saw that there was no one holding the candle. There *wasn't* even a candle, only a blue flame hovering in mid-air in the centre of the passageway.

His startled cry had summoned the servant who'd been waiting patiently in his bedchamber to help his master disrobe and settle for the night. He'd hurried out with his own chamber stick and the disembodied flame had instantly vanished. Naturally, his master had said nothing to him. But Cecil had lain awake half the night, unable to banish the vision from his mind. Finally, he persuaded himself that he had seen a reflection of his own candle, perhaps in mirror or a glass, or a shiny metal ornament in the hallway.

In the morning he found himself unable to resist searching for what might have caused the illusion, though he had sworn he would think no more about it. And when he found nothing that might have reflected his candle flame at that spot, he had tried to convince himself that a hanging or tapestry must have been drawn away from the wall, exposing some object that had now been covered again. Perhaps like the meat, it was simply tired eyes playing tricks. He prayed it was that, and not that his wits were wandering.

The steward bowed out of the small chamber, and Cecil tried to pull himself back to the point of this interview. He had not invited Inigo Jones to supper for the pleasure of his company. Not that he ever invited any guest for so trivial a motive, and Jones plainly knew it, for he was looking as nervous as a prisoner who'd been shown the rack.

'Are you planning another entertainment, my lord? Do you wish me to design another set for a masque? I am at present amid feverish preparations for the masque Queen Anne has commissioned as a gift for the King for the eve of His Majesty's Accession Day, but of course, when that is concluded, I should be pleased to oblige you. Queen Anne has asked Master Jonson to write his verse on the theme of King Solomon and the Queen of Sheba. It will be staged—'

'I do have a task for you, Master Jones, but it is not an entertainment,' Cecil cut in quickly. He was in no mood to listen to another tedious description of a play that evening. He resettled his aching back against the cushions. 'There is a man currently in the Fleet prison, Tobie Matthew, the son of the Bishop of Durham. Perhaps you have heard of him?'

His gaze darted sharply to Jones's face. Cecil was already aware that the two men had been friends in their youth. Tobie was in his thirties, perhaps only five or so years younger than Jones.

'As you may know, Master Jones, Matthew was a promising young Member of Parliament, but four years ago, he was permitted to travel to Italy, where he fell under the malign influence of Catholic priests who converted him. Naturally, that marked the end of any career in Parliament he could have hoped for, and neither a spell in the Fleet prison nor the personal intervention of the Archbishop of Canterbury has since persuaded him back to the Protestant Church. Matthew has, however, pleaded with the Privy Council to be allowed to go into exile in Spain and that mercy has been granted to him, together with a period of grace of six weeks to put his affairs in order before he departs. He will be required to live under the offices of a guardian for those weeks, and you have been suggested as a man who may be relied upon to keep a firm hand on the prisoner until he departs these shores.'

Cecil did not see any reason to inform Jones that the condition he had imposed on Tobie Matthew's exile was that he was to become one of the spymaster's many pairs of ears and eyes in Spain.

Jones's face flushed and not simply from the heat of the fire. A look of delight and relief crossed his face. 'My lord, it would be an honour to be entrusted with his guardianship.'

'As someone who was raised a Catholic yourself, Master Jones, though as one who has rejected its excesses, you seem to be the ideal person to win Matthew's trust, without yourself being at risk from his corrupting influence.'

Inigo beamed, visibly swelling up with pride at the trust the Secretary of State was placing in him. He was man of great ambition, as Cecil knew, but was forced to fight a continuous battle to try to ingratiate himself into Court circles.

'I will watch him constantly, my lord. You need have no fear. I will exercise the utmost diligence in carrying out my duty to you and the Privy Council.'

Cecil nodded. 'From Matthew's correspondence with me, I am persuaded that he respects you and your judgement, Master Jones, so there is one other small matter I would like you to attend to for me. A property belonging to Tobie Matthew's father, the Bishop of Durham, borders my house here. You will no doubt have passed it as you arrived – that monstrosity, Durham House. It was leased out to various tenants, including Walter Raleigh, now incarcerated in the Marshalsea prison. He and most of the tenants have vacated the premises, but Matthew still owns a lease there. Obviously, since he is going into exile, he will have no use for it, but he will require the means to support himself in Spain. I am sure you will agree, it would be entirely in his interests if you could persuade him to sell the lease to me before he departs. You may suggest a figure of, say . . . one thousand two hundred pounds. No more, but I am willing to offer that much, which will keep him in relative comfort abroad for a few years.'

'That is a very generous sum, my lord.'

'Then let us hope you can convince Tobie Matthew of that, Master Jones, *before* he sails.'

If Inigo Jones was curious about why Robert Cecil was so keen to acquire the lease, he had the wit not to ask. Cecil had, for some time, been planning to build a rival to the Royal Exchange. His New Exchange, crammed with a hundred shops, would sell only the best and most lucrative merchandise. Located on the Strand, it would capture all the wealthy city trade. Only Tobie Matthew now stood in his way.

'MASTER JONES looks pleased with himself. He strutted past me like one of his mechanical peacocks,' Jeremy Northwood said, settling himself in the chair that was still warm from Jones's backside.

Cecil regarded his visitor with irritation. After the business of Tobie Matthew had been dealt with, he'd planned to retire to his bedchamber to read his letters. He was drooping with exhaustion and his back was paining him. He needed to lie down.

'Filling your house with players and playwrights, my lord? I hear Ben Jonson was telling everyone he was insulted that you had seated him with Jones well below the salt. Said he'd been invited to sup with you and couldn't even see you, he was so far down the table.'

'Is that so?' Cecil snapped. He was well aware that his agent took a malicious delight in stirring up trouble, but for once, tired and irritated, he allowed his temper to get the better of him. 'Then Master Jones need not trouble to come here again.'

Northwood grinned, helping himself to wine. 'I heard about that trick with the maggots this evening.' He glanced at Cecil, but Lord Salisbury's face gave nothing away. 'Interesting. You know, of course, His Majesty has had a few of the same jests played on him. That is, if they were intended to be jests. A waxen image served up with his morning bread, but you know about that, of course, you were there. And I dare say word reached you that he found a toad with pins through its heart in his chair of ease-ment three nights ago, and yesterday a slip of paper with magical symbols scrawled all over it stuck to the sole of his boot. He's convinced they're curses, of course.' He glanced over his wine-glass at the spymaster. 'You did know?'

'I have been informed,' Cecil said coldly. Maggots in the meat were a child's jest, not a witch's curse, but all the same he did not like being the butt of a joke in his own household, in front of his guests.

'I don't believe in such things myself,' Northwood said, 'but I dare say it doesn't matter if the curses themselves have no power. If they can make a man run mad, thinking dead toads and wax dolls can hurt him, then they've done their work. And they've certainly put fleas down James's breeches. He'll not sleep in the same bedchamber two nights running and has his private rooms searched twice a day, top to bottom. Is that the intention, do you think, to make him jump at his own shadow?'

'To what end?' Cecil asked.

Northwood shrugged. 'I was hoping you might tell me. Though if this man they brought in through Battle is planning to make another attempt on the King's life, he'll hardly need to set light to a barrel of gunpowder. If this carries on, James will fright himself into Bedlam, or off the top of the Tower, without the assassin even needing to pull a knife.'

Cecil glanced at the door. It was firmly closed and well-padded against eavesdroppers. 'And young Oliver Fairfax?' he said, abruptly changing the subject. 'What do you make of him?'

'He's loyal to his cousin, which is only natural. Lord Fairfax is his sponsor at Court. But Richard humiliates and belittles the boy. It is breeding a simmering resentment in him, which I am sure a man with your talent can exploit, my lord.'

The amusement in Northwood's tone and expression only increased Cecil's irritation. 'Is that *all*? I trust it is news of more import than that which brings you here at this late hour. Battle Abbey? Is our man still there and still not suspected?'

Northwood nodded. 'He would be dead if he were. But he can't stay there much longer. The old dowager is ailing and he says her physicians agree she will not live to see this summer through. Our priest will stay to learn all he can about where his fellow priests are being sent next. It seems likely Lady Magdalen's chaplain will start to move them on soon. Smith knows that once the old woman dies, Little Rome dies with her, and he for one will have to find another rat hole to scurry into. But now that Lord Buckhurst is dead and no longer able to influence the Privy Council, I think I can promise that the Council will move to crush Little Rome once and for all.'

Cecil folded his arms. 'See that they wait. Much as I would like to see her end her days shivering in the Tower, she is too well loved in Catholic quarters. If we're patient for another few weeks until she is safely buried, then it will be easy to arrest the servants and all those involved, without anyone bothering to protest. You have the names?'

'The priest will supply them, a full list. Smith is grown careless. He's certain that the man he sent to his death on that ship was working for you, and now that he believes he's disposed of him, he's relaxed his guard.' Northwood laughed. 'Your fake priest has done well to fool a man like him. Smith checks thoroughly, I am told.'

'But we laid a trail that could be checked. The Yena's work has been excellent. Better than I could have hoped, and as a genuine priest, he knows exactly what questions a man like Smith will ask. He can supply both the papers and an authentic story. And he confirms the intelligence you gathered from Battle, Northwood – the man who was smuggled in on that ship through the Abbey is already in London. They will strike soon.'

Northwood inclined his head as though he were graciously accepting the compliment that his intelligence had been sound. But Cecil derived some satisfaction from watching his fingers tighten on the glass. He was annoyed that his information had been checked. Good! Northwood needed to be reminded that the watcher was also being watched, just in case he got any ideas about deviating from the truth.

'Does the Yena know how and where the attempt will be made, my lord?'

Cecil evaded the question. 'It will not appear to be an obviously Catholic plot. The Papists learned how swiftly the commons turned against them when the Gunpowder Treason failed; even the ordinary men of their own faith were appalled by it.'

'As you ensured they would be, my lord,' Northwood said acidly, evidently still smarting. "The Devil of the Vault" – wasn't that the phrase you fed to the broadsides and pamphleteers, my lord? Malicious conspirators burrowing away beneath the beds of innocent children and the kitchens of their wives and mothers, ready to burst up through the earth and slaughter them all like demons from the pit of hell. Some in the Privy Council are surprised you didn't order a tunnel dug. You could have charged the commons to view it and made enough money to keep the King in new clothes for a year.'

Cecil spoke as though he hadn't been interrupted. He was in no mood to be baited tonight, and his tone was icy. 'I believe that they will make it seem to be the work of a lone madman, or even an unfortunate accident – the sabotage of a bridge or a building, so that bad workmanship can be blamed, or it can be laid at the feet of malcontents, like those who rose in the Newton Rebellion. That is, after all, still fresh in the minds of the commons and the broadside writers.'

'Perhaps they mean to make it look like witchcraft, one of those curses come true,' Northwood added slyly. 'But I wager you've learned more of this plot than mere conjecture, my lord. Do you intend to let it run again, like the Gunpowder Treason, then expose it at the last minute? Another anonymous letter to the King with hints so broad even a child of six could fathom it out, while you feign complete surprise and awe at his wit? Not even James will swallow that a second time, much less the broadside scribblers.'

Cecil rose, his face in shadows. 'My duty is to keep this realm safe. And I will do what I deem necessary to ensure that – *whatever* I deem necessary. No one, whoever they are, or whatever good offices they have performed in the past, will be permitted to get in the way of that.'

Chapter Twenty-eight

LONDON

DANIEL PURSGLOVE

By THE TIME I reached the inn where I was lodging, its parlour was in darkness and I knew the maids would long be in their beds. I plodded up to my own chamber and stripped off my wet clothes, but not before I'd pushed the hatch-table in front of the door. It wouldn't stop someone determined to enter, but it would mean they couldn't come in without waking me. My dagger close by my hand beneath the blankets, I lay down and tried to sleep. I was exhausted and cold, but sleep would not come. The faces of Sibyl, Myles and Erasmus swam pale and bloody before my eyes each time I closed them.

I had neither tortured nor murdered them, but I might as well have plunged my own knife into each one of them. For I knew that it couldn't be a coincidence that I had met with each of them before they had been killed. But their deaths made no sense. Sibyl might well have had information about Catholic fugitives, which she would not be persuaded to divulge except under torture. But if Myles had known anything of value, he'd have willingly sold that information for the promise of a few coins, and mere threats would have been enough to loosen Erasmus's tongue.

What if those poor souls had not been the quarry but the bait, the dumb beasts slaughtered to lure the real prey – me! Richard would love to see me dead, but not even he would have tortured those people just to take revenge on me. I could think of only one man who would have reason to pursue me so ruth-lessly. I had quested after Spero Pettingar; were these murders intended as an elaborate warning of what would happen to me if I didn't abandon the hunt? No, that didn't make sense. Sibyl and Erasmus were both loyal Catholics – as, I assumed, was Pettingar. The Gunpowder Treason was, after all, a plot to fur-ther the Catholic cause. Besides, if Pettingar wanted to throw me off his track, why not simply kill me and put an end to the threat I posed?

But it was not the first time I had born the guilt for the deaths of innocent and defenceless people, slaughtered because of what I had done.

Bodies of slain men, women and children lying broken and crushed among the reeds in that Irish lake, their faces white and frozen in terror, blood streaming from their sodden hair and clothes, turning the water scarlet. And their frightened eyes, all open, staring up at me. *Why, why have you done this to us?* The boy whimpers for the woman who will never come to him, never kiss away his pain, never save him. *A mháthair . . . A mháth—* The word, like the child, dies in my arms.

I tried to convince myself that if I'd dreamed, then I must have slept, but as I dashed water over my face and struggled into still damp boots, my aching body wasn't convinced. I lumbered down the stairs as clumsily as a man twice my age and found a place in the parlour where I could eat while watching the door.

The scowl on the face of the serving maid doling out the breakfast deepened as the customers groused about the meagre amounts of coarse bread and butter they were served. The sprats which the innkeeper offered to make up for the lack of bread would not keep a man's belly filled until dinner, as they were quick to point out. Most ate swiftly and hurried out, anxious to be about their business. But I made what little there was last as long as I could, sitting there until the girl returned to clear the empty trenchers. She glowered at me, clattering the jugs and beakers to show her irritation that I had not finished eating, but I refused to be dislodged.

Then, when I'd almost given up, the door was thrust open again and the maid I had been waiting for came through, nudging the door aside with her hip and staggering beneath the weight of fresh coals for the fire, a broom and cloths. I took the pail of coal from her, setting it down by the fire. She looked surprised to find the parlour still occupied at that hour, but thanked me.

'I was hoping I might see you,' I said.

She gave a faint smile, but avoided looking at me and busied herself, making it plain she did not have time to talk. Although that morning she was rather dishevelled, a smear of soot on her face and her tangled hair slithering out from beneath her cap, she was still a comely young woman, with fetching dimples in her plump cheeks. I'd no doubt she was well used to men at the inn demanding more than a tankard of ale from her and she'd learned to be wary of any man who tried to get her alone. But I needed to do just that. I glanced around to ensure that no one could see me talking to her if they happened to look in through the small window from the street. I did not want her to become another victim.

I waited until she had knelt down in front of the fire to sweep the scattered ash from the hearthstones.

'Yesterday, you gave me a letter that a man had asked you to deliver to me. Do you remember?' I kept my voice low and my head down, appearing to be occupied still with my breakfast.

Her head jerked round and she stared at me anxiously. 'I didn't take nothing from the letter, sir, nothing. Only what he gave me for my trouble.'

'I know you didn't. The seal wasn't broken. You are not in any trouble. I only wanted to ask if you can remember what the man looked like?'

She rocked back on her heels as she considered the matter. 'There's customers come to the inn all day and all evening, sir, so many of them. Don't remember their faces, barely have time to glance at most of them, if you want the truth. Well, unless they're . . .'

'Young and good-looking,' I suggested.

She giggled.

'But I don't think this man would have been young. Was he as old as me, do you think? Older?'

She craned round to peer at me again.' Like I say, sir, I don't have time to look. The master and mistress keeps me that busy, it's a wonder I don't meet myself coming back.'

'But you'd remember this man. He must have spent a while explaining carefully who you had to deliver the letter to. And he paid you well, I dare say.'

I skimmed a coin across the floor towards her and she caught it deftly, darting a nervous glance towards the door to the kitchen as she squirrelled it away.

'Maybe he was a bit older than you, sir, but he'd no flesh on him. That always makes it hard to tell. Can't say as I can recall his face, not enough to describe it.' She gave a bright little nod. A new thought had struck her. 'It's 'cause I was looking at his beard, that's why. It was coal-black, like his hair, but it had this white streak straight down the middle of it. There was one of our old gentlemen used to ride here with a horse like that whenever he came to London. Black it was, but with this white streak straight down its nose and another through its tail, like someone had daubed the creature with limewash. He used to boast it'd never be stolen, 'cause you could spot that horse a mile off. But it was thieved though. All the priggers had to do was to dye the white streaks black, easiest thing in the world.'

'This man's beard was trimmed into a sharp point?'

She glanced at my own bushy beard before nodding vigorously. 'So sharp that if he starched it, I reckon it could put a girl's eye out. You know the man, then, sir? Friend of yours, is he?'

There was no mistaking him. Gaunt face, black hair and the black beard with the distinctive white streak in it. The same man that I'd seen in the Lusty Tup in the Ridings and in Bristol. The same man I'd seen before Sibyl and Myles had been murdered, and now he was here in London. He had drawn me to the Hunting Lodge, where he knew I would find Erasmus dead, knew because he had killed him, as he had killed Sibyl and Myles. I had suspected that Myles and Sibyl had both been killed by one of Cecil's pursuivants. The torture they'd endured had all the hallmarks of one of his henchmen. Now Erasmus, like the others, had been tortured and murdered by one of them too and there seemed no doubt who that pursuivant was – Badger-beard.

'I know him,' I said grimly. 'He's a dangerous man, not one you'd want to tangle with. So, I want you to swear you won't tell anyone I was asking questions about him.'

I bowled another coin towards her and rose to leave, stuffing the last fragment of sprat into my mouth and washing it down with the dregs of the ale. 'If you should see him again, make sure he doesn't trap you alone in a room or out on the street.'

Her eyes widened in alarm, but her chin jerked up. 'I can take care of myself. I've met men like that before,' she added defiantly.

'Not like this one, girl. If you had, you'd be floating face down in the Thames with a rope round your neck and worse.'

Chapter Twenty-nine

I STOOD IN THE DARKNESS of my new lodgings and pulled open the wooden shutters of the casement a crack to stare out. An alleyway ran between the two warehouses on the opposite side of the street, and the gap between the buildings allowed me to see a strip of the Thames. Red and gold slithers of light darted across the oily black water from torches and lanterns and from small fires burning along the banks. Shouts, cries and raucous laughter mingled with snatches of music from inns or tenement courtyards, their notes clashing like rutting deer as one group of musicians tried to drown out the neighbouring ones with their own favoured tune.

Though it was an hour or so after sunset and a light rain was falling, wherries still ploughed up and down the river, their lanterns dangling from poles in front, luring the boats to follow them. Some men were travelling home from their business in the city; others were setting off for the evening, eager to sample the many pleasures offered by the inns, playhouses, gambling tables and stews. A few people hurried up the alley, turning along the street below my window. This area was much better lit than many of the backstreets of London, and no one appeared to be lingering to watch any of the buildings.

I had resolved to leave the inn where I'd been staying as soon as I'd learned who had delivered the message sending me to the Hunting Lodge. I wanted to keep the serving maid from coming to any harm, if I could, and, moreover, I had a healthy desire to keep my own carcass out of the Thames.

The room I had found was above a workshop. It was sparsely furnished, but the owner had tried to charge an exorbitant price, and it took a great deal of haggling to get him to reduce it. But though it lacked comfort, it had certain advantages. One entrance was through the small workshop. No one could slip in that way without the owner seeing. At night, the workshop was locked, as was the door which led from it to my attic staircase – the landlord plainly didn't trust his tenants – but I knew I could get out that way if I was cornered. The second way up was by a flight of wooden stairs at the back of the building from a ground-floor storeroom. It was unused by the owner and was piled with an odd assortment of old furniture, including a battered table, too long to fit my small chamber, and a throne-like chair with a missing leg.

I closed the shutters, dropping the iron bar in place to secure them, and wedged rags beneath and between them to ensure no glimmer escaped into the darkness outside, before lighting the candle on the rickety table. I did not want to announce the room was occupied yet, though I knew word would get round soon enough.

It was not Badger-beard who was concerning me at that moment. If he'd wanted to kill me, he'd already had a dozen chances. Anyone who could get in and out of the Hunting Lodge with a body – and I was sure Erasmus had already been dead or close to it before he was planted in that room – could have found a way to murder me long before now, if my death was his objective. No doubt he had other plans for me. He would eventually find me here; maybe he already knew where I had gone. No, it was FitzAlan I was more anxious to avoid just now, or rather whichever of *his* men might have tracked my return to London.

As soon as I had learned of the plot against the King, I'd known I should report it to FitzAlan, and leave it to him and that polecat Cecil to uncover the details and make their arrests. They'd done that many times before. For all I knew, Cecil's agents had already informed him of this new threat. Maybe that was why Badger-beard had been following me from one city to the next, 'questioning' people I knew. He thought I would lead him to the ringleader and his fellow conspirators. That's why I hadn't yet found myself choking with a rope around my neck and my hands crushed in his iron gauntlets. He was letting me run.

I should go straight to FitzAlan, tell him what little I'd gleaned. It would be safer for me and those around me if I did, for I'd no longer be of any use to Cecil or Badger-beard. And if I didn't tell FitzAlan all I knew, I could easily find myself on the scaffold. The charge of misprision of treason carried no lesser penalty than treason itself. The Jesuit Henry Garnet had been hanged, drawn and quartered for not speaking out when he got wind of the Gunpowder Treason, and he had pleaded the seal of the confessional. I didn't even have that excuse.

I could flee abroad, of course. Leave James to whatever fate they had in store for him. After all, what did I really know? Some plot was afoot to kill the King, but how, where or when I had no idea. I didn't know the identity of the mysterious woman who had visited the old fortune-teller and Zephora. I couldn't even be certain the woman's fears were real. Half the wives in England must have heard their husbands grumble that the country would be better off if King James and his family were wiped out, and maybe they were right. Only the Scots had profited by his accession; England had been bled dry for it.

But the flaming star that heralds the violent death of kings drags war and destruction in its wake. James's murder would plunge the whole kingdom into civil war, and once bloodshed begins, it's the defenceless and the innocent who suffer worst of all. I was already guilty of the death of too many innocents; I would not have more on my conscience.

But if I told FitzAlan, I would be condemning others to the same fate as Garnet's. Robert Cecil would order the arrest, not just of the conspirators, but anyone remotely connected to them. The ringleader had been brought into England through

Battle Abbey. Lady Magdalen, her ward, Katheryne, and even the servants, including my erstwhile drinking companion, Arthur, would be arrested and questioned. I didn't much care if Father Smith was taken; in fact, I'd almost enjoy the sight of him being dragged on a hurdle through the streets. There had been times in Battle Abbey when I'd gladly have placed the noose round his neck myself. Smith was as guilty as any man who ever conspired to lay a match to a barrel of gunpowder, but priests like him have a habit of slinking away, vanishing into the night, leaving the Arthurs of this world to hang in manacles until they suffocated or their guts burst open, because the poor bastards cannot confess what they do not know.

And if Waldegrave was one of those arrested? I had wanted him dead, but when I believed he was, I had felt cheated. Could I stand there and watch him be stretched naked on the block, watch them drag his guts from his belly and cut off his cods, to expunge his descendants as if they never existed, as if *I* had never existed?

The only way to protect the innocent was to save the guilty. James must live. The Serpent must not be allowed to strike.

I dragged myself off the bed and cracked the shutter open once more, peering out into the street below. Solitary figures hurried along, their heads bent against the rain and gusting wind, so intent on reaching their destination, they scarcely seemed aware of those that passed them. The cutpurses would earn a good sum tonight. But the foul weather was a mask that I also could make use of: with a hood drawn low and a muffler covering most of my face, I would not attract a single curious eye on a night like this.

As soon as I slipped from the comparative shelter of the narrow alleyway, the wind, always keener along the river, pounced, snatching the breath away. Rain rattled like musket shot on to the churning black water.

Acrid smoke from a thousand chimneys, workshops and cooking fires gusted down over the river, making the eyes water and the throat sting with its stench of burning whale oil, coal, tar and burned bone. Fistfights spilled from the taverns on to the quayside; insults and curses were hurled in a dozen different languages. I wove an erratic path along the quayside, dodging mis-aimed punches, piles of horse shit, ropes, barrels, heaps of sailcloth, stray dogs and all the other hazards that might pitch the unwary straight into the icy river.

A small knot of men was gathered on the edge of the bank, raining angry threats and vicious blows down on someone in the centre of the group who had been stupid or unlucky enough to offend them – most likely a wherry boat customer who'd refused to pay up, or a clumsy nip who'd tried to steal their day's takings. Just as I passed them, one of the men stepped back to get a better swing, moving straight across my path. As I sidestepped him, he slipped on the mud-slimed stones, crashing down on his backside in a puddle of filth. Still sitting on the sodden ground, he cursed me roundly for getting in his way. Neither his dignity nor his temper were soothed by the gales of laughter and ribald jeers of his fellow boatmen, who had turned to look, momentarily distracted from the lesson they were inflicting on their captive. Between us, one of the wherrymen and I hauled the man to his feet.

'Lucky you didn't end up in the river, brother,' I told him. 'I'd not try to settle a quarrel so close to the edge on a night like this.'

The man who'd helped his companion up gave me a malicious grin, revealing a jaw full of broken or missing teeth. 'We was just explaining the very same thing to this one here. Lucky he hasn't found himself floating in the river already. Dangerous business working these waters, if you don't know what you're doing. Accidents happen all the time, don't they, lads?'

The others grinned. 'Nasty accidents,' they chorused. 'Very nasty.'

'We've pulled some of 'em from the river so battered their own mothers wouldn't have known them.'

The group of men had parted slightly, revealing a young lad crouching in the centre of them. The beating having been temporally halted, he staggered to his feet, cowering, evidently expecting another blow to fall. As he warily raised his head, a stream of scarlet blood trickled from beneath a shock of tow hair, running into one of his pale, frightened eyes. Though his lip was cut and swelling, and his cheek badly bruised, his face was vaguely familiar, and for a moment or two, I thought I must have seen him in one of the inns. Then, as he glanced beseechingly in my direction, an image flashed into my head of a boy staring at me before with just such an imploring expression, a boy standing beside another river, telling me how he longed to leave Breighton. *I don't want to be a ferryman here, forever going back and forth over the same little bit of water for the rest of my days like him.*

The ferryman's son, Dob, looked even more skinny than when I had last seen him, every bone and joint pressing out through his skin. It seemed that only the grip of the man holding him from behind was preventing the wind from picking him up like a twig and tossing him into the river.

'I know this lad,' I said quickly. 'Runaway apprentice. His master's looking for him, means to give him the whipping of a lifetime when he gets his hands on him. Got notions about running off to sea to make his fortune in the New World. Old seadogs have been filling his head with tales of Spanish treasure, reckons he'll come back as rich as Captain Drake.'

All the time I was talking, I was inching towards Dob until I could grab his shoulder. 'You come along with me, lad. Your master will be only too glad to give you a taste of the sea-life – a sound flogging and a week of bread and water, just like on the ships. He might even sprinkle a few weevils in it to give it a proper flavour.'

By now the men were laughing heartily and throwing in their own suggestions for what the boy might expect. The man holding him by the arms had relaxed his grip and I pulled the lad forward, jerking him from the man's grasp. Holding Dob tightly, I marched him rapidly away, as the men continued to shout jokes after him.

As soon as he was at a safe distance from them, he tried to squirm out of my grip, plainly not remembering who I was. He kept protesting that I'd mistaken him and he was no runaway apprentice. I ignored his complaints and when I judged that we were far enough away, I pushed him through the door of a small alehouse, feebly lit by a few poor candles.

I shoved him on to a stool in a corner, and seated myself so that he couldn't push past me.

'You may not have run away from any master, but I'd wager you didn't have your father's blessing to come to London.'

A girl set down two beakers of strong beer in front of us, without troubling to ask what we wanted, and took the coins I dropped into her hand without a word.

Dob lifted his beaker with a shaking hand and drank awkwardly, dribbling and wincing as the liquid touched his cut and swollen lip.

'What did you do to rile those men?' I asked him.

'Only asking for work,' he mumbled. 'Laughed at me. Said I was too skinny to row, so I started to untie one of the boats, just to show what I could do. That's when . . .'

He trailed off, rubbing his arm. Given the blows he'd taken on his body, he'd be lucky if he could stir from his bed come morning when those bruises stiffened.

'You're fortunate they just gave you a beating. They could have killed you for stealing one of their boats, and I doubt even the watch would have stopped them, because it would save the city the expense of paying the hangman to do it.'

'Wasn't stealing!' Dob muttered indignantly. 'I was just going to show them I could row as well as any of them.' He clamped his hand to his mouth. It was plainly hurting him to talk.

'Work on the wherries is handed down from father to son, like with your own father's ferry. They don't take kindly to outsiders muscling in.'

He peered at me and I cursed myself. I'd given him advice like that before.

'I know you . . . crossed on ferry in the flood. You had a fine horse. Bubwith men came looking for you,' he added breathlessly, now alive with interest. 'They were asking if you'd crossed back, said if you tried, we were to hold you and send word. But you never came.' He leaned closer, and gasped, holding his bruised ribs. 'That owd lass that got murdered, did you really do it?' he whispered. There was no fear in his face, but his eyes glittered with the kind of excitement that lads show when listening to tales of vicious pirates or bloody battles.

I assured him I hadn't. He looked positively disappointed, but seemed to believe me.

'I know of a cheap lodging house, Dob. You'd be obliged to share a room with several others, probably have to share your bed too. But the woman who runs it is a motherly soul. If you tell her you're newly come to the city and got set upon by some Scots lads, she'll take you in. She hates the Scots.' I gave him directions and, fishing out a few shillings, grabbed his hand and thrust them in it. 'That should buy you a few nights and enough to fill your belly till the worst of the bruises have faded and you can manage to walk without groaning. Then as soon as you're fit to travel, set off and head straight back home, lad. It's where you belong.'

He had taken the money without protest, but at this last piece of advice, he stared sullenly down at the table.

'I could work for you,' Dob suddenly blurted out with as much eagerness as his cut lip would allow. 'Folks are always laughing at me. Reckon I must be nesh, 'cause I'm as skinny as a reed. But I am stronger than I look. I can best the Derwent even when it's in flood. You'd not be sorry you took me on.'

'I've no need of a servant,' I told him firmly. 'If you won't go back, then when your face is mended, try taking yourself to one of the inns like the Wrestler by Bishop's Gate. They keep coaches and horses there. You'd make a good stableboy. You like horses, don't you?' From the way he'd handled Valentine, I already knew he did.

Though he continued to plead, I rose, making the excuse that I needed the jakes. I did not intend that he should be seen again in my company. I slipped out into the street and found a dark corner where I could watch the door of the inn to ensure the boy wasn't followed or waylaid. I waited with growing impatience, but after what felt like half an hour, Dob seemed to finally realise that I was not returning and limped out of the inn. He had evidently taken my advice, for after a few false turns he headed in the direction of the lodging house I'd suggested. No one appeared to be trailing him and I deliberately walked the opposite way, squelching through the mud and filth, trying to avoid the worst of the overflowing gullies as the rain beat down.

THE RAIN AND icy wind had driven most men and women off the streets, either into the inns and gaming houses or to huddle close to their own hearths. I passed a few beggars sheltering in doorways and was splashed with icy water by the wheels of a gong farmer's wagon as it rumbled through the streets with its kegs of shit. The driver kept up a constant stream of mumbled oaths as he passed, though he seemed to be alone with his reeking cargo. I hoped that Titus would not bother to venture out on such a night, but when I slipped inside his lodgings, he had evidently not been home long, for I found Zephora kneeling in front of him by the small fire, dragging off his sodden boots and hose while he slurped a mug of steaming ale.

Catching sight of me, he nudged Zephora with a grimy bare foot. 'Lock the door, and you'd best brace it too. It won't stop this one getting in or out – Danni could break into the King's treasury, if he'd a mind to – but it might give us a bit of warning if his bloodhound decides to join us.'

'Bloodhound?' I asked, a cold chill gripping me.

Titus ignored the question, occupied with peeling off his remaining hose. He wrung it out and draped it over a stool next to the hearth, where it began to steam, stinking like Smithfield meat market in the high summer. He heaved his bare feet towards the hearth, wriggling his hairy toes in the warmth. Zephora nudged them aside as she crouched close to the fire, heating a poker to mull more ale.

'So, what brings you out on a night as foul as the Devil's piss, Danni?' Titus finally said.

'I've a proposition for Zephora.'

'Too late, Danni, she'll not be accepting any more propositions now. She's mine and I'm keeping her to myself.' He chuckled, leaning forward to pat her affectionately on the rump. She turned her head to smile fondly at him.

'And you'll be able to keep her like a lady in silks and sugared almonds, if this works.'

'What works?' Zephora spun round, giving me her full attention, the firelight turning her milky eye demon-red.

Titus nudged her shoulder with his empty mug. He had heard too many promises of riches before in his lifetime to believe any of them. Zephora took the mug impatiently, filled it, and thrust the hot poker in. It hissed and steamed. Then, pushing it back at him, she edged nearer to me.

'What are you scheming?' she demanded.

'First, have you found the Yena, Titus?'

He shook his head, hooking his foot up into his own lap and picking at a broken horny toenail. 'Early days, Danni. If a man don't want to be found, there's plenty of rat holes in this city where he can go to ground. But word's out. If he's in London, I'll ferret him out, don't you trouble yourself about that. Now, like Zeffy says, what scheme are you cooking up?'

'That woman who visits you and Mary in her cottage, Zephora. I need to find out more about the plot her husband is involved in.'

Zephora's saffron mane of hair swished across her cheek as she emphatically shook her head. 'Mary has told her she can't come back. Told her Avery won't speak to her no more. Mary's old. She's afraid. She don't want to get mixed up in anything like that, and no more do I.'

'You're already mixed up in it. If the plot is discovered, like the Gunpowder Treason was, then they'll find this lady and they'll torture her until she tells them everything. By the time they've finished with her, she'll be begging them to take her husband, her mother, her children, anyone she cares about, and inflict the agony on them instead of her. She'll give them you and Mary in her first breath.'

Zephora, trembling, shrank away from me, pressing her face into Titus's thigh. He wrapped his arms about her.

'Now see here, Danni. You and me have been friends for a good long time and I've always stood by you out on them streets, but I swear on my mother's grave, I'll see you lying in the gutter with your throat cut and rats feeding on you if you go frightening my Zeffy.' He stroked her hair. 'Said I'd take care of you, girl, and I meant it. I'll not let anyone harm you.'

'I don't want to frighten her or see any harm come to either of you. That's why I've come up with a way to keep you both safe from any threat of arrest. And you could find yourselves handsomely rewarded into the bargain if all goes well. Just hear me out, will you?'

Zephora slowly raised her head and regarded me warily, but at least she was listening.

'I'd wager this woman is desperate to talk to Avery again, especially if he can give her a charm to protect her husband and enough riches to escape the country.'

'But I told you, Mary won't let her in again,' Zephora protested. 'She'd not do it, even if you offered her a ship full of Spanish gold.'

'We will not involve Mary. I will find a place and prepare it. You will bring the woman there. That's all you have to do, Zephora, persuade her to come. And I will do the rest.'

It took a lot of persuasion to get Zephora even to agree to that, and a great deal more to convince Titus. The fire was burning low before I finally rose and made for the door. As I lifted the brace away, another thought struck, something I'd almost forgotten.

'My bloodhound, Titus . . . who did you mean?'

For a moment he looked bemused, his mind clearly still on the mystery woman and Zephora. 'Bloodhound? . . . Aye, one of my street-lads spotted a man seemed to be taking an uncommon interest in you. Saw him twice, but the boy said he probably wouldn't have noticed him, except for his beard. Made him stand out. Black it was, with a white streak right through it. Mean anything to you, does it, Danni?'

Chapter Thirty

WHEN THE KNOCK finally came on the stout oak door, it reverberated through the small stone watermill like thunder. *One, pause. One, two, pause. One, two, three. Silence.* Somewhere among the stones, a raven croaked and the door creaked open, moved by an invisible hand in answer to the knock.

I heard Zephora's voice, urging, 'In there, m'lady. Master Belizar is waiting. He'll not let harm come to you. He's a great magician and a proper gentleman. I'll be waiting right outside with the horses to see you safe back to the city again after.'

The woman hesitated on the threshold, as well she might. It could have been a trap. It *was* a trap, but she walked in. The mill wasn't in darkness. I didn't want to scare her, not yet. I knew she would already have been fearful about coming here. Two candles burned on pricks to light the rickety wooden stairs and four more glowed down from the room above, flames to entice the moth to flutter closer. Shutters covered the small casements and I had stuffed cloth and wool into any slits that were uncovered. Out here, in the country, a single glimmer of light would stand out like a beacon at night. On all the approaches to the old mill I had marked the crude symbol of a knife pointed outwards, a sign well known to vagrants and outlaws, telling them that tonight the mill was occupied by those who did not welcome intruders and if they wished to see the dawn, they would do well to look for another shelter.

I had discovered the mill a few miles from the city after I had been forced to flee Ireland. The watermill and the small forge it had once powered had been abandoned. Some said that the whole family who'd lived here had been found dead: *plague*, a few said; *murder*, others whispered, not even the dog left alive. They claimed you could still see the rusty bloodstains on the walls and boards. *Cursed*, most insisted: the Devil had gathered up the souls of the blacksmith and every living creature on the farmstead and dragged them screaming down to hell. The truth was doubtless more commonplace. The leet which carried the water had probably dried up, the stream which fed it choked or diverted, and the mill-owner forced to abandon the site. But that explanation wouldn't have served half as well in keeping the forge empty and prying eyes away.

Now the great millwheel lay still, covered with green oozing slime. Slow, steady drops fell with hollow ring into a pool of stagnant water and mud below, like the distant echo of ghost hammers. Chill air rolled up from it, washing into a room blackened with soot from long-dead fires. Rusty iron shafts and crumbling anvils lay covered in the husks of dead insects, the droppings of mice and rats, and the dust of decades.

As soon as the woman stepped over the threshold, the door shut with an echoing thud behind her and she gave a muffled shriek. For a moment, I feared the woman was going to wrench it open and flee, but she took a deep breath, lifting her head to gaze up at the glow of the lights in the room above. Through a gap in the floorboards, I could see her standing below me, caught in the candlelight on the stairs. She was enveloped in a coarse, ankle-length, mud-splattered cloak that appeared to have been borrowed from a serving maid. As she edged towards the steps, I glimpsed riding boots and breeches.

I stayed out of sight, letting my voice drift gently down to her. 'May the golden orb of the blessed spirits surround you. Come, enter into their presence.'

I cringed at having to spout such bilgewater, but I'd listened to enough fake fortune-tellers in my days on the road to know what the woman would be expecting.

The slow, measured creak on the stairs told me she was obeying, albeit warily. As she clambered up the last step, the flames of two candles below her snuffed out, plunging the staircase into darkness. She started violently, taking a rapid pace into the room, towards the light.

'Have no fear, m'lady, it is the sign that the spirits are close by.'

I had positioned myself at the far end of the room, dressed in voluminous black robes, a black silk cloth wound about my neck. A mask covered my eyes, nose and cheeks, set with silky black cockerel feathers that trembled and gleamed in the candlelight at the slightest movement of my head. She glanced nervously at the dark hole through which the staircase vanished. But her attention swiftly darted back to the scene I had prepared behind me.

I had dressed this room so that, in contrast to the one below, it looked like a fairy-tale palace. The broken, throne-like chair, stealthily removed from my new landlord's storeroom, had been draped with swathes of cloth to disguise where I'd roughly mended it and it now stood behind me. Titus had been pressed into finding a cart to carry the furniture and help lug it up the stairs. He hadn't wanted to, of course, but I'd reasoned with him – less chance of any harm coming to his adored Zeffy, if no one else was involved.

In front of the throne, I'd spread the long table I had also *borrowed* from my landlord with a white linen cloth, and furnished it with a flagon, a pewter goblet, and plates of glistening confit fruits – I'd had a hard time keeping the mice off those. And I'd scattered dried rose petals and sweet herbs across the cloth, around bowls of jewel-coloured liquids – translucent red, gold and green – to enhance the magic. A pleated canopy was draped gracefully over the scene – it was the only way I had been able to stop dirt, spiderwebs and insects in the rotting boards above from falling down on the table below. On the floor a little way from the table, I had drawn a red pentagram inside three concentric circles, filling the spaces with every magic symbol and Hebrew letter I could ever recall seeing and a few I'd made up to complete the effect.

I gestured to the low stool I'd placed in the very centre of the pentagram. 'M'lady, if you are ready to begin, I would ask you to lay aside your cloak and seat yourself inside the magic circle, which I have protected with strong charms and signs.'

She dragged her attention from the glowing bowls of liquid on the table. 'You can really summon him? Summon Avery? Zephora said you could ask him for a powerful amulet to protect my husband and . . .'

She trailed off. Zephora had also promised her escape money too, but I suspected the woman was reluctant to admit that for fear it might appear that wealth was all she wanted. Her accent was curious: I'd wager she'd been raised in a noble Yorkshire house, but had spent time among the ladies of the Royal Court, maybe even with James's Danish wife. My old master, Viscount Rowe, had told me that many of the ladies at Court were starting to acquire Queen Anne's manner of pronouncing certain English words. Could the plotter's wife be a lady-in-waiting to the Queen herself? After all, Robert Catesby, leader of the gunpowder plotters, had been a hunting companion of the King.

'Avery has made it known to me that he wishes to help and protect you, m'lady, but he can only do so if you trust him. Any doubts you have must be banished from your mind, for he will not come to those who do not truly wish for his help.' I gestured towards the table. 'I have done all I can do to welcome him. Now you must welcome him in your heart.'

'I will! I do!' she breathed.

'Then let us not keep the great spirit waiting, for he may become impatient and restless, and bestow his blessings on others instead of you.'

As I'd hoped, she threw back her hood and unfastened her cloak, dropping it on the floor in her eagerness to comply. Then she stepped carefully into the pentagram on tiptoes, doing her best to avoid treading on any of the signs and symbols. She lowered herself on to the stool and rearranged the position of her hands several times, plainly uncertain which pose would be most suitable for the supplication of a spirit.

'Whatever you see or hear,' I warned, 'do not step outside of the circles. For then you will be at the mercy of jealous and malicious spirits, who will be drawn to this place as wasps are drawn to honey.'

Now that she was in the pool of light cast by the candles, her face was visible for the first time. She looked to be in her late twenties, with a long, straight nose and prominent brown eyes. Her hair, piled upon her head, gleamed bronze in the candlelight. I studied her carefully to commit her face to memory.

I had drawn another single circle with its symbols in front of the throne and table and I now made a show of stepping into that. Then, with dramatic flourishes that could have earned me a place on stage among the King's Men, I called on Avery to appear. The woman sat as still as a rock on the stool, but her eyes, wide with anticipation, darted wildly around the room. I kept her waiting, pacing around the edge of the magic circle, calling out to Avery again. As I circled, one by one the candles flared with glittering sparks and each in turn was snuffed out by an invisible hand, until only a single flame was left burning. My own right hand was still a little stiff from the injury, but I could work these tricks well enough.

The room was in near-darkness, and from the tail of my eye, I saw the woman press her hand fiercely to her mouth to stop herself from crying out in alarm. Then, as I circled again, a cold blue flame appeared in the throne, hovering in mid-air. The woman was on the point of rising, but seemed to recall my warning and gripped the legs of the stool beneath, forcing her body to remain still.

'Avery is come! Avery will hear you,' I said in sonorous tones. 'Ask him for what you most desire.'

It was some time before she was able to speak and when she did, her words came out in a squeak. 'Grea . . . Great Avery, I wish for a spell . . . I mean an amulet, one that will protect my husband, keep him safe.'

'Avery must know what you want to protect him from. There are many kinds of danger and each requires a different magic.'

'So that he will not be killed or . . . arrested.'

I bowed and addressed the throne, using what little ancient Greek I could remember from my lessons as a boy and trusting she would not understand the words. Waldegrave always told me I would need it one day, though I suspected he had never imagined this kind of occasion. The blue flame guttered and bent in response to the *magic* words.

'So that he may weave his magic against them, Avery commands you to name aloud those enemies who would harm your husband.'

'He . . . he fears Lord Salisbury and his agents . . .'

'The great spirit, Avery, already knows which enemy your husband intends to destroy. It is the King. Avery will help your husband prevail, but only if you speak the truth and tell him all. You shall not lie to him. He will know and he will punish you.'

She buried her face in her hands, rocking back and forth. 'Henry never confides in me. Just things I overheard. I don't know if he even means to do it. He always says that I get things wrong . . . misunderstand what people are saying. I don't know if what I thought I heard is true,' she added with a wail.

'Avery will know. Tell him truthfully exactly what you heard.'

'I can't! I dare not! I shouldn't have come.' She half rose again.

I moved swiftly to stand between her line of sight and the throne, bowing again towards the table. A light flared up above one of the bowls of liquid. Without turning back to her, I spoke haltingly to give the impression I was translating another's words.

'The Serpent's head is here . . . The Serpent lies coiled in the heart of the city . . . The circle is closing . . . Serpent shall strike with its tail . . . but it is the head that commands. Speak soon or the Serpent will be destroyed. If she does not speak tonight . . . it will be too late to help her.'

Behind me the woman moaned. And I knew by the creak of the stool behind me that she had sat down again.

I slowly turned. 'Avery already knows what you will say, but you must speak the words aloud so that they can be woven into the amulet to protect your husband and save you both from the Tower.'

With a flourish I produced a small wooden box concealed under my robes and offered it to her. 'Open it!'

She did. 'It's empty. There is nothing inside.'

'Close it and return it to me.' Taking it from her, I placed it on the table in front of the throne. 'Will you speak the words, that Avery may weave his magic into an amulet of protection?'

She took a deep breath and nodded.

'Name the hour and place where the King will die.'

'I . . . heard talk of . . . a masque at Denmark House, Queen Anne's house, the night before the Accession Day tilt. The King will be the guest of honour to mark the beginning of his reign, but . . . but midnight will bring its end. That is all I know, great Avery. All, I swear!'

There was a flash of fire over the table. When the smoke cleared, the blue flame in the throne had vanished. I picked up the box and gave it to her, again instructing her to open it.

She lifted the lid and gave a little cry, looking up at me with a mixture of awe and gratitude. She lifted out the object that lay within and dangled it by its chain in the light of the one remaining candle. It was a wolf's tooth set into a silver mount, engraved with Arabic letters. The top was crowned with a piece of polished red coral. I'd found it in one of the little dark shops that trade in trinkets brought in by foreign seamen or returning mariners, desperate for money. I had no idea what the letters meant, but I was sure the woman and her husband wouldn't recognise them either.

'The tooth of the wolf to give him the courage, strength and power to overcome any foe. Silver to guard against those who wish evil upon him, and coral to protect him. Avery has inscribed the silver with his own magical charm to bind them. You must—'

'Riders coming this way!' Zephora's voice rang out urgently from below.

The woman gave a small cry of fear, her gaze darting wildly about, seeking a place to hide, and with good reason. It would mean an agonising death for us both if we were caught conjuring spirits, even fake ones. I had come within a breath of that fate once before; I had not the slightest hope of escaping execution if I was accused a second time. I grabbed her wrist and dragged her to the top of the stairs.

'Go down quickly, and get out. The darkness will cover you.'

I didn't wait to see if she obeyed, but I heard the creak of the stairs as I dragged off my robe and hurried to extinguish the last remaining candle. There was no time to dismantle the scene. I could only hope that once they saw the derelict state of the mill, they would not risk climbing up the stairs in the dark, with no certainty of how sound the boards and beams might be above. But I couldn't wager my life on that.

In complete darkness, I inched back to the wall and gingerly followed it to the stairs. One false step and I'd plunge straight down them. I was still only on the first step down, when I heard a noise below me. Someone had entered the mill. Heavy boots scraped on the dirt-gritted flags. There was a dull thud, a growled oath as the intruder collided with something in the darkness. I stepped back up and crept back along the wall until I felt the casement shutter.

I pulled out the wood and rags I'd stuffed into the gaps in the casement and dragged back the warped and swollen shutters, cursing silently as a rotten board broke off in my hand and fell to the floor. The wood was wet and the sound was not as loud as it might have been. All the same, the footfalls of the man below me stopped abruptly. He had frozen, listening, or was he himself afraid of being heard?

From the window, I could see five or six riders approaching, led by one holding a blazing torch. The yellow and orange flames were guttering wildly as the wind snatched at them. The dull glint on their helmets and the leather jerkins warned me they were men-at-arms.

Several times the man with the torch reined in his mount and circled, holding the light low to the muddy ground, searching for tracks. They were following someone, and it was likely that the watermill was not their intended target, but if the tracks continued in this direction, then they might well search it. The man below in the forge might be their quarry, or merely someone like me who had seen them approach and had his own reasons for not wanting to be stopped and questioned.

I had hastily worked loose more of the rotten planks of the shutters, all the time watching the riders coming closer. As yet, the night sky was too heavy with clouds for the mill to be distinguished at a distance from the black sky, but as they drew closer, the torch-bearer pointed to the tracks ahead and at that moment must have seen the outline of the mill. The others caught up with him and formed into a row behind him. They advanced rapidly. As soon as the torch-bearer was close enough to the door of the mill for the corner of the building to cut off the light, I began to scramble out through the hole I'd made in the shutter. I focused on speed rather than silence. The men-at-arms were not yet through the door and the man below me would not dare to move from his hiding place to investigate any sound from above.

The top of the great water wheel lay directly below the window, and beside it the chute from the leet which would once have poured water down on to the paddles of the wheel. I clambered out, clinging to the lip of the casement. The wooden paddle was wet and coated with slime. As I tried to lower myself on to it, I felt the wheel groan and shift. The locking mechanism had rusted away. Even if I did find something to hold on to, when my full weight pressed down on the wheel it would begin to turn and I'd plunge off it, probably becoming trapped beneath it. I would have to clamber back inside and lie low, trusting that once the men found their quarry they would not trouble to search further.

The crashes and shouts from below drifted out through the window. There was a yell of triumph, pounding feet and a cry of pain. The wheel on which I was still balanced juddered violently. Something heavy had struck it from below. The paddle beneath my feet lurched downwards, and I was left dangling by my arms from the casement, scrambling to find a purchase on another paddle that was every bit as slippery as the first.

Shouts and commands were rattling out from below, and a man's anguished pleading. There was a pause and then I heard feet climbing the stairs and saw the glow of the torch slowly filling the room from which I hung suspended. I should have realised that the cornered fugitive was bound to tell them he'd heard sounds from above – anything to buy himself time, and who could blame him? But my time had just run out.

I dropped, twisting sideways and grabbing for the two sides of the chute that fed the wheel. Shouts from the upper room to those below told me they had just discovered the elaborate scene I had created – candles, pentagram, all it lacked was a cauldron of bats and boiled babies. Not even the most beef-witted of guards could fail to recognise what had been going on there, and sooner or later, someone would peer out of that window. I hauled myself upwards by the sides of the chute. The rain had made the mud, weeds and filth that had accumulated in it slippery enough to slither over, but if I lost my grip, I'd slide back down and crash on to the wheel . . .

All the time, I was trying to listen for sounds from the room. As I heard a voice at the window, I pressed myself face down into the chute, and tried to keep still. I was losing my grip on the sodden wood – I could feel it slipping through my fingers –

but just when I knew I would have to move, someone shouted an order from further back in the room, answered by the man at the window as he turned away.

I was hauling myself up into the leet above, when I heard them leave the mill and remount their horses. I risked a look, wanting to be sure that they had all departed and had not left anyone behind to guard the sorcerer's lair, though there would be few volunteers willing to spend a night with witches and spirits.

I watched them ride off, their prisoner's wrists tied to a long rope and fastened behind one man's horse. They would run him back to the city to be questioned. Whatever other crimes the wretch stood accused of, he would now also find himself on trial for sorcery.

I crept back into the building, working swiftly to remove anything of value and stow it back in my horse's saddlebags; then I obliterated the marks on the floor, scattering dirt over the floors and steps as I retreated back down the stairs, so that no sign even of the footprints of the men-at-arms would be visible to anyone who might return to collect evidence. I wasn't sure it would be enough to save the man, for the guards would testify to what they had seen, or what they imagined they had seen, but with luck, it might make them look like fools.

I SPENT THE NIGHT huddled in a wood, planning to slip back into the city among the crowds surging though the gates in the morning, having washed off some of the mud and filth from that dried-up leet in a puddle. It was too cold and wet to sleep, but I doubt I'd have slept even if I'd been in a feather bed: my thoughts were swarming through my brain like ants from a broken nest.

I had deliberately not asked the woman her name. She might well have thought a great spirit like Avery should have divined it already. But even if she had answered truthfully, I had no wish to be in possession of any names I could be forced to divulge. Besides, I could only make use of a name if I was prepared to give it to FitzAlan before any attempt on the King's life was made, and that I was not willing to do. One name would lead to another, the circle of arrests spreading ever wider, like ripples from a pebble tossed into a lake.

And if I was to attempt to prevent the assassination at the masque itself, a name would be as much use to me as a plough on the ocean. All of those courtiers taking part would be dressed in extravagant costumes, women clad as men, nymphs or goddesses, men as beasts or helmeted warriors, to fit whatever theme Queen Anne had dreamed up. But all would be masked and disguised, with dozens of actors, musicians, dancers, cooks and servants milling among them and enough weapons, real and fake, to slaughter half of London. *The King will be the guest of honour to mark the beginning of his reign, but midnight will bring its end.*

Chapter Thirty-one

LONDON

'ARE YOU SICK?' the messenger demanded.

He took a step backwards and raised his lantern, studying Peter Frilleck's face. The apothecary was not flushed, but he did look ill. Since the messenger had last seen him, his face had become haggard. His skin had acquired the yellowish pallor of parchment, and his hair hung in lank rat tails beneath his nightcap. But his eyes burned like a man with fever, sunk deep inside dark sockets.

'Plague? Sweating sickness?' the messenger demanded, shining the lantern in the face of the apothecary's wife. 'Is there a fever in this house?'

Susanna flung herself on this suggestion, like a drowning soul grabbing wildly at a rope. 'Sickness, yes!' she gabbled breathlessly, her arms wrapped tight around herself, clutching the folds of her voluminous nightgown. 'We have sickness in the house! My husband cannot come. He is ill. And you should leave straight away, save yourself from the contagion.'

The messenger regarded her with disdain and turned back to Peter. 'If you really have a contagion, I will leave you. But that will not be the end of the matter. A physician will be sent to examine you to see if you really are too ill to attend. Refusing a summons from the palace is a serious matter. Do you want to be dragged out by guards in front of your neighbours? Your wife too, if she is found to have lied to the King's servant. Are you quite sure you want to claim there is sickness in this house, Master Frilleck?'

Frilleck glanced at his wife standing in the doorway of their parlour. The chamber candle was clutched in her shaking hand, and her eyes were red and swollen, staring at the messenger in fear.

'My poor wife has slept and eaten little these past weeks. It has made her sick so that she doesn't know what she is saying. She is ill, but it is not a contagion.'

'Then you should prepare her a sleeping draught and something to coax her appetite. An apothecary will soon start losing customers, if word gets round that he cannot cure his own family. Now hurry and get dressed – the boat is waiting and our journey downriver will be swifter if we can catch the ebbing tide. You may serve me some wine and meats while I wait, Goodwife Frilleck. Quickly now!' he snapped, as Frilleck and Susanna stood staring despairingly at one another.

The apothecary watched a moment longer as his wife turned and padded towards the kitchen, but not before he'd glimpsed the shine of tears welling in her poor, exhausted eyes.

A VICIOUS, ICY BREEZE gusted up the river, giving an unpleasant swell to the oily dark water. There were few craft abroad at this hour, mainly those that were reluctant to be seen by day, sliding as black shapes through the water, any cargoes they might have been carrying hidden beneath ragged sailcloth. Caught fleetingly in the lanterns on the King's boat, they sped away like cockroaches scuttling from a sudden light. The boats of the corpse collectors alone kept their steady pace, their lanterns held out on the ends of long poles, men leaning over the gunwales, searching for the bodies of those who had jumped, fallen or been flung into the churning water.

In all that great expanse of darkness, the Tower loomed up, bathed in its hellish glow. The Tower was not sleeping. It never slept. Tongues of blood-red light flickered through the slits of the unforgiving stone. Torches burned on the grim walls and writhed through the spiked portcullis that marked Traitors' Gate, revealing the dripping green walls of the cavernous maw behind. Despite Jonah, no one swallowed by the gaping jaws of that leviathan ever expected to be coughed up alive from its belly.

Frilleck's hand strayed again to the bag next to him, tracing the shape of the heavy jar inside. He had not intended to tell Susanna what he had been commanded to do when he had returned from the Palace of Placentia, brushing it off as nothing, a small request, that was all. The summons had been an honour, he had assured her, just like she'd predicted: if he produced this minor physic to the King's satisfaction, then he might be entrusted with bigger, more valuable commissions.

He might, he'd said, in time, earn enough to set up a business in the wealthier part of the city, buy a house there too, acquire new customers, ladies who were willing to pay handsomely for an ointment that would cure some fancied blemish or a draught to soothe a little headache. So that was why he had to take such care over the preparation of this physic, close his shop for hours at a time, so that he could concentrate, work on it day and night, if necessary, to ensure it was the very best. He had squeezed Susanna's arm, giving what he'd hoped was a confident smile.

But they had been married for nigh on twenty years, wed just as soon as his seven-year apprenticeship had ended and he was finally permitted to take a wife. And any woman who has lived and worked alongside a man that long knows when something is troubling him. Even if she had not, the nightmares that jolted him out of sleep when he finally came to bed and sent him scurrying back down to his shop in the middle of the night would have alerted her, and she had coaxed and cajoled until he was finally forced to tell her what he'd been commanded to make.

'But suppose it doesn't work, or the King should drink it and it makes him ill or even . . .' She had clapped her hand to her mouth, the thought too terrible to be spoken aloud. 'If he *was* poisoned by an assassin and they didn't know who'd done it and blamed you . . .'

He'd pretended to be offended. 'You think your husband so poor an apothecary that he cannot follow a simple recipe.' He had not, of course, shown her that list of forty ingredients. 'I expected my own dear wife to have more faith in me.'

But though she'd assured him she knew he was the best in London, the best in the whole realm – he must be, why else would the King have chosen him from out of the whole guild? – Frilleck had known Susanna was not convincing herself, much less him. Out of love for each other, both had pretended they were reassured. But even when he eventually collapsed into their bed in the middle of the night, he would feel her lying stiff and wakeful beside him, and her clumsy accidents in the kitchen and irritation over the smallest mishap were not simply the result of tiredness. She had been frantic with worry.

Had she too been remembering that story Frilleck's father had told so many times before his death? How when he was a boy, he'd seen a cook boiled alive for poisoning seventeen guests of Bishop Fisher, causing all of them to be ill and two of them to die, though the bishop himself had not eaten the pottage, and so was mercifully spared. When he learned of the crime, King Henry had persuaded the House of Lords to declare the crime of murder-by-poison to be treason, for all that he'd later had Bishop Fisher beheaded for a treason of his own.

Frilleck's father said they had hung the man in a gibbet cage which they lowered repeatedly in and out of a vat of boiling water below, until he finally died, and that had taken hours. His screams and roars could be heard clear across London, so his father had said, and several women had fainted at the sight, though Frilleck's father boasted that, as a boy, he had watched avidly. Frilleck had shuddered again at the memory of the tale, which had grown more vivid with each retelling over the years.

If you could be boiled alive for killing the guests of a bishop, when the bishop himself had not even been sick, he could hardly imagine a lesser fate awaited a man who poisoned the King of England and Scotland, even if, by some miracle, the Sovereign lived.

By the time the apothecary had been conducted to the same small antechamber as before, he was no longer sure he could even stand unaided. His legs had frozen and his brain was so numb with apprehension, he could barely remember his own name.

He expected to be forced to wait again. He was hoping that, at least, would give him time to unglue his tongue, which seemed to be welded to the roof of his mouth, and force his knees to bend so that he could actually kneel. Remembering the last time, when the King had slid into the room from beneath a tapestry – which one had it been? – he had resolved to kneel as soon as he arrived in the room, so that he would be ready. But as he entered, he found himself standing in a pool of light cast by candles which had been arranged so close together that, after the darkness outside, it was too bright to see the far end of the room.

Rubbing his eyes, he shuffled sideways to evade the glare, but the messenger grabbed him, pulling him back into the bright bubble of light and pressing down hard on his shoulder.

'Kneel, Master Frilleck,' he hissed in his ear.

The apothecary sank to his knees, almost sending the bag containing the jar crashing to the ground as he fumbled to balance. He was vaguely aware that the messenger, standing behind him, had bowed low, and he heard his footsteps retreating and the door softly close.

He tried to focus his tired eyes beyond the light, and thought he saw something move, then heard the sound of heavy panting. For a moment, he thought it might be his own breathing. Two eyes glittered in the candlelight. He saw the flames reflecting in them. But they were the same height as his own. It did not make sense. There was a soft grunt and then a clicking, like claws on wood, as the eyes came closer, and before he could register what he was seeing, a large hairy head thrust out of the shadows, straight at his face. He gave a cry and toppled backwards as the creature stood over him, a wet tongue licking his mouth, its breath stinking of raw meat.

From out of the gloom came a single short bark of laughter. 'Not afraid of a wee hound, are ye, man? Down, Labros!'

The dog lifted its great head to look at the speaker, and obediently flopped on to its belly.

'So, have ye brought the theriac, Master Frilleck, and the receipts for the ingredients as I bid ye?'

The apothecary tried to speak, but the words came out as a croak.

The King seemed to take that as a yes. 'Well, then, what are you waiting for? Put them on the table. The list I gave you, you have that also?'

Frilleck was not sure if he was permitted to rise, so attempted awkwardly to shuffle towards the table on his knees, until James impatiently ordered him to his feet.

'You'll find a spoon laid ready. I want you to take a measure of that theriac and give it to my hound Labros.'

'But . . . but Your Majesty,' Frilleck stammered, aghast. 'What might strengthen a man could kill a dog.'

'Aye, and what would poison a man will also poison a dog.'

With a trembling hand, Frilleck broke the wax seal on the lid, pulled it off and dug the spoon into the thick syrup. Even to his own nose it was nauseating, and he had smelled nothing else for days. He held the spoon out to the dog. Labros scrambled to his feet, took a pace forward, sniffed at the proffered spoon and gave a low short howl, backing away from the stench.

'Your Majesty, it is usually advised that a theriac be mixed with wine or dragon water to aid the swallowing of it and mask the taste. But the dog . . .'

'Labros does not take kindly to wine, any more than a theriac. Lift up that cover and you'll find a dish of lights, blood-gravy and bread, mix it in with that. It's the hound's accustomed meal, and he has not been fed since yesterday. He'll be ravenous.'

Frilleck lifted the cover and at once the hound bounded up, almost knocking the table over, and trampling heavily on the apothecary's feet as he tried to mix the theriac into the gravy before the hound snatched its feast. The apothecary bent to position the dog's dish on the floor, but before he could set it down, Labros sent it flying from his hand with a single butt of his huge head. The bowl clattered to the floor, splattering the rich gravy-soaked bread and offal across the boards. Labros was on it before the dish had even stopped spinning. He licked up every scattered morsel and polished the bowl more thoroughly than any maid with a scouring brush, scraping it noisily around the floor as he searched for every last scrap.

Frilleck was aware that the King was leaning forward, watching the dog intently. He could still barely see him in the shadows beyond the candles, but he seemed to be clad in a long loose gown trimmed with a broad collar and cuffs of fur, and a close-fitting cap rammed over his cropped hair. He, like the apothecary, had been roused from his bed.

There was silence in the chamber, save for the scratching of the dog's claws on the wooden boards as it prowled around, its nose to the floor, determined to ensure not a drop of the blood-gravy remained. Finally, with something like a sigh, it lay down on its side and stared up in the direction of the King, scratched its ear with a hind paw and chewed the corner of one of the tapestries dangling tantalisingly in front of its nose.

Frilleck suddenly realised he hadn't been breathing and took a great gulp of air.

'The hound seems none the worse for his physic, Master Frilleck.'

The apothecary found himself sweating again, in spite of the chill of the chamber. He was desperate to explain that a dog might indeed come to no harm – after all, they had been known to eat all manner of foul, decaying creatures, even the shit of other beasts, without injury – but the King himself had devised this recipe. How could a mere apothecary warn a king that the theriac might be lethal without suggesting that his Sovereign could have made a grave error?

As though he knew what Frilleck was thinking, James grunted. 'Dinnae fret, there are men awaiting execution who are willing to try any physic offered to them, knowing if it kills them, it'll be a quicker death than the noose or gibbet, and if it doesn't, then they'll be pardoned. Your King will not take a drop till he's sure it'll do him no harm.'

For the first time since he'd received his commission, Frilleck felt the screaming tension in his chest and body ebb a little. He should have realised the King would take no risks. It was going to be alright.

'You have done well, Master Frilleck. And this is for your trouble.' A leather bag was tossed on to the floor at his feet, landing with a clink of many coins. Labros raised his head for a moment, hoping it might be more food.

'If the theriac proves to be all that I hope, I shall require more from you in due course, but for now, let me warn you that you are still bound to silence. Not one word of this is to escape your lips, apothecary. If it does, be sure I shall hear of it. The King has eyes and ears everywhere.'

'Your Majesty, I swear on my life, I shall not breathe a word of this to a living soul.'

'Then your wife and your bed await you, Master Frilleck. You may depart. The messenger is waiting outside the door to take you back to the boat.'

Seldom have such heartfelt prayers of gratitude risen to heaven as those that the apothecary silently offered up to His Maker, as he wobbled out of that chamber.

JAMES WAITED UNTIL he heard the boots of the messenger and uneven tread of the apothecary retreating. Then came a soft knock and a discreet cough from behind one of the tapestries.

'You may enter.'

A figure in dark doublet and breeches stepped into the room, bowing low.

'Is Master Frilleck's chamber prepared and ready in the Tower?'

'It is, Sire, just as you instructed. It is comfortable enough, with a bed and fire. I have personally ensured his cell is well above ground and as far from the river as can be managed, so that there will be less danger from prison fever. Master Frilleck's wife should already be on her way to join him there.'

'Let Frilleck think he is being taken back to his shop, but conduct him straight to the Tower. I want them both to be treated well; I may have need of his services again. Good food and wine, and plenty of fuel for their fire. I do not want him to fall sick. But no one may speak to them. No visitors or messages, in or out. You are certain they have no living relatives who will try to search for them?'

'None, Sire, since Frilleck's father died. They had three children, but none survived infancy.'

For a moment, there was a heavy silence, as if the King was recalling his own lost children, the last taken just six months before.

His voice when he spoke again seemed thicker. 'And the servants?'

'Only Master Frilleck's apprentice and a maid-of-all-work employed by Mistress Frilleck. They will be told their master and mistress have been called away. The apprentice has already been found another post in the north. The maid will be dispatched from the city. The house and shop will be thoroughly searched as soon as they are gone for anything that might have been written down. I shall supervise that myself, Sire, using my own handpicked men. You may rest assured they are to be trusted.'

'Anything ye find is to be brought straight to me. Ledgers, recipes, books. I will examine them. Straight to me, Lord Fairfax.'

Richard Fairfax gave a faint smile, too faint for his Sovereign to perceive in those shadows. He bowed low and backed gracefully out of the chamber.

Chapter Thirty-two

DENMARK HOUSE, LONDON

DANIEL PURSGLOVE

'CALL THAT SINGING? My mother's old tom cats sound better than you,' the stout man jeered, already turning away from the sallow-faced youth standing in front of him. He frowned, peering closely at the sheaf of papers he held, rubbing his eyes, evidently having trouble deciphering the writing.

'Go on, Master Styward, hire the lad,' a grinning servant called out, nudging me to share the joke. 'Everyone knows King starts snoring in the first five minutes of any masque. The lad's yowling might wake him up a bit. Certainly give him the only laugh he's likely to get.'

'Haven't you taken those harnesses to the platform yet?' Styward barked. 'They're waiting to test the flying eagle, and if there's an accident, you'll find yourself up there dangling by your cods.'

The servant laughed. 'Still want to take part, do you, boy?'

The lad nodded eagerly and as Styward waddled off, the boy dodged around him and positioned himself firmly in front of him again. Styward was shaped like a barrel, with thinning hair which, like his beard, was dyed a curious shade of oxblood red. A long lovelock trailed from beneath his plush velvet hat, which resembled the tail of a bedraggled mouse. But there was no mistaking the man's importance, for a heavy silver chain hung from his neck and his stubby fingers and thumbs bore several thick gold rings, studded with large red and green stones.

He tried to walk around the lad, but the boy dodged back into his path again.

'I can act too, play any part – soldiers, princes, even girls,' the lad added, adopting what was probably intended to be a coquettish pose but which was about as alluring as a hog in a gown.

'Every actor, dancer and musician in London has been here, all of them desperate for work after the plague. Even if you could sing like a nightingale, dance like Salome and act like Richard Burbage all at the same time, I couldn't hire you. All the roles are cast. Now be off with you before I have you whipped out.' Styward cuffed the boy aside, one of his heavy rings catching the lad hard on the ear and sending him reeling.

Glancing up, Styward caught sight of me standing a little way off. 'And if you're here looking for work, the same goes for you too. We've all the performers we need. Try your luck in the kitchens. There's an army needed in there. They must have bought up every beast in Smithfield market.'

I nodded and marched off, appearing to take his advice. I had taken care to keep my face half covered with a muffler and my hat pulled low. I didn't want him to remember me when he encountered me again, and I was determined that he would. I had no intention of working in the kitchens, though, I needed to be in the centre of the masque and I'd come prepared.

The gardens were spread across the whole of the front of the complex of buildings that made up Denmark House on the north bank of the Thames. Walks lined with small trees, still bare at this season, ambled around knot gardens, flower beds, arbours and a large circular fish pond. At the far end of the gardens, the waters of the Thames lapped against the high wall which kept them at bay, and the tips of masts, their flags and pennants streaming in the ever-present breeze, glided past the top of the wall, the boats and passengers hidden from view. In the centre of the wall was a wide gate, leading down to a set of stone steps which thrust far out from the bank so that even when the tide was out, boats could discharge their passengers and cargoes. Either side of the steps, two archways led to boathouses concealed beneath the gardens, where the Queen and her visitors might discreetly leave or arrive without being seen from either the river or the palace.

From the river, you could see little of the palace, for the wall hid the gardens and much of the buildings themselves and whenever I'd passed on a wherry, the water gate had been locked, as too had the stout iron grids which guarded the subterranean boathouses from intruders. But today, at least, the water gate stood open and a relay of men were unloading a long boat moored in front of it. Boxes and crates were being passed up the steps, then loaded on handcarts inside the wall, from where they were trundled towards a stage that was being erected close to the house. I grabbed the back of a handcart one of the servants was preparing to pull away. I gave it a shove from behind to get the wheels rolling and held on to steady the cart as it rocked and yawled between the trees. The man dragging it turned his head to nod his thanks.

In front of the stage, a great archway had been erected, concealing a narrow platform that ran the length of it above, from which several harnesses were being raised and lowered, dangling on ropes wound over wheels. Carpenters were hammering away below, like a descent of woodpeckers, and a man of about my own age with a frown of anxiety etched deep into his brow was circling the pillars of the arch with a plum line, trying to determine if they were straight. As we lifted off the boxes, he glanced at us worriedly.

'Have a care with those! They're for the Queen of Sheba's bower,' he called, wincing as the heavy crate we had almost lowered slipped at the last moment, the corner striking the ground with a loud crack. 'It a took a week to fashion that, and the masque is the day after tomorrow. There will be no time to replace anything if it's smashed!'

'Taking the greatest care, sir, don't you fret,' the servant sang out. Then, as he came closer to me, he muttered, 'He's always like this, dancing around like a dowager with a mouse up her skirts and a spider down her back. We'd all get on a lot faster if he'd leave us to it.'

'Who is he?'

The man grinned at me. 'You've not been long in the Queen's employ if you haven't met her lapdog. That's Master Inigo Jones, that is, designs all this lot for the masques and he draws the costumes too. You wait till you see what some of the ladies will be wearing. 'Course it's a closely guarded secret, but one of the maids took a peek and she says it would make a bawd blush. Mind you, I quite fancy having a job like his – there's a few gowns I wouldn't mind seeing one particular lady-in-waiting wearing, or *not* wearing, given what he has them prancing about in.'

'But it's not just the ladies of the Court taking part, is it?' I said. 'They've hired professional actors too.'

''Course they have. The Queen and her ladies don't speak their parts, just like these mechanical peacocks here.' He tapped one of the boxes. 'Only there to look pretty and move about a bit. They have real actors who do all the hard work. And I don't envy their job. You think Master Jones flaps about like a hen who's laid a square egg. You want to go and have a listen to old Jonson putting the players through their lines – he explodes a dozen times an hour, he does. That's him ranting now.'

He jerked his head towards a large tent that had been erected away from the stage. The roar of what sounded like an enraged bull came from inside and several of the carpenters exchanged glances, grinning.

I made myself useful for the remainder of the afternoon, helping to unload boats, shifting boxes, holding planks in place while they were nailed or drapes as they were hung. As long as I kept busy, no one questioned who I was, but all the time I kept watch on the tent where the actors were rehearsing. Finally, as the sun was beginning to sink, the flap was lifted and a thickset man with a large head and closely cropped beard strode out. Barging aside two young servants who were lighting lanterns for those craftsmen still hard at work, Jonson made for one of the buildings at the back of the gardens, without so much as a glance in the direction of the stage.

When they deemed it was safe to do so, the actors emerged in twos and threes and joined a procession of workmen making for one of the high gates that led out of the gardens into the streets beyond. The two guards waved most of the men through unchallenged, occasionally peering into a bag of tools or a knapsack to ensure that no one was leaving with stolen property. I caught up with the actors and sauntered out after them.

I followed them across the square outside, where the company began to break into small groups heading for their lodgings or inns, and fell into step with two men who turned towards the river. One, with flaxen hair, had fine, delicate features which might have fitted him for the roles of girls in his youth, but now sported a neat beard. The darker man's features were coarser, but his skin was loose and his cheeks slightly sunken, suggesting he had recently been ill or starving, or both. The clothes of both men were worn and the bright colours faded, but the fair-haired man's attire was neater and cleaner, which I guessed might be connected to the cloak pin in the form of lover's knot on his shoulder.

'I could swallow a whole flagon of beer without drawing breath after this day's work,' I said with a sigh. 'Jones has been a bear on our backs all day in case we break one of his precious toys. Nothing satisfies that one.'

'You think he's bad. We've had to suffer Jonson all day, telling us how his lines are to be said, how to stand, how to walk, how to gesture. Anyone would think we'd never set foot on stage before! *You're not putting enough feeling into it. A block of stone has more expression than you lug heads.* What kind of feeling does he expect when you're reciting a few flowery verses about kingly virtues? Give me a good love scene or a bloody murder, and I'd soon show him feeling.'

'There's a cosy little alehouse just along there,' I said. 'Mistress of the place keeps a keg or two of special brew out the back, if you know to ask for it.' I tapped my nose. 'What do you say? I reckon we've all earned it.'

The dark-haired man nodded enthusiastically. 'And we can raise a tankard to the damnation of all playwrights, what say you, Parry?'

The other seemed to be wavering.

I swiftly gestured towards his lover's knot. 'It's my betting Parry has something even more tempting than beer waiting for him at his lodgings, isn't that right? And I'll wager she'll have a hot supper ready for you.'

'Come on, Parry, she'll still be waiting after a flagon or two.'

The actor grinned sheepishly. 'She be waiting alright, waiting to tip the supper over my head if I stay out too long. She's a little wildcat if she's baited and she's got a tongue shaper than Jonson's when her claws are out.'

'Then run for the hills, my friend,' his companion advised, 'before you put a ring on her finger and she puts one through your nose.'

Parry laughed and slapped him on the back. 'Enjoy yourself, Nat.' He nodded affably to me. 'Don't let him get too bumpsy. He can't remember his lines when he's sober, never mind when he's got a head full of hammers.'

Nat grinned and feigned a kick at his friend's backside as he walked away, calling out, 'At least I can walk across a stage without tripping over my own arse.'

I took the arm of my new friend and steered him into the Kraken, an alehouse that was favoured by sailors whenever they could snatch time ashore. Three small rooms all on different levels were squeezed together to make up the alehouse. Behind was a yard where Ma did her brewing next to a stinking jakes, which is what gave her illegally strong brew its body and flavour, her customers joked, though never in her hearing.

I led Nat to the darkest corner and sought out Coppersnout, who took the money and the orders from behind a stout grille.

He was a huge man who filled every inch of the cubbyhole into which he was crammed. He had acquired his nickname because he had a metal nose where flesh and blood should have been, kept in place by two leather straps fastened round his head. He swore his old nose had been bitten off by a shark as he leaned over a ship's rail, but others speculated that it had been sliced off as punishment for some crime, or that he'd lost it to the pox.

One of the serving maids set a flagon of the thick dark beer between us and two tankards. Nat gulped his measure greedily, wiping his mouth on the back of his hand before setting it down.

'Spouting those lines all day brings on a fair thirst. And Jonson has us repeating them over and over again. And for what? They're not going to sound any less pompous, whichever way we say them.'

'That bad, is it?'

He rolled his eyes. 'It'll look well enough with all the mechanical devices and the dancers. The King likes to see the Queen dance and the lads too if they're nimble and can leap well. But he won't listen to a word of the verses, never does – bores him witless and I can't say I blame him.'

He glanced round to see if anyone was listening, but it seemed that the weather-beaten men supping their ale and sucking the pipes around us had even less interest in Court masques than the King did.

'So, what is the theme of this masque, then?' I asked him. 'Jones tells us nothing except it's all a great secret.'

'Always is,' Nat said morosely. 'He'd make all the craftsmen work blindfolded if he could, for fear that someone is going to let slip the secret of one of his magic tricks and spoil the surprise. I don't know all they've got planned. They won't tell us more than we need to know for our parts. But from what Jones and Jonson have let drop between them – not that they're on speaking terms – the Court of King Solomon comes into the masque somewhere and the visit of the Queen of Sheba to test his wisdom. Young Prince Henry is to play Solomon, though considering he's only fourteen, he'll need a deal of makeup and a false beard. There's to be all kind of tricks for those scenes. Queen Anne is to play Sheba. And the prettiest of her women are to pose as the nine graces of a sovereign, with us speaking the words for them in a tableau.'

Nat reeled off the graces, counting them on his fingers. 'There's Temperance, Verity, Bounty, Perseverance, Stableness, Verity – no, I've said that one – Lowliness, Devotion – that's it, then Justice and Mercy – they'll appear together, of course, "in equal measure". Jonson's as smug as pie for thinking that one up. He took the line from one of the King's own books, which he probably reckons will please him, if his Royal Majesty is still awake by then, or even listening, which I doubt.'

I poured him another measure from the flagon. He didn't see the small bottle I'd palmed tipping over it. 'So, which grace are you playing?'

'Temperance,' he muttered gloomily, taking another deep draught from his tankard. 'There'll be singing and dancing, of course, like always. The wild dance first with the savage pagans, then the Court dances for when King Solomon has civilised them with his wise and beneficent rule, and brought peace and prosperity to all his subjects, just like our own noble Scottish lord.' He swept his arms out theatrically, almost knocking the flagon off the table. Several of the seamen around us glanced at him suspiciously, as though he was a strange sea creature they had pulled up in a net of cod.

He rambled on, grumbling about plays he'd been in which had been stopped after just one night or not been performed at all, because some fool had complained they were seditious, without giving a thought as to how starving actors were supposed to pay their rent and fill their bellies. His voice was becoming ever more slurred, his movements so uncoordinated that he could hardly lift his tankard. When he did, the beer dribbled out of the side of his mouth and dripped from his beard.

'Your friend can't hold his drink, can he?' one of the men said at the next table. 'You want me to help you get him out back to sleep it off?'

Wrapping Nat's arms around our shoulders, we hauled him to his feet and steered him out into the small yard. We sat him down on the back of a handcart, but his head flopped down on to his chest so we dragged him back until he was lying in it, his legs dangling over the end.

'He's dead to the world,' the mariner muttered.

I hoped he wasn't just plain dead. I had not intended to kill the poor bastard.

'If the watch finds him in that state,' I said, 'they'll ask what he's been drinking, and he might just tell them when he sobers up, especially if they drag him before the magistrates. I don't want to bring trouble to the Kraken's door. Where else would we get beer like Ma brews?'

'What you going to do with him, then?' the seaman asked. 'Even if you cover him, they see you trundling a cart through the streets after dark, they're bound to stop you to find out what you got on it, case its filched.'

'Thing is, my friend has got himself in a bit of trouble. That's why he was trying to drown himself in drink. He could do with getting out of London for a few months, till things settle down. I was thinking, if there's a ship sailing on the morning tide . . . one that's already loaded, so I could get him down into the hold without anyone finding him before she's at sea? I've known him sleep a full night and day when he's taken this much and by the time he wakes . . .' I pulled a purse from out of my shirt, holding it where the mariner could see it. 'I'd give a lot to help out my friend.'

The seaman cupped the purse in the great horny hand as I dangled it, weighing it thoughtfully as he considered the matter. Then he pinched one of Nat's limp arms. 'I suppose he'd do. Got a bit of muscle on him, not much, but a few months at sea will see that right. Hold hard.'

He re-entered the alehouse and in a short while returned with another man following at his heels. He jerked his head towards the man behind him. 'He's from the *White Bear*. She's laden and ready to sail as soon as the tide is high enough. Cargo's already been checked by the searchers and the Exchequer's men, so they shouldn't be back, isn't that right, Gannet?'

Gannet came closer, peering down at the unconscious Nat. He lifted Nat's sleeve and rubbed his own calloused hand over Nat's palm. 'Not as tender as some landlubbers, but they'll crack in the salt before the week's out. You sure he wants to go to sea? It's a hard life if you've not been brought up to it.'

'He came to the wharf wanting to find a ship,' I said. 'But all those sailing tomorrow have a full crew and he needs to get out of the city quickly. He can't risk waiting.'

Gannet's head snapped up and he regarded me suspiciously. 'What's this trouble he's in? I don't want to find myself spending months at sea trapped with a murderer or thief. Always causes trouble for everyone on board if things start go missing and accusations start flying.'

'Nothing like that – his trouble comes in the form of a woman.'

Both men laughed. 'He'll be in good company, then. But we'll have to get him aboard quickly. There were only two left aboard on the second dog watch. The rest were given leave to go onshore, seeing it's our last night in port. Those two will let us cart him down to the hold, if their palms are well-enough greased, 'cause they spent all their pay days ago. But the first watch'll take over at eight bells, and one of them is the captain's nephew and his snitch. You *have* got a good deep purse, haven't you?' he added, suspicion once more in his voice.

I pulled it out again and he raised no more arguments. We tucked Nat's legs up inside the cart and covered him with a torn piece of sailcloth we found draped over some kegs in the yard. Gannet and I wheeled him along the wharf, while the other man went ahead, keeping a sharp lookout for any watchmen, so that he could warn us.

We reached a flight of steps around which several wherries were clustered, anxious to pick up any passing trade. Gannet guided the cart into a dark alleyway close by, and the other mariner came back to join us.

'No sign of trouble, but we'll have to take him downriver and walk him round the bridge. The *White Bear*'s at her moorings on the other side, in the legal quay. You can leave your friend to us now. We can manage him between us. They're well used to mariners being carried aboard the worse for drink on their last night ashore. There'll be plenty of willing lads around to give us a hand. They've more than likely had someone do it as a favour for them in the past.'

Gannet held out his hand for the money to pay the wherrymen and the two men on the *White Bear* and waited until he considered I'd handed over enough recompense to them for their trouble.

I stripped the cloak from Nat as they hauled him upright. It wasn't a garment any seaman would own. I used that movement as a cover to slide the papers out from inside his jerkin without the two mariners seeing. Then I waited until they had lifted Nat safely into the wherry and the little craft was heading downriver towards the great bridge of London, watching until the lantern lights in its stern and bow were just two among many dots of lights weaving through the darkness of that broad river.

I tried to persuade myself that Nat might take to the life of a seaman. After all, he didn't seem to be enjoying himself much as an actor and even the most hard-bitten sea captain might seem mild-mannered if you'd worked for Ben Jonson. But I couldn't afford to dwell on it. I pressed my chest, feeling for the sheaf of papers I had lifted from the unfortunate man. I had lines to learn. It was going to be a long night.

Chapter Thirty-three

A SNAKE OF early-morning mist hung over the river, obscuring the opposite bank. Wherries and other craft emerged briefly through the gauze curtain and vanished almost at once. The cries of the boatmen and those hailing them drifted through the chill air like the souls of the damned. I yawned and shivered as another knot of men arrived to show their papers at the gate to the gardens of Denmark House, and were ushered inside. I remained in the doorway, where I could watch those approaching. I needed to be sure the two seamen had kept their word.

I caught sight of a curly flaxen beard and face I knew and stepped out. 'Parry!'

He looked a little startled, but then recognition dawned.

Before he could speak, I babbled on. 'Danni,' I said, touching my chest with what I hoped was a theatrical flourish. 'I've been waiting for you – got a message for you from Nat.'

His forehead creased in a frown. 'Not still in bed, is he? I warned him to keep a clear head. Jonson will have him thrown out if he turns up late again. He's not worked for months, he can't afford to lose this.'

I put a hand under his elbow and led him a little way off. 'That's why I'm here. He's sick. No, not the plague,' I added hastily, seeing his eyes flash wide in alarm. 'But as you say, he can't afford to lose this work. I said I'd cover for him, split the wages. He's lent me his papers and I've learned his lines. But Jonson worries me. Do you think he'll notice?'

Parry considered the question. 'We're rehearsing in masks and robes. Jonson insists. Wants to make sure we're used to the masks, so his lines aren't fumbled. That's all that concerns him, how his precious lines are delivered. You *are* an actor, aren't you?'

'I've been acting for years. Not in London, though. When my wife died, thought I might try my luck here. More work for actors in the city.'

'And more actors chasing it,' Parry said, grimly. 'But it's good of you to help Nat. I'll tip off the others, so they don't say anything within Jonson's hearing. But we best hurry and get a mask on you before Jonson turns up. He barely looks at us when we're not rehearsing, but all the same he might realise he's not seen you before.'

We lined up behind three other men while the guard at the gate, shuffling from foot to foot in the cold damp air, examined the identification papers and permissions proffered to him. As I glanced around, ready to dart away should Nat make an appearance, I saw a figure standing where I had been waiting for Parry. He was muffled up against the damp mist, as were we all, but he slowly drew something from the pouch dangling from his belt and raised it in the ghost-light. It was small, human-like, a hand, freshly skinned, the flesh raw and bloody. For a sickening moment I thought it was the hand of a small child, but the fingers were too long and the thumb too short. It must have belonged to some kind of ape or monkey. Then the man pushed the ghastly trophy back into his pouch and pulled his scarf away from his face and neck. Even as a swirl of mist spun about him, I could clearly see the stark white stripe in the dagger-point black beard.

Parry elbowed me in the ribs, jerking his head towards the guard, who was now impatiently beckoning me to come forward. I presented Nat's papers. As he studied them, I turned to stare back at the place where Badger-beard had been standing, but the doorway was empty.

'You going to stand there all day?' the guard demanded, jabbing me in the chest with the papers he'd been trying to return. He rolled his eyes at his fellow guard. 'Actors! Can't even walk through a gate without waiting for someone to applaud.'

Parry hurried me over to the tent and thrust a long, hooded robe trimmed with a moulting rabbit collar and cuffs at me, and a violet mask, the symbolic colour of Temperance, being midway between the blue of intellect and the red of passion. It covered the top half of my face, leaving the mouth clear to speak the all-important words. As I dressed, he hurriedly whispered an explanation to those actors who had already assembled. Several glanced over at me curiously, but nodded in a friendly enough way. But before anyone could speak, Jonson strode into the tent and began growling orders, handing out new pages of the script to some of the other actors, with fresh changes he had made. Parry groaned as he received his and others were protesting loudly, but Jonson ignored them.

'This afternoon we'll rehearse on the stage, *if* Master Jones has finally managed to complete it. But this morning we'll go through changes I've been working on *all night*, to make it easier for those dolts who couldn't get their lumpen tongues around perfectly simple lines.' He paused, glowering at those who had complained.

'Anyone who doesn't have new lines to rehearse, you are excused, but you are not to leave the gardens. You would be well advised to find a quiet spot and rehearse privately. I expect every man to have learned every word of his speech by this afternoon. There are a hundred men in this city alone eager to take the place of each of you. And they shall, if you have not learned your parts when you step on to that stage this afternoon.'

I left Parry with those who had lines to learn muttering darkly in the tent, and slipped out of with a handful of others who had been spared. Most tore off their masks as soon as they were outside, but I kept mine on. If that vermin Richard Fairfax had managed to inveigle one of the many courtiers' roles in the masque, I could not run the risk of being recognised by him.

On the other side of the gardens, near one of the great palace buildings, the drapes on the stage were looped back to reveal a painting covering the whole of the back of the stage, depicting what I took to be a distant scene of Jerusalem, with myriad little houses climbing the slopes of an immensely steep hill crowned with a golden temple. The blue sky above was buzzing with tiny angels and colourful birds with long, trailing tail feathers.

Servants were dressing the front and sides of the base of the wooden stage with swathes of evergreens and garlands of impossibly vivid scarlet roses, blue cornflowers and bright yellow celandines, all fashioned from silk. Others stood on ladders, hanging huge, gaudily coloured fruits on the fake trees that lined the edges of the acting area, while over their heads, a sun and moon with cheery faces travelled through the sky, so that as one set in the west its celestial brother rose in the east. Both were revolving on a large wheel cranked by a small lad whose attention and strength seemed to be waning, for the wheel was moving at an erratic pace and sometimes stopped turning altogether, until a bellow or slap jerked the lad back to the task.

But all this was merely the backdrop to the throne of Solomon, which had been positioned on the centre of the stage. Six steps led up to the chair itself, representing the six kings who, it was foretold, would sit upon Solomon's throne. On the sides of each of the steps was a pair of gilded animals: a golden lion sat opposite a golden ox on the first step, a wolf and a lamb on the next, then a panther and camel, an eagle and peacock, a wildcat and cockerel, and a hawk and pigeon. All gleamed in the weak sunlight.

Master Styward was lecturing a gangly youth who wore a trailing oversized robe draped over his own clothes. The lad was sent to the far side of the stage and instructed to process towards the throne, on a signal. He hitched up the robe, which was falling off his narrow shoulders, and started forward, but seemed to have entirely forgotten how to walk. His uneven, stiff-legged gait brought a ripple of giggles from the girls hanging the garlands. The lad's cheeks flushed scarlet and he glanced miserably at Master Styward.

'You are standing in for Prince Henry, not a camel!' Styward yelled. 'Walk like a prince.'

The boy's second attempt was even more ungainly, not helped by the jeers and ribald jokes from the servants and workmen who had paused in their own tasks to watch.

'Forget the walk,' Styward said with an exasperated sigh. 'Just go to the foot of the throne and mount the steps – slowly, mind. Place both feet on each step as you climb up, then sit down, so we can see if the throne works.'

The boy shuffled to the foot of the steps, but the instruction to place both feet on each step seemed to baffle him, and for a moment it seemed he would attempt to jump up, holding both feet together.

'No!' Styward bellowed. 'Step up with one foot, then bring the other up. Then stand and wait before you mount the next step.'

The lad did so and as the weight of both feet pressed down on the first step, the golden lion and ox swivelled to face each other and slid forward until they were almost touching the boy's legs on either side. He gave a yelp, and, throwing up his arms as though the lion had bitten him, rushed on to the next step. The wolf and lamb turned and slid towards him. He was better prepared for the action this time, and by the time he reached the wildcat and the cockerel on the fifth step, he was plainly enjoying himself. He stepped firmly on to the sixth step, but his robe had slipped once more, and the hem caught in the hooked beak of the cockerel, jerking him backwards. He came crashing down, knocking against the bird as he fell. Two men clambered on to the stage and dragged the lad unceremoniously off the steps, dumping him aside like a sack of wheat, before carefully examining the bird and testing the movement. Meanwhile, the boy sat on the boards, rubbing his bruised shin and groaning loudly.

From somewhere behind me, Jones came hurrying up. 'Has he broken it?' he demanded, while the boy moaned louder, wailing that it was his leg that was broken. Jones rounded on Styward. 'The mechanism is delicate. If that mewling clot-pole has bent it . . .'

'Gilding scraped that'll need touching up,' one of the men grumbled. 'But it still moves as it should,' he added grudgingly, glowering at the lad.

'You, boy, take that robe off before you do any more damage, then get up there again and this time sit down on the throne,' Styward barked. 'We still have to test that.'

The lad clambered sullenly to his feet. Limping with great exaggeration, he approached the stairs, mounting them gingerly, holding himself as far away from the golden beasts as he could. He looked relieved when he finally reached the top and gingerly sat himself down, staring round apprehensively as though the throne was a spiked torture chair. For a moment or two nothing happened, but then a carved golden eagle with wings outstretched and a crown held in its talons slowly descended towards the boy's head. He glanced up, cringing lower and lower in the chair as it approached, leaning away from the outstretched claws.

'Sit up, boy! Sit straight and hold your head up like a king. It won't touch you.'

The eagle inched downwards in its magnificent flight, coming to rest so that the jewelled crown in its claws was positioned just above the boy's hair. He glanced up and, seeing that the eagle had stopped moving, he relaxed. A grin began to spread across his face. He gripped the arms of the throne and lifted his chin regally, gazing down upon his kingdom, relishing his moment of princely glory. Everyone in the garden was looking up at him and his delight was plain to see.

There was a sudden creak and the eagle jerked down – only by a couple of inches, but it was enough to ram the crown down on to the lad's head, trapping him in its claws. He squealed and tried in vain to push the eagle up, while the men rushed forward, bellowing at him to stop or he'd break the mechanism. Eventually, he seemed to realise that the only way to get out of the bird's grip was to slide down the seat. He wrenched his head out of the crown with a great effort, blood trickling from the scraped skin of his forehead and temples, then wriggled out from under it and galloped down the steps, his injured leg forgotten in his haste.

Styward, almost purple in the face with rage, rounded on Jones. 'What if that had crashed down on Prince Henry's head? You could have killed the heir to the throne. The King would have had you boiled alive, and me along with you.'

'It's those clot-poles you employed. My calculations were correct, but those two joitheads there couldn't follow instructions on how to scratch their own backsides!'

The two men were protesting that it was all the fault of that frog-witted boy falling on the cockerel.

'And suppose Prince Henry knocks against one of those beasts of yours like the boy did,' Styward yelled at all three of them, 'and the same thing happens, or worse?'

'We were going to put a block in so that it can descend no further,' one of the men said. 'We were just waiting for the boy to test it so that we could judge the height.'

'So, young Prince Henry's life is to depend on a little block of wood, is that it? And what if it should fall out?'

What indeed? I thought as I slipped away. There were so many *accidents* that could occur: a pin removed here, a harness cut there. And anyone from a nobleman in the Court or the lad who cranked the wheel to make the sun revolve could, wittingly or unwittingly, be the one who dealt the fatal stroke.

The water gate once more lay open and a procession of men and boys ambled past, hefting sides of mutton and venison, sacks of vegetables and baskets of live chickens. The human ants followed each other in single file towards the kitchens. I felt the empty glass vial in the leather pouch beneath my shirt. That was not something I should be caught carrying in the grounds of a royal palace, yet how easy it had been to physic Nat's beer, how simple it would be to slip a few drops or a pinch of powder into a dish or pie. Maybe not with the intention of killing someone outright, but to make them drowsy and clumsy enough to cause an accident to themselves . . . or to someone else.

Chapter Thirty-four

'You look a little better than when last I saw you. Body less stiff now?'

The bruises on Dob's face were still visible, but the swelling had subsided on his lip and he moved more easily and without wincing. He was sitting on the end of one of half a dozen beds crammed together up across the wall of an attic room in the lodgings to which I'd sent him. The other inhabitants of the long narrow chamber were absent, for though it was dark outside, it was still early evening and no visitor to London would take himself to bed when there were all the temptations of the city to be sampled.

I had managed to get through the afternoon rehearsal without forgetting my lines or falling over my feet, which appeared to be the two capital crimes that drew down the divine wrath of Jonson. He appeared not to notice that his masked Temperance was no longer the same man and as the day wore on and Nat did not appear at the gate, protesting that an imposter was inside, I began to believe that Gannet had indeed been as good as his word and that the actor had found himself on an unexpected sea voyage.

As soon as we had been dismissed, at dusk, I left Denmark House, placing myself in the centre of the crowd of actors and labourers in case Badger-beard was outside the gates. Parry had quietly asked if I thought he should call upon Nat, but looked relieved when I assured him that I would tend to him and that he should hurry home to the angel who awaited him. I had followed a circuitous route to the inn where I hoped I'd still find Dob, retracing part of my route several times and even crossing to the other bank of the great river and back again on two wherries, in the hope of losing any pursuer. I couldn't expunge the image of the flayed hand from my mind, nor the face of the man who'd taunted me with it. I had deliberately distanced myself from Dob, even before I'd seen that hand, for fear of the danger I might be dragging an innocent lad into, but I needed him now and I could think of none other to help me. I had convinced myself that what I'd planned would actually keep him safer.

I sat patiently watching Dob devour the humbles pie I'd bought him. He gobbled it down so swiftly that it was plain he had eaten little since he'd arrived in the city. He licked his fingers with great concentration to catch every last drop and crumb.

'Was that as good as your mother makes?'

'No one makes humbles like Ma.' But the wistful expression that had settled on his face was swiftly replaced with a look of stubborn defiance. 'But I'm not going back! Not till I've made my fortune.'

'And I haven't come to persuade you to, quite the opposite. How would you like to work in the royal palace for a day, for Queen Anne herself?'

He gaped at me, his eyes blazing with excitement. 'For . . . the Queen? . . . In a real palace?'

'You'll be able to tell your parents and friends that you served Her Majesty. Imagine how proud your parents will be of you and how jealous you'll make the other lads in your village.'

He nodded eagerly, a slow smile spreading on his face. I knew he was already imagining himself recounting the tales to an awe-struck audience. He looked a little less enthusiastic when I told him he'd probably be working as a kitchen scullion.

'Peeling and plucking all day?' he said doubtfully. 'Couldn't I look after the Queen's horses? I'm right good with beasts.'

'Maybe in time, if you prove yourself, but this won't be any ordinary day.' I tried to explain what a masque was, but it was so far beyond the boy's experience that I might have been telling him tales of a fairy kingdom. He did understand what a great feast was, though he probably imagined something like the harvest feasts or church ales he was accustomed to back home. But when he learned the King, the Queen, the Prince and many nobles in all their gold and finery would be there, his eyes sparkled.

'There is a more important reason for you to be in the kitchens, Dob.' I rose to check that no one was lingering on the stairs outside the door to the attic. 'I want you to swear on your mother's life that you will tell no one what I am going to tell you. You know what such an oath means, don't you?'

His expression grew serious. 'If I break it, she will . . . die?'

'She *will* die,' I repeated. 'So, are you willing to swear?'

He hesitated, but curiosity overcame him. 'I'll not speak a word of it, I promise. I . . . *swear* on my ma's life.'

'I think someone will try to cause mischief at this masque, murder even. I want you to keep your wits about you while you're working, watch what others are doing. See if anyone comes into the kitchens and acts secretively, perhaps slipping something into a dish of food while they think the cooks aren't looking. Whoever might attempt it, they would never think they were being watched by a scullion – that's why you might see something that the guards and I could not.'

'Poison?' his eyes were wide, but there was more excitement in them than fear.

'Possibly, or it may be something to make people sleepy or appear more drunk than wine alone would make them.'

Dob nodded eagerly. 'Remember how you and my father were talking about the old lord's accident after we brought you across Derwent? Well, the servants who were sent away, they were talking back of our cottage while father was tending to the ferry, and one of them said the stableboy was acting right queer the night before it happened, like he was half asleep or cat-hawed, but no one saw him sup more than the measure of small ale he was always given of a night. They told the young lord that the lad had been addled that night, and he said it was more proof the stable lad had cut the strap, done it when he was drunk. But the servants reckoned that whoever cut that strap had slipped him something without him knowing, so as he'd sleep like the dead, because he always bedded down in the hayloft right above where the leathers were kept. That's why he got the blame, see, because the young lord said no one else could have tampered with the saddle without him hearing.'

'And someone might be planning another accident like that at the masque,' I told Dob.

Maybe even the same young lord who had so carefully planned the accident that killed his own father.

Chapter Thirty-five

THE TOWER OF LONDON

'THREE OF MY PRIZE DOGS he's stolen now, do ye ken that? Has them wandering the palace of Saint James, and he'd have taken this pard too, except that she clawed the face of one of his men when they were trying to get her into the wagon. Laid it open to the bone. That'll teach that laddie of mine not to be so soft.'

James poked a piece of raw meat towards the panther through the bars of the cage on the end of a long, sharpened pole. The creature snarled, her ears laid flat and her lip curling back to reveal her long fangs, gleaming wickedly white in the small dark space. The underground chamber was cold and damp, and the musky smell of the beast and reek of feline dung and piss in the sodden straw made Robert Cecil's eyes water.

'Prince Henry doesn't enjoy watching the animals fight each other, Sire. He has a weak stomach for such spectacles.' Standing well back from the cage, behind the King's back, Cecil mopped his eyes with his kerchief before pressing the scented cloth discreetly to his nose, but not even his ambergris perfume could overpower the odour of the caged panther. 'I am given to understand he was fond of those particular dogs and concerned that they would be badly injured if they—'

'See this!' James raised the bloody titbit above the animal's head, wriggling it tantalisingly just out of its reach, then dragged the pole swiftly out of the cage as the panther sprang towards the retreating morsel, landing with all four paws clanging against the bars. She spat and hissed, clawing wildly through the bars in an effort to grab the meat which James held just out of her reach. 'See!' James repeated triumphantly. 'These beasts love to fight. It's in their blood.' He waved the scrap in front of the panther's nose, and gave a bark of a laughter as the furious animal slashed out again.

'If my son paid better heed to his studies instead of trying to turn fighting dogs into pap-fed lapdogs, he might learn the craft of kings. He wastes all his time at the tilt or charging about with pistols on horseback, plaguing every captain and officer with questions about war and its machines. And the beef-witted commons applaud him for it! I've told him, the womenfolk will not still be cheering and tossing flowers to him when he has their husbands and sons marching off to war, dragging them half across Europe to be maimed and slaughtered for his glory. He should be learning how *not* to plunge his people into bloodshed. He should be studying the art of negotiation and diplomacy. He thinks war a game, and he'll likely provoke a conflict just to play it. I've warned him that if he does not spend more time attending to his books instead of playing soldiers, I'll make his brother, Charles, heir to my throne. At least the wee lad is a scholar.'

Cecil had little regard for Henry, who in turn had never hidden his contempt of him, but the prospect of Henry's younger brother, Charles, becoming king was even less to be welcomed. Scholarly he may be, but he was a sickly and petulant boy, not above demanding jewels, daggers or anything else he fancied from the courtiers, if he saw one of them wearing something he wanted. Given that Henry was undoubtedly the lesser of two evils, Cecil had started to send some of the ambassadorial reports to the fourteen-year-old Prince. Henry was keenly interested in affairs overseas – mainly, as his father said, the ones that might led to wars – but the boy might learn something from them, unlike the ancient Greek philosophers whom James demanded he study.

The panther had given up chasing the meat and had flopped down as far back in her cage as the small space would allow. James resumed his efforts to coax her into action again.

'The Queen has devised a masque with Ben Jonson for the eve of my Accession Day. She tells me her wee protégé, Inigo Jones, has designed the scenery, which no doubt means Anne has bought up every last yard of gold cloth and every bag of pearls to be had in London, for she's laid on so many of these entertainments and masques since she came south, I canna imagine there are any of Queen Bess's old gowns left to plunder for jewels or embroidered silks for her ladies' costumes.'

'I understand the masque is to be in the grounds of Denmark House, Sire.' Cecil cursed himself again; he'd only learned it was to be held in the gardens when they had started building the stage. If he had allowed Jones to ramble on about the masque that night after supper, he could have forced him to tell the Queen it would be impossible to stage it outdoors. It was that wretched business with the maggoty meat that had distracted him.

'Sire, such an ostentatious display and so much expenditure at this time will not sit well with either Parliament or the people, especially if the tilt procession the next day is also a lavish affair. There is already hunger, and there will be worse in the coming months. I fear there is a grave danger that an open display of extravagance at this time might well trigger another uprising, like the Newton Rebellion.'

'They'd not dare rise again, Lord Salisbury! Not after the lesson they were taught in Northamptonshire. They tell me fifty of the rioters objecting to the enclosures were cut down, including that tinker Captain Pouch, who roused the rabble. That man actually had the effrontery to claim he had my authority for the revolt. Mine! As for that magic pouch he claimed would protect those gowks who followed him, do you know what they found in it when they hanged him?'

'Cheese, Sire,' Cecil muttered wearily.

'A piece of stinking cheese – that was his divine protection.'
James gave another bark of laughter.

'All the same, Sire, if you could persuade the Queen that a
more modest celebration, held *indoors*, might sit better with the
commons in such a year of hardship, when so many are going
hungry . . .'

'Aye and you know why they go hungry? Because the landowners are here in London, instead of back in their shires seeing
that the food is fairly distributed and ensuring scoundrels and
merchants don't make a fortune at the expense of poor folk by
stockpiling grain so that they can increase the prices. There is
more than enough food to last until the next harvest, Lord Salisbury, if people don't buy more than they need and hoard it. They
must be prevented from doing that. I'll deal with the landowners,
chivvy them back to their shires to do their duty by their people.
But I'll not have the commons thinking they can take what they
want by violence from those set to govern over them.'

Finally bored with the panther, the King flicked the meat off
the stick into the cage and gave his full attention to Cecil. 'If a
man is in want, Lord Salisbury, then he must humbly pray to
God for his needs. He canna storm heaven and tear down the
celestial throne, and if he tries, God will strike him down for his
presumption. A king is God on earth. If his people have needs,
they may petition him, but they canna take what they want by
force, else he too will strike them down. I answer only to God,
Lord Salisbury. I'll never answer to a rabble of men. As for the
masque, I can think of a thousand better ways to spend my time
than sitting through hours of Jonson's turgid verse.'

'Such as hunting, Sire? I recall you once said your kingly
duties were the hunting of witches, prophets, Puritans and hares.'

James chuckled. 'And so they are, but don't leave out *dead
cats*, Lord Salisbury. I said dead cats too.' He prodded the panther
on the rump with the sharp pole and the beast turned, snarling.
'But the good Queen likes nothing so well as her masques and I'll
not deny Her Majesty her few wee pleasures. She's mother to the

heirs of this realm, and as such she's mother to the people. They canna question what she does, any more than a child questions the orders of their own mother. The masque is Anne's accession gift to me and I'll not refuse it.'

A *gift* which the people of England would have to pay for, Cecil thought sourly. But then the King would undoubtedly see that as his due.

'Where's the steward?' James suddenly demanded. 'This beast is sluggish. Too much meat. Give a hound too much meat and it blunts his appetite for the chase.' He shouted for the steward and, leaning heavily on his stick, limped towards the door, where guards snapped to attention.

'Sire,' Cecil said urgently. 'There is another reason that it would be wiser to have the masque performed *inside* Denmark House.' He spoke low and rapidly, knowing that James already considered the matter closed. 'Intelligence has reached me that there will shortly be another attempt on Your Majesty's life.'

'There are a dozen plots hatched every day, as well you know, my little beagle. What would you have me do, cancel every engagement and cower in my chamber for the rest of my days like a wee mouse?'

'A man has returned to England to lead another plot, Sire. One that is in every way as serious and potentially deadly as the Gunpowder Treason.'

James stopped dead, and turned, taking a few paces back toward his Secretary of State. 'The man who has returned. Does he go by the name of Spero Pettingar?'

'*If* he has ever used that name, then he travels under another now, but that is only to be expected. He would hardly use one that is known to us.'

'And what manner of attack does he mean to use? Do your intelligencers tell you that, Lord Salisbury?'

There was only the briefest moment of hesitation before Cecil spoke. 'Open gardens on the banks of the Thames cannot ever be secured as well as the interior of a building, Sire.'

'I'll remind you, Salisbury, the House of Lords was a building and I recall ye could nay secure that, for the gunpowder was planted right beneath us in front of the very noses of the guards. Seems to me I'd have been safer out in the open air that day, for there are no cellars in the gardens.'

'I do not believe they will try that method again, Sire; nor will they attempt anything that risks the perpetrator being seized in the act and persuaded to give up his confederates, as Guy Fawkes was.'

'Poison, you think, do ye? They tried to me poison before at that entertainment you organised. The cook died in prison before he could be questioned, but we both know he was not the assassin. Is that not so, Lord Salisbury?'

Cecil kept his face impassive, recalling another poisoning in this very Tower which had been kept hidden from the King.

'If that's their plan, they can attempt it as well indoors as outside – more so, I dare say.' James clapped his hand on Cecil's shoulder, his mood suddenly and inexplicably buoyant again. In spite of his own twisted leg, he loomed over his crook-backed Secretary of State and seemed to derive satisfaction from that.

'Dinnae fret yourself. Your King will not drink a drop or eat a crumb that's not been tasted, and you can search under every blade of grass and toadstool for the smallest whiff of gunpowder, if it'll content ye. But I'll not be frighted into a cage, as my son would have me keep this poor beasty here, away from harm and as powerless as an old hearth cat. Keep me safe, my little beagle, that's your job, but you'll not do it by locking me up.'

Chapter Thirty-six

DENMARK HOUSE

DANIEL PURSGLOVE

'HERE, CAN'T YOU examine these?' I demanded of the second guard at the gate, thrusting Nat's identity papers in his face. 'Master Jonson's got the temper of a baited bear and you making me late won't sweeten it.'

I had deliberately pushed to the front of the queue of men and boys who were waiting to have their papers examined. A second guard stood on the other side, keeping a watch on anyone who might try to slip through unchecked. As I'd hoped, the line of men broke ranks and tried to elbow me aside, brandishing their passes at the two guards, all complaining that they too had masters with equally short tempers. As the guards attempted to restore order, I gave the signal to Dob, who slipped adroitly between the gatepost and the distracted guard, turned swiftly towards the river, and then sauntered through the gardens like one who had worked there all his life.

As soon as he was clear, I slipped to the back of the queue, standing in line as though I had never had any intention of doing anything else, and freely joining in the grumbling about those who wouldn't wait their turn.

I had instructed Dob to hang around near the water gate. Since the masque was to take place that night, I had every reason to suppose last-minute provisions for the feast would again be brought in by river. Dob was to seize a sack or basket and follow

345

the others towards the kitchens; once he'd managed to inveigle his way inside, he was to carry out any orders shouted at him, while keeping a close watch on all who came and went.

Chairs and stools were being carried out and placed under a huge canopy facing the stage, which afforded the guests shelter from the cold breeze from the river. A high-backed chair with a footstool had been placed on a raised dais under the middle of the canopy; this and the less ornate chairs and stools were heaped with cushions and draped with furs and rugs. These were for King James's party, with the Gentleman Pensioners flanking three sides of the dais to protect their Sovereign.

To one side of the stage, a low, flat platform had been erected for the dances that would form part of the masque, and that too was decorated with garlands of improbably huge fake fruit, gaudy silk flowers, and wooden birds covered in real feathers. On the other side of the stage, dark cliffs rose up created from painted canvas and gauze, stretched over wooden frames. A linen cloud concealed the giant eagle with outstretched wings, suspended from a hoist, which would carry King Solomon up from the stage to the dark cliffs where the fallen angels, Uzza and Azazel, would be chained. Solomon would command them by means of a ring of a power to reveal all the mysteries of the universe.

Parry had told me that Jonson had been ordered by Archbishop Bancroft to add another verse, making it plain that this ring had been given to Solomon by God. The Archbishop had wanted to ensure none of those watching could mistake it for the magic rings used by the false magicians who plagued London, claiming to be able to bring wealth and fortune to their customers.

I thought of the man in the mill who the men-at-arms had taken prisoner, convinced that they had caught a sorcerer in the act of raising spirits. The poor wretch was probably still trying to talk his way out, or maybe he had already been put to the torture and confessed to being in league with Beelzebub himself.

But the question that still gnawed away at me was how those men-at-arms had happened to be at that remote and lonely spot. I could not believe it was mere chance. I had not seen any sign of Badger-beard since he'd taunted me with that little flayed hand outside the gate, but I knew he must be close by. I'd taken care to ensure Dob and I did not arrive together, and I had warned Dob that once inside he was to stay well away from the gates, in case Badger-beard was lurking outside. I could only hope he wasn't already inside these palace walls.

The morning was spent putting the actors, musicians and dancers through their final rehearsal, concealed in the tent or behind screens. When I wasn't rehearsing, I prowled around the empty stage, searching for anything that could be used to harm the King, but I could see nothing. There was plenty of opportunity for accidents to happen to those on the stage, but nothing obvious that might reach the King, unless the threat was under the platform on which the King's chair had been placed.

But I was not the only one who had considered that. Several times I saw guards checking beneath the dais. A cohort of them also descended the steps which led from the gardens down into the boathouse, to ensure that no barrels of gunpowder had found their way beneath the grounds. But the plotters would surely not be foolish enough to use a method that had already been foiled so publicly. The cellars and tunnels would have been thoroughly inspected in every building that the King was due to visit, ever since that fateful day.

The water gate was continually opening to receive fresh produce from the cargo boats. Alongside them, barges painted scarlet and gold were gliding through the twin arches into the boathouse beneath, disgorging passengers dressed in their best finery. As they emerged inside the gardens, they were swept straight into the palace buildings by obsequious servitors, clearing the way before the guests with silver-topped staves and barking at anyone who did not step aside smartly enough.

A procession of ladies of the Court and two cherubic-looking children, the latter dressed in rags, were ushered across the gardens and behind the stage. Styward was puffing around them, marking people off on a list he held, like a shepherd's dog trying in vain to corral a flock of skittish sheep. Several drapes had been lowered at intervals across the stage on either side of the throne. Each of the women was carefully positioned behind one of them, posing as a kingly virtue. The actors were being summoned one by one to stand beside them. They were to declaim the verses as each drape was lifted in turn.

'If I could have Justice and Mercy and the children? Ladies, this way, if you please.' Two of the women turned towards Styward. The first was clad in a striking black robe trimmed with white fur, a white rope around her slender waist and a wide white lace ruff encircling her neck. A black mask covered the whole of her face, glittering with diamonds, and she clasped a small sword with a jewelled hilt. That I assumed was Justice. The other figure, Mercy, was dressed in a scarlet gown with a vivid blue cloak, which trailed several feet behind her on the ground. With a lurch, I realised who I was staring at – her long straight nose, the prominent brown eyes. Today her bronze-coloured hair was flowing about her shoulders, not piled up as it had been on the night I'd conjured Avery for her in that desolate mill.

I had known she would be here; of course, she would. But even so, seeing her again jolted me into the chilling realisation of what her husband intended to do. In hours, the King and perhaps his heir Prince Henry, the Queen too, could be lying dead. Would they die alone or would others be slaughtered with them, as the gunpowder plotters had intended? Surely, if that was the plan, her husband would have made some excuse to keep his wife at home. Only the most fanatical or callous of men would risk his wife being injured or killed, however dedicated he was to the cause.

There was a great deal of giggling coming from behind the billowing drapes, along with thumps and curses as some prop was dropped or knocked over or ladies overbalanced. Jonson was evidently making a great effort to sound patient, but his tone was growing increasingly terse and strained, which only elicited more laughter from both ladies and actors, who were relishing the opportunity for flirtation.

Another group of nobles emerged from the boathouse steps, and swaggered towards the house, passing the spot where we were waiting. Sword hilts gleamed from beneath the half-cloaks, their lacy ruffs starched and bleached whiter than a fall of fresh snow. Watery sunshine glinted on the jewels in their hats, their dangling earrings and their gold and silver chains and brooches. The opportunity to impress the ladies of Queen's Anne's Court was a rare one, since at the King's Court they were mostly in the company of men. They nudged each other, making ribald comments about paupers and cattle-thieves in the hearing of any Scot they recognised. There was going be trouble before the night was old, especially after the wine began to flow.

Then, as the little knot of men drew level with the stage they turned to stare at the actors waiting below in masks and costumes, and I saw the two men I had least wanted to encounter that night. The first was Richard Fairfax, and the second, at the back of Richard's party, was Badger-beard!

Richard looked straight through me. My violet robes and mask were plain compared to the multicoloured costumes of Bounty, Verity or Devotion. In any case, actors were of no interest to him; I suspected he didn't even register that there were real men behind the masks. But as I stared at Badger-beard, our eyes met. His expression didn't change, and I swiftly looked away, but I could not be sure if there had not been recognition in that glance.

Badger-beard was a pursuivant. Was he keeping company with Richard because he suspected him of treason? It was Cecil's favoured tactic, to let the plot run until the last possible moment and catch the conspirators in the very act. No, Badger-beard was too close. If he'd wanted to give Richard rope to hang himself, he'd have kept his distance. Richard would not act if Badger-beard was in his party.

But suppose Richard had betrayed his murdered father's faith and he too was now working for Cecil? If both Badger-beard and Richard were here to catch traitors, then if the assassination plot was attempted, I would find myself caught fast in their net. Between them, they'd ensure that I was the one fish who did not get away.

Several sharp jabs in my ribs jerked me back, and I realised someone was shouting for Temperance. I stumbled up on to the stage and, like a child's wooden doll, allowed myself to be positioned behind a gauzy drape, next to a young lady-in-waiting who could have been no more than sixteen.

Temperance was dressed in a long, diaphanous violet gown with golden cords crossed around her bare breasts. Elaborate wings made of swans' feathers were fastened to her back by a small harness and she wore a gold chaplet on her loose hair. She giggled, twisting round to show off her figure to its best advantage, and pouting when I made no attempt to flatter her. But my thoughts were still racing at the sight of Richard and Badger-beard together.

She was barefoot, standing on a grassy tussock studied with silk violets. Next to it was a little pool of shallow water. The bottom was formed from a piece of glass, bounded by chunks of crystal, giving the illusion that the water was much deeper.

'One foot is supposed to be in the water, madam,' Jonson instructed. 'Temperance is the balance of all things, and you must balance between earth and water.'

The girl lifted her skirts up to the knee to reveal a slender bare leg, even though the water could only have been a couple of inches deep, glancing at me sideways to see if I was watching. She wobbled and I offered a hand to steady her as she lowered her foot into the pool, then snatched it back up again. 'It's too cold! I shall be frozen to death if I stand in this.'

'You will only have to suffer it for as long as it takes for the actor to speak the verse, then the drape will fall again and you can move your foot,' Jonson said, his jaw clenched. 'Besides, the candles concealed on the other side will soon warm so shallow a pool. Please try once more, madam. Her Majesty the Queen desires it.'

All the time Jonson had been coaxing her, she had kept her hand firmly in mine, though she hardly needed my support to stand on the grass. She looked up at me. 'Do you think I shall catch cold if I stand thus? This gown is so thin and the cloth so fine, I feel as though I'm wearing nothing at all. I might as well be naked.'

'Wear a cloak until just before your drape is lifted,' I said tersely. I was itching to have done with this and get back outside. The image of Erasmus, his face grotesquely swollen, his hands flayed, swam before my eyes. I needed to know that Dob was safely in the kitchens and warn him if I could.

Sulkily, Temperance set her little foot down in the two inches of water and accepted a pair of twin silver goblets from Jonson. At his instructions, she dutifully poured wine from one to the other and back again in a graceful arch, while I galloped through my lines. The candles burning behind the pieces of crystal rock sent light rippling through the stream of wine and shimmered on her gown. She was right, the cloth was almost transparent.

I hurried out as soon as we were released, ensuring that my mask remained firmly in place. I made for the kitchens on the far side but was forced to halt as another procession of men and boys crossed my path, carrying baskets from a small boat piled with loaves, manchets, pies and other fare too plain to be intended for the guests, no doubt brought in to feed the army of workmen, soldiers, actors and musicians. Glancing along the line, I glimpsed Dob standing by the water gate, staring vacantly out at the jumble of craft of every size and shape, jostling each other as they fought to pull into the jetties and steps on both sides of the great, grey river.

I strode towards him, grabbed him by the arm and hauled him into the shadow of the wall. He gave a startled squawk, staring up at me in fear; he had never seen me in my mask and costume before, and had no idea who I was. With my back to the gardens, I lifted the mask for a moment or two before pulling it back into position.

'What are you doing out here, Dob? Didn't they give you any work in the kitchens?'

He nodded vigorously. 'Emptying the pails of guts and peelings, cranking the spits, feeding fires and chopping—'

'Then why aren't you in there doing that and making yourself useful to everyone?'

I glanced around to ensure no one was close enough at hand to hear me. 'Didn't you understand what I told you last night? I need you to keep watch.'

'I was watching!' he protested. 'But they sent out anyone who could be spared to help bring in the vittles for them that's working here. There's so much to be prepared for the feast, they don't have time to bake for owt else. And I'm starving – it's smelling all those roasting meats and not being allowed to taste a scrap of it, not even suck a bone.'

'Then carry one of the baskets back inside and do some work,' I snapped. 'You won't get fed if they find you standing idle, gawping at the wherries. I'd have thought you'd have learned your lesson after that beating you took. The watermen of London are never going to let you ply your trade on the Thames.'

'Wouldn't want to now I've seen 'em work,' he said scornfully. 'My father knows more about rivers and boats than all of them put together. I was watching one of the boats moor up by yonder steps. Cack-handed as a cow on ice, they were. Didn't know how to use the ropes and currents to bring her tight alongside bank – even a bairn in clouts knows you don't tie off a mooring like that.'

'Look,' I growled in exasperation. 'I know you're sour about the roughing-up they gave you, and with good reason, and yes, I'm sure you could teach them a thing or two about boats. But I told you, even if you were a master mariner, they still wouldn't take you on. You can sneer at them as much as you like tomorrow, if it makes you feel any better, but tonight you've got work to do. A man's life depends on it, maybe more than one.' I gave him a shove towards the kitchens. 'And whatever you do, don't start telling the cooks how your ma makes better pies than they do, else you'll find you're the one being skewered on a spit and roasted.'

He angrily turned to walk away, but I grabbed him again. 'If there's any trouble here tonight, if anyone asks you if you know me, pretend you've never heard of me. Say you were looking for work and you heard some men in the street say they needed kitchen-hands. And one more thing, Dob. Remember that man I warned you about with the white streak in his beard? He's here to watch the masque, so you need to stay out of his way. He'll do you more injury than a whole boatload of rivermen. Don't leave the kitchens and don't go off with anyone.'

He glowered at me, then shambled away, his shoulders hunched, turning back only once to dart me a furious look.

The ladies-in-waiting had returned to the palace and Prince Henry had appeared. Inigo Jones, Styward and several of the men responsible for the mechanical apparatus, hoists and harnesses swept him up on to the stage to demonstrate his part. Each part of the apparatus had been examined, pulled and pushed a dozen times over, not I thought from any fear of sabotage, but rather from the anxiety that it would jam and fail to perform. I had not seen the young Prince before. Although he was engrossed in the discussion he was having with Jones with an air of gravity of a man three times his age, he nevertheless acknowledged the curtseys and bows from those who passed with a nod of his head and a radiant smile, charming all.

The Prince was not yet in costume, but wore moss-green breeches and doublet, a soft white linen collar and a large-brimmed green hat with a great bunch of feathers over his closely shorn brown hair. At fourteen, he was still beardless and he was blessed with a smooth, clear complexion many a girl would have envied, with large brown eyes and even features, unlike his father's. He also had the easy, fluid gait of an athlete or dancer, in marked contrast to King James's weak and twisted legs. Even at a distance, it was clear to see why he was far more popular with the ordinary people than his father, except among the Catholics, for he was rumoured to be a Calvinist and that did not bode well for Catholics under his future reign. If it was planned that James would be dead before this masque was over, it was likely that young Henry would be joining him, if not tonight, then very soon after.

Chapter Thirty-seven

THE CHILL TIDE OF DARKNESS had oozed into the city. Torches had been set blazing every few feet on the walls surrounding the gardens, both to illuminate them and to ensure no one could scramble over them without being caught in the light. The flames guttered yellow, orange and red in the cold breeze from the river. Flowers of coloured glass, each with a candle flame glowing at its heart, studded the bare branches of the fruit trees like gems on a gown. Candles in bronze bowls of black water shimmered along the edges of the paths, their dancing flames reflected a hundred times as the water beneath them riffled in the breeze.

The gardens were filling up with nobles, jewels glittering in their hats, wrapped in fur cloaks against the night air. They sauntered between tables laid with roasted birds redressed in their own feathers, pastries, fruit, and subtleties of marchpane and sugar made into castles and scenes from the Holy Lands in which basilisks petrified travellers with a glance, crocodiles fought lions and doves nestled among serpents. A fountain of wine sparkled in the torchlight, while musicians tried to make themselves heard above the hubbub of chatter and laughter, the rattle of dishes and shouted orders to servants, and the ever-present clangs, bellows and shouts from the commoners outside the walls, plying their trade on the Thames and her banks.

A fanfare of trumpets silenced the din and the water gate was flung wide. The guards on either side stiffened, the wickedly sharp gilded blades of their ceremonial halberds shining blood-red in the torch flames, like the blades of executioners' axes. By a miracle, the sea of guests divided, lining the path from the gates.

I only glimpsed a flash of red and gold as the King's barge moored at the bottom of the steps. I assumed it must be too wide to enter the boathouse tunnel, or perhaps he wanted everyone in the gardens and out on the river to witness his grand entrance.

A line of Gentlemen Pensioners – his elite bodyguard, recruited from the fittest and most loyal young nobles in the realm – mounted the stairs, taking their places in pairs on either side of each step. Should the King stumble as he slowly climbed, taking one step at a time, his weak leg dragging behind him, they would ensure there was no danger of him plunging into the swift, icy current of the great river. I searched the faces of each of them I could see. My former master, Rowe, had been one of them before Richard had had me dismissed from his service, and I had no wish to encounter him again, at least not here. I was relieved to see he did not appear to be on duty.

When James at last stood framed in the gate, another fanfare greeted his appearance. The King made his solemn procession, his hand pressing down on the shoulder of a page-boy, a gaggle of courtiers and officials trailing in his wake. He was clad in a heavy black cloak trimmed with panels of gold thread. Curled black feathers gleamed in the high-crowned black hat, fastened there by an immense square brooch set with black stones and white pearls framing a deep red garnet which glistened like a fresh wound. His wrinkled hose were patterned with red and brown stripes, which had the unfortunate effect of making his legs look even more spindly.

As he advanced towards the canopy, it was like watching a ship cut through water, for a wave rippled down through the crowd as they bowed low and curtseyed as he passed, then straightened and surged behind him. Unlike his son Henry, James did not acknowledge any of them, except with a deepening scowl, and when at one point those in front had crowded too close, he waved his hand like an irascible old crone to clear his path.

The King and those in close attendance were settled beneath the canopy. Furs were laid across his lap and pages processed with a variety of dishes. As they approached the King, they paused before two of his own tasters, who took it in turns to select a pastry or a morsel of meat from each platter and take a bite from it, which they swallowed; they then dropped the remainder of the piece they'd sampled into a basket at their feet before waving the page-boy on. The King was taking no chances of being poisoned here. The pages then knelt before James, holding the dish up high for him to inspect. A curt nod meant that His Majesty would sample it and it was placed on one of the small tables on either side of him. An impatient flick of his fingers was a signal to take a dish away. The guests in the gardens crowded outside the canopy, watching, like children being entertained by the feeding of caged bears.

As soon as I saw the elaborate ritual, I realised I'd been a fool to imagine the assassins might poison the food. So how would they attack?

I slid to the back of the knot of actors and dancers. The lanterns and candles had been lit around the space where the dancers would perform, illuminating the wooden sides of the stage. I edged along it, looking for any signs that the boards had been recently prised open, but all appeared in place. None of the garlands of silk flowers showed any sign of having been disturbed. Then something caught my eye: a thin blade of light flickered across a tiny gap beneath the drapery above me. It had appeared so briefly, I decided it must have been the wind gusting one of the torches. But then it was there again.

I edged to the back of the stage and slipped behind the painted backdrop. The lights which would soon blaze out from it had not yet been lit and most of the stage was in darkness. But there was one light burning, low to the ground, shining up on to the profile of a man kneeling on the boards at the foot of the hoist that carried the giant eagle. He had a weighty iron spanner in his hand and was attacking one of the bolts that secured the upright beam of the small crane.

I crept closer. He was so intent on his work, he noticed nothing moving towards him in the shadows, but several times as loud noises from the gardens rattled through the scenery, he stared anxiously over his shoulder at the backcloth as though afraid that any minute it would fly up and he would be discovered.

As he glanced around for the third time, the spanner slipped from the bolt and clanged down on the boards. I sprang forward, bringing my boot down on it and lunging for the man. With a yelp, he toppled backwards before I could grab him. The whites of his eyes flashed wide with fear in the lantern light. I snatched up the spanner and held it over his head, silently threatening to bring it down on his skull.

He cringed, one arm raised protectively. 'You'll not get out of here alive!' he squealed. 'The moment they find my . . . corpse, they'll seal the gardens. It's crawling with soldiers and guards. They'll do worse than hang you.'

'And do you know what they do to assassins and traitors?' I growled. 'You'll be begging for death before they've finished with you.'

'I'm no traitor,' he retorted, indignation overriding his terror. 'There's no more loyal man than me in London. I wouldn't see a hair harmed on their Majesties' heads, especially young Henry. No more Christian a prince has ever drawn breath in this land.'

'Then what are you doing with this?' I brandished his spanner.

'Saw someone slipping off the back of the stage when trumpets were sounding for the King's barge, someone who I reckoned had no business up here. So, I came to check. Couldn't find nothing amiss, but when I gave this the eye . . .' He pointed to the base of the crane. 'The bolt's loose. It's still in place but it would have popped right off as soon as any weight was put on it. Whole thing might have come crashing down. Could have killed the young Prince and likely anyone sitting out there who was in its path. And this pole is long enough to have dragged the canopy down on to the heads of the King and all the guests. Can you picture it? If they were all under it, fighting their way out! And if a lantern had smashed and set fire to that oiled cloth with them trapped beneath it!' He shuddered. 'A man could fright himself into his grave just thinking about it.'

I moved closer to peer at the bolt, still grasping his spanner. He shrank back again, with a terrified glance up at my masked face.

'Do you think it hadn't been tightened?' I asked.

'It was me that put it in there when we were building the crane. 'Course I tightened it properly!'

I handed him back the spanner, crouching to help hold the bolt in place as he wrenched it tight. 'Could it have worked loose?'

'Not unless some joithead was messing around with it. But there's enough sodden-witted clot-poles have been working on this masque for that to have happened. Out of all the men looking for work in the city that he could choose, Styward has a talent for picking an army of idiots and knaves.'

'Did you recognise the man you saw coming off the stage?'

'Only saw a glimpse of him, just enough to know it was a man. Could have been anyone, even one of the nobles just being curious. But I reckon he did me favour. If I'd not seen someone lurking around, I'd have had no reason to check this again, 'cause it was as solid as the Tower of London an hour ago.' He stood up and picked up the lantern, then grabbed me by the elbow. 'Come on, the music's stopped. That means the masque is finally about to start.'

The tension in my chest eased a little. Was it over? Had we done it?

We marched off the stage just as two women began to sing. Light-bearers and male and female dancers resembling Trojan warriors and their consorts emerged from between the fake trees next to the stage, led by two male figures, dressed as Discord and Harmony. The former was in black robes trimmed with silver, clutching a silver lightning bolt. His crown was formed from a nest of poison-green snakes, with glittering red eyes and with forked tongues in the fanged jaws. The tongues, like the snakes themselves, were threaded on wire so that they darted back and forth as he moved. Harmony, with a sheathed sword hanging from his waist, wore robes of shimmering blue silk and a crown in the form of the sun. He carried a live dove in a gilded cage in one hand, while on his other arm was a hooded falcon, perched on a gauntlet. Though the falcon couldn't see the dove, the dove could see her; far from being the image of peace and calm, it was flapping its wings frantically in a bid to escape.

I slid through the group of actors and clambered up on to one of the bower seats to try to see the audience. As Discord and Harmony began to recite their arguments on the role of kingship and government in lengthy verses, James attacked the array of food on the small tables around him, glancing up only to talk to a flaxen-haired man seated on a stool next to him, who appeared equally bored by the performance. I assumed this was the King's current favourite, Robert Carr.

Only when the lively tune was taken up by the musicians was the King's attention drawn back to the performance. Something resembling a smile twitched across his lips as the dancers began cavorting wildly, outdoing each other in leaps and turns. The King's hand drummed against the arm of his chair in time to the music and several times he leaned in towards Carr, jabbing his finger in the direction of a dancer he evidently thought was giving a particularly fine performance.

I leaped down from my perch and edged around to where I could get a better view of the audience. The speeches of the kingly graces were not to be delivered until the third section of the masque, so there was time enough before I had to take my place.

The action now shifted to the stage, as the golden throne of King Solomon was revealed in all its glory. Tiny lights twinkled from the windows of the houses in Jerusalem painted on the backdrop behind, and as the moon rose on its cranked wheel into the painted sky, lights shone down through holes in the canvas, giving the illusion of myriad stars. The audience shouted their appreciation.

The shouts redoubled as Prince Henry processed in as an extremely youthful Solomon, dressed in cloth of gold and scarlet, his long silk train carried by page-boys in colourful breeches. Girls in diaphanous gowns followed, cradling lyres, baskets of fruit, green and yellow parrots, and chattering monkeys tethered to their arms by silver chains. The boys, who wore only thin sleeveless jackets over their bare chests, were visibly shivering in the cold Thames breeze.

Henry slowly mounted the throne steps and the golden animals obediently swivelled and slid towards him. Being far more accustomed to robed processions, he did not stumble as the unfortunate servant lad had done. The eagle bearing the crown descended slowly down over the Prince's head, coming to rest safely this time about three inches above it, while Henry sat calmly and regally beaming at his subjects. Perhaps word had not reached him of the earlier accident?

While most of the audience cheered and nodded to each other, James regarded the boy without smiling, and with a perceptible tightening of his jaw. The hunchback, Lord Salisbury, seated on the other side of James, was glancing from father to son, and he also remained unsmiling. I searched the faces of the crowd from my new vantage point. Then I finally spotted Richard. He was sitting under the canopy near the far back corner. I only saw him now because he had leaned forward across the youth sitting next to him to speak to a man on the other side. The man had a corpulent belly and red-gold hair which, if he'd been an actor, might have fitted him for the role of one of the Tudor kings. Badger-beard was sitting behind them on the end of the row of stools. He was not talking, but was watching the performance on the stage with the intensity of a man who is waiting for something he knows is about to happen.

Another fanfare of trumpets heralded a procession of dancing girls and men bearing boxes and urns, painted to look like solid gold. There was a rumble of wheels as a small chariot, flanked by two giants of men carrying enormous ostrich-feather fans, was drawn on to the stage by a miniature dappled-grey horse. The horse drew more excited gasps and comments from the crowd than the occupant of the chariot herself, for few in London had ever seen such a diminutive or elegant little beast.

Queen Anne, dressed as the Queen of Sheba, was assisted down from the chariot by the two fan-bearers. They say James had been enraptured of her beauty when he took her as his wife when she was just fourteen. Now in her thirties, she had matured into a striking woman, tall, with pale golden hair. She looked every inch the queen of legend in a white dress, caught at the waist by a golden girdle. A chaplet of diamonds and sapphires crowned her hair, from which a long gauze veil hung down, sweeping the floor.

She paused, facing the audience, smiling and kissing her hand to her husband. He had been in the act of drinking and lifted the goblet in his hand to return the salute. It was a cordial enough greeting, but James's attention waned again as soon as a man appeared beside her to deliver another lengthy speech, describing how the Queen of Sheba, having been told of the legendary wisdom of Solomon, had come to question him to see if it be true.

A curtain was drawn aside to reveal a huge model of the Sphinx. The creature rolled towards the audience, pulled by men dressed as winged seraphs, and a voice boomed out of it, posing riddles to King Solomon. Several times, a man in the audience, well in his cups, called out the answers – usually the wrong ones – before the young Prince could speak. The man's friends giggled and slapped him on the back, while anxious courtiers tried to lead him out, but James held up a hand to stop them, evidently finding his interruptions more amusing than the words Jonson had so carefully crafted.

Then, at Prince Henry's command, the great eagle with out-stretched wings slowly dropped from the hidden crane as Henry descended from his throne. I turned to study Richard. He had shuffled forward in his seat, his gaze seemingly riveted to the scene. Henry sat astride the eagle. It slowly rose, then the bird moved towards the cliff where the two fallen angels lay chained. The wooden crane creaked and groaned; the eagle juddered and tipped on the end of the rope; Henry was jolted forward. There was a collective intake of breath from all watching, but he was his father's son on horseback and regained his seat as expertly as any skilled rider in a joust. The eagle descended again, and Henry sprang off, holding up the magic ring with which he would command the disgraced angels to reveal all the mysteries of the universe.

A hand gripped my arm. 'Come on,' Parry urged. 'We have to take our places on stage before that golden goose flaps its way back.'

I glanced back towards Richard. He was no longer watching the masque, but seemed to be examining something in his hand.

'Hurry!' Parry ordered. 'If you miss your scene, they won't pay you and, worse still, they'll likely fine you for ruining the Queen's masque. And where does that leave poor Nat? Don't forget it's him they'll go looking for, because it's his papers you're using.'

I took my place and recited my lines with a haste that out-raged the young lady posing as Temperance, and would, no doubt, give poor old Jonson apoplexy. Then I slipped off stage while the Queen of Sheba led her ladies and others in the final stately dance and song of the masque, celebrating the peace and harmony that flowed through a kingdom wisely ruled by a just sovereign.

Outside, the other actors were busy pulling off their cos-tumes and masks, anxious to start stuffing themselves at the groaning table of food and wine which had been made ready for them in one of the halls in Denmark House. But though my belly was crying out to join them, I slipped back along the side of the gardens to the place from which I could observe the audience.

That loosened bolt had been no accident. Even if the carpenter's fear of a burning canvas dropping on the heads of King and company had not come to pass, and the young Prince had been merely injured by the fall from the eagle, in all the chaos and noise that would have ensued, no one except the assassin would have been looking at James. A single, well-aimed thrust of a stiletto would have been all that was needed, and the assailant could have slipped away before the King had even crumpled to the ground.

The stage and the two areas either side were now filled with performers led by Justice and Mercy, weaving the intricate knots of the labyrinth dance around Prince Henry. Some of the courtiers had joined in the dancing, and the rest of the audience were watching with interest, but it was too sedate to please the King, whose attention had wandered back to the food, wine and Robert Carr. Richard's attention too had wandered: he was watching the King, muttering something behind a raised hand to the red-haired man beside him.

The illuminations on the stage were so bright, in contrast to the space under the canopy, that it was only as one of the torches guttered that I saw the gap in the audience. I edged closer, wondering if what I'd seen or rather had *not* seen was just shadow. As Richard leaned across the youth to the man next to him, I had a clear view of the row behind him. There was a space – Badger-beard was gone. If he had come here to catch conspirators in the act, he'd been defeated. This thought had scarcely formed in my mind before it was shoved aside by a more chilling one. If Badger-beard had seen me with the carpenter and realised *I* had helped to undo the Serpent's handiwork and lost him his chance to catch the traitors, then he would take revenge. Showing me that little flayed hand outside the gates had been a warning for me to stay out of his way or else.

I began to search frantically for his face among the crowd. The gates were still locked and guarded. Badger-beard could not have left the palace grounds, so where was he? Lying in wait for me? But he could hardly attack me in here nor expect I would go quietly off with him to my death . . . No, no, that *wasn't* his plan. It wasn't my life he'd take to punish me. He'd make me pay, not with pain, but with guilt. For a man like him, that form of vengeance would taste far sweeter. And I had offered the victim to him, like a goat dropped into a lion's pit.

Chapter Thirty-eight

I WOVE AND BARGED through the milling crowd of servants and mechanics who had gathered around either side of the stage, trying to glimpse the glittering spectacle which was the finale of the labyrinth dance. Ignoring the shouted invitations from some of my fellow actors, who were already crowding towards their promised food and drink, I tore towards the kitchens and charged through the open door.

It was as if I had stepped straight into a baker's oven. Though the kitchens were two storeys high, the air was as thick as treacle with smoke and steam. Fires blazed in two huge fireplaces, filling the room with a blood-red glow, which almost smothered the feeble yellow light from candles set on sconces on the walls. As the carcasses of birds and beasts turned on great ladders of iron spits, fat infused with honey and spices ran from them, mingling with the bloody juices of the meat, dripping and sizzling into the troughs below. Copper pots boiled and rattled over the holes in a long stone bench, beneath which a dozen more fires burned.

Voiding baskets full of dirty platters and glasses were heaped by the doors, ready to be scrubbed, while fresh platters were being filled and decorated on the long tables. A great vat of ale stood near one of the tables to slake the thirst of the cooks and scullions. Overhead, the sergeant of the kitchen was edging up and down a narrow gantry, alternately consulting the papers in his hand and leaning over to bellow down at some cook or scullion below, or gesture towards a spit that was not being cranked smoothly enough or a pan that was boiling over.

A score of men and a few women were bustling from table

to ovens, whisking platters in and out through the far doors, or gulping down mugs of ale, their faces flushed and shiny with sweat, their stained shirts damp and clinging to them. In that maelstrom, trying to distinguish one face from another was like trying to distinguish a single soul in the paintings of the damned in hell. A dishevelled lad, catching sight of me standing in the open doorway, started violently slopping the syrup of spices he was beating. I was still wearing my mask and robe and realised how sinister a figure I must seem, suddenly appearing, lit up by the hell-red glow of the fire.

I ripped my mask off and held my hands up. 'No cause to get alarmed, lad, I'm just one of the actors. But I need to speak to a friend of mine, just started here today. Lad by the name of Dob.'

He frowned, raising his hand to his ear, as I tried to make myself understood over the cacophony of shouted instructions, clattering dishes and the crackling of flames and fat, without drawing the attention of everyone in the kitchen. 'A new lad, calling himself Dob. Have you seen him?'

He looked blank for a moment or two, his face pinched and tired, his eyes red from the haze of fat smoke. Finally, he nodded, gesturing back towards the door. 'Think he went out a while back.'

'Was he alone? Did someone come in to find him? A man with a white streak in his dark beard?'

'Someone fetched him. Heard her say something about a message, but—' The lad started again at a shout from the gantry above and bent to the vigorous beating of his syrup.

'Her?'

The lad shrugged, his eyes rolling upward in mute appeal to leave him alone before more trouble descended on his head.

I hurried from the kitchen and made for the darkest part of the gardens, discarding my robe and mask. All the dancers and players in the masque had now removed their costumes and I knew I would stand out in mine now if I continued to wear it. Richard would still be milling around somewhere, but if I could keep away from the torches, he might not spot me, especially if he was not expecting to see me. I sped across the gardens to the gate on the far side through which we'd entered. If Badger-beard had sent a woman in to entice Dob out into the grounds, he would not loiter and he would hardly risk killing him in the palace grounds. But the guards at the gate were adamant that no one had left that way since the King's arrival and nor would they.

'No one leaves anywhere before the King, neither man nor mouse,' one said.

'Be clapped in irons if we opened this gate before His Majesty has departed and he'll be going the same way as he came, by barge,' the other added. 'Anyway, why are you in such a hurry to leave? It's not often you get to fill your belly at the King's expense; it's usually the likes of us paying for him to stuff his chops. If I wasn't on duty, believe me, I'd be guzzling all the meats and wine I could grab while I could. I'll wager they'll be the best you've ever tasted.'

'You may as well,' the other agreed. 'We'll not get our orders to open up this gate for the commons till all the nobles are safe away by boats. And there's to be squibs and a cannon salute for the King and young Prince over the river as they leave. That'll be a sight worth watching.'

A single word burst through my head like a musket shot. *Boats.* I had been so annoyed with Dob for leaving the kitchens to gaze idly at the river that I hadn't listened hard enough to what he had said. *Didn't know how to use the ropes and currents to bring her tight alongside bank – even a bairn in clouts knows you don't tie off a mooring like that.* Dob was right: no genuine wherryman would make such a mess of bringing a boat alongside. That meant the loosened bolt could never have been the assassination attempt on James and Henry that the Serpents had been planning. That was far more likely to have been the work of a lone malcontent, paying back an offence offered to him by one of the carpenters, or wanting to make Inigo Jones look a fool.

But out there on the river, fuzzled by the strong wine they had been imbibing all evening, the King and his courtiers would be fowls trapped in a net, and the Gentlemen Pensioners unable to defend them.

Even if I could have got through the water gate ahead of the King, I'd be stranded. The river washed right up against the wall of the gardens. The steps leading down to the boathouse tunnels were guarded and though I could easily have picked the locks on the grilles between the boathouse and the river, I'd little doubt that a strong cohort of guards would be on duty there, for no one would risk an assassin creeping into the grounds under cover of darkness from the Thames.

I hurried back towards the kitchens. Several trays of aniseed jombils and little marrow bone pies lay cooling on some racks. As soon as the sergeant up on the gantry had his back to me, I grabbed a basket from a stack by the door and piled some of the pies and sweet pastry knots into it, covering them with a piece of sacking.

'Sergeant will have your guts,' a voice whispered at my elbow.

Dob was standing behind me, his face flushed from the heat and his hair plastered to his forehead with sweat. A momentary surge of relief washed over me.

'Want to get out of here?' I mouthed.

He nodded vigorously.

'Grab one of those sacks by the far door and march out with it. Look like you've been sent to deliver it somewhere. Keep going and I'll follow.'

I waited until Dob was on the other side of the room, then sent an egg rolling into the path of one of the men carrying a large joint of roasted meat on a platter. The egg broke beneath his foot, and he slipped, meat and plate clattering to the floor. The sergeant whipped round, raining down curses on the man and ordering him to clear up the mess. Dob slipped out and I swiftly followed.

Another kitchen lay beyond the first, but everyone there ignored us. They were well used to servants passing through. Beyond that was a maze of low corridors lined with stout oak doors, probably leading to stores, wine cellars and sculleries. But finally, after several false turns, we found a narrow door at the end of the passageway. A cold breeze hissed through the small metal grille set into it, confirming to me that it was an outer door. I only hoped it didn't simply lead to another closed courtyard.

A guard almost fell on top of me as I dragged the door open: he must have been leaning against the wood. Dob gave a nervous giggle, which only served to infuriate him more.

He took a couple of steps backwards and jabbed the spear point of his halberd at my chest. 'Just where do you think you're going, sirrah?'

I pulled a face. 'There's an old biddy lives a few streets away, confined to her bed. Used to be a servant of Lady Elizabeth's family,' I told him, certain there would be more than one Lady Elizabeth at Court. 'Seems her ladyship still has a fondness for the crone, wanted her to have some marrow bone pies for the Accession Day celebrations tomorrow, but, of course, her ladyship can't leave the Queen's side tonight, so I'm sent to go traipsing round there. I've been running from pillar to post since before dawn and I still haven't had a bite to eat myself.'

'You and me both,' the guard agreed. 'And it'll be worse tomorrow with all the processions and the tilt.' He twitched aside the sacking covering my basket, peered in and grabbed a couple of the small pies. Stuffing one whole into his mouth, he chewed with evident satisfaction. 'You want to help yourself to some of those before you hand the rest over. 'Cause I tell you this, no one is going to bother fetching you and me any pies when we're in our dotage. And you know they'll throw the rest of them on the floor tonight, don't you? Happens after every masque. Cooks are ordered to prepare a whole table full of cold meats and pies, then the Scottish nobles deliberately overturn the whole mess of it without tasting a bite, and call for the cooks to spread the new table with hot food for them. They think it a rare sport.' He stabbed at the sack that Dob had slung over his shoulder. 'What you got in there, boy?'

Dob was staring in frozen panic at the lethal blade of the halberd flashing inches from his face. I had no idea what Dob had grabbed, but though the sack was bulging, he seemed to be carrying it with remarkable ease.

'Feathers,' I said, with sudden inspiration, 'for the old crone's pillow.'

'Then you want to do yourself a favour and keep those well away from her,' the guard said. 'Can't die quickly if you sleep on feathers, my father always told me that. And you don't want to find yourself waiting on the old besom for months to come, do you?'

I laughed and pushed the basket towards him again. He extracted another pie and two of the sweet pastry knots, which he stuffed beneath his hat before unlocking a wrought-iron gate. I propelled Dob forward and the guard waved me through as cheerily as if we'd become blood brothers. Dob almost broke into a run as the guard locked the gate behind us. But I pulled him back.

'Slowly, lad. If you start running, you'll look like a thief and he'll call out the watch.'

I made him trudge beside me towards the end of the street, though he kept glancing back anxiously over his shoulder. As soon as we turned the corner, I stuffed a pie in his mouth and another into my own, for I was starving. Then, ignoring Dob's muffled protests, I thrust the basket into the hands of an urchin sitting in a doorway, who whooped with surprise and delight at his unexpected supper. I tossed Dob's sack over a wall and we ran down an alleyway in the direction of the river.

A stiff breeze was blowing along the river. Lanterns outside the buildings lining the banks licked gold and red tongues of flame into the dark, icy water. Moving dots of light, far and near, marked where wherries and private boats still criss-crossed the Thames, even though the hour was late, and the skies as black as tar. I glanced back along the bank towards Denmark House. The curve of the river meant that I could just glimpse the King's barge below the steps leading down to the water. In the stiff breeze, royal pennants of blue, red and gold streamed out from the top of a long, gilded cabin with glass windows, which protected the King and his favoured guests from the chill night air. Torches blazed on the barge and the gilding on the cabin gleamed so brightly that where it reflected on the black water, the barge seemed to be floating on liquid gold.

I stared across at the opposite bank, where the flames of numerous torches silhouetted an ants' nest of scurrying figures. The cannons which would salute the King's departure and the squibs which would be fired into the sky above were being made ready.

'That boat you told me about earlier, Dob, the one where the men on board didn't seem to know how to moor it properly, do you see it now?'

Dob, shivering in the cold wind after the heat of the kitchen, stepped as close as he could to the water's edge. 'Is that the King's barge?' he asked in awed tones.

'The red and gold one, yes, but can you see the boat you were watching before?'

He stepped back. 'They tied up behind where the King's boat is. It wasn't nearly as tall or long as the King's. It might still be there, but I don't know, 'cause I can't see round the royal barge.' He turned to stare again at the sight, but I dragged him away and back along the narrow wharf path.

An old man was lifting a small crate containing several indignant ducks from a sculler on to a narrow wooden jetty.

'That boat, Dob, do you think you could handle it?'

'That pinny? It's so small anyone could manage that.'

'It might not be as easy as you think, there's a swift current on the river.'

It was too dark to see Dob's expression, but from his stance I knew it would be scathing. I picked my way along the slippery boards.

The old man snatched up an oar, plainly thinking he was going to have to fight me for his ducks. He was even more wary when I asked to hire his boat, assuring him that the lad was an expert waterman and the sculler would be returned safely. But he could not resist the sum I offered him and finally, after I'd carried the duck crate to the bank for him, he reluctantly agreed.

The tide was flowing in and Dob had to pull hard against it. It would be easier coming back – if we lived long enough to make it back. I could tell Dob was anxious to get as close as he could to the barge, but I ordered him to stay well clear of it. The guards on board would doubtless have orders to deal forcibly with any craft that approached too near, especially an old tub like this one, stinking of rotting fish and duck shit.

The hour was late. This was not to be a great river procession like those that would take place over the next few days, when as many as a hundred craft of all sizes would be following in the wake of the King's barge. Tonight, only three other barges, all smaller and less ornate than the King's, were moored along the bank in front of his, facing downriver, waiting to fall in behind the King's barge after his had passed them. On the first of them, a large group of musicians had taken their places and started to play, in readiness for the King's arrival.

Dob had stopping rowing, allowing the incoming tide to push us back up towards the great barge again. I kicked him.

'The boat you saw before, can you see it now?' He reluctantly dragged his gaze away from the King's barges and scanned the moorings.

'There it is.' He pointed with his chin. 'They've moved it downriver.'

'Are you sure it's the same one?'

He nodded.

'Then take us down there. Not too close, and row beyond it.'

His body strained with the effort of pulling on the oars against the current. I hunched low in the little sculler, glancing up at the other boat as we slid past. It was half concealed behind another of the many wooden jetties that bristled into the water. Five – no, six men were inside. Two already had oars in their hands, though the craft was still tethered to its mooring at the stern. The bow, through freed, was being pushed against pillars of the jetty by the current. Two of the other men in it were grasping long, metal-tipped boathooks. There was no lantern on the front of their boat, but there was the glow of one shining up from below, where it had been placed in the bottom of the craft.

I told Dob to row down to the next little jetty, moor up and wait for me. I crept towards the men along a small stretch of the bank, keeping to the deep shadows, and settled down to watch. The men on board had stripped to look like watermen, dressed in breeches and shirts, with sleeveless leather jerkins to allow free movement of the arms. But the leather gleamed too new in the glow of the lantern below them. It was not cracked or worn as regular boatmen's would have been.

If they were the would-be assassins, though, I could not see how they intended to attack. They could not expect to grapple the King's barge and clamber aboard, and I couldn't see any weapons in the boat, except for the oars and boathooks they held. Maybe they were simply singers, dressed as watermen, positioned there to entertain the King as he passed.

They were not watching the barge. All of them were staring fixedly across the broad stretch of the river towards the opposite bank. Something caught the attention of one of them and he gestured towards it. A few yards downriver, beyond the gusting orange lights of the torches illuminating the cannons, was the rhythmic flash of tiny light from the darkness. It vanished, then repeated again and again – someone was using a signal lantern.

One of the men in the boat bent to retrieve the lantern below him. As he leaned forward, I caught the glint of silver as a pendant swung down from his neck into the light he was lifting. I recognised it instantly. The bone-white of the wolf's tooth, the silver mount, and the flash of the polished coral, red as a drop of freshly spilled blood – the amulet Avery had *conjured* for the lady in the old water mill to protect her husband.

I scrambled back to the jetty and down on to the boat, where Dob sat shivering.

'Row to the opposite bank,' I told him, unfastening the mooring rope nearest to me. 'We need to be a few more yards downriver too, but we have to get there quickly. The King's life may depend on it.'

Dob gaped at me, but he cast off the other mooring with a swiftness no waterman on the Thames could have bested, and he rowed with all his might, telling me, in his father's voice, to keep a sharp lookout on both sides for any craft that might slice through us. Once more we found a small wooden jetty, this one rotten and sagging into the current.

'Stay here. Keep low in the boat and whatever happens, whatever you see, don't show yourself or make any sound.'

The planks of the crumbling jetty rocked and groaned beneath my weight as I scrambled ashore, slipping on slimy boards. The ground on this side of the river was a large expanse of low-lying marsh, bordered on one side by the Paris Gardens and playhouse and on the other, some distance away, by Lambeth Palace. I could just make out the lights of both in the far distance on either side of me, but the stretch of shore on which I stood lay in darkness. Upriver, opposite Denmark House, a dome of flickering orange light from the torch flames lit up a row of men standing by the cannons, ready to give the gun salute as the King's barge pulled away. But the signal light had come from somewhere between me and them. A rough path, raised up on a low bank, ran between the water's edge and the treacherous marsh behind. Keeping low and using the reeds and willow scrub on the bank for cover, I inched along it. Bright pinpoints of flame ran like a string of rubies along the river's edge ahead of me as the soldiers lit the match cords twisted around linstock poles, ready to touch to the cannon fuses.

I continued to inch forward, silently cursing as my boots plunged deep into icy mud. I kept stopping to listen for movement, but the roar of the river, the rustle of the wind in the reeds, the music from the barge and the bellowed commands and answering calls from the men covered any other sounds. A whole butchery of killers could have been camped out on that wasteland, preparing to attack, and I wouldn't have heard them.

Then, just as I thought I must have walked past the spot where I'd seen the light, three flashes from the opposite bank were answered by three flashes on my side of the water. They were brief, but enough to illuminate the metal barrel of a small cannon, standing alone on the darkened bank.

I veered off the path and down on to the marshland behind, praying to every saint and demon I could name that this particular stretch was firm enough to bear my weight. I squelched across it for a few yards, until I was behind where I'd seen the signal. The glow of the torches from the palace gardens on the opposite bank, though they did not reach this side of the river, were enough to throw the figure on the bank above me into faint relief. I could make out very little detail, except for the movement of a man bending low, and the silhouette of the cannon's muzzle. It was aimed straight across the river, level with any passing barge.

I knew with chilling clarity what was about to happen. As the other cannons fired the salute and the squibs exploded in the sky, one more shot would boom out, under the cover of their noise. The red-hot ball would not be large. It wouldn't need to be. It might not kill the King and his heir outright, or even wound them, but the barge itself would be mortally wounded. It would sink and the King and Prince would find themselves struggling in their heavy robes in the icy black waters of the river. I finally understood what role the man with the wolf's amulet and his friends would play. Boatmen, gallantly trying to rescue those thrashing around in the river with their long metal-tipped boat-hooks, which could just as easily ensure that a man was pinned beneath that dark water until he drowned. Every man at Court knew that James had refused to allow his son to learn to swim, for fear of the danger of the sport. Now he was about to pay the price.

Chapter Thirty-nine

A FANFARE OF TRUMPETS announced that the King was leaving
the gates of Denmark House. I could see little of what was happening, but I could hear the cheers of men and a rattle of musket
fire, the tiny balls glowing red, flashing like fireflies through the
night sky. A small flame glowed in the darkness above me. The
assassin had lit his cord match, ready to touch it to the powder.

I crept closer, until I was directly behind the spot on the bank
on which he stood, and crouched in the chill, wet mud. The musicians had struck up a lively tune. The man was staring at the river
with the intensity of a cat hidden in the bushes, watching a bird
hopping blithely towards it. A shouted order and the cannons
upriver began to fire, one after the other, great booms echoing
across the water and bouncing from the stones of the buildings.
A rush of yellow light above each of the great guns as the loose
powder was touched by the match, then an explosion of red fire
as the cannon blank fired. While overhead, coloured squibs burst
in the sky. The great barge would be moving slowly against the
incoming tide in the centre of the river, putting it within range
for far longer than had it been a moving man or horse.

I saw the glow of the match trailing through the darkness
above me. I stormed up the steep bank and in my haste, slipped
on the mud. The assassin must have sensed the movement behind
him, for he half turned as I dug my boots in and ploughed on,
dagger in hand. I aimed the thrust upwards into his back, but
his sudden turn, together with the thick leather jerkin he wore,
deflected the blow and it pierced his arm instead. If he cried out,
I couldn't hear it above the explosions.

I dragged the dagger out and his hot blood gushed over my hand. His left arm hung useless, but he was still holding the linstock pole in his right hand, with the smouldering match twisted on the end. He thrust the end of the linstock towards the cannon's touch hole. He was facing me now and I struck him again, stabbing into the bare flesh at his throat. With a gurgling cry, he dropped the pole. His hand clawed at his neck as blood sprayed out between his fingers. I felt the scalding drops on my own cheeks and lips, stinging my eyes, so that for a moment I was blinded. Then he tottered backwards and toppled into the water.

I turned to grab the linstock, which had fallen across the cannon barrel, but I was too late: the burning match touched the gunpowder. There was a hiss and a crackle as red sparks fizzled above the touch hole, then an ear-splitting explosion, as the ball, red-hot and burning bright in the dark air, shot from the muzzle. The recoil hurled the cannon backwards, tipping it over the bank. There were screams as the ball missed the cabin of the King's barge, which had just rowed clear, and tore through the prow of the musicians' boat following it, sending the pennant pole crashing into the water.

The hole in the prow was above the waterline, but the smashed wood, caulked with tar and wadding, had already burst into flames. Men began tossing buckets on ropes into the river, drawing up water to douse them, while the rowers pulled frantically for the shore. The barge rocked perilously as the musicians and those nobles and servants travelling with them stampeded towards the stern to escape the flames.

King James's barge had pulled closer to the far bank. The rowers were trying to speed the craft away downriver, but they were having a hard time of it against the tide. Several red flashes burst from the stern of the boat, and as I saw the white spray boiling beneath me in the water I realised the King's guards had opened fire towards the spot where they thought the rogue cannon lay, though they were being carried further and further out of range.

I turned to stare upriver as shouts, bangs and more bursts of scarlet exploded through the darkness along the bank. Flaming torches were moving towards where I stood, and I realised the explosions were no longer squibs, but musket fire. The soldiers were coming this way, searching and firing as they came. The assassin's body had vanished into the water and would already have been carried away in the swift current. The corpse would be battered against every pillar and stone in the river. Bodies of men who'd met a violent end were pulled from the Thames every day, and even if the assassin's carcass were found, I wouldn't be able to identify him, much less prove that he had fired the cannon. On the other hand, if the soldiers caught me here, they wouldn't trouble to look any further for their would-be assassin.

I dropped down on to the lower ground behind the bank, running and splashing back towards the boat where I had left Dob. There was a cry behind me and the flames of the torches merged and then paused. They had evidently found the cannon and were now casting in ever-widening circles around it, searching for whoever had fired it.

As soon as I stood up on the bank, they would see me silhouetted against the lights on the other side of the river. I needed to make that moment as brief as possible. Ignoring the mud, I crawled up the bank and rolled over the top, hoping that I had not misjudged the distance and that I was as close as I could be to Dob and my only means of escape.

I found myself just a few feet from the jetty. I could see the prow of the little sculler jutting out on the other side. Still crouching low, I edged down the slippery boards as they swayed and cracked beneath me.

'Dob! Dob! It's me, lad. Get ready to cast off and row downriver.'

There was no answer. The boat was in darkness in the shadow of the landing stage. I dropped down into it. He was not curled up in the bottom. The sculler was empty. Another musket shot rang out.

I needed to get out of here. But if Dob had climbed up on to the bank somewhere to get a better view of the royal barge or the squibs, he'd walk right into those soldiers. God's blood, maybe they'd already seen him and were firing at him. Then, with relief, I heard a creak on the jetty.

'Dob! Get in! Quickly!' I crouched to unfasten the mooring rope, fumbling to find it in the dark.

Something fell across my face, but before I could react, it slid swiftly to my neck and tightened. I was caught in a noose, being jerked sideways. My head was smashed into the wooden pillar of the jetty. The boat rocked violently beneath me, and I was pitched into the bottom of the sculler, dazed and choking from the rope tightening around my throat. I grabbed my dagger, but the man standing over me stamped down hard on my wrist, forcing it from my fingers. I felt the prick of his own knife against my neck.

With his free hand, he pulled the end of the noose from the pillar and wrapped it around the plank seat behind me, lashing me by my neck to the wood. Blood pounded through my head, till I thought it would burst. I could do little to prevent him binding my ankles and my hands; the cords were so tight that I could already feel my fingers swelling. I was struggling to draw any air into my lungs. Each move I made pulled the cord around my neck tighter.

'Keep still and keep silent,' my captor hissed in my ear, 'or this will be your last breath. If you draw those soldiers towards us, I will kill you before they can set one foot on the jetty.'

He unfastened the mooring rope, took up the oars and pushed us out into the current, rowing away downriver. A cry went up from the bank and there was another crack from a musket; I saw a red streak and heard the whistle as the shot went over the boat and hissed into the water. The man bent lower, pulling harder, only straightening when he judged that we were out of range. From the drag of the current and the way the stinking icy water in the bottom of the sculler was swilling around, I could tell he was trying to cut diagonally across the river to the far side. Then he turned, letting the boat drift upriver with the tide.

Chapter Forty

THE COLD WATER soaking into my clothes at the bottom of
the boat was at least helping to clear my head from the blow.
I tried to ease the noose away from my windpipe to gulp the air.
Moving my legs an inch at a time, I felt for my knife, which I
knew must be lying somewhere near me. A boot shot out, slamming into my kneecap. I jerked in pain and almost blacked out
as the rope wrenched violently against my throat.

'I told you to lie still!'

We passed the barge which had been damaged by the cannon
shot. The flames had been extinguished, but from the shouts and
orders, they were still pouring water on the smouldering prow
to ensure the wood didn't rekindle. They were too busy to take
any notice of the sculler sliding through the darkness far below
them on the river. Men were swarming all over the barge, trying
to recover the musicians' instruments and inspect the damage.
The glow from their lanterns did not penetrate our craft, but it
was enough to give me the first glimpse of my captor's head and
shoulders as he pulled back on the oars – a black, dagger-point
beard and the flash of a white streak.

My first instinct was to lash out with my bound feet and
attempt to knock him into the river, but the force that would
take to kick him overboard could easily break my own neck, and
if the boat capsized, I would be as helpless as a puppy tied in a
sack and tossed into a lake to drown. He was right: all I could
do was lie still and wait.

The boat was crossing back to the south bank of the river
and we were once again in darkness. We were upriver now of

the cannons and the search being made by the soldiers. There was nothing between the city and the village of Lambeth except open fields and marshland. The sculler bumped against something, jolting me forward, the rope cutting deep into my neck. I couldn't breathe. I thought my eyeballs were going to burst. A cold paralysis was seeping down my limbs. I slowly surrendered to an empty blackness and then I knew nothing more.

A STINGING SLAP roused me and I heard groaning, which I slowly realised was coming from me.

'Here, drink this. Swallow it, damn you, unless you want me to force it down your throat.'

I was sitting propped up against a rough wooden wall. My wrists and ankles were still bound, but it took me a minute or two to realise that the noose that had been around my neck now hung loose on my chest, for my throat was so swollen I could hardly breathe much less swallow, and my skin burned as if the cord was still biting into it.

As my senses gradually revived, I realised I was in a small hut, smelling of rotting cabbage, a damp earth floor beneath me. The door was shut, but a stream of cold air blasted in through some kind of window above my head, which was covered by a sack. A small fire burned in a pit, dug into the floor, the flames twisting and flattening in the icy draft. The dull red and orange glow from the fire, which offered the only light, sent shadows crawling spider-like across the walls.

Badger-beard was pressing the mouth of a leather flask to my lips, tipping it towards me. Thirsty as I was, I tried to resist the liquid, convinced he was trying to drug me or poison me. He forced me to swallow: it was sweetened wine, which could mask the taste of anything. I spat it out and he rocked back on his heels, laughing.

'As you please, Master Pursglove, or whatever name you are using this night. But, trust me, you'll be begging for it before dawn.'

I raised my bound hands. 'Do you intend to do to me what you did to Sibyl and Myles and Erasmus? Or do you only torture old women and young boys?' I was desperate to know if he had taken Dob, if the lad was floating dead in the river or worse. But I bit back the question. If Dob was hiding out somewhere, I didn't want to put him in danger by letting this killer know he'd been in the boat with me.

He poked the fire with a branch and left it there until the end caught alight. Then he lifted the stick out and rocked back on his haunches, studying the flame for a long time before he spoke.

'I confess your question disappoints me, Master Pursglove. They told me you were intelligent. Or should I be addressing you as *Matthew*? That was the name bestowed on you at baptism, wasn't it? *Matthew Issott.*' He enunciated the name slowly, chewing it over in his mouth. 'Matthew the tax collector. No, I'm afraid your parents made a bad choice there – it really doesn't suit you. You'd never be content to settle for any occupation as steady and mundane as that. *Daniel*, on the other hand, is much more apt. That Jew was always getting himself into trouble, playing with fire, putting his head in the lion's jaws, just like you.'

'And you? What shall I call you?' I croaked. 'What name fits your nature? Judas? No, he didn't kill for pleasure.'

By the light of the burning stick in his hand, I saw a lazy smile on Badger-beard's face, amused by my outburst. 'Some call me the Deacon, one who serves God and man.' He pressed his hand to his heart and mockingly inclined his head.

When he straightened, his tone had changed again. 'You do realise those soldiers would have killed you if they'd caught you this night? If you were fortunate, they would have clubbed you to death, or else tied you in front of the barrel of a cannon and fired. I've seen that done in Spain and, trust me, only a lucky few die instantly. But even that would have been painless compared to what Robert Cecil would have ordered for you in the Tower. The King does not forgive the treachery of those he has trusted. But as the old proverb says, *In trust is treachery*. You don't need me to remind you of the truth of those words, though, do you, Daniel?'

'Then why didn't you let those soldiers arrest me? It would have saved you the trouble of murdering me. Or was it that you wanted to work on me yourself, as you had Erasmus and Sibyl. Does it give you pleasure to inflict pain? I hear it arouses some men better than any jade's tricks. Carry on, then, if that's what you brought me here for, but if it's information you want, you're wasting your time. There's nothing I can tell you.'

'No, there isn't anything you can tell me,' he agreed. 'But there is something you can do. Something that you *must* do.'

I laughed, though my throat was so mauled, it came out as a growl. 'Why would I do anything for a man who has tortured and killed an innocent woman and lads who could not possibly defend themselves? If you mutilated and murdered them with the intention of frightening me into doing whatever it is that you want, you've gravely mistaken my nature.'

Badger-beard thrust the burning stick back into the heart of the fire, staring at the flames as they leaped up around it and consumed it. 'Tonight, you foolishly thwarted an attempt on the King's life. Theirs was a clumsy and ill-thought-out plan, drawn up by fools. The King might merely have been wounded or even escaped injury altogether, and that would have served to make him feel even more invincible than he already does. A little strutting god with the divine right to rule and God's omnipotent protection to do it. And even if they had succeeded in killing him, those taking part would have been caught. They were relying on an uprising to help them escape, but word has to be spread, men have to be roused, such things take time. Time which those men on the boat and the man you dispatched did not have.

'Nevertheless, it was intended that the plot should be allowed to proceed, but then you lumbered in and you prevented it. Actions have . . . *consequences*. Consequences which one among us hoped he could have spared you, if you had only listened to his warning. But then you never heed warnings, do you, Daniel?

Just like your namesake, and look where that landed him. Beware the lions.'

'Who?' I demanded. My throat felt skinned from the inside and talking wasn't helping, but I had to know. 'Who intended that the plot should go ahead? Who wanted those men caught? Robert Cecil?I Is he the master you serve, Deacon? What you did to Erasmus and the others, it had all the hallmarks of a pursuivant, a man like Richard Topcliffe. Did he teach you how it is done? Is Cecil running schools for torture now?'

'Consequences,' he repeated.

The Deacon laid another stick in the fire until the end was well alight, the tip glowing red beneath the flame, and shuffled towards me, the burning brand held out. He swept within an inch of my face and I steeled myself not to flinch from the heat.

'Hold out your hands!'

They were bound in front of me. I could not move them away from him any further than my side and he knew it.

'You hesitate, Daniel. Could that be cowardice I see? Fear? It seems you would not hold out as long in the Tower as some of us have wagered. We must ensure, then, that you are never put to that test. Your hands, if you please.'

Iced water flooded my bowels, but I was determined not to give him the satisfaction of seeing me flinching away. Hatred steels a man much more than courage and my hatred for this man was white-hot.

He grabbed my sleeve as I thrust my arms out towards him. He smiled, then blew out the flame on the end of the stick and pressed the smoking end to the rope, holding it there until the cord had almost burned through. He retreated until he was out of reach of my arms. Then he dropped the stick back in the fire and drew his dagger, pointing it towards me.

'I think you can manage to break that bond yourself now, and I will leave you to untie your own feet, to spare you the temptation of kicking me. But I warn you: I will not hesitate to stick this blade into you if you make any attempt to move from where you are sitting until I give you leave. And I do not bluff when I say our skills with the knife are equally matched. My advantage is that I have one in my hand and you do not.

'Now the first thing you need to know, Daniel – and I intend to tell you only what you need to know; it is for others to offer you explanations, not me – is that I did not torture and kill your three friends.' He said it quietly and without emotion. He might have been discussing the meat to be served at table.

I dragged my wrists apart, fists clenched. The cord snapped.

He raised his dagger. 'Toss that rope over here, just in case you are inclined to use it. And keep your temper in check, Daniel. I repeat, I did not torture and kill them. Why would I? Sibyl had always proved extremely loyal to the Catholic cause. Myles was a mere boy who might have seen much, but in truth understood little of the games being played around him, and was certainly no threat. Erasmus, yes, I will admit that had he been arrested that would have proved dangerous for all of us, but he was keeping out of the way and he could have been silenced in the Tower before he was persuaded to talk. I did not kill him. What reason would I have? As I said, there is nothing I could have learned from them, or you, that I did not already know.'

'I am not a fool,' I rasped. 'You sent me the message telling me to meet Erasmus at that den they so aptly call the Hunting Lodge. The maid at the inn described you perfectly. You intended me to find his mutilated body, probably even to be arrested for his murder.'

The Deacon emitted a grunt of mirthless laughter. 'I imagine they are no strangers to violent death or murder in that establishment, whether or not those involved ever actually use that word. And what is the difference, I wonder – *killing, murder, execution, assassination* – such interesting nuances of conscience and consequence. But whatever you choose to call it, I suspect none of the deaths in the Hunting Lodge are ever reported and no one is arrested for them.'

'So, you knew you could torture and murder Erasmus as you

pleased and escape justice. How many more have you murdered in that place?'

The Deacon gave a grunt of amusement. '*Jaculus has news of your friend. Descend the stairs at the ninth bell tonight, and ask for him.* Wasn't that the message you received, Daniel? It doesn't mention Erasmus. *I* didn't mention Erasmus. I was sending someone else to meet you at the Hunting Lodge. I didn't know the young man would be there, much less that he would be . . . dead. But I assume that the manner of his death was the same as that of Sibyl and your young friend Myles.'

'Then who?' I demanded. 'Who murdered them?'

The Deacon shrugged. 'You said yourself, their mutilation and death had all the hallmarks of a pursuivant. Does that not seem the most likely explanation?'

'But you were there, in every village, in every town where I went. You didn't even attempt to hide. You wanted me to know you were following me. You wanted me to know what you'd done. And yesterday morning, outside the gate, the flayed monkey's paw.'

'That was a warning, Daniel. I was trying to remind you of what had happened to those who got involved with you and what lay in store for you, if you didn't back away from disrupting this plot. I was there in every town and village to protect you. That was why I was sent to follow you: to watch over you and ensure that you didn't meet the same fate as Sibyl. You have enemies, Daniel, men who would baulk at nothing to have the satisfaction of listening to you begging for your life, or watching your agony on the scaffold. Nothing would delight them more. And their reach is long, maybe longer than you can possibly imagine. Someone wants you dead and it is my job to keep you alive . . . for now, at least,' he added drily.

'You read those broadsides I had pasted up; I watched you do it. *A barbarous traitor and vicious murderer is lately absconded from Newgate gaol . . . He passes by diverse false names, most recent Daniel Lyrypine, Father Montague, John Willitoft and*

Joseph Pursglove. Didn't you have the wit to understand the message I was sending you in those words? It was to warn you that others knew where you were and who you were. I was ordered to hound you back to London, by someone who knew you to be as obstinate as the tide. Arguments would not have persuaded you to return. I suppose I should thank whoever it was who did kill your friends, for it seems little else would have goaded you back here.'

In spite of my numb and swollen fingers, I had managed to untie the rope binding my feet, but I kept a firm grip on this one.

'Who do you serve, Deacon? Who gives you these orders? And why do they want me back here, in London, where I am most in danger, if they want, as you put it, to *protect* me?'

'I said I would tell only what you need to know. I offer no explanations.'

'So, what else do I *need to know*?'

'That I have instructions to take you to someone tonight. Someone who wishes to speak with you.'

'And if I do not choose to go?' I brandished the rope between my two fists. It wasn't a knife, but I could still use it as a weapon.

'I would advise you to co-operate on this occasion,' the Deacon said calmly. 'Though I know that to obey any order sticks in your craw. Your young friend Dob – whose health, I confess, I am surprised you have not inquired about – is unharmed for now, but if you wish him to remain so, then I would suggest you do exactly what I ask.' The Deacon clambered to his feet, his dagger still in his hand

'Stand up slowly, Daniel. Keep your back to that wall, and drop the rope. Even in this small space, you'd never reach me in time to use it. I've been known to spear a scurrying rat across the width of a Great Hall. And I am sure you would prefer to walk in on your feet, than to be delivered tied and bound to the Yena.'

Chapter Forty-one

'YOU MAY UNCOVER your eyes now,' the Deacon said. 'We don't want you falling over and breaking your neck.'

I dragged the thick hood off my head, gulping the cold air, though it could hardly be called fresh; there was an overpowering stench of old sweat, mould and musty cloth. By the light of the lantern the Deacon held up, I saw we were standing at the end of a large, enclosed undercroft. Baskets and bundles bound with cord were stacked along the grimy walls. Heaps of old clothes, piled on rows of rickety tables, were sorted into different types of garments – breeches, gowns, shirts, shifts, smocks – alongside a great pile of wool rags and another of linen.

'A palterer rents this undercroft. It has it uses.' The Deacon nodded towards the baskets large enough to contain a crouching man and the bundles of clothes which might conceal anything.

He bent to open a small doorway behind one of the pillars that supported the vaulted ceiling. It wasn't exactly concealed, but it wouldn't have been visible, even in daylight, to anyone walking in from the outside. Behind the door was a stone spiral staircase. Without waiting to see if I was following, the Deacon led the way up, vanishing almost at once, leaving only the glow of the lantern behind him.

The door at the top was already open by the time I trudged up. The Deacon stepped aside and ushered me in. 'I'll wait for you below to see that you leave . . . *safely*.' He stepped out, closing the door behind him.

The room, in contrast to the filthy undercroft below, was clean, though small. It was well warmed by a fire, the chimney breast, probably installed long after the house had been built, curved sideways. The smoke funnelled into the chimneys rising from other fires in nearby rooms, so that from the outside it would be impossible to see where it was coming from. The room itself was wedge-shaped and windowless. It was simply furnished with a bed, several chests, a table with a chair drawn up to it and a high-backed settle standing near the fire. A cooking pot dangled in the hearth. Half a loaf of good wheaten bread had been set on the table, together with a dish of butter, a cheese and some salt pork, along with a flagon and goblet. It appeared that the old man was eating a great deal better here than he had in Bristol. But only a single candle burned on the table, with a glass globe in front to magnify the light for reading or writing. Other candles had been set on sconces around the walls, but none of these had been lit.

In the dim light, I had glimpsed a figure in the winged settle by the fire, his face in shadow. His body was so still, he might have been asleep, or dead. I didn't want to look at him. I did not want to see him, to speak to him, even to be in the same realm with him. And yet part of me was itching to stride over there, to drag him out of that chair, demand answers, force him to show some remorse for what he'd done to me all those years ago, force him to acknowledge who I was. I wanted to wrap my fingers around his scraggy old throat and see fear dawn in those eyes, watch that fear grow into terror. I wanted to hear him beg, and then I wanted to cut him out of my life, to sever *his* life, as you'd cut off a stinking, gangrenous limb. I wanted him dead, as he was supposed to be.

'You will never change, Daniel. I warned you in Bristol to leave well alone, but you ignored me. If you had walked away when I told you to, I could have saved you. But not now. I cannot protect you now.'

He hadn't moved. The voice came from the shadows, as though uttered through the unmoving lips of the alchemist's legendary brazen head – *Time is, time was, time is past.* Too late to listen. Too late to hear his omnipotent words. Too late for this little god to save me.

'You were always an obdurate and refractory child.' The enunciation of each word was measured and precise, every syllable carefully selected and thoroughly examined before being deemed worthy to escape those thin, dry lips. 'No matter how many times I tried to teach you obedience, you would go back and do exactly what you had been told not to do, precisely what you knew would bring down trouble upon you.'

'Then it seems I take after my father in that.'

For the first time since I'd entered the room, he moved, leaning forward slightly from the shadows of his chair, so that the firelight licked across his face, as a candle flame lights the skull carved on a tomb. His eyes were sunk even deeper into the dark sockets than I remembered. The silver-white stubble that had frosted his chin had been allowed to grow into an uncut but well-combed beard. The frayed and faded black doublet had been replaced with one that was russet brown, but like the thick, ankle-length coat he wore over it, it hung so loose on his frame that I assumed the clothes had once belonged to a man several times his girth. I wondered if they had come from one of the palterer's heaps of garments below.

'Your father? You speak as if you know who that was, Daniel.'

'*Is*,' I corrected. 'I know who he *is*.'

Waldegrave said nothing, but his hand lifted to the left side of his mouth, and though I could not see it in the guttering firelight, I knew he was pressing it against the spasm that had twisted lips. It gave me an unexpected moment of satisfaction.

'The Deacon must have told you that I went to Bubwith, to the Church of All Saints where the burial records are kept. *Matthew Issott, died eighteenth of August fifteen-eighty, aged four* – the same age that I was when I was dragged from the arms of my mother, Elena, and taken to George Fairfax's manor. All my life I wondered, why me? Why was I chosen as the boy to be

393

raised as companion to Richard? There were surely children born to a better station in life who might have been more suitable, or if George Fairfax had wanted to take a charity child into his household there were hundreds of foundlings and orphans you might have selected. Why me?

'But then at Bubwith I met a woman who had birthed all the babies in those parts and she remembered me, remembered this.' I lifted my beard and pulled down my collar. 'My gallows mark. No other child was born with anything like it in the village. She remembered something else too. A priest from Willitoft who came to say secret Masses in Bubwith, who frequently visited Elena's house after dark to hear her confession. Why so often, old man? Was Elena such a sinful woman that she needed to confess more frequently than the other Catholics in the village, or was it that she needed to confess *after* your visits? Who was buried in the place of four-year-old Matthew Issott? Because as you can see, *Father* Waldegrave, the dead child lives! A miracle, isn't it?'

'A miracle you are still alive after the number of foolish things you have managed do in your short life, Daniel.'

Before I even thought about what I was doing I snatched the poker out of the fire and grasped his neck, pinning him to the settle, holding the glowing tip of the metal inches from his eye. 'Answer me!'

Though his face twitched and his eye watered from the heat, he neither flinched nor attempted to push me away. Somehow that only infuriated me more. I wanted to see the terror in his face. I had waited years to see it. But I saw only a faint smile. My threat meant nothing to him. It even amused him. I stood over him a few minutes more, suddenly conscious of the metal poker cooling in my hand and the coldness of his fragile parchment skin under my fingers. Only the pulse of his neck, faint as a bird's, told me he was still alive, and that pulse hadn't quickened. It hadn't even fluttered. He didn't care what I did to him. He didn't *care*.

I snatched my hand from his throat, flung the poker down on to the hearth with a clang, and turned away. What did it really matter whether he spoke the words or not? We both knew the truth. It would hang between us, like an iron chain binding the necks of two felons together, until we both lay rotting in our graves.

'I was told you were dead, dragged out of the Avon,' I said dully. 'Then in Bristol I learned that someone had given Castle Joan a weighty purse to swear the corpse was yours. The last time I saw you, you didn't have pennies enough to put on a dead man's eyes. So, I'd wager that purse didn't come from you, nor from the castle rats you worked for when you were forging papers for them. Who paid for you to disappear? Who had you brought here? Who is paying for that?' I gestured towards the bread, meat and cheese on the table.

'You are welcome to share it. You must be hungry after your night's exertions. Eat. Hunger can make a man choleric.'

I cut a good-sized chunk from the bread, buttered it and piled meat and cheese on top. He was right about one thing: I was starving. I hunched down in the vacant chair by the table as I ate. I could just see the gleam of his eyes in the shadows as he turned to watch me.

There was silence in the room except for the crackle of the flames in the hearth and my own chewing. Somewhere behind the wall, I heard the faint sound of a lute and someone singing. Did those who owned the house and cellar know Waldegrave was here? Probably, for neither he nor the Deacon had troubled to keep their voices muffled.

Ravenous though I was, it was painful to swallow and I could only manage tiny fragments without choking. I drank some of his wine to try to ease the mouthful down my swollen throat. The Deacon had been right when he warned me that I'd be desperate for a drink before the night was over.

'Tell me about the Serpent, old man. Is he the one who pays you to forge documents now? I know he ordered a man in Battle

Abbey to kill a pursuivant. And I know a man was smuggled in from Europe through Battle. It was no ordinary priest, but someone who planned to finish what the gunpowder plotters began. An attempt was made to kill the King tonight, but you already know that. You and the Deacon were waiting for it to happen, and I prevented it. Have you brought me here to warn me not to interfere a second time? Not to prevent Spero Pettingar from carrying out what he came back to England to do?'

Waldegrave laughed, but the laughter quickly cracked into a hacking, wheezing cough. 'And . . . how many times . . . have I warned you, Daniel? If I said to you now, do not interfere, do you think for one moment . . . I would believe that it would have the slightest effect? The easiest way to get you to do something is to tell you not to do it.'

I ignored his mocking tone; I'd been raised on it. 'Is the Serpent – is Pettingar – behind what happened tonight? Do you work for him? You owe me that much, old man.'

'I owe you nothing, whelp. But I will tell you. Because it is necessary for you to know. The Serpent was behind this attempt on the King's life tonight. But Spero Pettingar is not the Serpent. No!' He raised his hand, pushing at the air, fending off the words I was about to utter. 'I have not had you brought here to answer your questions; that in any case would be as futile as Sisyphus endlessly wrestling a boulder up a hill, for your questions never end. No,' he repeated. 'I am here only to give you your instructions. You are to join the circle of the Serpent. You are to see that another assassination on the King and his cubs is planned and this time you are to ensure it succeeds.'

I gaped at him and found myself laughing in disbelief. 'You expect me to help this . . . this Serpent, whoever he is, murder King James? Even assuming I wanted James and the princes dead, what on earth makes you think I would risk ending my days being tortured on the rack, then hanged, drawn and quartered on the block, for a cause to which I have no allegiance, whatsoever? You are asking me to commit murder and treason. Not even you could be so arrogant as to imagine I would agree to that. What makes you think I won't go straight to Robert Cecil and repeat all that you and the Deacon have said and done?'

'If you were going do that, you would have gone straight to the spymaster and told him the moment you learned of the plot that was to take place at the masque tonight. If you had, you might well have expected a handsome reward, a position in the King's Court or in Robert Cecil's employ. But you did not, and that makes you as guilty as the man who fired the cannon tonight or the Serpent who gave that order. I need hardly remind you that misprision of treason is punished on the quartering block just as brutally as treason itself, as Father Garnet discovered to his cost. And I know you will assist the Serpent to bring about the King's death, because you have already committed both murder and treason. A man who has killed once, I am told, finds it easier to kill again.'

'On the battlefield, yes,' I said. 'I will freely admit to that, and I killed again tonight, but these were killings in the service of my Sovereign and my country. Not treason, quite the reverse.'

Waldegrave nodded. 'Those, I grant you, the King would not consider treason. Men have been knighted for doing what you did in the heat of battle or dispatching an assassin as you did tonight. But to lure your commanding officer to a place of solitude and then beat him to death – that is murder and that is treason. Men are not honoured for that. It takes a certain kind of courage, I will grant, knowing you would be condemned to the most agonising of deaths if you were caught. But you were not caught, were you, Daniel? The Irish were blamed, and you fled.'

The blood in my veins had frozen as he spoke, but with this last word it suddenly boiled up inside me. 'I did not *flee*. I walked away – away from the slaughter of helpless men, women and children. I was sickened by what they'd done. I wanted no more part of it. What I did to that officer was not treason. It was justice!'

The child's skin is so cold. My shirt is wet with his blood. Hands reach up, clutching at my legs; eyes stare up at me out of broken reeds, pleading for help, pleading for answers – why? why us? The huts on the crannog where they sought their pathetic refuge, charred and burned, still smoking, floating in a lake of blood, their blood. And all around me the cries, screams, moans, sobs and whimpers of the dying. 'A mháthair! A mháthair!'

I found myself on my feet, pacing the room, without even being aware I'd risen. My fists were clenching and unclenching; I couldn't stop them.

'How did you know? How could you possibly know, Waldegrave?' I rounded on him.

Had he conjured a demon? Because no angel could have witnessed what happened that day. No angel could have stood by and watched that. Only the Devil was there, sitting on horseback, watching them run, listening to them scream, smiling in satisfaction as the swords hacked them down and mothers fell, still clutching their infants, trying in vain to keep their terrified children safe.

'Who told you, Waldegrave?'

The old man crouched between the dark wings of the settle, the firelight licking round his skull. 'Your secret is known to the person whose instructions I am obliged to relay to you. And they will use that knowledge to destroy you, make no mistake. Whatever grace and favour you might have gained in royal circles for the past services you have rendered will become as dross the moment the truth is revealed. Worse than dross, for where trust has been bestowed, the sting of treason is felt more keenly. You have no choice, Daniel. You must do it. If all transpires as some men hope, then you will be amply rewarded, and if does not . . . If the plot should fail . . .' He spread his hands. 'You know what awaits you. What awaits all of us.'

Epilogue

HE STOOD MOTIONLESS in the far corner of the palterer's undercroft, behind a stack of cloaks and coats, worn and stinking. These, he hoped, were less likely to have been dragged from the corpse of some wretch who'd died of the plague or some other contagion than shirts or breeches. The only lantern was in the hand of the Deacon, who was hovering by the door at the other end of the undercroft, but its light barely penetrated an arm's length. The Deacon glanced down, towards where he knew the man was standing, and held up a warning hand. He could evidently hear something stirring above on the stairs. Moments later, the door opened and Daniel stepped out. Although his face was masked in shadow, there was something in his stance, his awkward movement, that suggested he was walking almost in a trance, hardly aware of his surroundings.

He took the thick hood that the Deacon thrust at him, staring down at it in his two hands. Lifting it to his head, he started to pull it on, then he seemed to come suddenly to his senses. He tore it off, balled it and hurled it on to one of the piles of clothes. Before the Deacon could stop him, he strode rapidly down the length of the undercroft, his fists swinging. Both men reached the door at the far end at the same time. The Deacon hung the lantern, still alight, beside the door post before hurrying out after Daniel. The door banged shut behind them.

The man collected the lantern from beside the door, turned the key in the lock, and picked his way towards the back of the undercroft, trying not to touch anything as he moved. The clothes that were newly acquired by palterers were often lousy and full of fleas, looking for any warm body to latch on to.

When the man reached the room at the top of the stairs, the Yena was leaning forward in the settle, toasting a lump of cheese on the end of a poker. A slice of bread lay ready beside him. He did not seem surprised to see his guest and held up the cheese in mute invitation, but the man shook his head, instead pouring a measure of wine from the flagon on the table into an exquisite silver beaker, chained to his belt inside his cloak. Then he drew the empty chair over to the fire.

He raised his beaker to the Yena in a silent toast. 'When your pupil left just now, he did not look happy, Father.'

'I have done all that I can to persuade him to work for you, but are you still convinced that he will do what you want of him in the end?'

'He will realise he has no choice. But he must be led there step by step. First to infiltrate the Serpent's circle, then to aid the plot. He has too much pride, too much experience on the battle-field and as a legerdemainist, to be able to resist helping them to devise a plan that will work. Once he is in that far, he will be unable to pull out. But the timing must be right. They cannot be allowed to proceed until all is ready. If they had succeeded tonight, our plans would have collapsed. It is vital that the Serpent is kept alive and stinging until the Wyvern is ready to strike. You have done us good service, Father, as you continue to do.'

The old priest watched the cheese bubble and brown. He shook it off on to the slice of bread. 'If you value the service I have rendered you, I ask only this in return. Daniel did your work tonight, though he did not know it. So, for my sake, can you not spare him the final act?'

'No one can be spared, not even you or me. If the sacrifice is demanded, it must be offered up. Willingly or unwillingly, it makes no difference.'

The Yena lifted his eyes from the scorched cheese, which he had still not attempted to eat, and stared levelly at his guest. 'The

Deacon tells me he is holding a boy hostage as surety that Daniel would come here tonight. Do you intend to release him?'

The man grimaced. 'He will be detained for a little longer, just until we are certain Daniel needs no further persuasion. And he will be kept safe, fed well at least, and subjected to no more discomfort than is absolutely necessary. Unlike Erasmus and the others, I imagine he knew little about Daniel before today, and even if he had been questioned by the most subtle of interrogators, there is nothing he could have told them. But, of course, now he knows that Daniel had knowledge of tonight's plot, he cannot be allowed to go free. He will have to be dispatched, when we have no further use for him.'

The Yena briefly closed his eyes, making the sign of the cross.

The man sighed. 'If it soothes your conscience, Father, rest assured it will be done swiftly and mercifully, as it was for the others. I certainly don't want any noise. Afterwards, the hands will be mutilated. It is a useful device: apart from ensuring the deaths are not investigated, it also reminds those who discover the corpse of the horrors against which they fight.'

He drained his silver beaker and replaced it on the chain on his belt, then stood, rubbing his hands over the fire and staring into the flames.

'You once reminded me of an old proverb, Father. "*Serpens ni edat serpentem, draco non fiet.* Unless a serpent devours a serpent, it will not become a dragon." And I offer you another in return. "Strike the serpent's head with your enemy's hand." Understand this, Father: in the end, it is Daniel's hand that will strike that blow. Daniel must kill the King.'

Acknowledgements

I am deeply indebted to my colleague – storyteller, harper, and talented historical novelist – Kristin Gleeson, who lives in West Cork in Ireland, for her generous help with the Irish Gaelic phrases used in this novel. Any errors in usage are entirely my own.

This novel is the third in a series set in Jacobean England, featuring Daniel Pursglove. The character of Daniel and the series would never have been conceived without the ideas, and the unfailing support and encouragement of Mari Evans, Managing Director of Headline, Frances Edwards, Senior Commissioning Editor at Headline and my agent Victoria Hobbs, Director of A.M. Heath. I'd particularly like to thank my editor, Frances Edwards, for her patience and endurance in reading all the drafts, and for all her thoughts and suggestions which shape and hone the plots and characters. My gratitude also to copy-editor, Katie Green, who has the unenviable task of checking and polishing the text and Jessie Goetzinger-Hall, Editorial Assistant at Headline for all that she does to bring everything together behind the scenes.

My grateful thanks go to all those at Headline who have worked on typesetting, proofreading, design, sales and publicity, especially Caitlin Raynor, Publicity Director, Headline and Tinder Press.

I'd also like to take this opportunity to especially thank all the people working in bookshops and libraries who, despite the extremely difficult and anxious times we are living through, steadfastly continue to feed and nourish our hearts, souls and minds.

But an unopened book is a story untold. Its characters lie sleeping. Their voices are silent. So, my greatest debt of gratitude is, as ever, to you the reader for opening this book, waking the characters and bringing this story to life.

Behind the Scenes of this Novel

Like many people, I acquired the impression from my early school studies on the 'Tudors and Stuarts' that the threat to Catholics under the Reformation largely came from the Crown and Government. I used to think that while priests could be hunted down and executed, if you were an ordinary lay Catholic, you could survive, provided that you didn't hide fugitive priests in your attic or cellar. It was only as I began to delve into Church and legal records to research this series, that I appreciated the extent to which ordinary citizens could bully and torment any members of their community who were of the 'wrong' faith. Petty disputes over boundaries or goods or personal grudges could quickly escalate, and if you were a Catholic, you had almost no redress under the law, whatever wrongs your neighbours inflicted on you.

The Protestant Reformation was slow to reach Yorkshire, particularly in the more remote villages and manors of the North and West Ridings. It didn't really take hold there until the beginning of the seventeenth century. In consequence, Yorkshire attracted a number of the wealthier Catholic families. In 1603, Thomas Lord Burghley, Lord President of the Council of the North, in York, expressed his grave displeasure at the number of Catholic ladies who had come to greet Queen Ann on her journey south to London, for she was rumoured to have herself converted to Catholicism. Many Catholics fervently hoped that the new monarchs, James and Anne, would lift the restrictions and cease the persecution that Catholics had endured under Elizabeth, even if they didn't actually make England a Catholic country again. But in this, they would be bitterly disappointed.

Following the failed Gunpowder Plot, new legislation stipulated that churchwardens and constables who failed to report the absence from Protestant services of any recusant over the age of nine would be fined twenty shillings for each one; as an incentive, they would be paid forty shillings for every recusant they did report. Recusants who refused to attend church were fined £20 per lunar month, and if they couldn't pay, two thirds of their property was seized. They were barred from the offices of the Crown, from practising law and other professions, and they couldn't graduate from university. Any recusant who was an heir to property could be prevented from inheriting it, and for the first time, wives, who had formerly *not* been fined for recusancy, on the basis that they were acting under the authority of their husbands, could now be fined and imprisoned alongside them.

Although the wealthier recusant families in Yorkshire could afford to bribe local officials and churchwardens not to report them, they were certainly made to pay dearly for it, with a constant threat that if they didn't pay up, they would be reported. But what intrigued me, and indeed formed the basis for the accounts of the treatment of Daniel's mother and Sir Christopher Veldon's brother in this novel, were the reports I came across of the harassment of Catholics by their own neighbours.

The Memorandum Book of Richard Cholmey, written between 1602 and 1623, details how Cholmey's neighbours and others in the locality openly invaded his land to steal his game, wood and live-stock, knowing that he couldn't take them to court. He says that he was violently robbed on several occasions, and threatened by one of his own tenants with a long thick cudgel with an iron spike on it, barely escaping with his life, but could do nothing about it. When he was briefly imprisoned in York Castle, all his livestock was stolen by his neighbours and sold in Thirsk market and a friend had to buy the animals back for him.

He was not the only one to suffer. In Bubwith, a yeoman farmer, John Barber, had already been forced to pay over two thirds of his living to the Crown, being left with only one third to maintain himself, his wife, children and elderly parents. Yet, despite that, three times in one year alone, the sheriff's men and pursuivants confiscated his goods and the cattle on his land, ignoring his protests that a number of the cattle grazing there did not belong to him. The sheriff's men then returned to take all his hay, corn and wood and any other items of value they could find in his house, which they offered for sale to his neighbours at a knock-down price. Barber was forced to beg one of his neighbours to buy the goods and cattle, which his friend kindly did, honourably selling them back to Barber at the price he'd paid.

But the yeoman farmer was beside himself with fear, knowing that if he started to grow crops again the following year or graze his cattle, they could all be taken from him again and he could not afford to keep buying them back. Between the law and their neighbours, it is little wonder that many Catholics prayed that deliverance would come in the form of Divine Justice or a Catholic invasion from Europe, for it seemed increasingly unlikely that their King was going to come their rescue any time soon.

But in contrast, some Catholics – those willing to outwardly conform, whatever their private beliefs – flourished under James's rule. Two of these were set designer and architect Inigo Jones and the playwright Ben Jonson.

Inigo Jones was born to a Welsh clothmaker of some means in Smithfield in London in 1573; it is believed that both his parents were Catholics. Whether or not Inigo himself actively embraced that faith is not known for certain. He was certainly baptised in a Protestant church, but so were many Catholics' children, to outwardly conform to the law and avoid fines. Certainly, as a young man, Inigo had many ardent Catholic friends, including the convert Tobie Matthew and Thomas Howard, the Earl of Arundel, then a prominent Catholic, though he later found it expedient to adopt the Protestant faith.

Inigo travelled to the Court of King Christian of Denmark in the retinue of the Earl of Rutland and it seems likely that Queen Anne was introduced to Jones through her brother Christian. Inigo was first employed to design the sets and costumes for a masque for her back in England in 1604, alongside the controversial playwright Ben Jonson, with whom he had a creative but stormy relationship.

Ben Jonson, though born the son of a Protestant clergyman, briefly became a Catholic convert. In 1598, he killed a man in a dual and was imprisoned, awaiting trial, for two weeks in Newgate. In that short time, he was converted to Catholicism by a fellow inmate. Jonson escaped execution by claiming benefit of clergy, but was branded with a T on his thumb, to ensure he couldn't claim the same defence again.

He was imprisoned a second time and only narrowly escaped mutilation for co-writing *Eastward Ho!*, a play which mocked the uncouth Scottish courtiers. Then, in October 1605, he was invited to dine with the ringleader of the Gunpowder Treason plot, the wealthy Catholic Robert Catesby. Everyone at the dinner that night was a Catholic and two of Catesby's guests were involved in the plot. So, when Robert Cecil summoned Jonson after the treason was uncovered, he must have thought he was about to be arrested, not least because a play he'd written in 1603, entitled *Sejanus*, bore significant similarities to the Gunpowder Plot.

But Cecil believed him when he said he had no knowledge of the plot, or Cecil chose to pretend he did, tasking the highly relieved Jonson to use his Catholic contacts to discover who else had been involved. But Jonson failed to discover anything. The playwright was accused of recusancy in 1606, but was never punished for it. Maybe it was simply intended as a warning shot; if so, it seems to have worked, for Jonson abandoned his new faith shortly afterwards.

Meanwhile, Inigo Jones found himself designing sets for royal masque after royal masque, his audience and royal patrons demanding that each should be even more spectacular than the last. Jones, using only candle and lantern flames, managed to create lighting effects that could suggest a moonlight glade with twinkling stars, or blazing deserts with a glittering sun. He produced moving clouds, and fake trees which half sank into the stage before opening their branches to reveal the performers. Once, he had a specially mixed perfume puffed across the audience at a key moment – the original smelly-vision – and he even invented the glitter ball: a revolving, large silver ball decorated with gold that hung above the dancers, sending sparks of light darting round the set.

Robert Cecil's choice of Inigo Jones to supervise the Catholic convert Tobie Matthew on his release from the Fleet prison was a clever ruse to get what he wanted from Matthew. Tobie Matthew had every reason to view Robert Cecil as his enemy. But Cecil permitted him to reside with Jones, a Catholic and an old friend whom Matthew trusted, rather than placing him with an ardent Protestant clergyman who would harangue him. It was a subtle and clever move. Did Matthew know at his release hearing before the Privy Council that it was Cecil who had had him arrested in the first place, even though Cecil pretended he had not?

When I read about this incident, it crossed my mind that Cecil may have been testing the allegiances of both men. The condition of Matthew's release was that he would act as an agent for Cecil, but Cecil could not be certain that, once in Spain, he would do so. Was Jones put in to probe Matthew's real intentions, or was Matthew placed with Jones to see if this close confidant of Queen Anne was still secretly harbouring Catholic leanings, maybe even influencing the Queen herself?

Jones succeeded in persuading Matthew to sell the lease of Durham House to Cecil so that he could build his New Exchange on the Strand, and Jones was well rewarded by Robert Cecil for doing so. Not only did Cecil invite him to design the staging for further entertainments, but, significantly for his future architectural career, Inigo Jones was invited to design the Exchange building itself. Sometimes being a Catholic wasn't such a disadvantage, just so long as the spymaster, Robert Cecil, thought he could make use of you.

Glossary

'B' – branding was a punishment which could be inflicted in conjunction with imprisonment in gaols like Newgate, or being pilloried, with the ears nailed to the sides of the neck restraint and then severed with a knife or torn off when the felon was released. Each type of crime was given its own branded letter. Branding with a 'B' often indicated the crime of 'attempted buggery'. It was a lesser offence than 'sodomy', which carried the death penalty, but in Elizabethan times being branded with a 'B' could mean the person had been found guilty of any kind of sexual activity deemed to be in violation of Church law.

BUMPSY – an archaic word meaning *drunk*, probably alluding to the unsteady gait of someone who is inebriated and frequently bumps into things.

CAT-HAWED – pronounced *cattored*. Yorkshire dialect word meaning *drunk* to the point of weaving around and fumbling words.

CHEWETS – small pies which might be filled with minced meat or chopped oysters, mixed with dried fruit such as raisins or dates, and flavoured with a buttery verjuice sauce made from sour or tart fruits. Chewets were a popular fast-food item sold by street vendors: they were easy to eat outside, but also, being small, didn't require a very hot oven or take long to bake, which saved fuel and meant the cook could produce a good number in a short time.

DENMARK HOUSE – today known as Somerset House, it was built in 1547 by Edward Seymour, Lord Protector and Duke of Somerset. In 1552, Seymour was executed for treason and so his house was forfeited to the Crown. The following year, the twenty-year-old Princess Elizabeth moved to Somerset House, where she lived until she was crowned queen in 1558. In 1603, James I's Danish wife, Queen Anne, took up residence in Somerset House, which was unofficially named Denmark House in honour of the visit of the Queen's brother King Christian of Denmark in 1606. Although Anne and James had seven children, three of which survived to adulthood, the couple mostly lived apart and had separate Courts. The name of the palace was officially changed to Denmark House in 1617, after Anne had the buildings and grounds remodelled. The name reverted back to Somerset House during the 1640s.

In 1604, the Treaty of London, which ended the nineteen-year Anglo-Spanish War, was negotiated and signed there. In 1609, Queen Anne invited the architect Inigo Jones, who also designed the costumes and sets for many of her masques, to redesign and rebuild the palace, work which continued until the Queen's death in 1619.

After the Civil War, Parliament tried to sell Denmark House, but no one was willing to buy it, although they did sell the contents for £118,000, a massive sum in those days. The last royal person to occupy the house was the wife of Charles II, Catherine of Braganza, who moved out in 1693. In 1775, following years of neglect, the original Somerset House was demolished and a new Somerset House was built on the same spot, designed by the architect William Chambers. Before the Embankment was constructed by the Victorians, the Thames lapped right up against the outer wall of the gardens.

DOG WATCH – when a ship was at sea, the crew was usually divided into two teams, so that they could work, eat and rest in four-hour shifts known as *watches*. First watch was from 8 p.m. to midnight; middle watch from midnight to 4 a.m.; morning watch from 4 a.m. to 8 a.m.; forenoon watch from 8 a.m. to midday and afternoon watch from midday to 4 p.m. But the last watch was divided into two *dog watches*, each of two hours: 4 p.m. to 6 p.m. and 6 p.m. to 8 p.m. This allowed both crews to eat supper at a reasonable time. It also meant they would automatically be on different shift times every other day, so that the same team wasn't stuck with the unpopular middle watch every night. These shifts continued when the ship was in port, but the captain might increase the number of men on certain watches to help with the loading and unloading of cargoes, or reduce the size of the team for other watches when moored up, to allow men to have shore leave or sleep.

DOUBLE-DOUBLE BEER – a strong beer which was then rebrewed using a fresh batch of malt. This made it extremely intoxicating even in small quantities. It also used twice as much fuel as ordinary beer at a time when wood was in high demand. In an effort to stop the worst of its effects, both in terms of loss of work and violent drunken behaviour, it was outlawed by Elizabeth I. This, of course, had the immediate effect of driving the trade underground. In his parliamentary journal in 1572, Cromwell summarises a bill 'restraining the bruing of double double ale or doble double beere within the Citie [London] . . . and no beere to be sould above 4s. the barrel, the strongest, and 2s. the single beere'.

(See also the entry for MARCH BEER.)

FOOTPAD – a robber who ambushed people on roads or tracks. These men operated on foot, in contrast to highwaymen, who did the same thing, but on horseback.

FOX TONGUE – raw meat or liver bound to a wound overnight was often used to draw out splinters or thorns, but the tongue of a fox was considered the most efficacious treatment. Parts of a fox were used in other folk remedies too. People carried fox teeth, which they thought would alleviate inflammation of the legs. The liver and lights (lungs) of a fox, when washed in wine and dried, were used as a cough cure. Fox fat rubbed into the scalp cured baldness, while the ashes of fox meat were eaten to help cure disorders of the liver or lungs.

FUDDLING CUP – a group of four cups with concealed holes, whose hollow handles interlocked, creating a series of siphons. Liquid poured into one of the cups would mysteriously drain away and bubble up in one of the other cups, using the same principle as the *Pythagoras cup* or *greedy cup* sold in Greece today. The fuddling cup was a popular adult toy in this period, especially effective if some of the party were drunk and couldn't work out why the wine kept vanishing.

FUZZLED – similar to *fuddled*, an Elizabethan term meaning drunk to the point where you weren't able to think clearly.

GALLANDINE or GALYNTYNE – originally a very thick, strongly flavoured bread sauce, made with stale bread, wine or wine vinegar and spices, particularly galingale or galangal, which is a plant root of the same family as ginger, but which tastes much more peppery. The sauce was served with both meat and fish. A royal recipe of 1390 advises the cook to 'take crusts of bread and grind them small, do thereto powder of galyngale, of cinnamon, of ginger and salt it, temper it with vinegar and draw it though a strainer & present it forth'.

GEE-HOES – the Bristol name for animal-drawn sledges used to transport heavy goods all year round in the city. These were low to the ground, making the loading and unloading of barrels and crates easier. But the main reason for using them was the fear that the vibration caused by iron-rimmed cartwheels trundling over the roads would shake the cellars and passageways beneath the city, ruining the wine that was stored there as well as risking the collapse of the vaults themselves. Sledges were also of more use in the country than wheeled carts if the ground was particularly muddy or icy, or loads had to be carried over rough pasture.

GREAT POX – syphilis. The old name, Great Pox, was used to distinguish it from an entirely different disease – smallpox, originally known as *small pokes*, meaning small pustules. By the middle of the sixteenth century, it was widely recognised that the Great Pox was sexually transmitted and had become an epidemic in Europe, particularly in the ports. Chief among the remedies offered by quack doctors and barbers were mercury salves rubbed vigorously into the lesions of syphilis, since mercury had been used to treat leprosy for centuries. But even at the time, many physicians recognised that the mercury was responsible for more deaths than the disease itself. Vitriol and arsenic, which were also used, were equally lethal. Wealthy men and women used guaiacum, a tropical wood, which, though it didn't cure the disease, was less likely to kill the patient, but since this was imported from the West Indies, it was way beyond the means of the poor prostitutes.

HaShem – Hebrew meaning *the name*. The Tetragrammaton, or Tetragram, the four-letter name of God, is so sacred it is not uttered by Jews. In prayers, it is usually replaced with *Adonai* (my lord), but even this is not used in conversation, for fear of breaking the Commandment against taking God's name in vain, so, *HaShem* is used instead.

HUFFCAP – a type of very strong, sweet, double-double beer. Huffcap also meant a swaggering, blustering bully.

HUMBLES, NUMBLES or UMBLES – the chopped or minced innards or 'pluck' of an animal, that is, the heart, liver, kidneys and the lungs or 'lights'. Seasoned with herbs and spices such as thyme, marjoram, borage, rosemary, parsley, pepper, mace or cloves, the humbles were mixed with mutton-suet to be used as the filling for puddings and pies – *humbles-pie*, a dish eaten by the lower classes, gave rise to the expression 'to eat humble pie'. The pluck from strongly flavoured meat such as venison was preferred, but in poorer households, the innards of any animal slaughtered for meat was used, so that nothing was wasted.

JACULUS – the name given to the so-called 'flying' serpent in natural history books of the period. The serpent was thought to 'leap' into trees, then fling itself down on any large prey passing by, like a 'javelin'. The concept of large snakes swinging down from trees in tropical forests might well have been based on real observations by early travellers, although those travellers probably didn't linger to discover how the snakes had got up there.

JENNY HANIVER – the carcass of a ray, skate or devil fish that has been tied into a monstrous shape and dried, resulting in a mummified specimen resembling a mythical creature. Since these fish have barbed tails, and also eyes and mouths that resemble human or mammalian faces, it was possible to make them look like demons or dragons, creating wings or limbs by cutting and shaping the body before drying. These fakes became very popular in the sixteenth and seventeenth centuries, especially in the ports of Belgium, where they were sold as curios to mariners and travellers to take back home, to show the strange creatures they'd encountered on their voyages. It has been suggested that one possible explanation of the origin of the name may be the French phrase *jeune d'Anvers* – youth of Antwerp – which English sailors corrupted into *Jenny Haniver*.

Jenny Hanivers have been crafted to look like imps, basilisks, wyverns and even the legendary 'sea monks' and 'sea bishops' which were believed to conjure storms at sea. An illustration of a Jenny Haniver appeared in Konrad Gesner's *Historia Animalium* in 1558, where Gesner firmly states that these are simply dried rays, and that people shouldn't be tricked into believing they are dragons or monsters. However, the tales of the animals and sea-creatures encountered by European sailors visiting tropical islands, as well as the skins and often badly stuffed specimens brought back by those exploring the Americas, only served to convince a public who had never seen such creatures that these fakes might be real.

JOMBILS or JUMBLES – pastries made from eggs, sugar, flour and aniseed, moulded into long thin rolls and each tied into a knot. They were then dipped in rose water and simmered in water before being fished out, dried and baked in the oven.

LAYSTALL – the official dumping site outside a town for the human excrement and waste from privies, cesspits and public lavatories known as *jakes*. The waste was allowed to weather in the laystalls before being transported to be used as a fertiliser for crops. The contents of the privies were dug out by *gong farmers*, also known as *night-men* or *night soil men* because they were only allowed to work at night between 9 p.m. and 5 a.m. *Gong* meant both the privy itself and was what was disposed in it, and comes from the old English *gang*, meaning *to go*.

LEGAL QUAY – a deep, safe harbour, just downriver of London Bridge, where sea-going and coastal ships were moored so that their cargoes could be loaded and unloaded, examined and assessed for customs duties. The ships could also be searched for any illegal goods or people that their captains might be trying to smuggle in or out. Many large, ocean-going ships were moored next to each other in long lines. Anyone wanting to travel upriver into the city from the Legal Quay would walk to the other side of London Bridge and catch a smaller wherry or rivercraft to continue their journey.

LINSTOCK or LINTSTOCK – a piece of equipment used to fire a cannon. A linstock was a long pole with a point at one end which could be dug into the ground to that it could stand upright, and a fork at the other end, around which a *slow match* was wound and lit. A slow match was a length of cord or hemp rope soaked in chemicals, so that it burned slowly, usually at the rate of thirty centimetres or one foot per hour. The smouldering end of the match would be used to ignite the loose gunpowder over the touch hole of a cannon to fire it. The match could be lit well in advance, so that it was ready to fire instantly whenever the order was given. The long linstock ensured that the person firing the cannon was able to stand well away to the side and was not in danger of being burned as the powder ignited or struck as the cannon recoiled.

MARCH BEER – one of the strongest beers, also known as *double beer* because it was brewed with twice as much malt as regular beers. Ale made with hops had to be drunk within a couple of days of brewing, but beer made with malt lasted for months and could be very strong. *Small beer*, supplied to servants and children, contained little malt and was much weaker.

MARIGOLD – or Mary's Gold. The rose and lily were symbols of the Virgin Mary in connection with her earthly life, but the marigold was the symbol of her assumption into heaven. The golden petals were likened to rays of light crowning her head. In Catholic churches, it was the flower often laid at the feet of the statue. But it was also known as *the flower of grief*: the marigold was seen to 'weep' on occasion, perhaps because the multiple petals retain the dew, and it was therefore also symbolic of Mary's tears and sorrow. It was the flower for Lady Day, 25 March, once the start of the New Year, so it also represents the dawn of a new age.

MARROW BONE PIES – bite-sized pastries filled with the marrow scooped out from beef bones, seasoned with ginger, sugar and cinnamon. The pieces of marrow were wrapped in pastry, then either deep-fried in beef fat or baked in the oven.

MHÁTHAIR – Irish Gaelic, meaning *mother*. Someone addressing their mother or calling to them would cry 'A *mháthair*'.

MISPRISION OF TREASON – the crime of concealing or failing to report your knowledge of a treasonable act or plot. To be guilty of this crime, you didn't have to be involved in the treason or even support it. You were guilty if you merely learned of it or suspected it but failed to report it. In this period, the punishment was the same as for the person actually committing the treason – execution.

MORT – a disparaging term for a girl or woman, meaning a woman who was not considered to be 'respectable', or who was the partner of a beggar or thief; for example, a *prigger's mort* meant the girlfriend or wife of a horse-thief.

MUMMY – a preparation made from embalmed human corpses for use in medicine. It was a practice that dates back to ancient Egypt, Greece and Rome, but even as late as the eighteenth century, mummy was still included in many English and European herbals. Mummy was used to treat humans, horses, hunting dogs and falcons. Mixed with other ingredients, it was said to heal wounds and skin problems, and cure paralysis, epilepsy and disorders of the liver, heart, lungs, spleen and stomach. Most importantly, it acted as an antidote to poison. Theophrastus Bombast von Hohenheim (1493–1541) invented the very popular *balsam of mummy* and *treacle of mummy*, but it could be taken in the form of elixirs, tinctures, pills, ointments and powders.

During the Middle Ages, Syrian merchants raided Egyptian graves to supply European apothecaries, but when the supply of Egyptian-embalmed corpses began to be exhausted, apothecaries turned to the use of modern cadavers, often buying them from executioners or prison warders. The herbalist Oswald Croll (1580–1609) particularly recommended the corpses of hanged male felons of ruddy complexion who were around twenty-four years old. In *Othello*, Shakespeare refers to a handkerchief 'dy'd in mummy, which the skilful conserved of maidens' hearts'.

PALTERER – someone who bought and sold old clothes, either to be used as garments or to be cut into rags to make paper. *Paltry* meant *rags* or *rubbish*. Palterers had a bad reputation for lying about who had previously owned the clothes, claiming they had been worn by some grand lady, or not admitting to the customer that the clothes had been taken from the body of an infected corpse. They frequently bought from thieves such as the lully priggers who stole wet clothes from washing lines to sell on, so *palterer* eventually came to mean any dishonest or unscrupulous trader, or someone who was deliberately misleading.

PEACH or PEACHER – an informer, or someone who betrays. It has been used in this sense since the fifteenth century, and derives from *pechen* or the earlier *apeche*, meaning *to accuse* or *ensnare*.

PINNY – Yorkshire dialect word meaning a small baby fish, particularly one that is newly hatched: a fish that is so tiny, it is not worth catching.

POOR JACK – dried salt cod, also known as *haberdine*. It was a cheap dish, but had little flavour, so all but the very poor ate it with large quantities of mustard.

POULTER – the older form of *poulterer* or *poultryman*, someone who breeds or tends poultry for a living, or a merchant who specialises in buying and selling poultry and eggs.

PURVEYANCE – from the eleventh century onwards, it was the right of the English monarch to purchase provisions for the royal household at a price set well below market value. Purveyance was hated by the commoners and merchants, not only for what the King commandeered, which could leave them financially ruined, but because the system was open to abuse by corrupt officials, who could requisition goods and sell them for personal profit. By the beginning of King James's reign, purveyance was worth around £40,000 per year to the Crown and became one of the major bones of contention between the King and Parliament, who wanted to put an end to the practice. But James refused to relinquish the prerogative without financial compensation. Although it was suspended during the Civil War, it was only officially abolished in 1660.

SHOT-ICE – Yorkshire dialect for sheet ice.

SLEECH – the West Country dialect name for soft, wet mud you would sink into, in contrast to *slub*, which is mud firm enough to bear your weight.

STAITHE – a landing stage, jetty or part of a riverbank used as a place for loading or unloading boats.

SUBTLETIES – sculptures made from sugar, marchpane or wax, presented between courses or used to decorate tables. They were not intended to be eaten but to entertain and impress the guests, displaying the wealth of the host. They could include animals, scenes of dancers, a chessboard complete with pieces, miniature gardens, a ship sailing on the sea with whales and mermaids, or even a model of the house or palace in which the feast was being held.

TENT – in the context of treating a wound, a tent was a roll of cloth or flax stuffed tightly into the open wound to keep it from closing over, to prevent the air, which was thought to carry infection, from reaching it, and to absorb the *laudable pus*, or discharge. Once the material was swollen with moisture and stinking, it would be pulled out and replaced, which must have been a painful process. The idea was to allow the 'proud flesh', or new flesh, to regenerate from the bottom of the wound upwards. If the skin closed over with infection still deep in the wound it could lead to gangrene or blood poisoning. The reasoning behind it is actually not so far from the approach taken to treating certain types of wounds and abscesses today.

TENTERS – when woollen cloth was woven, it had to be scoured to remove the natural oils and dirt, and beaten or trodden with fuller's earth to make the fibres bind together, so that the cloth would not become full of holes when it was worn. It was then stretched on long frameworks of wooden poles, like rail fences, and left to dry vertically under tension. The cloth was held on the frames by sharp metal hooks – *tenterhooks* – pushed through the edges of the cloth, which is said to be the origin of the expression 'to be on tenterhooks', meaning to be in a state of tension while you wait. (The name comes from the Latin *tentus*, meaning *stretched*, from which we also get *tent*, where canvas or other material is stretched over a support.)

THERIAC – a universal antidote both to poisons and plagues, first created by Mithridates VI, King of Pontus, who died in 63 BC. He experimented with single ingredients by trying them out on condemned criminals, then combined all the effective substances into one antidote, to produce a universal prophylactic against poisons and plagues which he consumed daily. By the Middle Ages, theriac was being produced in Venice and exported all over Europe. In England, it was called *Venetian treacle*, treacle being a corruption of *theriac*.

In London in 1586, the Master and Wardens of Grocers' Hall discovered *Jeane Triacle* (Genoa treacle) being sold, which was declared to be 'unwholesome, being compounded by certain rude and unskilful men'. They successfully petitioned that the recipe for theriac's proper manufacture should be kept at Grocers' Hall, and only one of their members, the apothecary William Besse, was permitted to prepare it for the whole of London and seven miles around.

TILT BOAT – a ferry boat rowed by two or four oarsmen which, unlike the wherries, had a canopy or awning over the passengers' seats to protect them from rain or sun. There were laws about the number of passengers the tilt boats and wherries were allowed to carry, depending on their size, but inevitably these would be broken on occasion by greedy watermen or passengers in a hurry, and since few people could swim, especially in the strong currents of the Thames, if the boat sank, many drowned.

VLOTHERING – an old Somerset dialect word meaning to talk incoherently, or speak nonsense.

WHILE – in some regional dialects including Yorkshire, *while* is used to mean *until*. This can initially confuse those from outside the region. For example – *Stay here while it's dark* – is sometimes wrongly interpreted to mean – *you should stay here during the hours of darkness*. But the speaker intends the opposite – *Stay here until it gets dark.*

WYVERN – a type of dragon or winged serpent, but the wyvern has only two legs, whereas a dragon has four. In place of its back legs, the wyvern's body tapers into a serpent's tail with a diamond or arrow shape at the tip. A dragon or wyvern was the emblem on the English battle standard, probably last seen on the battlefield in 1066. The wyvern was the bringer of death and destruction, and in the Middle Ages it was thought to fly through the night sky, spreading plague and pestilence to both humans and livestock.

YENA – the old name for a group of animals which included the hyena, said to live in tombs and feast on the dead. They were thought not to be able to turn around, because their spines were rigid, but they were believed to be able to change at will from being male to female. The yena or hyena was said to carry a stone in its eye, also called a yena, which if placed under a human tongue would enable that person to foretell the future and divine where treasure was buried. Naturally, this belief fuelled a lucrative trade in fake yena stones.

About the Author

KAREN MAITLAND is an historical novelist, lecturer and teacher of Creative Writing, with over twenty books to her name. She grew up in Malta, which inspired her passion for history, and travelled and worked all over the world before settling in the United Kingdom. She has a doctorate in psycholinguistics, and now lives on the edge of Dartmoor in Devon.